The Seventh Angel

The Prophet Series

Ande Edwards

Published by Naked Moose Publishing, 2018.

THE SEVENTH ANGEL
First Edition. August 31, 2018
Copyright © 2018 Ande Edwards.
Written by Ande Edwards.

DEDICATION

In honor of those who have dedicated their lives to helping victims of human trafficking and to the amazing men and women who have escaped and found the courage to share their stories. The Lord God Almighty has heard your cry.

Acknowledgments

What a bumpy ride this has been. You don't write a book about spiritual warfare without expecting to enter a great battle. And yet, when the attack came, I was utterly unprepared. It made me feel woefully inadequate. I questioned myself through nearly every step of this process. I would have a good writing day, or a powerful God moment, only to find myself overcome by discouragement and doubt the next. I told myself it was battle, but that didn't seem to miraculously resolve it. I clawed, fought, and prayed my way out of the fight, only to lose my grip and fall back into self-doubt and start the process all over.

Through it all, God sent me people that would lift me up, those who could be strong when I no longer could. People who could speak truth through the darkness that threatened me, and for that, I am eternally grateful.

Thea, you have prayed me out of many dark holes, thank you. Thank you for always being willing to discuss an idea, brainstorm a roadblock, and of course, read and reread my drafts. I am so thankful that God intertwined our lives all those years ago. This is not a journey I could ever have taken without you, and I am so grateful that He knew that and prepared you to journey with me.

Nat and Melissa, thank you for being willing to read very rough work and help me polish and refine it, then read it again and perhaps again. It is no small task to read the same book over and over. Thank you for listening to me prattle on about the story, the writing process, and my frustrations. Nat, thank you for talking me off the cliff each time I convinced myself I had no business writing such a book. Melissa, thank you for letting me peer into the mind of a real scientist and reminding me that most of the world, reads and works from left to right. Thank you for embracing the ridiculous way in which my own brain seems to work.

The three of you are such a powerful support network. You kept me afloat when the devil made it his business to bring me down. I sank over and over again, and each time you showed up with a life preserver. I can never thank you enough.

"Bob," you are an inspiration. You truly are an amazing woman; I feel so blessed to have you in my life. Your wisdom, splattered with pizzazz, is something for the rest of us to aspire to. Thank you for the encouraging words along the way, for prayers that crackle with power, and for always sharing in my enthusiasm.

To my brother, an incredible writer in his own right, thank you for telling me to stop writing like a professor and paint a picture instead of a description. I hope you see the picture this time.

To my sister, thank you for walking through this crazy life with me. Thank you for your encouragement as I ventured into very unfamiliar territory.

I could not have anticipated how challenging this journey would be. But I am so thankful that God, in his infinite wisdom, saw fit to bring me on it.

Prologue

The demon led Titus into the study where Lucifer waited. An overflowing ashtray sat on the desk still smoldering from a cigar freshly extinguished. The room was full of the holiest of all books. It was evident to Titus that Lucifer was searching the Word for something.

"My Liege," Titus offered in greeting kneeling on the expensive Persian rug.

"Titus, I assume you have a good reason for coming uninvited to my home, for interrupting me, and for usurping your position," Lucifer drilled. But Titus was not concerned by the harsh tone. He knew that what he brought would be pleasing to Lucifer. He would not have taken the risk otherwise.

"Yes, my Liege," he answered humbly. Being confident did not mean he need be arrogant. While Titus understood the value of the gift he brought Lucifer, he also realized he was in a precarious position. Lucifer was the Prince of the earth; he was not to be trifled with. Titus would proceed with deep respect never overtly revealing his betrayal of Morax or his own personal quest for power.

"Get up!" Lucifer snapped at him, irritation, and disgust evident in his voice.

"I bring you news of Platitude," Titus offered as he stood.

"Platitude? The King's college we are taking over?" Lucifer asked, as if he didn't already know.

"Yes." He paused briefly observing Lucifer for any signs of anger.

"What is your report then?" Lucifer prompted, fighting visible agitation.

"There was a prophet at the college," Titus once again paused giving Lucifer plenty of time to process the information. He cunningly laid his cards out for Lucifer to see and was instantly rewarded. A small ripple of excitement pulsed through Lucifer. But that excitement was chased back by a hint of fear that Titus would never acknowledge seeing. All who were wise feared the King. It was only right that Lucifer should as well. After all, who knew better than Lucifer what the King was capable of?

"Go on," Lucifer prompted in a slightly softer tone, his interest piqued.

Lucifer listened intently as Titus filled him in on the critical elements of the battle in Platitude. Titus did, of course, leave out many key facts, facts he was sure would only work against him. He would leave that bit for Morax. Lucifer listened, asking only what had become of each of the humans. Titus relayed what he knew which wasn't much.

"Find them and destroy them all. But bring me the prophet alive," Lucifer ordered.

Chapter 1

The earliest memory Aegeus had, was of standing under the sturdy branches of the Tree of Life and looking into the eyes of his creator. A rush of electricity had flooded through him, filling him with a power so magnificent that it knew no equal.

As the King announced Aegeus's name to all those present, the tree filled the sky with a beautiful array of silver lights. With one voice, the angels celebrated the creative hand of the King and the birth of a warrior.

Michael, donning his formal dress uniform, escorted Aegeus to stand with the other warriors, as the King continued to create. Seneca was the next one created, and dark blue lights filled the heavens sparkling and fizzling until they faded gently for the next angel, Kfir. As Kfir stepped forth, the tree erupted with orange lights which danced and twirled across the sky, shimmering slightly, before they too eventually gave way to the lights of the next angel.

The King proclaimed each angels name as he created them -a name that would define them, a name that suited them, a name chosen by him with great thought.

He made many types of angels that day: warriors, guardians, researchers, proclaimers of truth, cherubim, seraphim, avengers, common, and ministering angels among them. Each type of angel was created with a unique purpose. Each one designed perfectly for the mission the creator had prepared for them. Each one wearing a band in the color the tree had chosen for them.

But perhaps the most notable was the final angel created that day, the seventh archangel. The King proclaimed his name Lucifer. Thunder rumbled the great tree, and a magnificent light display soared high into the heavens as they celebrated the morning star. Aegeus watched mesmerized. Although Aegeus had not witnessed the creation of the other archangels, he felt certain Lucifer had been ushered in with as much celebration as any. Later, Aegeus had watched as Lucifer was cast down from heaven. That had certainly been a memorable day.

Aegeus remembered standing there looking beyond the great expanse trying to grasp what had just happened. The King, the mightiest of all warriors, had dealt with the revolt swiftly, but the memory of it lingered, great was the sorrow of the King.

Things changed after that. Uriel was chosen to replace Lucifer as the seventh archangel, and all the heavenly beings once again gathered around the Tree of Life to bear witness to and celebrate Uriel's promotion.

The King chose an angel of every type to bestow their gifts upon Uriel. As each one came forward, they would kneel and present their offering. Uriel laid his hand upon them, and their colors would swirl and mix together creating a magnificent display of heavenly light. Uriel would then share in their power. He would be able to fully understand their gifts, their contributions, and their challenges. This was the life of the archangel. By possessing all the gifts of the other angels, the archangel could more fully share in their joys and sorrows. Knowing their strengths and weaknesses enabled the archangel to serve the angels in their charge more fully. It was a great responsibility, it meant doing everything in your power to support and help the angels in your charge. It meant putting them ahead of yourself.

It meant understanding that truly leading came only through serving others and not by being served.

Today Aegeus would stand beneath the same tree and receive that honor. Today he would become an archangel. His mind raced with excitement, not for the promotion itself, although that was a tremendous honor, but he was excited to understand what life was like for the other angels.

Aegeus was pleased that no one had arrived for the ceremony yet; he wanted a few minutes to collect his thoughts. Walking closer to the tree he laid his rough hands against its bark brushing them lightly over the beautiful carvings, each one ornate and unique, each put there by the tree itself. Each serving a purpose, telling a story, if only one were willing to listen and able to hear.

Of course, he supposed that could be said of everything the King created. All of them were important, all of them served a specific purpose. Aegeus found himself thinking of the King's children and how desperately they needed to hear and know this truth. Too few of them truly understood how beautiful they were; so, few were able to see it.

As he slid his hands gently along the tree, images flittered through his mind. Scenes of things past and promises of things yet to come. Peace filled him.

Aegeus was searching for something specific, so he continued his way around the trunk letting his battle-worn hands glide across its ornate surface until finally, he found an area that felt warm. As soon as he touched the carving of the horn memories of the Twelfth flooded his mind.

He stood still and savored the memories now dancing through his mind like a movie. Memories of their first encounter when Sanyi released her into his charge. The moment when he first realized that she was indeed a prophet, the nights she fell asleep cradling her child in her arms and the look on her face when her dog unexpectedly fell to the floor and played dead during a dinner party.

That memory made Aegeus snicker. Reluctantly, he withdrew his hand from the tree afraid that remaining in the memories any longer would inevitably bring to mind things he would rather not recall. He could feel the tree calling to him, beckoning him to see more, to journey further into the memories. But memories of the Twelfth were tied tightly to so much more, and he didn't care to remember everything. Not today.

Instead, he stood peacefully relishing the remaining scent of the few memories he had indulged in. He let his mind linger briefly over Platitude and each of the twelve and their families. They were flawed and imperfect and beautiful. Because of them, Aegeus was finally able to understand why the King loved his children so much. It was the twelve who had helped him see.

The Twelfth wasn't what he had been expecting, and yet his encounter with her had been precisely what he needed. Aegeus had no doubt that that had been the King's plan all along. He basked in the memories a bit longer smiling and shaking his head as he recalled Kfir making himself smell like bacon, so a dog would chase him.

But not all the memories were pleasant, some of them carried great sorrow. Lavi had given his life to protect a girl without the Light. Haywood, battling to save the Fifth, had been destroyed before their eyes. And tragically, despite his sacrifice, she had been lost. Aegeus feared Meir would ever be the same. And of course, angels and humans alike would never forget that fateful day in the barley field.

Aegeus had believed that he would die that day. In fact, as Titus stood poised over him preparing to cut his wings off, Aegeus believed it to be unavoidable; it would be his honor to die in the service of the King. His sole fear had been for the Twelfth.

At that moment, when death seemed inevitable, his thoughts were submerged in the knowledge that she would witness it. How was it that she could see him? Would she now pay the price for that sight? He had been sent to protect her but had failed, and he feared she would pay the price for his failure. He worried how it would affect her and if she would fail to fulfill her purpose because of it. In anguish, Aegeus had prayed that Meir would help the Twelfth forget.

Memories of the mission and the Twelfth were not the only ones that carried sorrow. Thoughts of Platitude also brought with them sorrow over Seneca. Over the centuries Aegeus had rarely allowed himself to think of Seneca. After all this time, seeing him fully transformed from the magnificent angel he had once been into the imposing demon he had become was difficult.

Despite Aegeus's resolve to remember only the pleasant things from Platitude, memories of the final battle in Platitude encroached on his otherwise peaceful mind. It had not been easy to kill Seneca, but it had been necessary. Seneca had posed a threat to the prophet, and more importantly, he stood in opposition to the King. In many ways killing Seneca had allowed Aegeus to finally heal that wound.

It also helped him to more fully comprehend when the Word said that your love for the King had to be so great that your love of others looked like hatred in comparison. He did not have to hate Seneca to hate what Seneca had become. He did not have to hate anyone; he just needed to love the King more, and he did. When he returned to heaven from Platitude, he had never felt closer to the King.

But the memory that Aegeus would treasure most was the awakening of the prophet. It was a precious thing to behold.

The Twelfth had been blind to her calling. But in that final moment, as Aegeus's life hung in the balance, she had accepted it. The power of the Spirit had been overwhelming, and Aegeus felt honored to have witnessed it. He would carry that memory with him forever, it was one that brought him great joy.

He realized that it was precisely the type of thing Meir would use to bring comfort and encouragement. Knowing this made him smile, and he wondered how his dear friend was doing. He hadn't seen her since she returned to heaven. Soon enough, as an archangel, he would have the power to minister to her. He planned to bring her the same comfort she so often brought to others.

Aegeus purposefully stepped further from the tree and turned to face the wheat. Closing his eyes, he stood quietly letting the gentle breeze blow over him. In the distance, he could hear the song of a thousand angels singing out to the King. The sweet scent of vanilla hung in the air sweeping the remaining fragments of difficult memories away.

Chapter 2

"You look like you're in heaven," the King said quoting Kfir's favorite joke as he joined Aegeus under the tree. The tree reacted strongly to the King's presence sending colored lights soaring silently into the air. The King walked to the tree and placed his hand against the trunk. Golden sparkling light radiated from every branch like glitter. It reminded Aegeus of the lightning bugs he had seen in Platitude.

"Memories are one of the most precious gifts I offer my children Aegeus." The King moved toward Aegeus who instantly knelt before his King.

"My children's lives are so short upon the earth. Memories are all they bring with them when they join us here. In some ways, they themselves are a spectacular collection of memories. Memories are powerful. Their power does not just lie in those that are collected but also in those they leave with others. Memories contain the power to stir hope or despair, joy, or sorrow.

It is memories that the ministering angels use to comfort, encourage, and inspire. Your memories of Seneca will one-day do the same. You can choose to remember him as the valiant angel he once was or the demon he became. While both are true, you choose which one you focus on."

The King placed his hand on Aegeus' shoulder filling him with the Light.

"Aegeus your heart is heavy. Rise and tell me what troubles you." The King said gently.

"What became of the Strongman?" Aegeus asked.

"The Strongman fled the battlefield as soon as he saw that the mark of the warrior was glowing. Eventually, he resigned from the college in Platitude. Currently, he serves in Washington D.C. providing counsel to their leaders."

"So, then Platitude is free?"

"There is no shortage of evil upon the earth, and there were many who were eager to take his place." The King waited patiently for he understood that this was not what troubled Aegeus, but it was not in the King's nature to rush an issue.

"So, we lost?" Aegeus asked.

The King smiled, "What was your mission Aegeus?"

"To protect the Twelfth," he answered confidently.

"Did you do that?"

"I did. But...." Aegeus reflected on the final minutes of the battle. The prayers of the King's children brought light into the darkness. In those precious seconds, amid the power of prayer, the King's children protected Aegeus, not the other way around.

The King waited for Aegeus to wrestle through what had truly happened in the barley field. He knew Aegeus would continue to learn from that experience to reflect on it and find new power each time he did.

"Protecting you was the only way the Twelfth could ever discover who she truly was. And knowing who she is is critical to the next phase of her assignment. You did well Aegeus. We did not lose."

"The Tenth failed," Aegeus said, sadness seeping into him as he remembered the death of the Fifth, something Aegeus attributed to the Tenth failing to find his courage. The King smiled.

"He did seem to fail Aegeus. But even that was used for good. The Tenth will never forget what his cowardice cost. He is my child, and he came to me for forgiveness which I freely gave." The King paused, examining the tree and its fruit. "He found his courage in time." The King closed his eyes briefly, and when he opened them, there were all new varieties of fruit on the tree.

"It is often through what seems like a failure that my children learn the most valuable lessons. The Tenth will never again fail to stand when called to." The King concluded as he pulled a small green, square fruit, resembling a date, from the tree and handed it to Aegeus.

Aegeus took the fruit and popped it in his mouth where its sweet, rich flavor began to melt instantly.

"It reminds me of chocolate," he said with his mouth still full.

The King smiled in response. "It seemed like the day called for something new."

The King understood how vital timing was. Even as he waited now, understanding that the next question was the one that was dearest to Aegeus' heart; the next question was the one that mattered, the one that had transformed Aegeus into who he was. The King waited with anticipation for Aegeus to ask.

Raising his eyes to the King, Aegeus asked what was in his heart. "And the Twelfth what becomes of her?" The King smiled. Now they could have the conversation he had been waiting for.

"We have lost six angels, Aegeus." He spoke softly, gently. For he knew that Aegeus had been present for the death of each of the six. He had felt the full impact of each death; he wore physical reminders of each.

The King had long ago established a secret sign known only to the King and the angels. With the death of the seventh angel, the end of the age would begin. They did not know the exact day and time, but they would know that it was near. But it was not the remembrance of the sign that the King waited for. Slowly as a cloud moves across the sun, realization settled in Aegeus's eyes.

"She is to be part of it?" he asked, his eyes wide with knowledge and concern.

"Aegeus," the King said softly, "she is already part of it."

Chapter 3

Aegeus wasn't sure why the news that the Twelfth was part of the end of this age startled him, but it did. She had barely accepted the truth of who she was. There was still so much for her to learn. If she were to be part of the end of the age, she would face great trials; she would need help. *She was not yet battle ready.* He felt a hint of panic wash over him, *who was with her now as she trained? Had Lucifer discovered her?*

The King watched as Aegeus wrestled through his emotions searching to find the balance between his concern for the Twelfth's safety and his confidence in the King. The King did not take it personally, in fact, he felt great joy for Aegeus. For in learning to trust the King, to trust him even when part of you was bound by fear, in those times when you relinquish that which you want to the will of the King it is then that you demonstrate true faith. Those moments were among some of the most pleasing to the King.

"Who is with her?" Aegeus asked, uncertainty peppering his voice.

"Adiel is her warrior," the King answered. Aegeus felt confident in Adiel's capabilities. She was a mighty warrior strong and true. The Twelfth was safe with her. And yet he still felt a sense of loss that he could not quite explain. Handing her over, not being there himself, somehow it didn't feel quite right. Something in his soul whispered that it should be him.

"And her guardian?"

"Emeka."

Aegeus knew Emeka to be an excellent choice. He was a powerful guardian and a member of the elite guard.

"Can she see them?" He wasn't quite sure why he asked.

"No. Nor can she feel them."

So, in some ways, Aegeus thought, she was starting over. He could imagine that she felt alone, abandoned, just as she had with him at first. He knew it wasn't true but still, it pained him.

The King watched silently as Aegeus considered the situation.

Aegeus walked closer to the tree, placing his hands on its trunk, a habit he had developed eons ago when thinking deeply. He slid his hand along the rough bark of the tree strolling around its trunk, something that never failed to help clear his head. Occasionally he would pause as if the tree were imparting wisdom to him.

About halfway around the tree, he stopped and stood perfectly still. In complete peace, he looked around savoring the sights and sounds of home. A gentle breeze caused the heads of the wheat to billow, and in the distance, he saw a giraffe ambling along toward the mountains. Beautiful purple lights emitted from the tree giving the sky a pleasing hue. And still, the King waited silently.

Aegeus knew that the King was patient; he also knew that time was of no consequence here and so he took his time. He did not want to rush into the wrong decision. As he looked around at the majesty and beauty of heaven, he did not want to leave, and he knew he never would, not for the Twelfth, not for any reason other than the will of the King.

He could ask the King the right thing to do, but he also knew that the King would remain silent. Aegeus needed to make the right choice from his own heart. It was only right that Aegeus should choose his own path. The King believed in freedom. Love that was not chosen was not true.

Aegeus resumed walking at a slow pace, carefully considering his decision. Becoming an archangel was a great honor. It was something every angel dreamed of. After a period of training under Michael, when Aegeus was ready, he would be given oversight of a host of angels. It was a tremendous honor. One of the rarest and greatest honors the King could bestow on an angel.

Aegeus continued walking, pondering, wrestling with his thoughts. Becoming an archangel meant he would no longer fight the battles other warriors fought. He would never again be assigned to an individual human or family. He would rarely ever go to earth. His role would be different. But Aegeus didn't mind different. Change did not hinder angels. He didn't consider this a reason to pass up this opportunity and return to protecting the Twelfth.

As one of the King's children, her life on earth was limited. Eventually, she would return to heaven, her true home. Her time on earth was nothing more than a blink of the eye. Would he really give up being an archangel-something that was eternal-to help in a situation that was not?

Couldn't he watch over her from here? He could petition to be assigned to the Americas. Adiel could care for the Twelfth, it didn't have to be him. Was his desire to return and protect her a holy desire or was he teetering on pride?

Although... hadn't he given her his word in Platitude? Even if she had not been able to hear him, he had given her his word. He had vowed to fight for her. When Aegeus had circled the tree and again stood before the King, his decision had been made. He once again knelt before the King.

"My King, you have greatly honored me with the opportunity to become an archangel. But with humility, I respectfully decline and request to be reassigned to the Twelfth." A smile spread across the King's face; Aegeus had chosen well. Pleased, the King placed his hand on Aegeus' shoulder.

"Aegeus upon your creation I named you the Protector, you have earned your name many times over. But it was for this very mission that I created you. It is with tremendous pleasure that I grant your request. There are many preparations to make. Rise and assemble a team."

Chapter 4

Now that his decision to return to earth and serve the Twelfth had been made, Aegeus was eager to get his team and start the mission. Despite this, he waited patiently for Kfir not wanting to disrupt the training session. Instead, he leaned lazily against the beautiful fence surrounding the training complex. The fence was exquisite, yet straightforward much like the carpenter who built it. The sweet scent of roses met his nose as he leaned against it causing his mind to wander back to when the Lamb had made it.

The Lamb had returned to heaven different. The difference was difficult to define, subtle really, but it was there. The physical scars were easier to see, easier to understand. But the Lamb had also suffered emotionally; when he returned to heaven, the scent of humanity clung tightly to him.

Being human, walking among them had made a difference. Being on the earth left a mark on one's soul, the longer you were there, the more pronounced the mark. The Lamb was no exception, and when he returned, he retained a small sliver of humanity. He was a high priest who could empathize with their weakness; he had been tempted in every way, just as the rest of the King's children. But he had not given in to temptation. He returned victorious both as the Lamb and as the Lion of Judah.

Initially, after his return, there had been a grand celebration in heaven. Death had been defeated, the Lamb had returned to his rightful place at the right hand of the King. There was much to celebrate. But after the celebration, the Lamb had sought solace, time to reflect and renew. For reasons only he knew, he had come to the training field to find it.

The Lamb spent his quiet time at the military compound far from the city where he stood, day after day, quietly watching Heaven's Armies run through their drills. Aegeus and the others were mesmerized by his presence. Distracted even. Who could be in the presence of the Lamb and not be distracted by it?

Michael, despite the urge to the contrary, had continued their training pushing them to their best, pulling their attention back to the task at hand. But the Lamb was there. Aegeus could feel him, and he longed for nothing more than to put down his sword and go and sit with the Lamb. Of course, the Lamb had that effect.

Aegeus assumed that the Lamb simply wanted some quiet, something he had been deprived of on earth. Something he had often sought there but with little success. But of course, Aegeus didn't really know for sure. What he did know was that one-day, without any ceremony, the Lamb began building a fence.

He could have spoken the fence into being, but he didn't. He used his carpentry skills and built a fence out of Brazilian rosewood. He dug each post hole himself, hammering every nail. For what the Lamb knew, but the angels did not, was that the Lamb was building a hedge of protection around them, for he knew the battle that was coming.

Each day, when the training session was complete, Aegeus would wait until everyone else had left and then he would join the Lamb. He never spoke unless the Lamb spoke first. Sometimes they would remain silent. The Lamb building the fence, Aegeus holding, lifting, or digging as needed. All of it without words. It suited Aegeus.

But sometimes the Lamb would regale Aegeus with stories of his life on earth. He shared stories of his earthly family or his disciples. Funny stories that Aegeus imagined were precious to him. They would build amid the stories and laughter, the smell of the freshly cut rosewood filling the air.

After several passes of fruit on the tree, Joseph too arrived quietly and without fuss. His faced beamed with pride over his son and for some time he stood at a distance admiring the Lamb's work as he so beautifully performed the skill Joseph had taught him. In time Joseph approached and embraced his son.

They chatted about their earthly family: aunts, uncles, grandparents, and then as Joseph picked up a hammer and worked alongside him, the Lamb offered a brief update on Mary and his brothers. For quite some time after that, they did not speak. There was no need to. Aegeus left them then, earthly father and son working on the project together.

There was no urgency to their work. They took their time enjoying their task, enjoying each other's company until finally the job was done. Joseph departed to continue the heavenly job the King had assigned him, and the Lamb went to the gate to welcome Stephen, the first to be martyred.

In time, the Lamb returned to the compound. But when he returned, he came in full combat dress and walked confidently into the center of the arena. His eyes flamed and without a word, he drew his sword. He took over their training and worked them harder than Michael ever had. For the Lion knew the final battle would be great, but victory would be his.

The next time he came to the compound he brought David and a group of those who had once walked upon the earth as men, those prepared by the King to be warriors. They too trained for the final battle. From then on, the angels and the King's children trained side by side for the final battle. David led the King's children; Michael led the angels. But often they cross-trained. On occasion, the Lion would join them leading them all in the hardest training of their lives.

Aegeus had seen many passes of fruit since that time. Beautiful flowers had grown up around the fence adding to the ornate nature of its simplicity. The wood was still smooth and silky against his arms. Things in heaven did not decay or waste away as they did on earth. The fence would stand just where it was, just as it was, for all eternity.

Aegeus loved everything about the training compound, it was one of his favorite places in heaven. The smells were familiar, the sound of swords clanking against each other was comforting; the welcomed sound of voices raised together in comradery brought him joy.

The last mission had not been easy. Physically he had faced much greater, yet in every other way, Platitude had challenged his very understanding of who he was. Facing Seneca had been particularly difficult, but it had also been good for him; he realized that now.

Aegeus let the memory of Seneca at Pas Dammin fill his mind. The look in Seneca's eyes when he had fallen would probably always haunt Aegeus. Watching someone you love walk away from the King was difficult. It was even more difficult for the King. Aegeus understood that now.

He also now understood that time would never change that. For all eternity, Aegeus would grieve the loss of his best friend and brother in arms. The King too would always carry that loss with him. Seneca had chosen his path; however tragic it had been. Seneca had chosen wrong even if, at the time, it had seemed right to him.

Like Seneca, many made decisions that they thought were right, honorable even. But no choice that was out of alignment with the King was ever good or honorable. While the path before the person may seem right, it ended in death. They simply did not have the power to see the end of the path from the beginning of the journey. Walking with the King was the only way.

Sounds of revelry snapped Aegeus back to the present. He looked up to see Kfir standing amid the other warriors flailing his arms about in a way that was causing everyone to roar with laughter. He was obviously recounting a story of some sort - with great gusto. It made Aegeus chuckle just to see his gesturing, he found himself trying to guess the story behind it. He waited patiently for Kfir, not wanting to rush him, and not wanting to be rushed. He didn't know when or even if they would make it home.

Despite that, he had to admit this was the first mission in a long time that he was excited to start. The flight to earth was difficult, and most of his prior missions involved arriving on earth, battling and then the return flight. But Platitude had changed all that. Serving a human, not just battling, had given him a chance to reconnect with a part of his soul that he thought had been lost.

Chapter 5

"Brother, we missed you in training," Kfir said embracing Aegeus in the traditional greeting of the warrior. "Are you ready for the ceremony?" he asked, referring to Aegeus's promotion to Archangel.

"That's why I'm here," Aegeus began. Kfir smiled knowingly.

"You may want to do something about your hair before you stand in front of everyone," Kfir teased.

With a quizzical look on his face, Aegeus reached up and smoothed his hair. Kfir laughed a loud, infectious laugh at the sight. Aegeus gave him a brotherly shove in response.

"This from the angel with corn rows?"

"Hey, I'm bringing it back," Kfir offered, striking a pose that made Aegeus laugh all the louder as he turned toward the city. Without words, they began to walk.

"I have declined the promotion," Aegeus said, his smile betraying his joy over having found the perfect path of the King. Kfir smiled too. The news was not shocking to him, in fact, the only one who was probably surprised was Aegeus himself. Kfir knew Aegeus well, and he knew that once Aegeus learned to love the King's children, he would also desire to remain in their service. It was who Aegeus was, a warrior fiercely loyal to those he loved. Kfir had known long before the barley field that Aegeus would remain connected to the Prophet, but he was pleased to learn that Aegeus now recognized it too.

"Well then. Where are we headed?" Kfir asked although he had little doubt of where they were going.

"We return to the Twelfth," Aegeus answered.

"Of course." Slowly Kfir began to walk faster. At first, Aegeus didn't notice the subtle change, without thought he adjusted his pace to match. Kfir again sped up. Aegeus adjusted likewise, a smile now creeping onto his face. Without warning, they both shot into the air racing toward the city.

"You are never going to beat me, old man," Kfir yelled over his shoulder as he soared past the mountains at top speed. Aegeus flew just behind him pushing himself faster, the sights and sounds of heaven zooming past at an exhilarating pace. Because Kfir was looking back taunting Aegeus, he did not see the hippopotamus emerging from the watering hole.

Aegeus raised his eyebrows and nodded his head giving his brother in arms a slight hint of impending disaster. Kfir turned quickly enough to avoid a direct hit but not fast enough to prevent clipping the hippo with his wing and sending himself skipping across the water like a well-thrown rock. He landed with a thud on the other side.

Laughing as he flew by, Aegeus let his hand skim lightly through the water leaving a brilliant display of color behind. Aegeus pushed himself even faster enjoying the speed, enjoying the way it made the colors blend into one, the way the smells mixed together as he rushed from one to the next.

"How do you fly with your hair blowing around like that," Kfir called from behind him. Aegeus laughed and looked behind him to see Kfir closing in. It was no accident Kfir had won every race they had ever had; he was one of the fastest angels in heaven. A strand of kelp from the watering hole was clinging to the back of Kfir's head flapping about as he sped toward Aegeus, but it was not quite willing to let go and return to the ground. The sight caused Aegeus to laugh so hard he lost his balance and fell bouncing along the ground as Kfir zoomed passed him taking the lead.

Aegeus bumped along the ground a few times and then was instantly back in the air just as heaven experienced a color shower, one of Kfir's favorite phenomena. Beautiful colors, new colors, freshly created by the King, covered the land. The colors swirled around, bathing everything in a variety of hues. Each new color took a turn and then they joined together, like a beautifully choreographed dance swirling about, drenching everything, if only temporarily, in their wonderful hue. Aegeus watched with joy as Kfir changed colors. Everything was saturated, reflecting each new color as it performed its glorious dance designed to announce its arrival and demonstrate the glory of the King. Aegeus flipped and spiraled his way through the colors enjoying the beauty of it, enjoying watching as his own body changed with the beauty of each new color until finally, the shower was over.

As they approached the city, navigation became more difficult. The sheer number of angels and humans in the city meant they had to weave between bodies. Reluctant to slow down more than was necessary, they whizzed, somewhat recklessly, between buildings and around corners. Kfir headed directly for the Throne Room, but Aegeus veered off the path. His change of direction caught Kfir's attention. Kfir made an abrupt turn around the side of a building and nearly collided with Elvis.

"Sorry!" he called over his shoulder as he disappeared around the corner. Elvis waved in acknowledgment smiling at the sight of Kfir with kelp stuck to his head.

When Kfir rounded the building, Aegeus was there leaning against the wall waiting for him. But Kfir was unprepared for the sudden stop and crashed directly into Aegeus sending the two of them tumbling back into the streets of gold. They laid there haphazardly laughing for several minutes. Getting to his feet, Kfir offered

Aegeus a hand which he readily accepted. He decided not to mention the kelp.

"Supplies?" Kfir asked, knowing that had to be where they were going.

"I prefer our food." Aegeus offered, giving Kfir a knowing look. Kfir laughed.

"Don't you like hot dogs?" Kfir asked with a wink to which Aegeus rolled his eyes.

"I assume you want cupuacu muffins," Kfir asked, knowing they were one of Aegeus's favorite bakery items. They were fluffy with just a hint of salt unless of course, you asked Adiel who described them as moist and smooth with the perfect hint of sweet. Moist and sweet would not ever be what Aegeus wanted in a muffin and try as he might, he could never taste it that way.

Kfir knew that it didn't really matter what he got, each item tasted as unique as the person who was eating it, each drink tailored to the taste buds of the drinker, but each angel still had their favorites.

"Why don't you get the supplies and meet me in the Throne Room?" Aegeus suggested, "I need to make one more stop."

Chapter 6

Aegeus loved the Garden of Souls. There was something particularly sacred about it. As he approached, he could hear the flowers singing their hauntingly beautiful song to the King. Aegeus had never heard anything like it. His mind became entangled in the melody, all other thoughts temporarily forgotten.

No one had ever told Aegeus that the garden of souls was especially sacred. It was something you just knew. You could feel it as you approached.

He entered quietly and saw the King sitting on a golden bench with Meir. He noticed immediately that her hair was a beautiful shade of pink and she wore a robe that glimmered of gold. Her wings were the same shade of pink as her hair, their tips sparkling with gold. The sight of her hair blowing lightly in the breeze made him smile. He hadn't seen her hair pink in quite some time. He considered it an indicator that she was healing well.

Peter stood beside the King and Meir with the Book of Names. He had already unfastened the two brass seals, the key on its chain now securely back around his neck. The ancient book's leather was soft; its pages were worn and slightly yellow. It seemed such a contrast to the flowers.

The King looked up; his eyes smiling in greeting, but he did not speak. Speaking was uncommon in the garden. Aegeus stood still. It was only later that he realized he was holding his breath.

The garden was full of flowers, heaven's version of the Diphylleia grayi, also called skeleton flowers by the humans. Aegeus thought the name fitting, given their purpose. The translucent petals of each flower centered around a beautiful sphere of colored light, the human soul. The petals echoed that light, giving the flower a soft glow reflective of the soul itself.

The scent of purity and innocence floated in the air, a precious smell that remained with the soul for some time. Even the King's children recognized it. They, of course, did not realize it was the smell of an innocent soul but they could smell it. They would hold babies close and breathe deeply taking in the smell. The King had designed it that way. It served as a soft reminder, a hint of nostalgia entangled with the desire to protect the innocent.

Meir reached into the flower closest to her and carefully removed the soul that rested inside its delicate petals. It was a brilliant shade of violet. Once extracted from the flower its shape was as unique as it was.

She carefully rolled it in her hands as Aegeus had seen the Twelfth roll cookie dough once forming it into a ball. When she had finished, she cupped it in both hands and held it up in front of her face, closing her eyes. Meir paused soaking in the magnitude of what she was doing and listening to the soul's song. Aegeus knew that Meir was also bestowing gifts on the soul, gifts that would be etched into it, buried deeply, but they would be there when needed. Gifts no other type of angel could give.

Bestowing these basic gifts was not something the King needed Meir for. He could, of course, do this himself. But it was considered a great honor for a ministering angel to assist in the Garden of Souls. Touching a human soul when it was so pure, so innocent, brought about a unique kind of peace. It renewed their faith in the King's children. You could not handle a soul of such purity and walk away untouched.

The King, in his wisdom, designed this process to benefit the angels. Angels like Meir who ministered to the King's children and knew their deepest wounds. It was possible that one-day Meir would minister to this person while on earth. Because she had held their soul in her hands here in this garden that soul would respond more quickly to her touch on the earth. It was a simple act that offered so much to both the angel and the King's child.

Meir turned to the King. Peter leaned closer and got his pen ready, his eyes wide with anticipation. The King smiled looking from Peter to Meir slowly. He laid his hand lovingly over Meir's without yet touching the soul. He met her eyes and spoke quietly.

"You have done well Meir." Aegeus watched as Meir reacted to the sound of her name coming from the King. A gentle shudder of pure joy ran through her. Slowly Meir opened her cupped hands and released the soul into the hands of the King.

"My sheep shall know my voice," he said. The soul burst into light, and for just an instant it blazed a glorious golden color then just as quickly turned back to violet, burning brightly, and filling the garden with its colored light. The King chuckled obviously pleased. Meir let out a sigh of relief. Peter opened the Book of Names to the appropriate page and waited, his pen poised.

The King then spoke the soul's name, a name it would not hear again for many years. A name it would not quite remember ever knowing. Peter recorded the name in the Book of Names, and the Spirit would write it on a small white stone.

When the soul returned to heaven, it would be tattered and damaged. Earth had a way of doing that to a soul. Then the Lamb would present the soul with the stone reminding it of its true name. Eventually, those stones would be used to form a Wall of Remembrance on the new earth. Of course, not all the souls would return.

The King then split the soul into two making sure it was equally yoked; he gently handed one-half back to Meir. He meticulously wove threads into the half he still held. Each thread contained things they would need to face the challenges of their life. The golden thread included personality traits, talents, dreams, and aspirations as well as critical experiences. After he finished weaving in the golden thread, he pulled a short royal blue thread from a small basket that sat on the bench between him and Meir.

The blue thread contained the King's laws which would be written in the person's heart. It also provided the deep-rooted notion that there was something more, that innate feeling that life had to have a purpose and the yearning to seek out that purpose.

He then pulled an emerald green thread from the basket. It glimmered as he knitted it into the soul. It contained the King's plan for the person's life. The human would be happiest and most satisfied when they found that path and stayed on it.

Picking up a silver thread from the basket he broke it in half carefully assuring that it too stayed equally yoked. He wove half into the soul he held. The silver thread would help the soul to find its other half once on the earth. On that simple small thread was the secret to how they would once again find each other. The secret to how the two would become one. The King knew that not all the souls would find each other on the earth. Some would give up too soon and join with another.

He finished knitting the soul together using a scarlet thread containing the day and time of their birth as well as their death. When the King had finished, he spoke a blessing over his child and then turned slightly toward Aegeus away from Meir. An angel, one Aegeus had not noticed, stood from a kneeling position, and held out a small vile. The King placed the soul into the vial sealing it carefully. The angel nodded to the King and left to deliver the soul to the womb of its mother.

That soul in transit, the King turned back to the other half, the half that Meir held gently, protectively. She held it out to the

King, and he repeated the same process knitting it together. This half would also get all its own threads. It would be completely unique and independent of the other half. They would share only the silver thread.

When both halves eventually returned to heaven, they would once again become one. Two halves of one whole, similar to how the King, the Lamb, and Spirit were three in one. The King took his time weaving in each thread. When he had finished, he once again placed the soul into a vial and handed it to an angel to be transported to its mother. Aegeus understood that while mere seconds had passed in heaven, the souls themselves might be delivered to the earth years apart.

He noticed that Meir had scooped the next soul from its flower and cradled it as she waited patiently for the King to finish his work with the previous one.

When he was ready, she handed it to the King. This time when he spoke, "My sheep shall know my voice," its light dimmed, flickered, and then turned a murky gray. The King sighed heavily. He had of course known this would happen; he had always known. Meir and Peter sat wide-eyed and ashen. Aegeus felt bewildered. He didn't fully understand, but it was evident something terrible had happened, of that much he was sure.

The King repeated the same process as he had with the prior soul. He declared its name then split it in half, something he did not necessarily always do and then he began to knit it together weaving in each thread. Peter recorded the name. But Peter knew that this soul had a high risk of never returning to heaven. This soul may not choose to return to the King; only the King knew for sure. As the King finished weaving the soul, the Lamb appeared in the garden. He nodded silently to Aegeus in acknowledgment as he walked toward the King.

"Father?" he said as he extended his nail-scarred hands toward the soul. The King gently placed the soul in the Lamb's hands. The Lamb held the soul up to eye level, and he stared deeply into it, whispering something to it that Aegeus could not quite hear and then he sealed it in its vial to go to the earth.

Chapter 7

Aegeus waited until the last angel had left the Garden of Souls on their way to earth with the soul entrusted to them. He sat still almost transfixed by the experience. Peter closed the Book of Names and sealed it until the next Releasing of Souls Ceremony.

"Will you be joining John?" the King asked Peter, a smile on his face.

"Unless you need something else," Peter said, more as a question than a statement. The King laughed, the sound of it filling the garden. Aegeus too laughed merely from the joy of it.

"Enjoy your time together. I understand the fish are biting."

"They always do when the Lamb is in the boat," Peter said with a wink as he departed.

The King stood from the bench he had been sharing with Meir. She too rose to her feet nodding slightly to Aegeus in greeting. Aegeus knelt before the King.

"Aegeus, I trust you are here to tell me you have assembled your team and are ready to depart for the earth?"

"Yes, my King."

"Come let us go to the throne room. Meir, join us."

Meir's eyes met Aegeus's, and she smiled meekly. Aegeus raised his eyebrows in question, and she nodded to reassure him that she

was ok, then she broke his gaze and without a word fell into step behind the King. Aegeus rose and joined them.

As they left the Garden of Souls and the song of the flowers faded, other sounds filled his ears. In the distance, he could hear children playing. He imagined they were playing toggle ball, one of his
favorite games, but he had no way of knowing for sure.

"Lion races."

"What?" Aegeus asked slightly unsure if he had missed something.

"The children, they have lion races today. Noah insisted." The
King had a teasing smile as if he and Aegeus shared a joke among
them. The King regaled Aegeus and Meir with stories as they continued the short walk toward the throne room.

When the savory smell of sacrifice and obedience wafted toward
them, they knew they were close. The King stopped and breathed it
in.

Turning towards Aegeus and Meir, he asked, "Do you know
what my children think heaven is like?" Aegeus had to concede that
he had never really thought about it. He had always known heaven.

"Many of them think they will sit on clouds and play harps for all
of eternity. They worry that it will be nothing but standing around
singing." The King said with a light laugh and a shake of his head.
"Can you imagine anything more boring?"

Aegeus could *not* conceive of anything more boring. Even the
long hours he had spent in the house with the Twelfth watching her
unpack and paint weren't as dull as laying on a cloud playing the harp
for all of eternity. And yet he was unsure of why the King mentioned
such things.

"Their understanding is limited," Meir offered.

"Indeed," the King responded. "It is important that you remind
yourselves of that as you work with them."

"I am enjoying my work here," Meir offered gently as if to imply she need not bother with the silly practices of humans. The King stopped and turned toward her, compassion filled his eyes as he looked at her.

"What is the name I have given you?" he asked gently. Meir stood still, her loose hair billowing around her face. Suddenly, her hair turned from pink to the color of gold. Her eyes transformed to the color of creamed honey.

"Giver of Light," she said proudly, standing just a little taller.

"And what have I designed you for?" he asked patiently.

"To minister to your children," she cast her eyes down away from his all-knowing gaze. The King reached out to her gently. A flare of light erupted from Meir as the King placed his hand on hers. She lifted her watery eyes to meet his loving gaze.

"You have done well here Meir. But I did not create you for this. You have been resting in my presence, as you should, but you must also be actively walking the path I have designed for you. It is there that you will be most satisfied, and it is there that you will bring me the most glory. It is time." He spoke gently, for he knew Meir well. He knew that her heart was tender, and she would respond easily. He loved that she felt safe in his presence and that she longed to remain there. But it was time for her to fully release her pain and step back onto the path he had created for her. The death of the Fifth had been devastating to Meir; he understood that. But he also understood that it was time for her to embrace that pain as part of who she was and to learn to use it to help others.

"You desire for me to join Aegeus on this mission?" she asked, understanding peppering her voice.

The King smiled. "I do."

Meir bowed her head to indicate her willingness to comply with the desire of the King. He squeezed her hand gently and then released it as he continued their walk toward the throne room.

Chapter 8

Michael was waiting for them when they arrived. He swung the large doors open leading the way inside. Kfir and the Lamb were already there chatting amicably. As Aegeus entered the throne room, the Lamb reached up and with amusement removed the Kelp from Kfir's hair. Kfir's face flushed for a minute and he shot a look at Aegeus who tried not to laugh.

As was the custom when leaving for a mission, the Lamb would offer them a blessing and the King would fill them full of his Light. Each of them knelt before the throne eagerly awaiting their turn.

The Lamb walked first to Meir and placed his hands on her bowed head. Her hair and wings turned a beautiful purple color bathing the room in the rich hue. Aegeus was pleased to see her changing colors so often, it meant she was truly healing and was ready to be back in the field.

"Meir, I have something for you," the Lamb said gently, "rise," Meir rose. The Lamb gave a subtle signal to Michael who once again opened the Throne room doors. One of the King's children stepped in. She walked slowly across the sapphire floor her head down her face somewhat hidden. Aegeus could not see who it was, but he could feel her emotions simmering just beneath the surface.

Meir must have felt it too. She shifted her weight, and her wings began to sparkle, something they did when she was preparing to minister to someone. The Lamb extended his hand toward the woman, and as she drew nearer, she reached out grateful to take his steadying hand. Aegeus felt her relax immediately.

When she reached the lamb, she lifted her head and recognition settled in all their eyes. Aegeus heard a slight gasp from Meir who instantly sank back to her knees. The Fifth, once again overwhelmed by emotion and no longer able to hold it back, rushed forward and embraced Meir. Aegeus stood stunned.

"I am so sorry. I am so so sorry," the Fifth cried over and over into Meir's ear as she clung to her. Aegeus could not understand what was happening. The two women clung to each other emotion rising from them and mingling into a beautiful display of color and lights. Slowly, Meir looked up into the eyes of the Fifth.

"It's you," Meir said shock filling her voice.

"Yes. I am sorry for what I did. For what I have put you through," the Fifth said, tears coursing down her cheeks.

"It is I who should be sorry," Meir began. "I failed to save you. Haywood gave his life, and I failed you both. I am so sorry," Meir added wrapping her arms around the Fifth to embrace her in the human tradition. They hugged for some time, before slowly, with reluctance, releasing each other. It was then that the Fifth could truly look into Meir's radiant purple eyes and see the full extent of the pain she had caused.

"Meir, I understand now that there was much the King had planned for me. Many things that he wished me to do on the earth. I am the one who failed. I allowed the darkness to overtake me. I refused to feed my soul or hear the truth. Being reunited with my husband and daughter has been amazing, but I now understand that it wasn't time.

I know that there was so much I failed to do on the earth. I just couldn't see it. You did all you could to save me. I didn't know. I thought I was alone. I know now that was a lie from the evil one. I had no idea. Haywood-" her voice broke with the utterance of his name.

"I am so sorry," she went on when she was able to, "I am sorry that I did not love myself better, that I fought so hard against you, that I caused so much harm to all of you." She said looking at everyone in the room. "I didn't know-" she faded off emotion again strangling her words as they tried to find their way out.

In those words of apology and forgiveness, love and sorrow, Meir found herself. Her hair turned dark blue like the sea on a stormy day, and her wings began to glow and sparkle. She stood to her feet still holding the hands of the Fifth, bringing her with her. Her tears were gone, and her voice was sure and strong.

Meir wiped away the tears of the Fifth offering her the comfort she had been unable to provide on earth. A smile crept across Meir's face, her eyes aglow with a fire she had not known since the Fifth's death.

"We have a bond that shall not be broken," she told the Fifth. "I have worn your blood. Through you, I have known my greatest sorrow, and through you, I have also known great healing. Thank you." With those simple yet powerful words, Meir once again embraced the Fifth.

When Meir released her, The Fifth nodded to each of the angels. Kfir waved awkwardly in return, and the Fifth turned to leave them. Meir now standing straight and tall turned to the Lamb.

"Thank you," she said. The Lamb smiled at her.

"It was an important step for both of you. Now you are both ready." He said smiling.

The King walked to each member of the team filling them with the Light of God, their most powerful weapon and their source of energy and power while on the earth. The King himself was the source of the Light. Being on earth, they would be exposed to demons which would deplete their strength, as did performing miracles and engaging in battle. But prayer and the unsuppressed presence of the Spirit refilled both the angels and the humans.

"Time has passed on the earth, it has been three years since you left. Much has changed, and much is at stake. Stop and see Sanyi on your way to the prophet. He is her Keeper." The King paused slightly to assure Aegeus understood the command. Aegeus bowed his head slightly indicating he did, although he had not known Sanyi was a Keeper.

The King continued, "This mission will challenge each of you in ways you cannot yet understand," he said to the team.

"Aegeus, remember that there is much to be gained from the journey. The process is as important as the results." The King walked to Kfir and gently placed his finger on Kfir's forehead. A quick flash of light was shared between them.

"Kfir, I have imparted new knowledge to you that I think you will both enjoy and find useful to your purpose. Use it wisely."

"Yes, my King," Kfir said smiling broadly, excited to discover what it was.

The King turned once again to Aegeus "the team is ready?"

"Yes. Adiel is already with the Twelfth as is Emeka. With Kfir and Meir that gives us three warriors, a guardian, and a ministering angel."

"You will need another," the King answered.

"Who?" Aegeus asked knowing the King had one in mind.

"Mordecai."

"I don't understand?" Aegeus questioned. "The Twelfth is his bloodline?" concern flooded his voice.

"Mordecai will know his mission and his charge when it is right that he should," the King answered. Aegeus had just let down the walls around his heart. But at those words, he began to rebuild, protecting himself from the tragedy that may ensue. He did not wish to lose the Twelfth; he resolved not to-but even that thought terrified him. The Lamb walked to Aegeus.

"Protect the Twelfth Aegeus," he said laying his hand on him and filling Aegeus with power and reassurance.

"As the King commands, so shall I do," Aegeus responded. Aegeus could not imagine ever violating the will of the King, no, he would always choose to honor the will of the King over his own. But needing a Sentinel was something unexpected, something that scared him.

Those who needed Sentinels, those in their bloodline, faced a tremendous decision. A decision that had the power to change not only their own course but the course of humanity itself. The Sentinel would protect their charge fiercely until the decision had been made. If the charge chose well, the Sentinel would remain with them throughout their entire life. But if the charge chose the way of the evil one, the Sentinel was forced to walk away.

As the angels departed the throne room, the woman with the wild red hair entered.

"This will be difficult for them all," she offered. The Lamb and the King acknowledged this truth.

The King turned to Michael, "Send a detail to Tanzania, there is someone there of utmost importance."

"As the King wills, so shall I do," Michael replied before leaving the throne room to see to the task.

When Michael had left, the woman with the wild red hair turned to the King, "This will be a great test for Aegeus."

"Indeed" the King answered. "But he must assure himself of what I already know, that his love for me is greater than his love for her."

The woman with the wild red hair nodded knowingly, it was indeed an important lesson for him. "I will see that all eleven are in place."

Chapter 9

Aegeus, Kfir, and Meir looked around at the rugged terrain of Death Valley, it was a harsh environment. The dessert was sweltering. Aegeus guessed it was easily one hundred and twenty degrees in the human world. He was grateful that angels were not susceptible to the fluctuating temperatures of the earth. Demons were not as lucky. In the distance, he could feel the presence of an angel, but he couldn't quite see them yet. As they rounded a boulder, they found the angel hovering over a cluster of large stones.

"We seek Mordecai, Sentinel of the King," Aegeus called out to the unknown angel.

"I am Mordecai," he responded stepping forward toward the group.

Having never met a Sentinel Aegeus was unsure of what to expect. Mordecai was powerful with long hair that seemed to be the muted color of human hair instead of the strong colors angels normally had. He emitted a power that was different from that of typical angels. It was hard to describe, but Mordecai seemed to transmit the feel of both an angel and a human.

"It's the tear I was forged from," Mordecai offered in answer to Aegeus's unspoken question. "The King drops the tear of a human to the earth, when it hits, well," he held his hands out to signify that it resulted in something extremely rare, the formation of a Sentinel.

"You can feel the humanity of it. But I assure you I am an angel committed to the service of the King as I know you are Aegeus." He extended his arm in the traditional greeting of the warrior, a sign of comradery.

Aegeus grasped his arm in return. "You know who we are?" he asked, his surprise evident.

"The King told me you were coming," Mordecai answered easily.

"He looks like Thor," Kfir whispered a bit too loudly.

"Who?" Aegeus said perplexed, not able to think of any angels named Thor.

"You know, Thor the legend?" Kfir asked expectantly as if it were obvious. Aegeus searched his mind, but still, he came up blank. Kfir shook his head in disbelief but resigned himself to try once more.

"The Twelfth and her family watched a movie about him one night. They had popcorn?"

"They had popcorn? That is the clue that is supposed to help me remember?" Aegeus asked jokingly shaking his head.

Mordecai laughed at the exchange.

"I assure you I am more powerful than Thor. You need not worry. But sometimes when I take a form the humans can see, it does make the sound of a low roll of thunder," he offered to Kfir. Kfir smiled appreciating the reference.

"Do you take a form they can see often?" Kfir asked intrigued. Taking a form the humans could see required a great deal of energy and most angels could only maintain the form for short periods of time, a day or two at most.

"It is easier for me than for most," Mordecai answered.

"Is it true you don't return to heaven between missions," Kfir asked as if it were show and tell day.

"It is." Mordecai kept his answer simple and direct.

"What do you do then?" Aegeus prompted. It was strange to him to think of an angel remaining on earth so long.

"There is much to do. I live among them, offering small acts of kindness and testing those with the Light."

"What kind of tests," Kfir asked.

"Whatever the King wills." His answer was the truth, yet he could see they were not satisfied. "Tests of patience are common or hospitality. I test their kindness, patience, gentleness, those kinds of things. Simply put, I test their fruit."

This the angels understood.

"Sometimes they are simple tests: tangled Christmas lights, lost luggage, a flat tire, a lost cell phone, a misbehaving computer, an unexpected visitor," he offered as examples. Aegeus was not familiar with some of the references, but he understood the concept.

"Other times the test is more advanced," he went on, "Will they be kind when I am dirty? Will they show me compassion when I am in a form they find repulsive, will they feed me when I am hungry? But the purpose is always the same. Reveal their fruit, draw them closer to the King."

"How long has it been since you were home?" Meir asked.

"Three hundred and two earth years." This answer shocked them. Meir could not imagine being away from the King that long. How had he managed it?

"The King has provided many paths by which I am filled with his Light and strength. Prayers are one, as I know it is for you, but there are also places on the earth that serve as recharging stations if you will. And of course, I can communicate with him constantly despite being on earth." He said hoping to encourage them.

"Recharging stations?" Aegeus asked.

"Sorry, I spend so much time among the King's children I have picked up many of their expressions. The King has created places on the earth where Sentinels can go to receive power and healing. This is one such place," he gestured around him.

"Death Valley is a..." Kfir stumbled for the phrase "recharging station?"

Mordecai laughed with obvious delight.

"Yes. There are others, some of them in rather remote places, others in the middle of cities. I prefer the remote ones, but I go to whatever is closest." Mordecai offered a smile.

The angels continued asking questions of Mordecai, and he patiently answered them all, not at all bothered by their curiosity. He realized he was different, something they weren't used to. He imagined they had never met a sentinel, few angels had. Eventually, the sun began to set, catching their attention and drawing the discussion to a natural close.

"I have been waiting for you." Mordecai offered "I understand I have a charge." The other angels nodded. Aegeus found himself cringing at the idea that the Twelfth was that charge. Mordecai looked around slowly taking in the desert that surrounded them. The sunset bathed the desert floor in glorious shades of yellow and orange. He found solace in this place; he wasn't quite ready to leave.

"Please join me in a round of Stones," he invited. Despite his growing anxiousness to get to the Twelfth, Aegeus agreed to the game.

Stones was a seemingly simple game, and yet Aegeus didn't quite get it. Kfir kept likening it to Chess, a reference that did not help Aegeus, given he had never heard of Chess either. While Aegeus did not fully understand the game, he did understand the premise, move the stones into a variety of strategic spots.

Eons earlier, the stones, sliding along the desert floor, had been noticed by the humans. No matter how discretely the angels moved the stones, they left a trail in the sand. It was a phenomenon the humans noticed and began to investigate.

The King's children made many attempts over the years to find the source of the mysterious sliding stones. The angels found that remaining undetected added an element of excitement to the game. They created a few rules out of necessity. They would have to control their efforts and work slowly, so the human eyes could not see the movement. They also created a rule that you couldn't use your hands to move the stones. For close to a century these rules brought an exciting new aspect to the game.

Scientist had also found it fascinating. At one time, large crowds had come to see the sliding stones, and the angels had mingled among them. The King's children were so fascinated by it that they spent nearly seventy years studying the game, not recognizing it as such. Eventually, they caught the movement on camera and developed a scientific theory explaining it away, excited to finally have the answer. With the question answered, some of the human's fascination with the sliding stones had passed.

Mordecai set up stones for Aegeus, Kfir, and Meir. He went first demonstrating his personal technique. Because there were no humans present to bear witness, Mordecai moved the stone a considerable distance. Kfir went next. Kfir tried blowing the stone forward. He managed to produce a substantial gale force wind moving his stone about a quarter of an inch and kicking up a lot of sand in the process. Aegeus using much the same technique, pushed his stone about half an inch. The other angels cheered.

"Well now we know you have more hot air than me," Kfir offered in jest.

Meir stepped up and gently waved her wings. They began to sparkle. Gold light emanated from them. The wind they generated became stronger, and the golden light swirled and danced in beautiful patterns around her. The light had so mesmerized Aegeus that he hadn't even noticed her stone gliding smoothly across the desert floor, the sand remaining in place, completely oblivious of the wind that whirled around it. When the wind died down, and the lights faded the other angels discovered she had moved her piece into a critical position giving her the advantage. Countering her move would require thought and strategy. But she had also left herself vulnerable. It was a bold move, one none of the other angels had expected.

Mordecai stepped forward. "Impressive," he offered sincerely. He would need time to ponder his next move. "Perhaps this is a good time to find the Keeper?" he suggested. Aegeus nodded in agreement. He did not wish to delay any longer.

Chapter 10

Sanyi was glad Aegeus and Kfir had agreed to meet him at the coffee shop. He looked around longingly; he was going to miss it. He had been serving in this part of the country for over a hundred years. It suited him, it was a nice way of life. There was lots of heat in the summer, rain, and mud in the spring, beautiful colors in the fall and an abundance of cold, snow, and ice in the winter. Each season was robust and distinct, but they faded nicely from one to the next. Each season on earth brought its own pleasures, and Sanyi had learned to appreciate them all, acknowledging that that was easier to do because the temperature of the earth did not affect angels.

Season changes were one of the things Sanyi had had the most trouble adjusting to when he first came to earth. In heaven, the temperature was always perfect for each person, rainstorms didn't get you wet, and a gentle fog would fill the valley with a quiet softness on rare but beautiful occasions.

Some beings preferred the heat. Others, like Sanyi, liked it cold. They wanted to bundle up in coats and scarves and in heaven, they could. It snowed sometimes, but unlike on the earth, the temperature never changed. The snow itself did not feel cold to your hands.

Sanyi loved when it snowed, perhaps it was why he enjoyed this part of the country so much, or perhaps his love of snow was why the King had assigned him here. Sanyi loved big snowball fights and building snow animals. He never tired of seeing Kfir lay in the snow making snow angels, something the angels had first heard about on earth.

The landscape here was also to his liking. Some areas were rocky and jagged, others were quite flat. The soil was rich, and the sun shone bright and clear like no other place he had ever been.

The cities were just the right size for Sanyi as well, not too big but not tiny. This town, where he had been serving for the last several decades, was among his favorite cities in the state. He would miss it. But the call to assist Aegeus had come at just the right time. His latest charge had turned twelve, so Sanyi would be moving on. The family guardian was quite capable, and the boy was a couch dweller, so the job had become rather undemanding.

Sanyi, in a form visible to the humans, stood at the counter patiently waiting for his coffee. If he had to leave the area, he could at least have one last cup of his favorite earthly drink before he went. Tanzania was a long flight.

The girl behind the counter smiled as she handed him his coffee, and he couldn't help but wonder if some part of her could feel the power that so often emitted from the angels. Some of the humans could. They rarely recognized what it was, but some of them felt it.

He thanked her for the coffee, put a respectable tip in the tip jar and then took a seat at a table in the far corner trying not to make eye contact with any of the King's children. It required a great deal of energy to appear in a form the humans could see, a form they would consider human. But the coffee shop was one of the rare instances when he considered it worth it. In fact, the coffee shop was a bit of an angel hang out.

The shop was built to look like an old log cabin, and the coffee was amazing. Sanyi's favorite was the Palomino made from white coffee and white chocolate. It was, to Sanyi, a little taste of heaven in a cup. The coffee shop had praises to the King decorating its walls and angels tended to flock there, initially because so many of the King's children did but soon because they liked it.

The angels would take a variety of human forms and mingle, undetected, among the humans, drinking coffee and chatting amicably. Sanyi tried to blend in and savor his last Palomino.

The shop was full but not crowded. He noticed there were nearly as many angels as there were humans. The angels milled about chatting and sharing stories of their charges as their charges too met with friends, chatted with family, and savored their coffees. He really was going to miss it.

"It isn't a very original name," Kfir said surprising Sanyi at the table. Pleased to see Kfir, Sanyi stood from the table and embraced his friend.

"I suppose not," he said smiling. "But try the coffee you won't be disappointed."

Kfir embraced the invitation, he loved trying new things, and something that came with an angel recommendation was guaranteed to be good.

"What do you suggest?" Kfir asked excited to order as many as possible. The journey from Platitude had taken longer than he had anticipated, and he was ready for a snack.

"I like the Palomino," Sanyi offered, gesturing toward his own cup. Kfir, already disguised as a human, walked confidently to the counter, eager to get himself a cup of coffee and something called a breakfast sandwich.

Aegeus introduced Mordecai to Sanyi, who had the same reaction to encountering a Sentinel that each of the others had had. Mordecai launched into his explanation of how the sentinel was formed, and therefore gave off a different feeling than most angels.

While Mordecai explained it to Sanyi, Aegeus let his eyes rove over the quaint shop. There were lots of the King's children happily chatting about their plans for the day while they ate bakery goods and washed them down with a host of coffees that filled the air with a smell that made him miss Lavi.

But more surprising was the number of angels who also milled about, some in their angel form and some disguised as humans. Aegeus wondered how long the angels had been gathering here.

Their disguises were well chosen. There was a table of guardians disguised as elderly men. To human eyes, Aegeus was sure they looked like a group of friends gathered to share fishing stories. Teenage girls at another table were, in actuality, a mix of ministering angels and guardians.

"It's one of the more popular angel hangouts," Sanyi stated, interrupting Aegeus's thoughts. "Sit," he offered, gesturing toward the empty chairs at the table.

"So, I hear you passed up the promotion of archangel?" Sanyi asked.

"It was the right thing," Aegeus answered with confidence. Sanyi nodded knowingly.

Kfir returned with his coffee and joined the other angels around the small table. He held the cup to his mouth and took a small sip of the hot liquid. Aegeus waited anxiously for him to make a crazy face or even spit it from his mouth. Instead, he closed his eyes and let his head loll back just a little. A look of tranquility crossed over his face, and he sat unmoving for a long time. It made Aegeus a little nervous.

"Kfir?" he asked a little worried, a little perplexed.

"It. Is. Heavenly," Kfir said opening his eyes slowly and grinning widely. "Aegeus, you MUST try this," he pushed the cup toward Aegeus who drew back appalled at the idea. He had no desire to try coffee, the smell was pleasure enough.

"It is really good," Kfir offered again.

"I'll try it," Mordecai said taking the cup from Kfir. One small sip and he too was convinced. "Try it Aegeus," he urged sliding the cup toward Aegeus.

Aegeus's face said more than his words ever could.

"It is really good," a ministering angel from another table offered. Aegeus looked up surprised. They had attracted the attention of most of the angels in the shop, all of them watching to see what he would do.

"Is this one of those times when you pretend something tastes good so that I will try it and share in your misery?" Aegeus asked Kfir. The angels all chuckled at that, but Kfir reassured Aegeus this was not one of those times.

"It is amazing, Aegeus. You have to try it," Kfir nodded in assurance.

Aegeus took the cup hesitantly, even if Kfir loved it, it was unlikely that he would. He found that most of the human's food was not good. Concealing the cup so that the humans would not see it, he lifted it to his lips and looked around the coffee shop. The angels all watched silent and with great anticipation. Hoping this wasn't a trick, he tilted the cup up, so the hot liquid flowed into his mouth.

His eyes shuddered just slightly as his taste buds reacted to the flavors of the coffee. Images of heaven flashed before his eyes; it was indeed a little bit of heaven in a cup. The angels around the room cheered in response to his obvious delight.

A broad smile lit Kfir's face. "I told you. Now if you want more, you must get your own," he said as he pulled his cup back toward him.

"I'll get us each one," Mordecai offered getting up from the table. Aegeus watched as Mordecai flew straight out the roof of the shop. They could hear a soft roll of thunder and then Mordecai walked back in the front door in human form. He went to the counter and ordered two Palomino's and then joined the others back at the table.

The angels sat for a while longer while Aegeus filled Sanyi in on all that had happened since he had turned the Twelfth over. When he was done with his update, he paused just for a moment and then plunged in.

"I did not know you were a Keeper," he said to Sanyi.

"Few know. That is the way it works best." Sanyi answered. Aegeus nodded knowingly.

"The King says you have information for us," Aegeus prompted.

"Part of my job as a Keeper is concealment," Sanyi started. "I specialize in using the humans' own tools and discoveries to conceal that which needs to be concealed, until the time of revealing. In this case, I have concealed all of those from Platitude associated with the Prophet, and the Prophet herself. Once she acknowledged that she was a prophet, she became quite vulnerable, all of them did. So, we have concealed them, hidden them from Tracker demons. Low-level demons cannot see the mantel of the prophet, so we don't worry about that. But we don't want the warriors to find her or the others." Aegeus and the others could appreciate the wisdom of those words.

"Because of this," Sanyi continued, "The demons cannot use simple, modern means to find them, but that, of course, means that neither can you," he said.

"How are we to find her then?" Aegeus asked.

"You will have to search as in days of old. It is the only way to keep all of them concealed from the demons now. Otherwise, Lucifer would do a quick search, find their location, and send a team to destroy them, to destroy her," Sanyi added.

"Return to the beginning, and you will be able to track Adiel and Emeka to find the prophet. But should you need to find any of the others, you will not find them as easily."

This news did not please Aegeus. But if it were the will of the King, he knew there must be a reason and the logic made sense, so he tried to dismiss the agitation.

"Do we need to find the others?" Aegeus asked, hopeful that they did not. He felt as if it would result in a great delay in getting to the prophet, and she was his primary mission.

"Their lives are intertwined Aegeus. What effects one, effects all. Even if they don't yet realize it. It is important that each of them travels the road laid out for them. If even one fails, they will all fail."

"And what is this road?" Aegeus asked, a sense of foreboding starting to creep up his neck.

"It is a road that will wind until they are all once again together. A road that will crisscross their lives until they are no more. It is a road that is dangerous. The Twelfth cannot succeed without them all Aegeus. They are the warriors she must go into battle with. It is important that you hear me say that, not as her former guardian but as her Keeper."

"So, we are to find them all?" Aegeus asked with poorly concealed disappointment.

"You are to find the Prophet. But you will need the others. Your paths will cross, and as they do, assure they are well covered, especially the Second and the Third. As prayer warriors, they are essential to the humans and angels alike."

Sanyi drank down the last of his coffee and stared into the empty mug for a minute before speaking again. "Aegeus, you need to know that when they are once again all together, there will be great sorrow for the Prophet."

Aegeus and Meir exchanged glances at that news. None of this sounded to Aegeus like what he had been expecting. Finished with what he needed to convey, Sanyi turned and chatted conspiratorially with Kfir while Aegeus consulted briefly with Meir on the best approach to finding the Prophet. Then with a last mournful glance and goodbyes to the group, Sanyi headed to Tanzania for the next phase of his assignment.

Mordecai stepped forward, "Where is it we are headed?" he asked.

Meir answered, a slight sadness washing over her words, "A little town in the middle of nowhere."

Chapter 11

In many ways, Platitude had not changed. The mountains still stood tall and proud, the brook still gurgled through separating the college from the rest. Demons still formed a dome blocking out the light although the coverage was not nearly as complete as it had been during their prior mission. The presence of so many told Aegeus that another Strongman had arrived. Lucifer had not given up on his plan to take over the college. The prior mission had not stopped them, but at least it seemed to have slowed them down.

"Do we know how many of them are still here?" Kfir asked Aegeus as they stood just outside the town limits in the same salvage yard that had served as their headquarters when they were here last.

"I know only that the Twelfth is not. Mordecai and Meir check their homes. See if you find any of them still living here." Secretly Aegeus hoped they would not find any of them. It was a particularly difficult place for their souls. "Kfir, go to the restaurant, coffee shop, library, and movie theater. Check every public place. I will check the campus. We will meet back here."

Each of them flew from the salvage yard to their respective assignments. Aegeus flew slowly through the streets of Platitude letting gentle memories brush past him as he did. He was pleased to see that more people had the Light than when he had been here last, and their Lights burned more brightly than before.

He flew passed Perks and instantly thought of Lavi who had given his life in defense of a girl without the Light, he wondered briefly what had become of her. The smell of newly ground coffee beans chased him for several blocks. A small line of college students waited patiently outside the door of a new bakery. As Aegeus rounded the corner the smell of freshly baked bread and vanilla wrapped around him mingling with the lingering scent of the coffee.

Aegeus tried to avoid areas that he knew would have a heavy demon presence, a warrior showing up among them would undoubtedly attract a level of attention that he did not need. Instead, he veered off the main street and flew around the edge of the mountain, arriving across from the campus near the barley field.

He ignored the memories that tugged at his mind. Instead, he focused on the mission at hand. As he got closer to the campus, the putrid smell of the cafeteria rushed up to meet him. He had nearly forgotten how bad it was. Trying to ignore it, he began a careful search of the campus.

Aegeus had covered about half the campus before he saw Titus in the distance. Titus stood near the Great Hall surrounded by a group of destroying demons. Two warriors flanked him. He seemed to be issuing assignments to them. Aegeus landed a safe distance away and quietly listened to see if he could tell who they were targeting.

"Find out where they are coming from!" Titus yelled at a low-level destroying demon unfortunate enough to be standing in the front of the small group. "And when you do, destroy the prayer warrior!"

"Yes, my Liege," he said and scurried away.

"What would you have us do with the Tenth?" One of the demons standing near Titus asked excitedly. Aegeus moved closer careful not to reveal himself, straining his ears to hear.

"We have him ready," the demon smirked, evil oozing from him, sulfur starting to seep from him in his excitement. "Tormenting demons have spent all day weakening him," the demons all giggled in response.

"Tell me," said Titus.

"I made his computer crash. Twice," the demons all laughed. The tormenting demon, Frustration, who Aegeus could now see clearly, bounced slightly up and down in excitement.

"He called for tech support," the demon erupted in laughter finding it difficult to finish the story. "They came to the office and found the computer working just fine. But when they left," the demons again laughed jubilantly. "I caused it to crash again," sulfur now poured freely from Frustration as he reveled in the cleverness of it all.

"Then when it finally booted up, I erased a document he had been working on and caused the machine to continually ask him for his password." Frustration was now laughing so hard he could not have continued his report if under threat of death.

Titus looked at Frustration with both contempt and pride. The demon was foolish, and his emotional display was well beneath Titus, but the simplicity of the plan was pleasing. Frustration was right, the Tenth was quite vulnerable. Now was the time for a more elegant attack.

Titus looked at the demon standing next to him, "Jealousy, cover the wife of the Tenth. We will use the message of the boy to drive a wedge between them. Distrust cover her ears. Once she feels betrayed by him again, we can rip open old wounds. He will be reminded of his wife's coldness; we can accentuate that, keep him focused on it." Titus looked at a tormenting demon who nodded in understanding.

"The Tenth will turn back to his master sin, and we will once again control him." Titus looked around as if searching for someone he knew was in the crowd but couldn't quite find.

"Deception?" he called out.

"Yes?" a beautiful demon stepped forward, her long flowing gown billowing about her. "Make the call," Titus ordered.

Chapter 12—The Tenth

The Tenth's hands shook slightly as he hung up the phone. He sat in silence letting the words wash over him, letting them sink it. It was a lot to take in. He wasn't sure he could even believe it, after all, he had no proof. He rose slowly from his desk his knees a little shaky, and he felt angry with himself for such a physical reaction to the situation. This was turning out to be a terrible day.

He walked to the large windows that encompassed an entire wall of his office. Stuffing his shaking hands deep into his pockets he leaned against the windows and looked out over the campus.

The aquatics center was a new addition to the campus, and it had been placed in the Tenth's direct line of vision. The center was a glass building, and by afternoon the sun was positioned so that the Tenth could see straight into the building. It could have proven to be a great temptation for him if things had been different. He often wondered if the man had known that, but he dismissed the idea as ludicrous. How could he possibly have known?

Even so, the Tenth tended to stay away from the windows. Now, the Tenth watched as two female coeds walked from the aquatics center towel drying their hair. It was a hot summer day, and the girls were dressed in long skirts and three-quarter length sleeves. The dress code of the new president. He had passed stringent new rules regarding what women could and could not wear, a necessity he said so that the students could meet their biblical responsibility for modesty. Of course, modesty had been defined by him.

The Tenth sighed loudly, but there was no one around to hear. He had taken a great risk challenging the previous president, but it had paid off when that president had been removed. Although it didn't seem like much had changed here in Platitude. Well, he supposed that wasn't fair. Things had changed just not necessarily for the better.

Removing the last president had been a great victory. However, the new one was even more legalistic than the previous one. Slowly he had ushered in rules restricting nearly every activity on campus. He had started small with things few people paid attention to. Little things like what food was being served in the cafeteria. Then he moved on to bigger things like what type of music students could listen to on campus. Not just in public places but in their rooms, on their phones, through their earbuds.

Everyone had agreed that some music didn't belong on a Christian campus. Initially, only explicit music was banned. But then someone had been trying to protest the censorship and had pointed out that even non-explicit music sometimes conveyed non-biblical ideas. The president, intentionally misunderstanding the point, had agreed. And shortly after, all music that wasn't faith-based was banned. Then he issued a list of approved Christian music groups because they had to be leery of music that claimed to be Christian but wasn't. He was the only one truly qualified to decide that of course.

The President would never admit that. Instead, he made broad statements about how they were all in agreement on these things, how they all wanted the same thing. He constantly stated he had sought input on the issues and in doing so, he implied that everyone was in agreement, that the decisions had been reached together. But that wasn't true. It was true that he had on occasion discussed his ideas with others. But rarely was there agreement. That did not, however, stop him from suggesting otherwise.

But it wasn't just menus and music that had suffered. Eventually, slowly, the President had encroached on everything. He changed the dress code, tightened the curfew, began censoring the entertainment, movies, plays and art exhibits on campus. He banned books from the library, forbid field-trips to art museums, and blocked many websites from campus. He quietly disbanded the student newspaper, it was too provocative. Anything that challenged him had to go.

Then he crossed a line that the Tenth thought would bring about revolt, finally bringing an end to the tyranny. He censored what was said in the classroom. Just like with everything else, he started with common ground, things they all agreed were inappropriate. Then he slowly crept forward. At first, people spoke up, they voiced their concerns. But he silenced them quickly; graciously thanking them for "their opinions" while completely ignoring them. Unlike the president before him, he fired no one. He simply did not renew contracts. He stopped granting tenure. Not officially, of course, it just worked out that very few ever earned it.

How and why they were denied tenure was always a mystery. The excuses were feeble and poorly construed. Their letters said generic things like their beliefs were out of alignment with the college. Which beliefs? Well, there wasn't time to nitpick over such trivial details. When questions arose, and they did, the President merely refused to meet with the person. Childish? Perhaps. But it was working. And all those non-renewals and refused meetings made the Tenth's job more difficult.

He had lost half of his staff over it. And because the hiring process had become so subjective, replacing people was challenging. While the college had no official policy stating that they weren't hiring women, the Tenth hadn't seen a woman hired in over a year. They didn't pass the interview with the President.

Of course, this new censorship of the classroom meant entire disciplines were no longer considered viable. Sometimes that decision was forced upon a department, and sometimes they came to the agonizing realization themselves. Such as the art department that could not visit art museums out of fear over what may be hanging on the walls. They could not show or discuss great pieces of art such as the Creation of Man because it was deemed sexually explicit.

In fact, The Creation of Man painting was also deemed a graven image and could no longer be studied for the masterpiece it was but must be condemned and avoided as an abomination and violation of the Second of the Ten Commandments. The art department had died a slow and painful death. But they weren't the only ones. Psychology had not survived the new censorship; the PA program had not survived. It was hard to train physician assistants if you couldn't teach them about the human body or how to examine it.

As each department came under fire, the other departments lowered their heads and kept their mouths closed. They would reassure themselves with the idea that they couldn't fight every fight. They couldn't put their necks on the line for someone else's department. Therefore, slowly bit by bit, department by department they had stood alone against a mighty force and they had lost.

While departments were dying, new buildings were sprouting up, and new departments were being born. Every female student on campus was now required to take the "Christian Women" minor. The courses had transcript worthy names but questionable content.

The Tenth had heard rumors that as part of one course, female students were taken to the President's house where they would do his laundry, clean his home, and prepare his meals as practice. But the Tenth had not verified that because he didn't really want to know.

The pool had been another new addition. It had been a great distracter as the theater department was being dismantled. A pool was evidence that they were not legalistic that they were modern thinkers. The president himself had selected the location for the pool right across from the Tenth's office.

Fortunately, the women were required to wear swim pants and tankini tops so there was precious little flesh showing. There were separate swim hours for men and women with a half hour between so that one group would be completely gone before the other arrived. As a result, the pool did not serve as a point of temptation. If anything, it served as a constant reminder of the hole the Tenth was currently buried in.

And if the situation in Platitude weren't bad enough, today, he had gotten the call that he had dreaded for decades. He didn't know how it was possible. He was always so careful. What would he tell his wife? Things between them had been better since they got to Platitude. Oh, he had been tempted since getting here, he had even made advances at women, but nothing had ever come of it, and that was years ago.

He had not had any affairs since arriving in Platitude. Slowly he had started redirecting his desire toward his wife. He bought the book *Fire Proof* and started working his way through the days. He had learned to see his wife differently, to value her differently, to appreciate her for who she was as a person. He took responsibility for her bitterness and the role he played in it, and he began to lead his home by serving his wife. By serving her, he had been able to demonstrate love, regain trust.

The transformation had been slow. His wife had been suspicious, but eventually, she had softened her heart toward him. She had begun to trust him once again. Things were finally going well. This would ruin everything, rip open old wounds, bring up bad memories best forgotten. Perhaps he didn't have to tell her? He didn't even know this child.

In fact, it wasn't even a child, not in the traditional sense. It was a man. A thirty-year-old man that didn't even know the Tenth existed.

He would never have to know him. He hardly remembered the boy's mother. He had been barely twenty at the time. If the boy's mother hadn't died, the Tenth would never have known the boy existed. The boy had a father, whom he believed to be his biological father. He did not need the Tenth.

With those thoughts, he convinced himself that he did not need to do anything. He didn't need to tell his wife. He didn't need to tell the boy. He didn't need to do anything. Nothing had changed. He walked back to his desk and picked up the piece of paper where he had written the boy's name. Damian. It was an odd choice; although he did not miss the irony of what the woman had done there. He crumpled the paper up and threw it away. This boy was not his son.

Chapter 13

Aegeus arrived back at the salvage yard ahead of the others. The salvage yard still fascinated him, and he strolled through it running his hand across the broken, dilapidated occupants that came here to rust. The idea of corrosion was so unknown in heaven that when he saw it, it mesmerized him.

He walked among the abandoned vehicles pondering their stories. Something about it stirred him, rustling something deep within his soul that he couldn't quite place. Slowly he made his way to the back of the salvage yard and entered the building that looked as if it too were salvage material long ago abandoned here by its owner.

"Memory lane?" Kfir asked, arriving behind Aegeus unexpectedly.

"It's a little weird," Aegeus admitted, not entirely sure what made it feel so odd.

"What is weird?" Meir asked, arriving with Mordecai.

"I guess being back here. Seeing how time has moved on. We have moved on and yet..." Aegeus let the thought trail off. He wasn't sure how to finish it, anyway.

Meir laid her hand gently on his shoulder; she understood exactly what he meant.

"Kfir, did you find anything?" Aegeus asked, ready to change the topic.

"I didn't see any of the eleven, but I was pleased to see there were lots of angels. Many of the students with the Light also had guardians. While the demon presence is still strong, the angels are plentiful."

"That is excellent news," Aegeus affirmed. "I found the Tenth," he offered by way of a report. "I didn't see what type of coverage he has, but I did see that the demons were working with Titus to plot his destruction." Aegeus looked at Meir and Mordecai when he was done.

"We found the Fourth," Mordecai reported.

"Where?" Aegeus asked surprised. All evidence of the program the Fourth oversaw had been erased from the campus. It made no sense that he would still be here.

"We don't know exactly," Meir contributed. "His son still dwells in their home, and there is evidence that the Fourth does as well, but he was not there."

"He wasn't on campus either," Aegeus added.

"He wasn't in town either," Kfir offered.

"Kfir and I will search the surrounding areas, if he still lives here he has to be working somewhere relatively close," said Aegeus.

"We also found the Second and the Third," Meir reported. Her hair changed colors to a radiant coral glow clearly pleased by the discovery.

"That would explain all the extra guardians," said Kfir.

"Let's start by finding the Fourth," said Aegeus, and although he realized it would delay them further, he added, "after we find the Fourth, we will tend to the Second and Third."

Chapter 14—The Fourth

The Fourth slouched further down. His back was achy, and the rolling stool he was sitting on didn't help. He imagined it was the wise choice when someone was designing the lab and crunching the budget. No sense in wasting money on overly comfortable chairs. The research equipment was much more important. Thinking that didn't make his backache any less, but it did remove his frustration over the low quality of the chair. It was the kind of stool he would have ordered if he had overseen ordering. He also thought of his beloved mother, long since gone. He could hear her voice telling him to sit up straight, so he did. He couldn't help but wonder if people ever stopped hearing their mother's voice in their head; he hoped not.

The intercom in the lab buzzed politely, and then he heard the voice of his lab assistant T. Of course, the boy's name wasn't actually T, but the Fourth had taken to calling him that because the boy seemed to need a nickname and the Fourth wasn't great at coming up with them. His given name started with a T so the Fourth had simply used that. It seemed to fit, and it had quickly caught on around the office until nearly everyone was calling the boy T.

"Pops"? The Fourth sighed. Why did the boy insist on calling him pops? The Fourth had had many nicknames over the years but pops? It just sounded old. Of course, he supposed he was old to the boy who wasn't really a boy but a young man in his twenties, a mere boy to the Fourth. The Fourth sighed more heavily realizing that thinking of a twenty-year-old as a boy did indeed make him old. Perhaps pops was a fitting nickname after all.

"Pops I know you're in there. I can hear that famous sighing of yours. Plus, I can see you on the monitor," T said teasingly. The Fourth started trying to mentally count the number of times he had sighed in front of T.

"Glad to hear the monitor is working. That means that you see I'm busy. What do you need?" The Fourth asked trying to sound foul but knowing that T knew him better than that. More importantly, he was eager to get to the point.

"The director wants to know if you have seen any changes in sample Z1412." Without answering, the Fourth finished with the sample he was working on and returned it to where it went. He turned to the computer and recorded the data he had collected before he forgot. Walking carefully, his bad knee had been bothering him more lately, he went to the case with Z1412.

There was a hand washing station by the case, but the Fourth didn't wash. Instead, he took off his outer gloves and added fresh ones over his base pair. Opening the case, he retrieved the sample and did a cursory examination.

The Fourth wasn't sure when or exactly how the sample had arrived, but no one had done any real tests on it yet. They knew only that it was a virus. Honestly, the Fourth wasn't sure how it got into the BSL2 lab given how little they knew about it. Just a precaution he supposed.

"Am I looking for anything particular?" He asked into the empty room.

"Director didn't say. Just said to ask if there were changes," T replied with the casual indifference that had caused the Fourth to like him. T wasn't indifferent. He was an exquisite scientist. Young, inexperienced but exquisite. The Fourth considered the fact that T didn't get rattled easily one of his best characteristics. He just seemed to take things in stride. He looked things straight in the eye and dealt with them. He didn't panic. He didn't exaggerate or downplay. T made the Fourth think of a younger version of himself.

"There are no visible changes," the Fourth spoke into the room knowing T could hear him. The monitors show no changes. I will need to do tests if he wants more than that." The Fourth put the sample back. He was starting to remove his outer gloves when T interrupted him again.

"Pops. Don't deglove. The director wants you in the decontamination wash. The team is waiting," T said over the intercom.

"What?" the Fourth asked unsure that he had heard correctly.

"Decontamination. Now." T said. There was no hostility to the tone, no irritation or even panic. Just a simple fact. Decontamination was common in the BSL2 lab. Stopping in the middle of something to decontaminate was less common. The Fourth left his gloves on and moved toward the decontamination chamber.

He rotated slowly in the chamber letting his body take over and do what it had done many times. Something about it triggered a memory of Platitude. He had enjoyed working there. Being part of training up the next generation of providers.

But staying had not been reasonable. Things had spiraled out of control toward the end.

When the position at the Biomedical Research and Safety lab opened, he took it. Being a physician with a Ph.D. in Microbiology gave him an edge over the competition and knowing the associate director didn't hurt either. The lab was driving distance from Platitude, so he didn't have to move, which he considered a plus.

The transition had been smooth, and he found that the quiet and solitude of the lab agreed with him. His prior experience with research had gotten him into the Biosafety Level 2 lab most days and the Biosafety Level 3 lab when he was lucky. The demand for focus and precision in the Level 3 lab agreed with him. The hint of danger kept him on his toes which he liked. The idea that he could be on the brink of discovering the next big disease had its own appeal. When you factored in that he could be part of finding an improved treatment or cure well, it rounded it out for him.

Of course, the solitude was both a blessing and a curse. It suited the Fourth, but that was, of course, the problem and he recognized it. He hadn't kept in contact with anyone from Platitude even though he still lived there. He hadn't really been close to anyone, anyway. Work wasn't the place to make friends in his opinion. He missed the students, he loved teaching, and the lab didn't really provide that.

The arrival of T had changed things for the better. T was fresh out of graduate school and full of ideas. He had an eager mind and a wit that the Fourth could appreciate. He had grown up without a father and battled the odds to go to college. But he had, and the Fourth had a great deal of respect for the young man.

The lab provided less flexibility in his schedule than the Fourth had had in Platitude but that also meant he had a more routine schedule which helped with his son. His son had been clean and out of rehab for three years. Time had been kind to them. The benefits of the change had outweighed any detriments.

When the decontamination process was over the Fourth entered the changing room where T was waiting for him.

"What was that about?" he asked.

"Not sure. But Z1412 is being moved to at least a BSL3. That lab is closed until the move is complete. There is chatter that it may be headed to the CDC, but I can't confirm that. That's all I know," T said tossing the Fourth a fresh scrub top and heading for the door.

"They think it may be a level 4?" the Fourth asked as T was walking out.

T shrugged his shoulders "it's just chatter," he said without turning around.

Aegeus was pleased they had found the Fourth but finding him in the presence of the King's wrath was alarming. The King had told them that the time of his wrath was near. He had been warning his children for thousands of years but finding the Fourth locked in a room with it was still surprising.

It was clear the Fourth did not recognize it for what it was, or he would have taken more caution. The odd suit and extra gloves he wore were not enough to protect him from the plague he held in his hands.

"Is that the plague of Zechariah?" Kfir asked in astonishment.

"It is," said Aegeus.

Aegeus tried to push the plague from his mind and instead refocus on the mission; they could not afford to be distracted. Knowing that the King's wrath was upon them, seeing it in front of him, brought a sense of greater urgency. He wanted to get this taken care of and get back to the Twelfth, that was, after all, what he had returned for. He looked at Mordecai with a questioning look.

"He is not my charge," Mordecai answered in response. Aegeus was both relieved and concerned by the proclamation. Each person that Mordecai encountered and cleared meant that the others were at increased risk. One of them would face a decision of immeasurable consequence. Aegeus did not wish such a thing on any of them.

At Aegeus's direction, the other angels conducted a complete search of the facility where the Fourth worked tending to the King's wrath. Their search did not uncover any warrior demons, nor did they see signs of demon concentrations higher than would be expected. Aegeus assumed this to mean that Titus had not yet targeted the Fourth. Clearly, the demons did not realize the wrath of the King was being housed there.

Aegeus arranged for reinforcements to stand guard over the plague of Zechariah. When it was time, the King would pour it out upon the earth. Nothing in all of creation could prevent it, but that fact wouldn't stop the demons from trying. It mattered not to Aegeus if the demons would attempt to stop it or expedite it, all that mattered was the King's timing. A guard detail would assure there was no demon interference in the timeline. Michael, agreeing with Aegeus's plan, sent a host of warriors.

That detail arranged, Aegeus was eager to secure the Second and Third. For he now understood that the prayer warrior Titus searched for was the Third. If Titus found her, he would launch a full-scale attack.

Platitude stood little chance without the power of prayer. The Second and the Third would need protection. Aegeus had a plan; they just needed to get to the Second and Third before Titus did. The battle had grown well beyond Platitude, the wrath of the King was coming.

Chapter 15–The Second and the Third

It was a rainy day. The sky was dull and gray, the rain falling in soft sheets. The grass drank it down in great gulps, but despite its effort, puddles had formed around the small yard. Two mourning doves bathed in the puddles flitting about and singing. The Third could not hear the birds through the window, but she imagined their song to be one of joy and hope. Their frolicking had drawn the attention of a drenched and miserable cat.

The Third watched, amused, as the cat temporarily forgot his misery and poised for a strike to earn a hearty breakfast. But despite his best attempt, he was rewarded with nothing more than a face full of muddy water. Looking dejected, the cat sauntered off, and the Third smiled as the birds returned, the disruption seemingly forgotten.

The Third sat on a small wicker love seat with a steaming cup of tea in her hand; the welcoming smell enveloping the room. The cup was quite dainty, and it clinked each time she placed it back on its saucer. She paused to enjoy the quiet clinking of the china against the backdrop of the rain.

The dullness of the sky and the slight chill in the air did not deter her from her morning. She let her mind linger over the phone call with the Twelfth. They had been chatting every Tuesday morning since the Twelfth left Platitude. The Third thought of it as their way of having coffee together. She didn't let the miles between them bother her. Besides, in the modern age of FaceTime and Skype, what were miles? Nor did she let the fact that she was having tea and not coffee bother her, there was no sense in getting caught up in insignificant details.

The conversation between the two women had been easy, and the time had passed quickly, as it always did, but the Third could see that the Twelfth was tired. She admitted she wasn't really sleeping, and that was taking a toll. The Twelfth had dismissed it but the Third could not.

When the call had ended, the Third could not quite shake the feeling that something wasn't right. Determined not to let it foil her day, she went to the King with it, praying for the Twelfth, for each of those who had been part of their Wednesday night group, for her newborn grandchild, and finally for her husband who sat quietly in the corner chair facing away from the large windows that encompassed the room.

The Second quietly read the morning headlines still preferring an actual newspaper to an app. The silence in the room did not bother either of them. They preferred it. Him reading the paper, her alone with her thoughts. She found that It was a beautiful place to be; she never knew quite where her thoughts would want to go. Today they wished to explore the possibilities of retirement.

Retirement didn't seem real. It made them seem so old. She didn't feel old but at least on paper, she was old enough. She released a sigh at the thought of growing old. She wondered when her mind, which felt so young so shocked when it saw the person looking back at her in the mirror, would catch up with her body.

She took another slow sip of tea savoring the smell and flavor of her favorite brew. As was her practice when thinking of something unpleasant, she decided to allow herself only until she swallowed the tea to entertain her thoughts on aging. She held the hot liquid in her mouth just a second longer than was necessary, giving herself plenty of time to indulge the thoughts before completely banishing them for the day.

Those ideas sifted through and encouraged to move on, her mind instead returned to the day and her lack of plans. For the third day in a row, she had not a single thing on her calendar. She wasn't used to that, and she wasn't quite sure what she thought of it.

Retirement may be worse than she anticipated. She reminded herself that this lull in activity was only temporary. Their schedule for the summer was quite full. The Second had been asked to guest speak at locations all around the world, and they would be traveling for most of the summer. In just over a week they would be headed to Tanzania.

They enjoyed traveling and were looking forward to it. But it was never easy for the Third to be reminded of all her husband had suffered. He had shared his story, their story, hundreds of times, and each time she felt an overwhelming need to give thanks for his life and for their continued life together.

A little rumble of thunder announced itself, pulling her mind back to the small sunroom and the present. Practical things once again filled her thoughts, and she began to plan for lunch. She had just brought in some fresh vegetables from the garden, perhaps she would put together something simple from those.

The ringing of the doorbell was completely unexpected and a bit of an intrusion into the otherwise tranquil morning.

Chapter 16

ordecai could feel the power of the Third even before she
reached the door. Aegeus had told him she was a powerful
prayer warrior, but she was more powerful than he had expected.
Over the centuries he had been among many of the King's children,
but relatively few had developed into the type of prayer warrior the
Third was. It encouraged his soul.

As soon as she opened the door, he took a subtle yet deep breath
breathing in her scent and that of her household. He would serve only the bloodline of the family whose tear the King had used to forge
him. Even then, he did not serve them all only those chosen, recognized by their smell.

She was not his charge, a fact that slightly disappointed him. He
could feel the power of prayer flowing from her providing him an energy that he treasured. It was something he sought out fervently because of the amount of time he spent away from the King. He had
to fight the urge to close his eyes and soak in the power that flowed
from her. He didn't think she would receive that well. Instead, he
tried to look non-threatening, to exude a feeling of safety and comfort so she would not be alarmed.

Meir had alerted Voog, guardian of the Second and Third, to
both the threat and the plan. Voog now stood watch on the roof of
the house helping provide coverage. Mordecai hoped Voog could feel
the small hint of concern that danced just behind the Third's smile

and that he would offer her reassurance in response. Things would be considerably easier if she let him in.

Mordecai had taken a human form that he hoped looked like a harmless missionary. But despite his efforts, when she opened the door, she looked at him the way a woman does when a strange man turns up at her doorstep. He was pleased that despite the caution that was evident, her eyes seemed more intrigued than suspicious. He wondered if she had any idea that one of the most dangerous demons that walked the earth was searching for her, determined to destroy her. From her easy smile and gentle manner, he doubted it.

"I'm John," he stated as if she should know who he was. He pushed his glasses up on his nose and then extended his hand in greeting hoping that Meir was coming through on her end. The entire plan was dependent on Meir's timing.

"Hello John," the Third said in welcome as she shook his hand. He watched her face carefully, aware that many humans, especially those who knew the King well, could often feel "something" when they touched or encountered an angel. It didn't always happen and when it did the King's children did not immediately recognize what the "something" was, but they did know there was something.

Her eyes immediately registered it. Mordecai smiled more broadly; he would expect nothing less from a prayer warrior, but he also knew It meant he needed to be careful.

"Forgive me John but was I expecting you?" she asked with grace and diplomacy. Mordecai knew she was not.

"Oh," he said in mock surprise. "I was under the impression you had gotten the call already, Um-" he shuffled his feet, something he had seen the humans do when in an awkward situation. Just then the Second walked to the door.

"John, so sorry we just received the call," he said apologetically extending his hand in greeting and opening the door wider as a sign of hospitality. "Please come in, let me get your bag."

Mordecai entered their home, grateful that Meir had completed the call just in time. He knew she was eager to get to the Twelfth and would remain in Platitude only until things were settled.

The Second explained quickly to his wife that John was a visiting missionary. The Third warmly welcomed him to their home. The Second went on to explain that John would be visiting for a few days. He would, of course, stay with the Second and Third during that time, as was the custom.

The Third showed him to his room where he could freshen up if needed while she prepared a lite mid-morning snack. Mordecai thanked her kindly and closed his bedroom door gently to begin the process of covering her and the Second from the demons. By doing so, the demons would not be able to see them. The Second and the Third, would for all practical purposes, be invisible to the demons. It required a great deal of energy to maintain such cover for more than an earthly hour, but Mordecai could draw strength and power from the prayers of the Second and Third.

He was unsure how long it would take Aegeus and Kfir to find the warriors they sought and return to Platitude with them. Mordecai felt sure that Aegeus too was eager to find the warriors and get back to the Twelfth. Aegeus did not seem to appreciate the side mission. Mordecai was hopeful it would not be more than a few days. Until then he would stay in Platitude hiding the Second and the Third from the demons bent on their destruction.

Chapter 17

As Morax approached the front door, he soaked in the stunning scenery that only Hawaii could offer. The colors, the mountains in the distance, the flowers, it was beautiful. From where he stood he could see a dirt trail leading down a winding path toward the ocean. He couldn't quite see the ocean, but he could smell it, and he could hear the waves crashing on the shore.

He took a deep breath knowing his purpose here was not a joyous one. He was in no hurry to deliver bad news to Lucifer. The fresh salt air cleared his lungs, and for just a moment he believed everything would be ok.

While some of Lucifer's homes were simple—others like this one were extraordinarily luxurious. At least that was what Morax had heard. If the outside was any indicator, what he had heard was true. This house was also quite modern and rumored to be Lucifer's favorite.

Morax could see why it would be among Lucifer's favorites. The entire house seemed to be made of glass, three stories of nothing but windows. Rumor was that with a simple voice command the glass would darken preventing anyone from seeing in, but Morax could see no other houses within a mile, so there was little risk of that.

He pressed the doorbell reluctantly and was surprised to hear the peaceful yet haunting sound of flute music filling the space behind the door. Interesting choice, he thought. But the music was so peaceful so captivating that he found himself yearning to push the bell again.

A low-level demon that Morax had never seen before opened the door. He did not have the requisite look of a warrior. Morax imagined that at some point he had been a ministering angel. Now he seemed to be a tormenting demon turned doorman. Although Morax did not know the demon, the demon seemed to know him.

"Morax," he said in greeting tipping his head slightly. He stepped aside to allow Morax free passage into the house. It was possible the demon had spent his entire existence as a demon opening Lucifer's door. Morax found the thought pathetic; he immediately felt even more superior to the door demon. He stepped confidently inside to face his fate.

The house was a little too cool—Morax estimated it to be around sixty degrees, an unpleasant contrast to the temperature outside. The rumor among the demons was that Lucifer had once killed a demon because one of his houses had gotten over seventy. Everyone knew he hated the heat. It was an unwelcome reminder of what was to come and of how far they had fallen.

Morax didn't know if the rumor about his killing the demon over the temperature was true or merely the stuff of legend nor did he wish to find out.

The windows on the east wall were dark enough that Morax got a glimpse of himself as he followed the door demon further into the house. He paused briefly to admire his new body. This one was much better than the last.

No longer did he have the overweight body of a middle-aged aca-demician. He now wore the body he deserved. His hair was thick and as dark as coal. His body young mid-to-late-twenties he estimated. This body was more reflective of the demon he was. Morax found it a pleasing upgrade from the last one.

The door demon noticed that Morax had stopped. The demon cleared his throat gently and offered a scathing look at Morax with a hint of insult tossed in. Morax might have smitten the demon had he not felt a hint of embarrassment over the situation.

The feeling caught him off guard, it was not a feeling he was accustomed to, it was more the behavior of the hairless rats. Morax, holding his head high and offering a menacing look to the door demon, resumed moving in the approved direction.

The brief but unfortunate encounter made him think about the hairless rats. They did not seem to understand that they too were spirit living in borrowed flesh. He shook his head as he considered their ignorance. If they were ever to sort it out, to realize that the bodies they looked upon in the mirror were not their true form, not their real self.... well if they ever figured it out, it would make his job more difficult. Little chance of that, he thought snickering.

Yes, this new body suited him, and he had not yet grown tired of looking at it. If given a choice, he would opt to be in his true demon form without the confining body of the hairless rats. But a body was one of the requirements of a demon of his position, and so, when required, he possessed a human body, taking over the vessel.

Like the angels, demons could appear in human form. But doing so, without taking over a human body, required a considerable amount of energy and none but Lucifer was powerful enough to maintain that form for long. Unlike the angels, who made themselves look human for a short time, the demons preferred to take possession of a human body. The angels never did this, but the demons found it an amusing sport.

They could not, of course, possess a body that already had the Light. And in the rare case that a demon should be possessing a body that managed to become filled with the Light - well it was not a pleasant sight to behold. Never-the-less despite the danger, tormenting demons seemed to revel in the prospect, sometimes piling as many demons in as they could.

And if he must be contained within one of the hairless rat bodies, it may as well be one that conveyed his prowess.

Lucifer generally arranged a host body for Morax to possess, something appropriate to the mission. Each mission called for a different body type; he had to look the part. His mission in Platitude had required him to look different, to be different, but here he had no such restrictions. Memories of platitude invaded his mind, he allowed them to simmer as he prepared for Lucifer.

To Morax's great disappointment, Seneca had been lost. It was a shame, Seneca had been a mighty warrior for thousands of years. It was a significant loss. But watching Seneca battle Aegeus had been exhilarating. Morax had been unsure of who would be the victor. Unfortunately, it had been Aegeus.

Morax comforted himself with the knowledge that all had not been lost in Platitude. Despite losing the battle and the Strongman eventually leaving, they had had some success as well. Yes, they had lost some ground, but another Strongman had been brought in, and they were still making progress, slower than they had hoped but progress none the less.

It was important, as he prepared to update Lucifer, that Morax not forget their successes. He knew that focusing on the wrong things in his report could get him tossed back in with the general population. He certainly did not want that. Life at the top suited Morax better. He knew that it was best to paint a pleasant picture and let the little details sift themselves out.

The low-level demon led Morax to a large atrium in the center of the house where with a nod and a scowl, he left Morax alone to wait for Lucifer. Each of the three floors opened to the atrium which contained an elaborate garden. Enormous rocks lined the edges of the garden and a beautiful waterfall cascaded from the third floor all the way to a pool made to resemble an outdoor stream on the ground floor. Surprisingly the waterfall was not as loud as Morax would have expected.

Morax wandered about the lush, green garden while he waited. Flowers of all colors and types were nestled together in ornate flower beds, some of them endemic to Hawaii, some not. But wild orchids, Lucifer's favorite flower, were the overwhelming favorite and filled the air with their distinct scent. Lucifer had included hundreds of varieties of orchids in the garden, some Morax hadn't seen outside heaven.

Aside from the overwhelming presence of orchids, Morax couldn't help but notice that the lush garden looked eerily similar to Eden. He wondered if Lucifer ever actually swam in the pool, as he had in Eden.

The similarity to Eden stirred up memories Morax had believed long forgotten. His mind drifted back thousands of years before he had been a demon. The memory was so foreign, so far removed from who he was now that it seldom surfaced. In fact, most days he completely forgot his prior life as an angel.

He liked to think that he had been among the best of them but that didn't make it true. And if he were being entirely honest, which demons seldom were, he would have to acknowledge that he hadn't ever been a protector of one of the hairless rats, a fact that on most days made him proud. The idea of having ever protected one of them was repulsive. No, Morax had been their enemy from the beginning, and he took pride in that.

Instead, he had been among the first to fall. The humans hadn't yet been created, so no one needed protecting. But he had enjoyed the training—at least that was how he remembered it.

Chapter 18

Morax's mind followed the memory trail to his friendship with Lucifer when they had both been angels. Lucifer had been one of the two archangels to stand beside the King in the throne room, a position reserved for the King's most honored. Morax and Lucifer had been friends from the beginning—the angels' beginning-long before Genesis.

It seemed so innocent when Lucifer first mentioned his dream of one-day being King. Morax had laughed and agreed it would be nice to be the King—being the very essence of love and power. He could not even begin to imagine the majesty of it.

They would chat about it from time to time over manna or as they went about their daily work. Slowly, without Morax really noticing it was happening, they began to discuss it more often. For Morax it had been a fanciful dream, an innocent desire to one-day become the most wonderful being in all of existence. Who wouldn't want to be the King?

But for Lucifer, it became an obsession. He began to gather supporters, to convince others that it was possible. They had been young and foolish to think they could ever overthrow the King.

As Morax remembered it, he had never really thought Lucifer was serious. He recalled being shocked when Lucifer had finally taken action and attempted to overthrow the throne room. What a debacle that had been.

Morax had acted impulsively joining in with his friend against his King. But the plan had not been thought through well. How exactly would you ever overthrow a King who knows your every thought? Of course, they knew much more about the King now than they had then.

They had never seen the wrath of the King before that day—they had not anticipated that. How naïve they had been. The King had acted swiftly. One moment Morax was standing in the throne room, another angel in his grip, and in the next instant, a flash of light sent him flying from heaven. The fall had been horrifying. It had happened so quickly he hadn't had time to open his wings. He slammed into the earth leaving an enormous crater. He laid there motionless trying to figure out what had happened.

At the time, the earth was desolate and formless. Darkness covered everything. Initially, he feared he had lost his sight altogether.

All he had ever known was the beauty of heaven the overwhelming peace and love from being in the King's presence. Darkness was new. Fear was also new. None of them had ever felt fear before, and they had no name for it, no understanding of what it was. He didn't even know what it was he was afraid of; he knew only that he lacked the courage to move.

Realization gradually settled over him as he lay there petrified in the piercing darkness. They had been cast out of heaven separated from the King forever. The horror of it washed over Morax until he felt he may drown in his own sorrow. How would they survive? There was no life apart from the King.

He resolved to find his courage and search for Lucifer; surely Lucifer would have answers—his wisdom was so great. But had Morax been able to find Lucifer, he would have seen that Lucifer was in shock too.

Gradually the fallen found their voices and called out to each other. The sound of familiar voices led to greater courage. It was enough for Lucifer to stand among them and assume the position of authority. While he was not the King he had aspired to be, he would rule over the fallen.

The darkness was thick and penetrating, stealing the life from your very soul. Morax had no idea how long they were in that state before out of the darkness came the sweetest sound he had ever heard — the voice of the King. And it brought with it reassurance and hope. In that same instant, shame swept over him—something else they had never experienced.

"Let there be light." And with that simple command, the darkness was gone, and Morax could once again see. But seeing had been more terrifying than being in the darkness. Because when he could see he became aware of just how far he had fallen. He had lost the Light of God, the greatest weapon an angel possessed, their source of strength. It was then that Morax realized there really was no way back.

While they were no longer in the presence of the King and they suddenly knew of evil, they did have the privilege of watching as the King created the earth. A unique power flows from the King when he creates. A power that he emits at no other time. The angels delighted in it. It was with awe that they watched each step of the creation.

It had been beautiful, glorious even—until the King created man. Lucifer cried out in rage, jealousy consuming him. He had assumed this beautiful, perfect creation was for him, for the fallen. Lucifer hated man instantly—these creatures who were so clearly the image of the King. These vile creatures who knew no fear, no rejection, or shame. They walked with the King every day and chatted with him in the garden. They experienced his love and peace something the fallen had thrown away.

Woman was the final piece of creation, the piece after which the King had declared it "very good," and finished his work to rest. She provided the means for more of "them" to be made. If he could destroy her; he could destroy them.

Before Eve, Lucifer had been the most beautiful creature God had ever created; he had carried the seal of "very good." He believed that he should be the summation of creation, the final perfecting piece. In his mind woman had stolen that from him.

With the simple words declaring it "very good" creation had ceased.

For six days, the fallen had wallowed in the glorious voice of the King and the beauty and power of his creation. For six glorious days, they had been able to be in his presence, to hear his voice, to tell themselves they were not lost. And then with the creation of woman it had ended.

Lucifer's hatred for the woman grew, and he vowed to destroy her.

Chapter 19

The King put a garden in the east, the beauty and splendor of which was unrivaled. Eventually, the fallen found their way there. Morax had seen nothing else like it on the earth; it reminded him of the King's personal garden in heaven. Being in Eden made him feel as if they hadn't fallen quite as far as they had. He could lie to himself, and some small piece of him would believe it—because he wanted to.

Butterflies of every color flitted about the garden giving it the illusion of moving color. The sweet scent of flowers filled the air. Birds sang out glory and praise to the King. Every creature roamed about the garden living together in perfect harmony. The water in the big pond sparkled like a thousand diamonds beckoning to all who passed. It was there amid that beauty and perfection that Lucifer had met Adam and Eve.

Lucifer had been patient, taking the form of a dragon the most powerful and cunning of all the reptiles. He would sing into the night as Adam and Eve rested. He filled Eden with the songs of heaven, songs of the angels. His voice was beautiful and soothing, haunting even and soon the man and his wife began searching the garden for the source.

Lucifer never pushed. He was never obvious—he waited gently, patiently, innocently for them to find him. But of course, it was not innocent. He baited them in with feelings of comfort and curiosity. He waited for them to grow trusting all the while studying them, searching for a way to destroy them.

He studied the man and woman day and night looking for weakness, and he found only one—the same one he had once had—naivety. They did not know of evil. That discovery put his plan in place, and Lucifer spent years preparing to cause the humans—these creatures that the King treated as children—to suffer the same tragic fate as him.

Morax aided him in every way, but Lucifer had been the one to befriend them. He gained their trust by spending endless hours with them over the years getting to know them, patiently waiting for the right opportunity. He couldn't be sure how long it had taken. Hundreds, maybe thousands of years, they did not truly measure time then because it was eternal. But eventually, he had tricked the woman into eating the fruit while her husband stood beside her and watched.

Lucifer had relished in their fall. He was giddy with pleasure as they scoured the garden to find leaves to cover their nakedness. An evil joy filled him as shame enveloped them. But the victory had been short-lived.

Mere hours after they had fallen the King arrived and once again his judgment was swift. Lucifer had not expected that. He had been ignorant believing that he had nothing left to lose. He could not have anticipated death—none of them had ever seen death. They knew nothing of it. Even the word as the King had uttered it was meaningless to the fallen - until it wasn't. Until with horror, he understood. Certainly, none of them had anticipated hell.

Each of them had been punished in turn. Lucifer stood defiantly—a sneer on his face as the woman realized he was not an animal at all. The King ripped the legs and wings from the dragon leaving it to crawl on its belly humiliated. The animosity between Lucifer and woman sealed for all time.

The woman would experience pain in childbirth. It was a curse none of them could fully yet appreciate, not having ever experienced pain. But the piece that Lucifer had laid hold of, the thing that had caught his ear was the struggle between man and woman. She would desire him, seeking out the love and companionship he could offer but man would rule over her, making her yearning a heavy burden. Lucifer clung to it, deciding right then to burrow into it and amplify it, exploit it. He would work day and night to assure that for all time men would demean and degrade women devaluing them. Women would see it, know it was there, but be incapable of suppressing their desire. If he could divide the man and the woman, he could better defeat them.

After the King had them all escorted from the garden, he posted angels at the entrance. Everything changed. The King assigned warrior angels to fight and defend his children. Guardian angels were assigned to protect them from harm; ministering angels were sent to care for them. Angels who had once been beloved friends were now the mortal enemies of the fallen. Lucifer was consumed with rage. Hatred overtook him. Jealousy blinded him.

Each day the fallen grew darker. The angels they had once been, were slowly transformed day by day into the demons they eventually became until finally, there was nothing virtuous left in them. The transformation happened gradually, quietly for all but Lucifer.

It would be hundreds of years before Lucifer stepped foot back in heaven, but even then, it was not the same. He returned as an enemy of the King. There was a chasm between them that Lucifer could never cross. Never again would the King look upon him as a loving and cherished angel. He had lost the Light.

Over the years, much had been learned. Lucifer had adjusted his tactics. Lucifer understood the demons destined fate. But it didn't mean they would march into hell without dragging as many of the hairless rats with them as possible. It was all they had left. If Lucifer had any say, and he did, they would indeed see the Lamb hungry and offer him nothing but scorn and judgment just as they had as he hung on the cross.

The thought shocked Morax. It was not often that he allowed himself to remember the Lamb's death. It had been a considerable blow to the demons and was something best forgotten, something never to be spoken of. It proved to be another example of their gross underestimation of the King and his plan.

There had been such celebration in the hours leading up to the death of the Lamb. Which of them would ever have expected the King to send his son to this fallen earth in the form of a human? It was unfathomable. That much might, and power confined in a human body? And to send him as a baby no less. So vulnerable. The demons had not seen that coming.

But the King had sent a mighty force of protection for the child. Warriors surrounded him and his family. Joseph proved to be very devoted to the King and no matter what tactic Lucifer tried he could not break through. So, Lucifer waited patiently until the Lamb was accompanied by one that Lucifer could corrupt. Judas had been the obvious target. The King had provided mighty Sentinel to protect him. The Sentinel had proven to be a worthy foe. But even the mightiest angel could not usurp free will; it was an unbreakable rule of the King. Fortunately, Lucifer had assigned greed to Judas at birth. His love of money was strong, leaving him susceptible.

The plan had been beautiful in its simplicity, Judas would betray the Lamb into the hands of the religious. The religious! Morax chuckled aloud as he remembered it. What better irony is there than that? Titus would have appreciated that had he been there.

That part of the plan had at least worked, and Lucifer continued with that tactic. If you could get the religious to do the damage, it made Lucifer's job easier. Corrupt the religious and use them to destroy themselves and repulse the lost. Who would come to the King once they had seen his children? So, flawed and imperfect, and perhaps if Lucifer had his way, so judgmental. Pride, Judgment, and Jealousy had worked very well, and they continued to serve Lucifer with distinction.

For just a moment Morax allowed himself to recall how happy they had been to see the Lamb stumble from the crowd bloody and torn. Each step toward Calvary had been taken in great physical pain. Lucifer had walked beside the Lamb goading him, mocking him, celebrating. The Lamb had never uttered a word in response. His mother walked not far behind them, her heartbreaking, her strength faltering.

Lucifer walked along the dust-covered road and listened as Mary wept for her son. He listened to the taunts and cries of the crowd. Taunts his demons had inspired. He walked along celebrating the distinct smell of the Lamb's blood as it dripped from his broken body and hit the dirt beneath his feet. If only Lucifer had realized just how powerful that blood was.

But as history had shown, the plan had not gone quite the way Lucifer had expected. The demons had seen to every possible detail. The Lamb had stumbled out exhausted, weak, and anguished. Blood poured from his mangled body, the flesh on his back shredded. Flies attracted by the fresh wounds swarmed around him landing on his back and head, his face swollen from the beating. The demons celebrated their victory. Their shouts of joy assaulted the Lamb's ears. His tired, sad eyes met theirs. But even then, even as he staggered toward his death, Morax was sure he saw a hint of fire in those eyes. A glimmer of something bigger, something more.

The thought made Morax feel nervous. Bile had risen in his stomach as he considered that maybe they were missing something. Perhaps this was a mistake. After all, how many times had the King surprised them with the unexpected? Hadn't it all been too easy? Why hadn't the Lamb called in warriors? Instead, there were ministering angels lined up along the dirt path near him, tears glistening down their cheeks. But the Lamb had signaled them to stay back. This was a trial he must bear. Each of them had knelt before him as he passed watching as the King's son was lead to a criminal's death.

Morax began to worry. But the celebration continued as they placed him on the cross; Morax could not control the jubilant cheer that erupted from him when the Lamb screamed out as the nails pierced through his flesh securing him to the rough bark of the tree. It dug deep into his already tattered back. For three hours, the demons had danced around the Lamb calling out insults, mocking the King's son. For three hours, he said nothing to them. He did nothing to defend himself. All that power confined to a frail human body. The power to give and remove life with nothing more than a word, and yet he did nothing.

They should have known it was a trap. They should have known that the King would never have allowed the Lamb to be treated in such a way unless there was a very good reason. The Lamb could have merely uttered a word and destroyed them all. Instead, he hung there in humility as the demons and humans alike mocked him. Morax sighed heavily, they really should have known.

But who could have ever imagined the truth? It was preposterous. Eventually, the Lamb called out to his father, but his father had turned away.

The demons, unable to contain their joy, had erupted into celebration. Surely this was a blow to the King. Surely the death of his beloved son would weaken him enough that Lucifer could gain ground. But that was not how it had worked. Once again, they had not expected the King's next move. They had played directly into his hand.

Morax once again sighed, something he seemed to be doing a lot of lately. Morax shook the unwelcome memories from his mind. He was no longer the same person. The darkness had consumed him long ago leaving no signs of the angel he had once been. Morax knew he couldn't fully trust the memories. They were tainted by his transformation. He wondered if Lucifer had similar memories when he was in this place. Surely not. Morax couldn't imagine the Prince of this earth indulging such thoughts.

Chapter 20

The smell of stale cigars and ancient books filled the room. The walls were lined with books, well one book. The book. Lucifer sat quietly pouring over the ancient manuscript. The sunset without him noticing and the light in the room faded. Human eyes would not be able to read under those conditions, but Lucifer did not see with human eyes. No, his eyes were much more powerful.

Lucifer had every possible translation of the Bible in every language it was available in. He had read them all. Hundreds, if not thousands, of commentaries, lined the remaining shelves in the room. All of them well-worn.

He had read the Word thousands of times, perhaps millions. In fact, he had memorized it centuries ago. He had had plenty of time to study it, but then again there was never quite enough time was there? The thought of limited time angered him; it was an unpleasant reminder that once that had not been the case.

Time was just one more thing the King's children had stolen from him. Was it not enough that he had been cast down from heaven never again to call it home? Oh, he had access, but having access and being welcome was not the same. It was no longer his home. Now each time he went into the throne room every angel present drew their weapon. And yet he continued to go because he simply couldn't stay away.

That was another thing he hated. He hated that deep down, buried under thousands of years of hatred and sin he was at heart, still a heavenly being. And even though he despised it, he like all created beings, needed the King. Part of him, a minuscule part that he loathed, felt.... lighter in the presence of the King, peaceful even. He hated it. Every part of him despised it, and yet, on a purely carnal level, some small piece of him yearned for it.

And worse, he knew that one-day he would suffer total separation from the King. He would be put away in a place so dark, so devoid of any good, a place the King himself designed to be the ultimate punishment, a place where he would never again feel the presence of the King, a place that he feared.

That was the most horrific part of all. Lucifer hated himself for fearing it. He hated himself for feeling any connection to his creator. All of it disgusted him. Thoughts such as those were typically left untouched, festering in the quagmire of hatred and evil that filled him, but occasionally he would let them rise to the surface and feed his lust for destruction.

He had sufficiently fooled the King's children into attributing hell to him. They had this idea that it either didn't exist or was run by Lucifer himself. That was quite laughable. Lucifer was not going to rule hell. He was going to be an inmate, imprisoned for all time by the King. He would face endless suffering for what he had done. He was in no rush to get there.

But he let the King's children believe that he ruled hell because then they did not realize that he ruled the earth. They felt safe because they falsely thought he was in hell running things from there. He chuckled to think of it.

An enemy who was far away ruling over the dead was little threat to the living. He became something they could almost pretend wasn't real. But the truth of it, the idea that he walked among them- that he slid his hands across their skin and whispered into their ears on this earth; well that was much more frightening. If they knew that to be true, they would better prepare for the battle.

And so, he perpetuated the lie that he did not walk among them. He worked hard to make them doubt his existence. He made them laugh at the excuse that "the devil made me do it." The King had told them through his Word that Lucifer hid waiting to devour them, but Lucifer had convinced them that that was not literal; because it made his job much easier.

Now rumors were coming in from the troops that something was stirring. Perhaps indications that the end of his reign was drawing near. Lucifer too was seeing signs, but he had been seeing signs for a thousand years. He preferred to keep it that way. In desperation, he continued to pour over the ancient text searching for the answers but not finding them. Frustration filled him. Why wasn't it clearer, he wondered in exasperation as he slammed the book shut. In his opinion, the King had left out a lot.

Lucifer was in no hurry to see the end. So often people attributed the apocalypse to him too, but of course, that was not him either. It was much worse. Lucifer could never impart anything equal to the wrath of the King, and a portion of that wrath would be directed at him. He planned to take full advantage of it, deceiving as many of the King's children as he could, but it was not something he was in control of. And so, he searched the Word daily for any clues he could find, anything that would alert him to his impending doom. He sought desperately for ways to stop it or at least slow it down.

Lucifer faithfully collected commentaries, visited churches, and listened to sermons, but the humans were utterly useless. Their attempts to understand the Word often made Lucifer and his demons roll with laughter. How could he have expected anything different? How could the blind ever truly see? No, he would not learn the secrets he sought from them. Trying to had proven to be an exercise in futility.

He searched his desk for the Hebrew and Aramaic manuscripts, their pages yellowed with age and worn from his constant review of them. He opened one to Daniel one to Zachariah and the last to Revelation. He had read them all many times and yet he knew that he was missing something. Despite all his studying, all the many translations and theories, he still was not able to answer the only real question he had. How much time did he have?

He searched through the night until the sun began to creep back into the sky, once again bathing the room in light.

"My Liege?" his house demon spoke softly, aware that the intrusion would not be welcomed. Lucifer looked up in anger. Thick black smoke began to billow from him quickly filling the room with the stench of sulfur.

"What!" he did not try to conceal his rage at being interrupted.

"You have a guest. I would not have interrupted you, but it's Morax. He says he has news of Platitude." The demon waited anxiously, acutely aware that Lucifer could devour him instantly.

Lucifer smiled slyly, he had been waiting for this.

Chapter 21

"Morax I am pleased to see you," Lucifer offered in greeting as he entered the room. "I trust this body pleases you?"

"Yes, thank you." Morax acknowledged the gift Lucifer had arranged. The body really was far superior to his previous one. He hoped it meant this assignment would be more to his liking.

"How are things in Platitude?" Lucifer asked as he handed Morax a cigar.

Morax gratefully took the cigar and painted a genuine looking smile on his face. He let out a slow, steady breath before answering. He had been practicing his response. He planned to focus on their successes.

"We had many successes. The Strongman strangled them with rules chaining them to legalism. He demeaned women and their roles and told them mental illness was nothing more than a sin issue that could be cured with repentance and Bible study," Morax added knowing that would please Lucifer. The smile that lit Lucifer's face was evidence he had been right. Morax lit his cigar savoring the sweet honey flavor before continuing. A false sense of security filled him.

"We stayed extremely close to the truth, twisting it just enough to keep them judgmental and feeling inadequate. We covered them in shame, guilt, and pride so they would never consider sharing their biggest struggles thereby assuring they would never truly be free."

Morax felt himself smiling at the memory of all they had accomplished. It really had been a successful mission when he thought about it.

"Of course," he said hesitantly, knowing this was one part likely to cause him problems, "Seneca was lost in battle."

This news caught Lucifer completely by surprise. Seneca had been a mighty warrior—the first angel to fall after the original group. He had been something of a novelty item to the other demons. Although technically fallen he was not yet truly a demon and yet he was no longer an angel.

Lucifer found Seneca wandering aimlessly outside Pas-Dammim. Seneca made no secret of his passionate and deep hatred for the demons. He rejected everything about them and no efforts on Lucifer's part could change that. Eventually, Seneca sealed himself in a cave where he spent hundreds of years alone. Each day the darkness took more of him. Without the Light of God evil overtook him. Hatred filled him; anger, pride, and self-justification consumed him. He emerged from the cave a demon.

Seneca quickly became one of Lucifer's favorites. They rarely spoke, Seneca usually kept to himself, but Lucifer didn't mind that. He admired Seneca's tenacity, his all-consuming dedication to the destruction of the King's children and to any angel he encountered. Seneca had hated being a demon; somewhere in his mind, he had convinced himself that he wasn't really one of them. And in many ways, he never really was. But he was a demon nonetheless, and he was one of the most merciless among them, and that was what Lucifer valued.

"How?" That was all Lucifer could manage on hearing the news.

"Aegeus," Morax knew he need not say more. Lucifer paced away toward the pool and Morax waited patiently.

"Why was Aegeus in Platitude?" It was the question Morax had been dreading—the one piece he was unsure of. This news could be what destroyed him. He proceeded cautiously, grateful that Lucifer's back was to him and he would not have to look him in the eyes when he said it. He puffed the cigar again to stall before answering.

"The Strongman uncovered a prophet." Morax kept it simple. Fewer details seemed better to him.

Lucifer turned slowly toward Morax his silk smoking jacket fluttering out from his side. The look of shock mixed with fear on his face told Morax he had been right to be worried.

"So, it's true? The King has sent a prophet?" His voice shook almost imperceptibly, but Morax knew Lucifer well.

"Yes. A woman." Morax had intentionally saved that detail; he hoped it would help soothe the situation.

"A woman?" Lucifer seemed astounded. A smile washed over his face as all traces of fear scattered.

"Yes, so you understand why the Strongman spent so much time demeaning women and their role," Morax offered with a small smile of his own.

"After all these years the King sends a prophet, and he chooses a woman?" Lucifer said more to himself than anything.

He paced forward, his face evidence that his mind was working to try to understand what the King was up to. "And to put her in a small town in the United States," he went on, deep in concentration. Morax stood perfectly still and silent letting Lucifer work it all out in his own mind.

"She was destined to be dismissed from the onset. It makes no sense," Lucifer went on. Thousands of years raging against the King had taught Lucifer that the King never did what Lucifer would do—what Lucifer thought made sense. That made it harder to anticipate the King's moves.

Despite all his efforts and the magnificent empire Lucifer had built he still knew deep down that he was always at least one step behind the King although, he would never admit it.

"I trust you killed her?"

Morax felt his throat go dry. "Seneca did not. Aegeus, Kfir, and Adiel protected her. But no one—not even she—believed she was a prophet. And while Seneca did not kill her, we did kill two angels, Lavi and Haywood." He had saved that last bit of information just for this moment, and he hoped it would ease Lucifer's anger.

The death of an angel was rare indeed, and the shock of it gave Lucifer a moment of pause. Only four angels had ever died, Lavi and Haywood made six. It was most unusual. Lucifer could not help but wonder what the King was planning. Something about it made him uneasy.

"Where is the prophet now?"

"We don't know. She left Platitude two years ago, and there has been no sign of her since." This was the last of it. The last of the bad news that may get him killed. He tried to look confident; after all, he was the second in command, the highest-ranking demon other than Lucifer himself.

Lucifer walked slowly up to Morax, rage burning in his eyes a sinister smile on his face and sulfur pouring from him filling the room with the smell the King had cursed them with as a reminder of their destined fate.

Scales began to form on his skin as his true form pushed its way to the surface. Morax realized this was dangerous territory. He did not care to see Lucifer transform into the beast. He felt the sweat run down his back a reminder of how much he loathed the hairless rats and their fragile bodies.

Lucifer stopped just in front of him their noses nearly touching. Hatred coursed through Lucifer's body, his eyes a deep pool of evil scales now covering his otherwise perfect skin. Black smoke poured from him filling the room with the putrid stench of demon. Slowly a smile twitched in the corner of his mouth, and his eyes softened. The sulfur stopped, and the scales were once more hidden.

"Do you dance Morax?" It was as if Lucifer had splashed cold water on his face.

"What?" he asked confused his heart still racing.

"Do. You. Dance?" Lucifer stressed each word pausing slightly between them his face jubilant his white teeth glimmering where only seconds before there had been a snarl.

"I don't much care for the hairless rats or their customs; you know that," Morax said with steely confidence although he did not feel nearly so confident.

"Well, tonight Morax you will get very personal with...the hairless rats." Lucifer was clearly enjoying Morax's discomfort. "Why do you think I gave you such a young, handsome body? You are to be my wingman. I need to leave more of my seed before leaving here. That should assure that at least one of them bears my child. Then I will be leaving Hawaii, and we will find the eleven from Platitude, and we will finish what you could not. Titus has already begun the search."

Titus? Morax was stunned. Titus had known that Morax was walking into a trap and yet he had said nothing, perhaps Titus had even laid the trap?

Morax's skin crawled. It became obvious to him that Lucifer must have already known what had happened in Platitude. While some of the details may have been a surprise, clearly Titus had already told him most it.

"You look quite ill Morax," Lucifer said, feigning sympathy. He was obviously enjoying Morax's discomfort.

With those words, he signaled to the low-level demon who came forward quickly to lead Morax to his chambers. He was to prepare himself so that he might assist Lucifer, an assignment that was clearly intended to be a form of punishment. After which, they would hunt and destroy the prophet.

Chapter 22—The Twelfth

The chamber was dark; so dark the Twelfth couldn't see her own body. The floor was damp and cold against her bare feet. Her clothes felt torn and saturated with what she couldn't be sure. The wooden chair she was in was splintered and worn. She was bound with chains to what she imagined was a stone wall, although she could not reach it.

She shivered uncontrollably in the freezing room. She tried to think logically without emotion to assess her injuries and figure out where she was. Her lip was swollen, and one eye would no longer open. Chains bound her hands and feet cutting into her skin; she could smell her own blood. Despair covered her.

She could sense him before he arrived, a sense of extreme dread and evil preceded him. The chamber itself shook with his approach. It was too dark to see anything other than his beady red eyes, hollow and void of compassion, piercing through the suffocating darkness of the chamber. His presence was overwhelming. He filled a room when he entered and sucked it dry when he left.

She struggled to pull her wounded body from the cold floor, wondering how and when she had fallen from the chair. But her skin had stuck to the floor, and her flesh began ripping away as she attempted to lift herself. She would have screamed, but she no longer had the energy. How long had she been here? She had no sense of time. Things were fading in and out, memories blurring together until she was no longer even sure what was real.

Giving in to the pain, she laid on the cold floor feeling vulnerable and exposed. Hopelessness washed over her each time he entered the chamber, and she felt sure that this would be the time that he killed her.

He took a different approach with her each time, but every time the purpose was the same. He was looking for something, for someone. Who? She did not know. She searched her mind to figure it out, if only she knew, she would tell him. She wanted to tell him, she wanted to make it stop.

Sometimes he would speak from a distance, but this time he spoke directly into her ear. His voice angry, hatred permeating each syllable as he demanded information, information she did not have.

"Where are they?" His breath felt like fire against her face and neck. Was it possible that it was fire? Her skin screamed at the assault.

A new sense of fear flooded through her. Her mind raced to figure out what was happening.

"I don't know," She was barely able to push the words out.

"TELL ME!" he bellowed. The Twelfth had never felt such rage from another. He exuded such utter and complete hatred.

Sometimes he would switch tactics and try to make his voice soft and soothing. He would promise her a quick death if she told him where they were. Other times, like this one, he resorted to beating her.

She couldn't tell what he was using to beat her, but she tried to focus on that instead of the pain. She tried to busy her mind with anything to distract herself from the pain, and from the fear. Whatever it was he was using, it tore flesh from her body with each strike. The smell of her blood filled the chamber working him into a psychotic frenzy making him giddy. He became increasingly excited lashing her repeatedly with the strange whip. He was gleeful as her feeble screams bounced off the chamber walls.

Chapter 23

Adiel watched as the Twelfth slept if you could call it that. Her body twisted and flailed against whatever it was she was fighting. Adiel again found herself wishing for a ministering angel. A ministering angel would be able to see what the Twelfth was seeing and offer comfort. But there was no ministering angel here, and Adiel could do nothing to comfort the King's children. She felt powerless. It was not something she was accustomed to.

The dream seemed to be coming more frequently, but Adiel couldn't be certain because the Twelfth didn't bother to mention it anymore. There was a time when she had group texted the Third and the Eleventh. The three of them had spent many hours over the last several years discussing the possibilities. She had even typed it up and sent it to the First via email, perhaps he could tell her what it meant. They scheduled a phone call to discuss it, but then his wife had gotten sick, and all else had been forgotten.

In time, the Twelfth quit mentioning it to anyone. Occasionally over morning coffee, her husband would ask, "did you have the dream again?" To which she would mumble a groggy, "yes," and then they would both let it drop.

They had analyzed it to death. They had discussed every possibility of what the dream could mean. Meanwhile, Adiel and Emeka, the guardian angel currently assigned to the family, had done the same.

They had listened with great interest when the Twelfth initially shared the dream with her husband. Many mornings had passed in which the four of them would sit around the breakfast table discussing the dream. Adiel and Emeka, undetected by the humans they were there to protect, were no less engaged in the conversation.

The angels had gotten no closer to solving the mystery than the Twelfth and her husband with one small exception. They recognized that dreams were important, that there was meaning in them. They knew that the dream of a prophet could be a warning, but the prophet herself seemed oblivious to this.

But to know anything beyond that, Adiel and Emeka would need a ministering angel. Only then would they be able to see the dream, fill in the missing pieces and decipher its meaning. Adiel didn't want just any ministering angel, she wanted Meir. In part, because they were friends, in part because Meir knew the Twelfth and in part because Adiel was worried about how Meir was doing after the death of the Fifth.

Adiel knew that the Fifth wasn't the first that Meir had attempted to help but had failed. She had been in the service of the King far too long not to have experienced that. But never quite so personally as what had happened with the Fifth.

The Twelfth continued to thrash and moan in her sleep until Adiel finally reached down and shook her gingerly. She may not be able to offer comfort, but she could put an end to the dream at least for today. The Twelfth awoke with a start her heart racing her breathing ragged and fast, but she had not screamed out, and Adiel considered that progress.

Feeling certain that the Twelfth was up for the day, Adiel returned to the deck to join Emeka for breakfast. Emeka had picked up fresh jam during his last visit home, and Adiel planned to savor it.

It was a chilly summer morning precisely the type of morning the Twelfth liked. The water from the lake glistened as the sun peaked out from behind the mountain. A peregrine falcon cried out in the distance as the Twelfth walked out onto the deck wrapped in a quilt.

Shuffling over to the wicker sofa she sat down and curled her bare feet under her making sure the quilt covered them. Steam rose from her coffee, and she took a slow sip before letting out a long sigh. The lack of sleep was taking a toll. She was weary, and no matter how many times she had the dream, it left her rattled and on edge. At one time she had believed it meant something, but now, she didn't know. Perhaps it was exhaustion or stress. The Twelfth slowly sipped her coffee trying to push the terror from her mind and savor the richness of the coffee.

Adiel knew that the Twelfth's husband would also be up soon. He would know she had had the dream again and he would attempt to distract her by reading her the morning headlines. They would drink their coffee together and discuss anything but the dream. It had become the way they eased into most days.

Then, they would part, each going their own way for the few hours the Twelfth was required to work. Her agreement to fill in at the small clinic was the only way they had been able to afford to spend the summer in Maine. The woman with the wild red hair had arranged everything.

Emeka walked to the Twelfth and sat down by her on the small sofa.

"What job do you think she will be given in heaven?" he asked Adiel. It was an interesting question, one she had not thought about. Adiel sat her breakfast down to look more closely at the Twelfth.

"I haven't ever really thought of her there. I have been so busy thinking about her job here." she began, as she considered the question. "There is no use for her earthly job in heaven, so it must be something based more on her skills."

After judgment, those who belonged to the King were presented with the place the Lamb had prepared for them, some in the city, others far from it. Each of them was given a dwelling in a location that was perfect for them and befitting the life they had lived on earth. Initially, they spent time renewing, resting, and celebrating their return. But in time, when they were ready, each was assigned a job, something handpicked by the King something perfect for them. Something their time on earth had prepared them for.

It was fun to watch as they discovered that work in heaven was nothing like work on earth. There was no "grind" as the King's children called it. They were given a job they loved, a job they were perfectly suited for. Work was redefined into something you longed to do. There were no set hours there was no vacation time allotted there was no need. Each person worked when they desired to do so. It was such a different life, a better life, an eternal life.

"Perhaps she will be a warrior, trained to fight in Armageddon?" Emeka offered. Adiel considered it, the Twelfth's husband would make a fine warrior, but that didn't quite sit right for the Twelfth. "Well I think we are safe to say she will not join Martha in the bakery," she laughed. Emeka too laughed, cooking was not one of the Twelfths skills.

The angels watched as the Twelfth struggled to pull the quilt tighter around her fighting off the morning chill that seemed to be seeping through. Her hand grazed the side of her neck causing her breath to catch and drawing Adiel and Emeka's attention. Gently and tenderly the Twelfth touched the area again and made a face indicating that pain coursed through her.

Adiel and Emeka exchanged a glance, their breakfast forgotten, they followed the Twelfth as she made her way to the small bathroom mirror. When she pulled her hair back, there was a burn just behind her ear. The Twelfth shook her head as if an impossible idea had pushed its way in and she was attempting to stop it.

Adiel and Emeka stood frozen in place looking at the burn. This could only mean one thing; it was a prophecy. Suddenly the dream made sense, suddenly they understood. Emeka looked to Adiel, and horror-struck said the thing they both now knew.

"The Beast is coming for her."

Chapter 24

Morax painstakingly climbed the stairs of the hospital. He was unsure why Lucifer had brought him here, but he was hopeful that inside they would have a cure for whatever was ailing him. His head throbbed, his stomach lurched with each step, and there did not seem to be enough water in the world to quench his thirst. He could not remember ever feeling this way before.

Lucifer seemed to have anticipated it and handed Morax dark glasses as they left the house. The glasses helped, but Morax could not help but wonder why he felt so sick. He let his mind wander and consider the possibility that Lucifer had poisoned him.

The previous night had served to solidify Morax's hatred for the hairless rats. Lucifer, Lou as Morax had been instructed to call him in front of the rats, had taken Morax to a bonfire on the beach. One Lucifer had apparently been invited to by a tourist he had met before Morax arrived in Hawaii.

They arrived to find a large fire with fallen logs arranged around it providing a form of makeshift seating. A small group on the far side of the fire was cooking something on skewers. Morax couldn't quite make out what it was, but the smell of pineapple wafted passed him as they approached.

The sky was full of stars lending a romantic overtone to the night. Morax noticed that a few couples stood at the shoreline letting the waves crash over their feet while others further down the beach seemed to be night fishing. The temperature was perfect. It was a truly captivating night. Morax doubted Lucifer had chosen this location by accident.

Lucifer located his mark and then settled in quietly around the fire. He gave his undivided attention to her, and her friend who it turned out was Morax's blind date. He noticed immediately that she had the Light, but because it was quite dim, he did not anticipate it being an issue for him. Insecurity clung to her winking at Morax upon his approach. Morax glanced around anxiously to see if she had a guardian with her. Seeing none, he relaxed a bit.

Morax hated the hairless rats. They repulsed him. His preference was to destroy them. Mingling among them in this way was not part of his M.O. But Lucifer had given him this assignment and failure would surely mean a punishment worse than death. Morax noticed the girl seemed equally uncomfortable, but he felt confident it was for entirely different reasons. Despite his personal aversion, Morax noticed, to his great horror, that his physical body seemed to be responding to the girl. Desire burned within him, and he felt torn between destroying her and devouring her. He looked over at Lucifer with horror in his eyes. Lucifer met his eyes, smiled cunningly and then turned his attention back to his own date.

Morax had to admit that it had been impressive watching Lucifer work. A simple touch, a graze really was all he needed to get inside a human's head. Once he had access to their mind the rest was easy. It did not take much to open the door.

Lucifer was attentive without being creepy. Aloof enough to keep her interest and of course an excellent liar. He brought mystery, charm, romance, intrigue, comfort, whatever it was she was looking for he would offer. Just long enough to lure her in. Slowly, gradually he became bolder, more daring. But it was done with such finesse that it went unnoticed.

Someone had come around offering drinks, something blue that Morax did not recognize. Lucifer insisted that Morax have one to help him relax. It was all a blur from there. Morax had only vague memories of more blue drinks, of dancing with wild abandon around the fire with one of the female rats. He suspected he may have run into the ocean fully clothed at some point and he was reasonably sure he had thrown up. He certainly wanted to throw up now.

Overall Morax would consider the night one best forgotten. He had behaved in a most unsophisticated way. But Lucifer seemed to have accomplished his mission, and Morax recognized it was better that way, no reason to further agitate him. Morning had come early. But of course, the Prince did not need sleep.

Lucifer made breakfast for the women before they left and then sent them off with promises that he would call, and they would get together again soon. Morax made no such promises to his date. Over breakfast, he noticed that she too acted as if she were not feeling well.

She seemed a bit embarrassed, and Morax wondered if she had done something humiliating that he could not remember. He hoped so. Her regret was palpable, and her eagerness to depart his company was poorly concealed. That gave him tremendous joy. Despite the way his body was feeling his spirit soared with glee at her discomfort. Several tormenting demons entered the room and clamored on her causing her light to dim even more. Their talons ripped into her flesh as they made their way up her body and settled on her back. They pierced deep into her spine feeling jubilant as her soul cried out in pain.

Watching her suffering seemed to embolden Morax in a way he had not experienced in prior missions. It was exhilarating. He wondered why she did not cry out to the King. Why did she not pray? The King would surely deliver her. He would remove her shame and self-loathing. But she did not, and as a result, her light grew dimmer.

It was glorious. Morax had never known such utter and complete satisfaction.

As they were departing, just when he saw her start to let out a sigh of relief that it was finally over he rushed forward and grabbed her by the arm spinning her around; he kissed her. He felt her body convulse from the shock. His breath smelled vulgar even to himself it pleased him to know she suffered through it. When he let her go, she would not meet his eyes. He nearly forgot his own discomfort as he relished in hers.

Chapter 25

A wave of nausea washed over Morax bringing him back to the present. As they entered the hospital he had to stop moving, he didn't trust his stomach. Lucifer turned toward him and rolled his eyes.

"You really need to get out more," he offered in criticism. Morax wondered why Lucifer didn't just remove his illness instead of mocking him. What good was he like this? But Lucifer was not known for his mercy. Trying to swallow down the bile that was creeping into his throat Morax followed Lucifer further into the hospital.

Demons and angels filled the space. The sound of swords clashing together caused Morax's head to pound; he felt tempted to rip his own ears from the sides of his head just to alleviate his misery. Why must the rats' bodies be so weak? He wondered.

A skirmish between two destroying demons and a guardian exploded out into the hall right into Morax. Lucifer did not pause. He walked purposefully on, toward his destination.

The angels and demons alike took notice of Lucifer's presence. By the looks on their faces, each seemed convinced that he was there for their charge. Angels began to line the walls swords drawn. They stood little chance on their own but together they would pose a significant threat.

But Lucifer seemed not to notice. He did not deviate from his path. He was focused and purposeful. The intensity of it struck

Morax, and he had to wonder what exactly they were doing here. They wound their way down halls and up flights of stairs until finally, Lucifer stopped abruptly.

Morax looked up stunned. They were in the nursery. Morax considered himself a warrior. His missions took him into battle against some of the best angels in Heaven's army. He specialized in strategy and covert operations. He did not "do" babies. They had a smell he did not like, his stomach churned, threatening to erupt.

He stood dumbstruck he could not remember ever being so close to a human child before. Certainly not so many at once. Lucifer stood silently staring through the glass at them a smile on his face as if he enjoyed them. Morax looked on horrified.

"What are we doing here?"

"I have work here Morax," Lucifer responded as if speaking to a dimwitted child.

"What work could you possibly have that involves babies? Is one of these yours?" Morax asked thinking perhaps he had solved the mystery.

"I certainly hope so," Lucifer said purposefully misinterpreting Morax's question. He stepped through the glass as if it were not there into the room where the babies were. Morax watched as Lucifer went to each baby touching them one by one. Their souls were so pure so innocent that it hurt Morax's eyes to look at them. He squinted slightly. Lucifer took his time with each one. Some of them he merely needed to touch, some he whispered too, others he picked up and rocked. When he had gone to each one, he stepped back through the glass and rejoined Morax.

"There are more," Lucifer stated and again walked away with purpose. Some of the mothers had their babies in the hospital room with them. Lucifer paused at one of the doors just long enough for Morax to catch up. He patted Morax on the shoulder immediately concealing him from the humans then they entered the room.

A young woman laid in the hospital bed nestling her newborn child. The child was tightly swaddled and had a blue stocking cap on that Morax took as a signal that it was a boy. The child's father slept quietly on a couch against the wall. Morax thought the man seemed to have had as rough a night as Morax had although obviously for different reasons.

The smell of a new soul permeated the room making Morax feel both nauseated and nostalgic at the same time. Two angels stood in the corner their swords instantly drawn when Lucifer and Morax entered.

"Relax Omri I am here for the child this is my right" Lucifer said to the bigger of the two warriors. Morax did not flinch two warriors were not much of a threat against Lucifer no matter how strong the angels. Even Michael would not fight Lucifer alone. Omri kept his sword drawn. His repulsion was evident on his face. He looked as if beetles crawled under his skin. Morax took pleasure in his discomfort.

Lucifer walked to the edge of the bed and then waited he knew that he could not touch the child when it was in its mother's arms that type of pure unconditional love was too powerful. And so, he waited. Eventually, she laid the child down, and Lucifer stepped up. He placed his hand on the child, and a smile spread across his face. It had only taken a second.

Instantly a flash of Light filled the room blinding Lucifer and Morax. They were forced to step back from the child and turn their faces away. Omri stepped closer now flanked by six additional warriors he placed himself between the baby and Lucifer.

"Leave," Omri ordered Lucifer, knowing the King demanded it.

Lucifer abruptly turned and walked from the room there was no reason to waste time. Morax followed him not truly understanding what was happening.

"What was that?" Morax asked perplexed.

"A prayer warrior must have prayed for the child," Lucifer answered matter-of-factly. "The presence of the warriors instead of a guardian let me know it was a risk. But fortunately, I found the right sin quickly. The prayer cover was too late."

"What are we doing here?" Morax asked quietly, his head still pounding from their night out.

"This is one of my favorite jobs. When each human arrives on the earth, they arrive innocent and pure. The King sends them with advanced preparation, gifts he bestows on them things they will need. But I too bestow a gift on them. I give each one a master sin." Lucifer let the words linger in his mouth as he savored the reality of what he was doing.

"A master sin?"

"It is a weakness, a single sin with the power to master them. "Their" sin if you will. A sin that they will love and hate at the same time. For some, it is lying, for others: lust, jealousy, greed, cowardice, rage or idolatry. There are so many good options. Addiction is more complicated; I am exceedingly selective about that one. But gossip and sloth can always be counted on. Self-centeredness, legalism, anger, lack of self-control, being judgmental, or my personal favorite, pride. The list is quite long plenty of options to choose from. A sin that flows from them so naturally, they will assume it is part of their very nature they will think they were born that way. Surely you have encountered a human who defaults to lying, cruelty, lust or greed?"

"Yes of course."

"The master sin, as I like to call it, is one I hand pick for them. I search their innocent little souls and find just the right thing. Something that will gnaw at them their entire life. Something that will perfectly undermine the task the King has laid out for them. Something that they will have to actively fight against, something that will creep in and cause them to doubt their position with the King. Doubt the

King himself. Something they will cling to even unto death." His eyes smiled as he considered it.

Morax contemplated the idea of it and found he had never been more impressed with Lucifer. He really was quite brilliant.

"You personally assign them all?" Morax was stunned.

"This will strangle them their entire life, it is not to be left to just anyone. When determining how to torment them over the course of their entire life, it is best to handle that with delicacy. Some take longer than others of course but it is time well spent and what is time to us? Doing this well reduces the work in the long run. Torment-ing demons will soon attach to them digging their talons deep into the child's heart. It will seem so natural they will not ever remember life without it. They will believe it is just "who they are." He said air quoting the last part. "I thoroughly enjoy it. You really must learn to enjoy your job more Morax."

Chapter 26

Meir arrived with a silent swoosh joining Adiel and Emeka at the cabin in Maine.

"Meir!" they said in unison responding with surprise and delight at her arrival. Meir's hair and wings flashed a beautiful orange color in response. She had been anxious about being back on earth, but it felt good. She did not enjoy the distance from the King, but it felt good to be fulfilling her purpose. One was always most happy when doing that which the King prepared for them, even when that thing was difficult.

"What are you doing here?" Adiel asked pleased to see Meir.

"I have been assigned to her," Meir explained gesturing her head slightly toward the Twelfth who was at the lake with her youngest son. From the looks of it, she was attempting to fish with him, but the boy kept getting his hook caught in the grass, the trees, and even his mother. Meir smiled to see the Twelfth had not yet lost her patience.

"Aegeus has returned. He is delayed with the Second and Third. The others will join us once he has secured a detail for them."

"Others?" Emeka asked

"He brings Kfir and Mordecai with him."

"A Sentinel?" Adiel was surprised.

"You know him?" Meir was equally surprised.

"I do," Adiel offered without expounding. "I don't understand. The Twelfth needs a Sentinel?" She seemed to be experiencing the same concerns Aegeus had earlier.

"We don't know. We know only that it is the King's will that Mordecai should join us. We don't know who his charge is."

"What is he like?" Emeka asked having never met a Sentinel.

"Different," Meir left it at that. She wasn't ready to share what she knew about Mordecai. What she could tell the instant she had touched him. He was a fierce and loyal being. But the small morsel of humanity that was in him made a big difference. He understood and connected to the Kings children in a way that even she could not.

Mordecai carried immense sorrow within him, a pain he bore willingly for his charges so that their own sadness would not be so great. Unlike Meir, who waded through their emotions helping them find the strength to bear their burdens and the wisdom to see their lives through the King's lens, Mordecai absorbed their sorrow like a sponge, taking it on as his own.

In addition, he was filled with his own sorrow when they chose wrong. He fought for them day and night sometimes for years, sometimes for their entire lifetime. When the charge decided to walk in the ways of the King, a Sentinel would experience immeasurable joy.

But when they did not, the Sentinel felt the gravity of that. Meir thought of the struggle Aegeus had felt when Seneca had made his decision and separated himself from the King. Aegeus had carried great anguish over it. She thought of her own sorrow over the death of the Fifth, and she knew that even that was not as great as the sorrow carried willingly by a Sentinel.

For centuries, if not millennia, Sentinels served only one family. The connection and loyalty a Sentinel felt for that family was unlike anything Meir had ever seen before. Mordecai would be connected to his charge in a way that most angels would never experience. His connection to his charge was so great, it was second only to his devotion to the King. No matter the test, no matter the person, no matter the circumstances, Mordecai would offer his life to protect his charge until the moment they made their decision. There was no cost too high.

He would look at the face of his charge and see all those who had gone before them, all the others he had protected in the bloodline. Mordecai would remember each one that had failed, and each that had not. He would understand the connection between them and see his current charge as a new hope for all those before them. But if his charge chose to follow the evil one, the Sentinel would have no choice but to separate from them forever.

Mordecai was also full of great joy. A joy that knew no bounds. When his charge chose to follow the way of the King, they would be bound together as long as the charge remained on earth. And when the time came, the Sentinel would be the sole angel to welcome their soul and escort them to heaven. It was a tremendous honor. But Meir kept all these things to herself for they were not hers to tell. Instead, she drew their focus back to the Twelfth which Adiel was grateful for. She too was not yet ready to talk about how she knew Mordecai.

"How is she," Meir asked nodding toward the Twelfth who was once again working to untangle the fishing line on her youngest son's small fishing pole.

Adiel and Emeka exchanged a look unsure where to start.

"What is it?" Meir asked.

"She is having dreams," Adiel began. "Well, really a single dream over and over. It is a prophecy. The Beast comes for her."

This news should not have been shocking. She was, after all, a prophet. Lucifer knew of Platitude and that the prophet had prevented his full success there. He was aggressively seeking the eleven for destruction, it was reasonable, expected even, that he should come for her. And yet, the prophecy still stunned her.

"Is she ready?" Meir asked. It was all that really mattered.

Adiel and Emeka again exchanged a glance. This was a simple question, but the answer was not as easy. They could not know for sure the state of the Twelfth. But what they did know was that she had not entirely healed from Platitude.

"Platitude is still with her," Emeka added carefully, sensitive to Meir's own wounds.

"It is still with all of us," Meir responded. "It is part of who we are now. The King did not give that to her so that she could bury it or forget but that she might use it for her own growth and for the growth of others. She must learn to draw from it without being consumed. I will work with her," Meir assured them feeling familiar with the path the Twelfth was on.

A shout erupted from the lake. Adiel drew her sword moving swiftly toward the Twelfth. She was upon them before she realized it was a shout of joy. The boy had caught a fish. It was barely the size of his small hand, but he and the Twelfth celebrated as if it were a leviathan.

Chapter 27

Meir immediately began working with the Twelfth. After a quick assessment, Meir determined her work with the Twelfth should focus on three primary areas: assuring the Twelfth fed her soul well so there would be plenty to work with at the time of testing, helping her see Platitude through the King's eyes, and helping her to recognize the dream as a prophecy. It was evident to Meir that the Twelfth needed help wading through the pain that held her back, keeping her trapped. It was important that the Twelfth see her feelings through the lens of truth instead of only pain. She must learn to see suffering as something more, something with purpose, something of value.

It felt good to be working again, to be fulfilling her purpose and Meir savored each precious moment. She wondered how she could have ever considered not returning. She had been made for this very thing. The King had designed her to offer comfort to his children, to minister to them. She could see so clearly now that doing anything else was purposeless.

Meir began by finding the strength buried within the Twelfth. She took her time slowly wading through the Twelfth's memories, enjoying the process, happy to be back at the King's work. At times, she found herself mesmerized by the Twelfth's memories and thoughts.

Meir cataloged memories within the Twelfth that would help support her in the journey that was to come. Occasionally she would pause to enjoy the Twelfth's childhood memories of picking apples at a nearby orchard, afternoons fishing with her father, and quiet Saturdays playing dolls with her best friend. Meir felt encouraged when she found memories in which the Twelfth was filled with compassion for others or memories in which she dared to stand up for what was right, even when it cost her.

It was fascinating to Meir to see which memories the Twelfth had saved in detail like the soft petal of a rose, the gentle trickle of a brook, and the smell of Thanksgiving dinners long passed. Meir was equally surprised by the places where the Twelfth's memories were shockingly void of details.

She hovered over the college years a time when the Twelfth believed she had lost her way. But Meir could see what the Twelfth could not. Meir saw each memory for what it really was, what it looked like through the eyes of the King. Meir knew that each experience was developing the Twelfth, molding her and teaching her lessons she would never forget even if she didn't remember.

Meir watched as the Twelfth learned courage by being afraid. She learned boldness by being timid in the wrong situations. She learned compassion through suffering. She learned the value of self-control by being rash. Never in all those moments that she would consider failure had she ever lost sight of the King.

Meir lingered over some of the Twelfth's favorite memories such as the smell of fresh-baked cookies or the sound of laughter as she played with her children. She savored the memory of a cool evening at the end of a long summer when the Twelfth walked along the boardwalk with a young man. She experienced the jolt of electricity as the young man who walked beside the Twelfth took her hand in his, and Meir would never forget the look in his eyes years later as the Twelfth walked down the aisle to become his wife. Memories of the crack of the bat and the smell of fresh grass as she played baseball in the backyard were also powerful. Meir could taste the dirt as the Twelfth slid into home.

Dinner failures were perhaps among Meir's favorites; the Twelfth was no master of the kitchen. Meir couldn't help but chuckle to relive the memories of her catching the cookbook on fire or discovering she had never actually turned the oven on. On most days Meir found that the Twelfth too would chuckle when those memories came to mind.

Meir also delved into speeches the Twelfth had heard, kind words that had been offered in passing and usually without further thought by the giver. Songs the Twelfth had heard on the radio would fill her with a sense of strength. This finding pleased Meir, it would make the job easier. Music could be a powerful motivator. To test it, Meir would sometimes cause a song to get "stuck" in the Twelfth's head repeatedly playing in her mind. The Twelfth would moan over it, but Meir learned it was effective to either encourage or distract her whichever was needed most.

The Twelfth had collected a lifetime of memories some of which she may not even remember she had. Meir waded through most of them softly, careful not to disrupt any memories best left undisturbed. Some of them were warm and lovely. Some of them were agonizing and difficult, while others were quite cold and sterile.

And though it was not easy, Meir caused the Twelfth to remember things she would prefer to forget. Meir brought these things to the Twelfth's mind because they reminded her that strength was buried within her. Often the memory of a failure could be used to motivate her to stay the course and find her inner strength.

There was little that Meir did not explore, but she did not rush it. She chose wisely which memories to bring to the Twelfth's mind and which to leave dormant. Meir studied the Twelfth's mind because she was determined that she would know the Twelfth well. She would know how to encourage her and how to motivate her. She did not want to ever lose another charge. When she needed to, Meir would know where to get what she needed. She would know how to help the Twelfth feed her soul and fill in the gaps.

When Meir was satisfied that she knew just where to find all that she would need at the time of testing, she refocused her efforts on helping the Twelfth view Platitude for what it was. She discovered the memories of Platitude banished, pushed back into the recesses of the Twelfth's mind the place she reserved for her worst memories. A place she never visited willingly. There Meir found much that brought sorrow to the Twelfth and so Meir tread carefully trying to climb through the memories without awakening them to the Twelfth. It was there that Meir listened as hurtful words were thrown at the Twelfth. Careless words that burrowed deep into her soul ripping holes along their way.

It was there that Meir watched the Twelfth grieve the loss of a child. And it was there that the Twelfth had stored the most difficult memories of Platitude. She had relegated the night in the woods to that place. The night she had watched as one of her friends was driven to their death. Meir stopped short when she came to it. It wasn't time, so she skipped it moving on to memories of the Barley field.

Meir had not been present for the battle in the barley field, and it seemed to be something the Twelfth preferred to forget. When Meir tried to ease it into the Twelfth's mind so that they could sort through it and see the purpose, the Twelfth stubbornly resisted.

Meir pushed the Twelfth because she understood it was important to draw from every experience the lessons to be learned, otherwise the lesson would be repeated. Meir urged her to remember, even as the Twelfth struggled to forget.

Chapter 28

Peace and calm returned to the barley field in an instant. Just as quickly Aegeus was gone. The Twelfth didn't really know what had happened. She couldn't explain it. One minute she had found her courage and stood over him shielding his broken body with her own. In the next, he was gone as was the threat.

And then just as suddenly no one there could quite remember what they had been so insolent about or why they had been attacking each other. But the Twelfth remembered. She remembered the fear she had felt as the Seventh was attacked. She remembered the pain as a fist collided with her face. She remembered the science professor standing in the middle of the field his eyes wild as spittle and hatred poured from his lips. She remembered the oppression.

Meir worked to help bring perspective, to remind the Twelfth that many of the people in the field were on their knees praying, crying out to Elohei yeshu'ati, the God who saves. And then, they were delivered. The threat was gone. The field was silent with only a few muffled cries as if from a vast distance.

Meir reminded her how the people had begun to help each other, each hoping someone could explain the madness. Memories of the goodness amid the chaos, that which was holy rising from the ashes created by that which was evil, helped moved the Twelfth forward.

Yet even as Meir helped the Twelfth see the good amid the pain, it didn't last. Time had ticked on in Platitude, and as it did, people

forgot their shame. Judgment and Condemnation were again welcomed, guests. Many of them spouted hatred in one breath and bible
verses in the next, blind to their own hypocrisy.

The Strongman had been shameless, his rhetoric and insolence
grew each day, until finally, one- day while he was preaching in the
Great Hall, the Tenth had found his courage.

The Tenth stood up and challenged the Strongman in front of
the entire school. Omri, a warrior, summoned by the prayers of the
Second and the Third, had stood beside the Tenth defending him
from Fear and Uncertainty. Angels had flooded the Great Hall banishing most of the demons that were present. Only Morax, Titus and
the Strongman had remained.

Free from the influence of the demons and emboldened by the
courage of the Tenth others had joined in. The Strongman had raged
against the Tenth pelting him with Bible verses and theology. The
woman with the wild red hair had arrived in glorious fashion, and
the battle was hers.

Initially, everyone was told the Strongman was traveling, then
ill. At the proper time, they were told a version of the truth that
served the demons purposes. The Strongman had gone to Washington D.C. to serve as a spiritual adviser to President Bowlinger. Morax
was appointed to run the college until a suitable replacement could
be found.

Meir stressed these ideas to the Twelfth, putting emphasis on
them as evidence that good could come out of the pain. Meir tried
to remind her that the choice was hers about which to focus on. She
pulled up memories of the Wednesday night group and how they
continued to meet and support each other throughout that time.

But the Twelfth twisted the thought, instead focusing on the fact
that the group eventually began to move away one by one. Meir reminded her that because of social media, occasional calls, and less
common visits, they had been able to stay connected and involved in

each other's lives. Instead of seeing this as her support network being disbanded, Meir tried to help her understand it as them spreading out and taking the love of the King with them. She tried to help the Twelfth see that they were connected in a way that simple geography could never extinguish. Being such temporal beings, it was hard for the King's children to truly understand this, the Twelfth was no exception.

In accordance with the King's plan, the Twelfth remained in Platitude to see the Ninth graduate.

It was hard to believe she had only lived in Platitude for two years, it felt like so much longer. But the first year, the year the Fifth had died, that had been a long year. The Seventh had left Platitude very soon after the death of Fifth. They had little contact now that the Seventh was gone, but occasionally the Twelfth would get a text from her. The Twelfth couldn't really blame her, to be honest, the Twelfth had longed to leave too. She wanted nothing more than to walk away and forget that any of it had ever happened.

The year after the barley field, the Twelfth focused on keeping her head down and trying to survive it. She focused all her attention on the students until finally the year was over and the Ninth graduated. The Twelfth left Platitude days after.

Staying there had not even been a consideration there was too much pain. Symbolically, she stopped at the town line, unknowingly across from the salvage yard the angels had been using as a meeting place, and there she shook the town's dust from her sandals.

The Twelfth and her family moved far from Platitude, desperate to be free. But just because she no longer saw it, no longer dwelt on it, didn't mean that it was no longer with her. Meir began gently bringing to mind pleasant memories from Platitude. Memories of the twelve, memories of the Wednesday night group, memories of all the students she had counseled.

Instead of seeing it as a burden, a task that was required because there was evil, Meir helped her understand that she and the others, were part of a resistance. God's resistance. She began to see that she was part of the solution instead of a mere casualty. She began to understand how vital voices of descent were. And in recognizing that one simple truth, she began to heal. She started to allow the light to creep into that dark space and fill it with beauty and hope.

As the days turned into weeks, Meir was encouraged that it was finally time to help the Twelfth see her dream for what it was, a prophecy. The dream had started shortly after she left Platitude and two years later it was coming more often. The Twelfth, with a little help from the internet, had concluded that the dream reflected her distress from Platitude. She hated that, it made her feel weak, powerless. She had expected time to release her from it, but when it didn't, she decided that it must be because she didn't know what happened to Aegeus.

Aegeus had been so insistent that she was a prophet, and she had finally believed him. But she had seen no sign of the angels after the barley field. She hadn't felt their presence, she hadn't seen Aegeus, and she had lots of unanswered questions. Questions that haunted her. The result was that she felt alone, forgotten, and abandoned. Thoughts of being a prophet were long gone, scars were all that remained.

It was clear the Twelfth wasn't entirely sure what made one a prophet. Meir chuckled to realize that the Twelfth still envisioned prophets as old men in sackcloth proclaiming doom and saying, "thus sayeth the Lord" but she, of course, was none of the above. Instead, she was a middle-aged woman with a husband, children, and a penchant for adventurous shoes.

Her lack of understanding had caused her to become lukewarm, if not cold, toward her calling. It was obvious to Meir that the Twelfth did not truly understand the gift the King had given her. She did not understand how to give herself over to it and allow it to use her. And her lack of understanding caused her to ignore it, to suppress it, and ultimately, to doubt it. The Twelfth had made very little progress toward developing into the prophet she was.

Chapter 29—The Ninth

The Ninth knelt to reach under her cot searching blindly for her duffle bag. Her hands brushed across the canvas, and she pulled the bag out from its dusty corner under the bed. The dust tickled her nose and eyes causing a rapid succession of sneezes as her eyes watered just a little. Standing up with a bit of a grunt she dropped the empty bag on the meager cot that had served as her bed for the last several months. She was sad to be leaving Peru.

She shared the thatch roof hut, in a remote village near the Ucayali River in central eastern Peru, with four other physician assistants. Her belongings included a few sets of scrubs, her stethoscope, a few long sleeve cotton pull-overs that she wore under her scrubs on cold days, her Bible, undergarments, one t-shirt, a pair of well-loved jeans, a hairbrush, a toothbrush, and a very well-worn pair of tennis shoes. It was all she owned in the world.

The young guide that had volunteered to escort her the few miles from the village to the boat that would begin her journey out of Peru knocked on the hut door.

"Are you ready?" he asked.

The Ninth took one more longing look around the room, zipped her bag, and nodded at the guide in affirmation. There was no reason to linger. She slid the bag strap over her head and shoulder and left the hut.

Her guide was a native to Peru and to the small village. His mother had been one of her first patients. The Ninth had done all she could, but the woman had needed more advanced care than their small team could provide in such a remote location. The best they could do was keep her comfortable.

The Ninth had lost many patients since graduating, perhaps more than she had saved. At least it felt that way. She supposed that was what happened when you set out to do global health missions. She had worked in some of the poorest regions on the earth. She had been in conflict zones, natural disaster areas and villages like this one—remote and without access to modern medicine. She had learned things they did not teach you in school, things you could only learn out of desperation.

The dirt path out of the village was muddy from the recent rain, and her shoes made a sucking sound with each step as the mud clung to them, attempting to pull them off her feet. It only took a few dozen steps before she was swallowed by the forest, forgotten by the village.

She had decided not to tell anyone she was leaving. Her guide had promised to keep her secret. She wasn't good at goodbyes. She found it easier to leave quietly without fanfare. They had chosen a time when the fewest number of people would be out. It seemed better this way and yet part of her yearned for someone, anyone to acknowledge her departure.

Leaving in this way almost made it seem as if she had never actually been there at all. But then again wasn't that her life? She was no more than a wisp. She fluttered in and out of people's lives without ever attaching to anyone. She wasn't there to develop relationships, she wasn't there to make friends or be known. She was there to provide medical service. And if she were honest, she was there to forget. This lifestyle suited her.

Her foot hit a large tree root, and she stumbled forward nearly falling. Her guide reached out for her offering a steadying hand accompanied by an eye roll.

"Thank you. I'm just glad it wasn't a snake," The Ninth said trying to strike up a conversation. But she knew he would not be so easily drawn into idle chat; he was a man of few words. He led the way through the winding path in silence.

The Ninth relished this slow method of traveling. She would walk for several miles before getting into a primitive boat. Eventually, she would take a bus through the winding mountains until she reached a more populated area where she would hire a taxi to take her to the airport. The travel time gave her time to reflect on the last few months and years.

She had left Platitude unsure of what to do next. Like all her classmates she had begun the process of applying for jobs long before she graduated or passed her certification exam. She had secured a job in a family practice clinic only hours from her mom. She shared an apartment with one of her college friends. Overall, things were going well.

But that didn't seem like enough. Something deep within the Ninth's soul beckoned to her, enticing her to leave the safety and security of her life and pursue something more meaningful. She tried to silence the voice, but she couldn't. Her discontent grew stronger and stronger each day.

"I had the strangest dream about you," her roommate mumbled as she poured them both a cup of coffee.

"What about?" She asked, only partially awake.

"You found an old pair of jeans in the back of my closet. A pair we had forgotten all about. In the pocket was a receipt that was stamped on the back with a passport stamp. You were so excited. Weird, right?"

The Ninth stood still the coffee cup poised at her lips, but she was not drinking.

"What?" her roommate asked looking puzzled. "Does that mean something to you?"

It did mean something to her; she was shocked that it didn't mean anything to her roommate. But it had always been that way, as long as she could remember she had been able to understand the meaning of dreams as clearly as if they were a hand-written letter sent from a dear friend.

This dream too was perfectly clear to the Ninth. She was going to run into someone from her past. Someone she knew but who wasn't necessarily someone she had been close to. And that was going to set her on an adventure that would change her life.

"No," she lied. Nearly as soon as she had realized she could understand and interpret dreams, she also understood that this set her apart. It had only taken once of being called a freak to assure she never told anyone again. She didn't want to be set apart, she wanted nothing more than to blend in.

Her roommate was unconvinced, but she knew the Ninth well enough to know when to push and when to let something drop, at least temporarily. Instead of pushing she changed the subject.

"Oh, I almost forgot. I got two tickets to an art opening tonight. A bit of a drive but I hear it's worth it. Don't make other plans." And with that simple declaration, she left for work completely oblivious that she was about to change the Ninth's life forever.

The roommates arrived at the art exhibit in Chicago surprised to learn that the artist was the Seventh. After seeing her work and hearing the amazing stories of all she had seen and heard while serving around the world, the Ninth knew that she could no longer ignore the voice that had been calling her to provide medical care overseas. A flood of desire opened inside her chest filling her with a sense of purpose, a knowing. Six months later she left the states for Haiti.

She had never regretted leaving. But the decision had consequences she had not anticipated. She had not anticipated that she would own nothing of any value. The material aspect of it didn't faze her but having no real contact with the outside world did. Initially, she had relished it. She felt free, far from all that troubled her in Platitude. But in time she recognized that she was isolated from her support network, alone, with no way to reach out to anyone.

Most of the places she went did not have internet or phone service. She had little opportunity to speak to anyone from her prior life. She supposed that had its pros and cons. In her dark moments, she felt isolated from all those who really knew her, those who loved her and could help hold her up. Only twice in two years had she found her way to a phone to call the Twelfth. Both times her soul had been encouraged, uplifted, and she had told herself she would make more of an effort. But that wasn't reality. The reality was that she lived in faraway places among people who had more pressing issues than cell phone service or internet.

She stumbled once more causing her guide to again look back and roll his eyes at her ineptness. She did not take it personally; it was just his way. She understood that he risked his very life by agreeing to escort her through the jungle to the boat.

A sense of sadness settled in as she followed him. She loved Peru as she had come to love each of the countries she had been to over the last two years. Usually, she stayed longer but an urgent need had arisen, and she had been asked to go. The village was doing well, and they were expecting two new doctors to arrive the following week, so she knew Peru would be well cared for. She was needed at a refugee camp in Tanzania.

Chapter 30 – The Seventh

After the barley field, the Seventh wasn't sure she would ever smile again. At the time, she had assured everyone she was fine, but she wasn't.

Every time she closed her eyes, she would relive it. Panic would fill her as memories of being surrounded by madness overwhelmed her. She would remember the weight of their bodies against hers, their hands pulling her, their insults lashing at her very soul. Fear pressed in all around her. She fought against them, she always fought, but they overtook her.

For months, the memory had given her nightmares that caused her to break out in a cold sweat. She was afraid to be alone. She was equally afraid to be in large crowds. Repeatedly she had lied to everyone that asked how she was. She assured them all that she was fine. Everyone but the Sixth. There was no sense lying to her; they knew each other too well.

The Sixth knew she was anything but fine. The Seventh couldn't explain it, and she didn't want to. She wanted to hide from it, to run. And so she did, and it had been the best thing she had ever done. There was nothing for her at the college, leaving seemed so natural.

She had prayed about the decision to leave, but she had gotten no answer. She considered that affirmation that she should go. She was the first of the twelve to leave, it would be over a year before any of the others left. But without hesitation, the Seventh walked away from Platitude and everyone in it, everyone but the Sixth. There was nothing left there for her. If God had wanted her to stay surely, he would have intervened. And look at what had happened since she left. She had done missions all over the world, and she had met Damian.

The Seventh let her mind wander back to the flight that took her far away from Platitude. The plane was full, and it seemed like everyone had overhead luggage that was too big for the overhead compartments. Trying to accommodate everyone had caused the flight to leave late.

She had a window seat, there was a young mother seated beside her in the middle seat. Somehow, the woman's children had been assigned seats across the aisle. The woman seemed frazzled and tired. Like a woman who hadn't slept in a very long time. The Seventh smiled at the woman then turned her attention out the window to watch the ground crew load the bags. She had no desire to chit-chat.

The Seventh became vaguely aware that someone had taken the aisle seat, a fact that clearly caused even more angst for the young mother. The Seventh glanced up briefly to see the passenger while being careful not to meet his eyes.

The new arrival was a young man about her age. His eyes were kind, his jawline strong and his hair completely out of sorts. He carried a simple leather duffle bag that he quickly stored under the seat. It took only seconds, after storing his bag, for him to realize what was happening. He was separating this young mother from her three children on the other side of the aisle. It took even less time for him to correct the situation.

And so as far as the Seventh was concerned, fate had stepped in. Damian had been the perfect person to sit next to her. He immediately recognized that she did not wish to chat and so he had left her to her silence. He let her have the armrest between them and made no move to control either the light or the air.

When the flight attendant passed out drinks, he passed hers to her without comment. Their hands brushed, and their eyes met for one powerful instant. His eyes were the piercing color of cold steel, and it electrified her. She spent the remainder of the flight trying not to think about him.

As the plane made its way to South America, she created a thousand scenarios in her mind of who he was and where he was headed. None of them had been as satisfying as the truth. While her heart and mind raced, he sat tranquility reading a travel guide written entirely in Spanish. She noticed that he made a few notes in the margin of the book, and twice he circled something on a map. She didn't speak or read Spanish, so none of it made sense to her.

The plane arrived at Toncontin International Airport, and everyone disembarked. The Seventh was grateful that she had packed light. She followed Damian through customs without appearing to be following him. He seemed to be very comfortable with the process, and she had no idea what she was doing.

As it turned out, they ended up on the same shuttle bus. Damian's fluency in Spanish was quite helpful, and without realizing what was happening, she found herself sitting by him for the long journey from the airport. They were both there for the same thing—a service mission.

She and Damian worked at an orphanage. Each day everyone would be divided into teams and given various assignments. Some of them would travel out into the poorest parts of Tegucigalpa. The Seventh was often assigned to wash the children's hair, and she did so with great attention. She watched from a distance as Damian also did whatever was assigned to him.

He spoke the language fluently and seemed completely comfortable among the locals as if he were one of them. It made him even more appealing to her. He had no agenda, no pre-conceived ideas

or sense of importance. Each day he tackled whatever job he was assigned with joy and pride.

In the evenings, she would sketch out scenes from the day. Scenes
she would later use to inspire a sculpture worthy of the place and
the experience. The sound of the charcoal on the paper brought her
peace and a sense of nostalgia.

At the end of the third day, the Seventh and Damian sat beside
each other at dinner. He was gentle and unassuming in his inter-
actions with her and yet he had a quiet confidence about him that
made her feel safe and protected.

Their relationship had been equally simple and beautiful. He
made no demands of her. He was constantly traveling, and when she
could, she would go with him. He had no home to speak of. When
he was between trips, he would stay with friends or go to his father's
house. He didn't speak much of his father, but she didn't find that
unusual. He didn't really speak much of himself not in a personal
sense, anyway.

But he would regale her with stories of places he had been and
people he had met. Beautiful stories of beautiful people that had
touched his soul. Stories of children living in garbage heaps with
smiles that could make you forget.

Those ten days with Damian spent in some of the poorest parts
of Honduras, had changed her life. For ten days, her heart ached
for their poverty and craved their joy. How could people this poor
have such joy and faith? Those ten days seemed magical, even as she
thought about them now.

Years had passed, and she still found him intriguing. They had
been to several countries together inspiring her to fill sketch pads
with pictures from their journeys. Her sculptures had never been
more passionate, her heart had never been fuller. Damian had taught
her about the world. He was unassuming and straightforward, he

had a talent for making those around him feel important. It was, in her opinion, his best trait.

Chapter 31

Night had fallen, and the house was quiet. Meir, Adiel, and Emeka were sitting on the back deck overlooking the lake, the mountains were just barely visible in the background. A loon called out its forlorn cry in the distance, and the water lapped gently at the dock just off the edge of the property. They had laid out a simple meal of wine, fruit, and manna as they discussed both the day and the progress of the Twelfth.

Adiel had spent the day removing the tormenting demons that were so regular around the family. Each day she expelled any demons that arrived, except those that clung tightly to the family, those Adiel could not expel. Today, a tormenting demon named Rebellion had latched tight to the oldest boy. The demon snarled and spat at Adiel when she drew her sword. He stabbed his talons deep into the boy's ear yelling desperately as Adiel approached. When Adiel was close enough to strike, the demon clamored over the boy searching for a place to hide, the demon's feet blistered and burned as he scurried around the boy. Amused by the sight, Adiel took her time with the strike.

Emeka was regaling the angels by reenacting the scene in ex-aggerated slow motion when the arrival of other angels got their undivided attention. Emeka immediately registered the presence of Mordecai, who was gracious enough to yet again explain that it was the drop of humanity within him that Emeka was noticing. Meir wondered how many times he had had to explain it. She imagined it was in the thousands.

Mordecai and Adiel greeted each other with a familiarity that made it obvious they had worked together before, and Meir made a mental note to ask Adiel about it later.

"So you gave up being an archangel?" Adiel asked as she offered Aegeus the traditional greeting of the warrior.

"It was the right thing," he said with only a hint of regret.

Meir watched as Mordecai's eyes were drawn to the fresh fruit from the tree in heaven and the manna from Martha's bakery. She wondered how long it had been since he had had the comforts of home. His eyes met hers, and he smiled a slightly embarrassed smile that was designed to assure her that all was well. She had seen the same smile on the face of the Fifth.

"Have something to eat," she offered the group in welcome not wanting to single Mordecai out. The angels joined together over the small meal, laughing, and enjoying each other's company.

"How are you?" Meir asked moving closer to Aegeus.

"Better now that we are here," he answered.

"Who did you find for the Second and Third?" she asked, knowing how important prayer cover was to the mission, but Aegeus wasn't listening. The Twelfth had walked out on the deck. A gentle breeze blew, and the Twelfth's hair fluttered in front of her face causing the smell of cherry blossoms to caress the surrounding air.

Emotion swelled in Aegeus, a response he had not anticipated. He felt the symbol of the horn tingle slightly on the back of his shoulder, and he saw that hers too was glowing slightly. He knew she could not see it, but he wondered if she could feel it. Did she have any sense that it connected them?

"I can feel you," the Twelfth whispered into the night, as if in response to his question.

The angels froze, unmoving, uncertain, all but Mordecai. He walked over to her, intrigued. He circled around her, brushing his hand gently through her hair and drawing in her scent. His eyes never moving from her. The other angels watched captivated by the scene of Mordecai studying her.

"I'm glad you're here," she whispered. "Please. Stay." And with that simple request, she turned and went back to bed.

The angels stood silently for some time, no one willing to break the silence. Finally, unable to wait any longer, Aegeus turned to Mordecai.

"Is she your charge?" He asked fighting back emotion.

Mordecai remained silent staring after the Twelfth. Aegeus too stood staring at the doorway through which the Twelfth had vanished. He had not anticipated his reaction to seeing her again.

After a moment Aegeus asked again, "Mordecai?" he prompted, more gently than he felt.

"No," Mordecai answered, still staring after her. Relief flooded Aegeus.

"I have never encountered a Prophet," Mordecai added looking at the others, his face radiating a soft but powerful glow. Meir had never seen anything quite like it.

"Do you think she was reacting to you Aegeus, or do you think she could feel Mordecai?" Adiel asked.

"Most likely it's the combination of you both. I doubt she can differentiate. It's equally possible that having so many of us here may be what she is feeling." Meir suggested.

"Do you think she could see you?" Kfir asked Aegeus.

"I don't know," he answered, handing each of the angels a small serving of manna and fruit to distract himself. Mordecai took his meal and walked out to sit in the thick grass by the lake; he wanted a moment to collect his thoughts.

Aegeus too wanted to take a moment. He wanted to follow the Twelfth and assure himself that she was prepared for battle. He wanted to know if she could see him if she knew he was there. He wanted to speak to her and hear her tell him she was ok. But he fought against that.

In order to distract himself, he briefed Adiel, Emeka, and Meir on the situation in Platitude. Meir, feeling the emotions swirling around the others, offered comfort. Mordecai looked up from the lake, and their eyes met, he nodded slightly, unaccustomed to such gifts. She felt the despair he carried, and it weighed heavily on her. She smiled at him and then returned her attention to Aegeus.

When Aegeus had finished his report, and he had answered their questions regarding the critical role of the Second and Third he once again turned the conversation back to the Twelfth.

"How is she?" he asked. He needed her to be battle ready.

"She seems to think her purpose is complete. She thinks that that moment in the field was her moment, her great calling in life. And while she has tried to convince herself helping you was as noble a purpose as any, she struggles. She doesn't know what happened to you. Therefore she finds it anticlimactic and devoid of answers," Meir said.

Aegeus found the Twelfth's reasoning quite bizarre in a way that he appreciated.

"She is feeling alone. She is unsure of where to go from here," Meir felt that best summed up all that had been done since she arrived, all that they had accomplished and all that was still remaining.

Kfir shook his head at the ludicrous conclusions the King's children drew over his silence. Americans rarely sat still and listened to the King's voice. Their lifestyles were so full of chaos. They seemed to take pride in how busy they were but, as Kfir lamented, they were usually busy with things that did not matter, things that the King had not assigned them.

Kfir struggled with the idea that he would leave his post and take on a mission that the King had not given him. It was beyond his understanding, and yet the King's children did it regularly.

They had not trained themselves to silence all the noise and listen only to the King. Often, he would speak quietly again and again, yet they did not hear him. Their days were so full of other distractions. It was a sad plight.

But the Twelfth had learned years ago to hear the King. What she had not learned was to be patient for his answer. She did not even acknowledge that there was value in waiting. Perhaps she had given lip service to the idea or considered it at some point, but it had not taken hold in her heart. She did not stop to think about why he may not speak in her timeframe. She had not learned to value his timing. Respect it yes, value the waiting, no.

Adiel filled the others in on the Twelfth's fear that she was alone, that the King had forgotten her. Adiel found that to be the most frustrating part of all. She could not understand how the King's children would ever believe they were alone. He promised them they would never be alone. To doubt that was to doubt him. She wished their eyes would be opened to all that was around them, the real realm, reality. But their sight was so limited, and Adiel had to remind herself of this often. Six angels currently surrounded the Twelfth and her family, fighting for them, defending them, ministering to them, and yet they believed they were alone? Adiel shook her head at the lunacy of it.

"They cannot see," Meir reminded them all.

"You have seen the dream?" Aegeus asked Meir. Meir nodded in affirmation.

"The beast is coming for her," she replied. "The prayers of the Second and Third will be essential. Are they ready?" she asked.

Aegeus knew this, and yet hearing it made him sick inside.

"They are," he responded. "They are heavily guarded, and the woman with the wild red hair is ever present. Is the Twelfth ready?" he asked.

"She is not yet ready, but I am," Meir replied.

Chapter 32

The sight of the water pouring over the rocks and into the swimming hole was amazing and well worth the hike. The Twelfth had promised the children a quick swim when they reached the gorge, but now that they were here she felt certain that the water was far too cold.

Aegeus was pleased to finally be with the Twelfth, doing what he had chosen to do. The hike through the woods was, in his opinion, the perfect start to the mission, his true mission.

Emeka had had a rough journey to the gorge. Aegeus had been told by Lavi when they first arrived in Platitude that the boy was accident prone, but he had had no idea just how true that statement was. Emeka had spent the entire hike tending to the child preventing missteps and calamities along the way. Aegeus handed Emeka his wineskin with a look of gratitude.

Meir had walked the path alternating between the husband of the Twelfth and her oldest son. As she walked with each one, she would place her hand in theirs, bringing thoughts and ideas to them. Aegeus wasn't sure what they were about, but she had seemed both focused and intentional in what she was doing so he left her to her work without interruption or questions.

Mordecai had spent most of his time with the family dog. The thing was no better trained than when Aegeus had seen it last although it had aged a bit which caused a natural change in behavior that seemed to agree with it. Several times the dog had darted from the path chasing a random squirrel, moth, or the unfortunate blade of grass that bent to the will of the wind.

On one such occasion, the Twelfth had yelled at the dog to "stop," and the poor thing had frozen in place just as Lavi had taught it. While the family had finally realized that it was the word stop that was causing the behavior, they still had not discovered what command was needed to undo it, so the husband of the Twelfth had had to traipse into the woods and retrieve the dog.

The angels and humans alike had laughed as the man returned from the woods carrying the dog who held his position with exceptional rigidity. The man put the dog back on the trail where it stood frozen until Aegeus gave the command releasing it.

Halfway through the hike, they decided to stop for a short picnic lunch. Finding a small clearing with a few fallen trees, they plopped down on the decaying tree trunks to share a simple meal. Each member of the family retrieved their lunch from the backpacks they carried. The angels joined the family having a small snack of their own, reminding Aegeus of all the time the angels had spent with the Wednesday night group in Platitude and how unified it felt. He missed that.

When the angels had finished their refreshment, Aegeus started to stand up, he wanted to do a quick patrol of the path. Adiel placed her hand quickly on his shoulder using it to push herself up instead.

"I'll go," she offered, "you stay here with the family."

"I'll go with you," Meir offered, standing up and joining Adiel to indicate there was no need for discussion.

"What did you want to talk about," Adiel asked when they were out of earshot from the others. She smiled when Meir looked slightly surprised. "You don't normally offer to go on patrols," Adiel said with a grin.

"How do you know Mordecai?" Meir asked.

Adiel looked down briefly, not because she minded the question, but because the memory was a difficult one.

"I met him in the holy land many years ago," she began. "I was assigned to the apostle John, and he was the sentinel for Judas Iscariot."

Meir's mind raced at that news.

"Mordecai's charge is in the bloodline of Judas Iscariot?" she asked stunned.

"It would seem so." The two angels walked along for a few minutes with nothing but the sounds of the forest filling their ears. Meir could feel the sadness that flooded through Adiel as she waded through the memory. Mordecai had battled valiantly to protect Judas from the demons who fought to destroy him. But when his true test came, Judas had chosen wrong. Of course, the King had always known he would, but Mordecai had not. Mordecai had nearly died as he battled thousands of demons in the final seconds of Judas' decision. Judas had been given every opportunity to make the right choice, the King had provided him with one of the strongest sentinels. Mordecai had fought with the passion of a thousand angels, his heart torn open as his charge betrayed the Lamb.

Meir now understood the sadness that Mordecai carried. A Sentinel was attached to their charge in a way that most angels were never connected to the humans. Their bond was similar to that of a human mother and her child. For Mordecai to have watched his charge betray the Lamb....in an instant, Judas had gone from being someone Mordecai would give his life for, to being someone Mordecai would have to stand against. Mordecai had been forced to withdraw from Judas and had watched helplessly as the charge he had been so devoted to was overtaken by demons and killed himself.

Meir let the idea fade, while she could relate, she realized it was not the same. The full horror of it was not something she could even conceive of, nor did she care to. Such an experience was among the most difficult for the angels. Neither she nor Adiel spoke, there was no need to.

Adiel and Meir finished their patrol and rejoined the group just as the humans were finishing their lunch and preparing to continue their hike. Kfir and Mordecai took point, scanning the woods for any signs of demons. Adiel and Meir brought up the rear.

Aegeus walked beside the Twelfth. At times, he spoke to her unsure of if she could see or hear him. It surprised him how much he wanted her to be able to, but if she could, she gave no indication of it. Other than the first day when she had whispered into the air she had shown no other signs that she knew the angels were there.

They had been walking the final leg of the hike when suddenly without warning the Twelfth's Light had flared brightly. She stopped in her tracks standing still, her mind clearly racing. Aegeus stood beside her eager to know what the Spirit had told her. Eager to know that she recognized it as such.

Her family continued their hike unaware of what had happened, but the angels all stopped, waiting.

"Aegeus?" Adiel was the first to speak. Aegeus just shrugged. It was a full minute before her husband also noticed she had stopped. He had been helping the youngest child retie his shoe into a triple knot so it wouldn't keep coming untied. Emeka was quite relieved to see the triple knot.

"You ok?" her husband called back across the short distance.

She looked at him and smiled, wrestling with if she should say anything or not.

"What is it?" he asked, concern starting to creep over his face. He turned and began walking back toward her. She resumed walking putting a smile on her face to assure him everything was fine.

"It's nothing, I just had the weirdest thought that's all," She said dismissively. The angels looked at each other anxious and hoping to hear the thought. Meir moved closer to the Twelfth just in case.

"What was it?" her husband asked. Aegeus could have kissed the man.

"Well," she said as they reached each other on the trail "let's just say if the nuclear Zombie Apocalypse hits I think I know the cure," she said with a laugh.

"Oh really?" her husband said amused.

"Yeah" and with that, she continued her walk trying hard to look as if everything were as it should be.

"Aegeus?" Adiel asked again as the angels all stood baffled.

"I don't know," was all he could offer. But he hoped the Twelfth truly had heard the prophecy clearly and recognized it as such because something much worse than the nuclear zombie apocalypse was coming.

Chapter 33

The Twelfth knocked lightly on the door of the exam room after which she walked in without waiting for an answer. She wondered just briefly if anyone ever waited for an answer. She couldn't really recall a time when a patient had answered. Aegeus and Kfir walked in beside her. They had never been in a doctor's office before this was a little new.

A pale young woman without the Light sat uncomfortably on the exam table. Fear and Worthlessness clinging to her. Fear had her talons deep in the girl's chest. Worthlessness had his arms wrapped tightly around her throat. But perhaps the most disturbing was Bitterness. Bitterness, a powerful destroying demon stood beside her gripping her arm tightly.

An older man was standing next to her. He too was covered in demons. Greed and Hate controlled him. Instinctively Kfir reached for his sword, the demons bristled unsure of what to do about the arrival of two warriors. They looked at the Twelfth and then back at the warriors slightly anxious.

"Oh, we have a hero," Hate taunted pushing his long talon deep into the man's head.

"I feel so honored," Greed added finding her courage, "the King sent the mighty Aegeus after us?"

Aegeus and Kfir stood their ground without responding to the petty taunts. The signal had not come.

The Twelfth closed the exam room door sealing them together in the small room. She introduced herself and sat down on the stool near the in-room computer.

"What can I do for you today?" she asked the woman who was clearly ill.

"She's sick," the man answered gruffly. The Twelfth looked at him only briefly but did not respond to him. Instead, she looked at the woman expectantly, as if he had not spoken.

"I'm sick," the woman mimicked meekly, her eyes darting to the man. Fear pushed her talon more deeply into the girl's chest, then twisted it so that it reached toward her heart. Kfir shifted, righteous anger flooding over him, but he held his position because the signal had not yet come.

The Twelfth had seen many victims of domestic violence over the years, the scenario was not new to her, but something with this couple seemed a little off, different somehow. She knew she needed to ask the man to leave, but she also knew that doing it in the right way was important.

"Tell me what's bothering you?" She asked as she checked the woman's temperature and blood pressure. Both of which were much too low.

"She's been throwing up," the man answered.

"Do you smell that?" Kfir asked, wrinkling his nose.

"Smells like death," Aegeus replied, stepping closer to the young woman. The demons hissed at him in response.

The Twelfth turned to the man, speaking to him for the first time.

"It was wise of you to bring her in," she said gratefully "Thank you," she was sincere in her delivery. "I am going to need to examine her further, please step out to the waiting room. I will come and get you as soon as I am done." She spoke kindly but with authority.

"She wants me to stay," he said not moving.

"I understand. But it is against our policy to allow you to stay," she again said without wavering.

"Then we will go somewhere else," he said, moving toward the woman, and grabbing her by the arm as if to leave. The woman with the wild red hair entered the room. The demons screamed with rage at her arrival. She stepped close to the Twelfth, their arms barely touching. She raised one hand to silence the demons and laid her other hand on the Twelfth filling her with the Light until it overflowed from her pouring into the room.

"You were right to bring her here," the Twelfth said "leaving would not be wise. Is there a problem?" She knew she was a bit too bold, but if she were right, the young woman was very ill, perhaps life-threateningly so. Somehow, she knew this approach was the right one.

The man walked menacingly toward her stopping a bit too close. Aegeus and Kfir also walked closer, flanking each side of her, swords drawn. The man stood silently for what seemed like a very long time, then begrudgingly and with an unnecessary warning glance to the woman, he stalked out of the room. The Twelfth turned back to the young woman.

"Can you lift your shirt above your belly and lean back on the table please?" she asked.

The girl was hesitant, but she lifted her shirt slightly and laid back on the exam table. Stepping to her side, the Twelfth pushed the woman's shirt up a little more, so she could see her abdomen.

"How long has this been here," she asked working to control her voice and sound professional. The woman with the wild red hair stayed beside her keeping her hand on the Twelfth's back. The young woman quickly grabbed her shirt and pulled it down trying to cover the obviously infected wound.

"Please," the Twelfth said struggling to control her emotions and make the girl feel safe. "It's infected. I need to examine you." Her voice was strong and sure but gentle. She waited as the young woman struggled to decide what to do. Fear raged at the girl screaming at her to leave. The woman with the wild red hair held up her hand again silencing the demon.

The woman with the wild red hair stepped closer to the girl. She leaned down and whispered into the girl's ear. The demons screamed out as they began to burn and sizzle from being so close to the woman.

The girl swallowed hard, fighting against the fear. The urge to leave was strong, but deep in her tattered heart, the young woman knew that she was sick. She knew that going would cost her her life. Slowly she laid back down and lifted her shirt, indicating that the Twelfth could examine her.

The wound was inflamed and full of pus and infection. It appeared to the Twelfth to be a series of cuts, almost as if someone had carved letters into the girl's stomach. The swelling made it impossible to tell for sure. After a quick examination, it was clear the young woman needed to be hospitalized. It was highly likely she was septic. She pulled the girl's shirt down and removed her gloves. As she washed her hands, she tried to sound casual.

"How did this happen?" she asked without judgment, trying not to let her anguish bleed through into her voice.

The girl didn't look at her. She didn't answer.

"You need to be hospitalized," The Twelfth said. The young woman's face gave away her fear over that statement. "You have a very serious infection from that wound. I believe it has spread to your blood. Without treatment, it will most likely kill you. I am going to call an ambulance to come get you."

"I can't afford that," the girl said.

"It's ok," the Twelfth reassured her.

The woman with the wild red hair winked at Aegeus and Kfir and left the room, although they knew she was never really gone.

A series of chimes suddenly filled the small exam room although the humans didn't seem to notice.

"What is that?" Aegeus asked, glancing about the room for the source.

"Oh, sorry!" Kfir exclaimed, pulling out a small device.

"What is that?" Aegeus repeated perplexed.

"This?" Kfir asked, equally perplexed.

"Yes."

"It's my cell phone," Kfir answered as if the question itself confused him.

"Your cell phone?"

"Yes."

"When did you get a cell phone?" Aegeus was dumbfounded.

"Sanyi gave it to me."

"What do you need a cell phone for? Who could you possibly be calling?" Aegeus asked befuddled.

Kfir shook his head at Aegeus's apparent lack of culture. "I'm not calling anyone. I got a tweet," he said as if it should be completely obvious.

"A tweet?" Aegeus was even more confused. A phone he understood. But tweeting?

"Yes, you know Twitter," Kfir again said, as if it were the most normal thing in the world for an angel to be on Twitter.

"What is Twitter?" Aegeus asked, confusion evident in his question.

"You know... Twitter, social media?"

"Social what?"

"You don't have a blog?" Kfir asked incredulously.

"A what?"

Kfir shook his head in disbelief. "Aegeus, you really need more cultural experiences."

Aegeus stood baffled for a moment before he realized that there was movement in the room. A nurse had come in, and the Twelfth had left. A ministering angel was attending to the young woman.

"What happened?" he asked Kfir who was preoccupied with his phone.

"Well, it seems like their President is tweeting again," Kfir said shaking his head.

"Not with your phone! With the Twelfth?"

"Oh...." Kfir made a face, acknowledging that he had no idea and slid his phone into his uniform. "I'll find her." He flew quickly from the room, searching the small office for the Twelfth. She had just hung up the phone when he came in. She quickly dialed another number and waited for it to be answered.

"Hello?" the voice on the other end was familiar to Kfir.

"I need the number for the National Human Trafficking Resource Center, and I knew you would know it," the Twelfth said into the phone.

"1-888-373-7888," the voice said. "Everything ok?"

"Yeah. Why?"

"Because you could have Googled that."

"Yeah, but then I wouldn't have gotten to talk to you. Plus, our internet is down," she added with a little chuckle. "Thanks," the Twelfth said preparing to hang up.

"Hey?"

"Yeah?"

"Call me when you get off work. I have something I need to talk to you about."

"Okay," the Twelfth answered.

"Hey?" the Eleventh called out, concerned the Twelfth had already hung up.

"Yea?"

"You already knew that didn't you?" she asked.

"Knew what?" the Twelfth asked confused.

"You knew I needed to talk, that's why you called isn't it?" the Eleventh asked incredulously.

"I called because I needed the number," the Twelfth reassured her hanging up. But a slight smile crossed her face. She had known. She didn't know how she knew, but somehow, she had known the Eleventh needed her.

The Twelfth quickly entered notes in the newly created electronic chart of the patient and called the hospital where she would be transferring her. Before she went back to the exam room, she sent a quick text to the Wednesday night group telling them she had a patient that needed prayer. The Third was the first to reply.

Chapter 34—The Eleventh

She didn't look fourteen. She didn't look eighteen either, but she didn't look fourteen. The Eleventh sat across the industrial table from the angry eyes and hoped that her own eyes didn't betray what was in her heart. Even with several years of this under her belt the Eleventh still hadn't gotten used to the intake meetings.

The girls were still angry and defensive at this stage. It would be months if not years before they were willing to trust anyone. Most of them wouldn't make it out of "the life" on their first attempt. If the Eleventh hadn't been broken too, she would never have understood how they could go back to a life they hated so much. But the Eleventh had once been broken, broken in such a way that she didn't think she could ever be whole again, and so she understood.

She understood that sometimes the devil you knew, was better than the one you didn't. She understood that when all that was left of you was scraps, you didn't think you deserved anything more than to be swept up and thrown away. She understood that when you had been told you were worthless, you eventually began to believe it.

So, the Eleventh understood the angry eyes staring at her across the table. She understood that this young girl, not even old enough to drive, had made the fatal mistake of trusting a man who had promised to love her and protect her. And she understood that that misplaced trust had cost the girl her childhood. Trust was a mistake the girl did not intend to ever make again.

This man who had vowed to love and cherish her had instead handcuffed her to a bed, then raped and beat her. He subjected her to gang rape repeatedly for weeks until finally, he had crushed her. This part of the story never got any easier to hear. Each time the girls told their stories the Eleventh would relive her own rape. At first, it had overwhelmed her, suffocated her. But time had taught her to harness it. Gradually she had been able to use those memories, to connect with the young women she encountered. It drove her to do all she could to free them from the clutches of evil.

This young girl who should have been at home playing with dolls was instead fighting for her life, the plaything of grown men. Men who convinced themselves she liked this life, that she had chosen it. Men who believed the lies she told them. Men who did not care to see that she was only fourteen.

The Eleventh also understood that it would be a very long time before the girl would set aside her anger and share her story. That would not happen at this intake meeting. But the Eleventh didn't need her to, not yet.

Most likely her story was like the stories of so many others the Eleventh had heard hundreds of times. According to Child Protective Services, the girl was an orphan whose parents had been killed in a car accident that she had been fortunate enough to survive.

She had moved in with her an aunt and uncle. Within the year her aunt died of breast cancer, and her uncle began abusing her. She had only been eight. By the time she reached eleven, she had met someone through Instagram. Someone who offered her promises of a home, a family and what she desired most, love.

Like most tweens, she was taken in by promises of belonging and being loved without the fear that comes from experience. She fled the home, where she was abused by her uncle, into the arms of a much older man who continued to brutalize her.

From there, her story resembled so many countless others. A young girl who was taught from an early age that love was expressed through her suffering. A girl who simply lived in the small moments between violent acts committed by a host of strangers.

Despite the familiarity of the story, the bitterness and sorrow of it were no less significant. It didn't matter how many times the Eleventh heard it, it broke her heart every time. But like the very girls she served, she had learned not to let that show. She wouldn't be able to do her job if she did.

She had learned to conceal quite a lot. Since leaving Platitude, she had never told anyone she could see demons. She knew to keep that to herself. Since the barley field, she had never again seen so many demons at once, but they were always there relishing in the destruction and damage they inflicted.

The Eleventh would go to the grocery store, the bank, the park, the library, the church, it didn't matter where she was. If there were humans, there were always demons. She thought back to that day so many years ago when she had walked into the abortion clinic and seen them for the first time. She thought of the woman with the wild red hair that she had met there. The woman had told her that the demons were everywhere the humans were, but the Eleventh hadn't fully understood that then, now she did.

The demons were indeed everywhere. When she worked with the women and girls in the shelter, she could see their demons. She saw how hard the demons fought to maintain control. The Eleventh had learned not to react to the demons; she didn't want to draw their attention. When she did things escalated. It was a lesson she had learned at a high price during her very first intake meeting.

Chapter 35

Angry, violent demons clung to the girl. They clutched her body
desperately, covering her mind in darkness. Some of them dug
their talons deep into the girl's head while others had their hands securely around her heart. One had bitten into her neck. The sight of it
was terrifying. But perhaps the most frightening of all was the immense demon who stood behind her, his wings partially wrapped
around her his sword drawn close to her neck.

The Eleventh had never seen a demon like him before, and as a
result, a small gasp escaped her lips as she entered the room. The girl
had completely misunderstood, but the demon had not. For a fleeting moment, the room was perfectly still, frozen in that small gasp.
And then everything had erupted in a flurry of demonic activity.

Demons swarmed towards the Eleventh teeth barred, daggers
drawn. She panicked. Fear flooded her, and she threw her arms up to
protect herself running from the room. She could hear the demons
laughing behind the door celebrating their victory. She could hear
the girl crying. The Eleventh stood outside the room shaken, crying,
and discredited. She called in another counselor to conduct the interview.

The Eleventh had been so rattled by that encounter that she had
called the Twelfth in tears, convinced this was a job she could not do,
a task too difficult for her. Her heart ached for these girls. She longed
to help them, to bring light into their darkness. But her own self-

doubt was so great, her own pain so deep that she feared she would never be able to do it. The Twelfth had talked her off the cliff that day, a favor she had repaid a hundred times over.

She had learned the hard way to battle the demons without revealing that she could see them. And despite the challenges, in many ways, it made life easier. She no longer took slights, insults, or attacks personally. She now understood who the real enemy was. When she looked upon these women and girls, she often measured how they were doing according to how many demons they had.

In time, she began to recognize that not all the demons were the same. Some were smaller clamoring up a person's body like a reptile. They would latch on to the person with their talons. Others would bite and claw at the person. These seemed focused on causing emotional and psychological damage.

Others were larger, slightly bigger than a human with a similar form. They seemed intent on causing physical suffering. The Eleventh watched it all in horror while not allowing her body to give any signs of what she saw.

The largest of all was also the most frightening to the Eleventh. They were powerful beings the evil from them palpable. Sulfur would pour from them quickly engulfing the room in smoke that most did not seem to notice. The Eleventh was not entirely sure what they did other than fight. They would just appear in the room weapons drawn and fight against things the Eleventh could not see.

She assumed it was angels although she couldn't be sure. What she did know was that the demons railed against something other than her, something significantly more powerful. The demons often hurled insults at whatever it was they fought against crying out their claim to the girls. Sometimes they were destroyed before her very eyes by forces she could not see, and occasionally they would dart into the girl finding shelter from the forces that hunted them.

Some girls seemed to have a power inside them that caused the demons to scream in pain. It would singe and burn them. On rare occasions that power would blast the demons from the room leaving the girl free from their influence. In those moments truth could flow between the girl and the Eleventh.

Learning not to react to any of it had been hard, exhausting really. She tried to focus on the girls and not the demons. She focused on praying for the girls praying that God would banish the demons. And she found that the more fervent her prayers were, the more effective it was at banishing them. She learned that her prayers seemed to power the forces that fought against the demons.

Sometimes to the Eleventh's great horror, the demons would touch her. They would caress her face or stroke her hair. From time to time they would jump on her back or grab her by her throat and occasionally they would clamor up her back and sink their talons deep into her. She wanted to scream and rip them from her body. But that, of course, was something that would surely land her in a padded room. Instead, she would close her eyes and try to silence them. She had learned that often prayer would send them scampering. Often, but not always. She wasn't sure why.

Sometimes she would get home at the end of the day and realize that three of them clung to her. She hadn't seen them attack her, she hadn't fought it, and she would wonder how long they had been there. What had she said and done that day that was at their bequest?

But perhaps the absolute worst of it was that sometimes in dark moments she would simply accept them. Sometimes, she embraced things they whispered into her ear. Often, they said things she wanted to hear, things that made her feel justified in her position or attitude. From there they could lead her far away to areas they knew were soft targets and she let them. She quit fighting and just surrendered to the worthlessness, offense, anger, self-justification or what-

ever other thing they offered her. Sometimes she rolled around in
their filth because their lies were easier to believe than the truth.

Chapter 36

Lightning lit up the small room, and a few seconds later there was a long slow rumble of thunder bringing her back to the present and the angry eyes that say across from her. A couple of the demons that were attached to the young girl hissed in response. Four of them clung to her filling her with lies, doubt, and distrust. They whispered to her constantly during the interview clinging to her body; their talons deep within the unsuspecting girl.

The Eleventh wondered if the girl had been able to see the demons that clung to her and if she knew they were pouring lies into her would it make any difference? If she were aware that her distrust was a result of a demon whose forked tongue was in her ear would it matter? It would have to make a difference, wouldn't it? The Eleventh had to believe it would because it had made such a huge difference in her own life.

The girl sat, arms tightly crossed a scowl on her bruised and beaten face, her eyes hard and cold staring at the Eleventh. The young girl was clean and well-manicured. Her nails were painted a beautiful shade of red. Her skimpy dress and high heels betrayed her profession if you could call it that.

The word "profession" implied choice, and the Eleventh knew that this young girl had no choice at least not the way most of us understood choices. Her story, like so many of the other girls the Eleventh had worked with over the last few years, offered only two choices; enter "the life" or be killed. The Eleventh didn't consider either to be much of a choice.

At fourteen, she was not the youngest girl the Eleventh had worked with, that distinction belonged to a not quite eleven-year-old that had been accepted 6 months ago.

This girl's physical wounds were not the worst the Eleventh had seen either. That distinction was reserved for the twenty-three-year-old that decided she could finally get out. Her pimp had not been so willing to part with her; he made sure that she would spend the remainder of her life in a wheelchair. Where was the choice in that?

The Eleventh had seen many girls over the years all in varying stages of hopelessness. They were angry and distrustful, and they had every right to be; the system had failed them. When the Eleventh had begun this crusade, she would sit with each girl and think of Mary Magdalene. It helped her look past the harsh, bitter exterior to the vulnerable young women who longed for nothing more than to be loved.

Women and girls who didn't really know what love looked like, their understanding skewed and distorted from years of abuse. Girls who society had written off, who were locked away in jail when they were, in fact, the victims. For the millionth time, the Eleventh said a silent prayer of thanks for organizations like GEMS and Thorn that had paved the way for smaller groups like her own.

Outside the thunder once again rumbled with a gentle groan reminding her of the low growl of a lion. The Eleventh was grateful for the distraction. Her young interviewee shifted uncomfortably in her chair; it was the discomfort of sitting too long and not the interview. The Eleventh knew better than that. These girls had learned how to survive, and they had learned the hard way. This young girl was no exception. She would not be intimidated by sitting in this room with the Eleventh.

And yet she wasn't sure what it was about this one that sat differently with her. She asked the girl a few more questions and then left the sterile room. She would, of course, admit her to the program. If they weren't a danger to others, and they were willing to join her, she took them.

On the drive home, she let her mind play a montage of all the girls and women that she had encountered since joining Hope, an organization dedicated to helping victims of commercially sexually exploited women, girls, and youth. Her department specialized in women and girls there was a smaller division focused on males.

Her mind raced through all the stories she had heard all the women and girls she had talked to, and she lingered over the ones that had gone back to "the life" when life on the outside was too hard, too strange, and overwhelming. They didn't know "the rules" in this new life.

They had many hurdles to overcome. What the Eleventh considered "normal" life was as foreign to these girls as their life was to her. There was so much working against them. Most did not have any form of identity; they had no formal education. Without those things, they couldn't go to school or get jobs or even prove who they were.

They came into the program with only the clothes on their backs and often those needed to be discarded. The girls needed clothes, they needed formal education, job skills, communication skills, life skills. Many had criminal histories or outstanding charges. Addiction was common. The journey was long and arduous. It took time and patience, and they faced harsh judgment. There was no shortage of people eager to cast the first stone.

It was exasperating on a good day. In addition, most of the girls had significant emotional and physical scars. The Eleventh could never have anticipated how many of them had been branded or had their pimp's names tattooed or carved into them. She made removing those marks a top priority. It was a treacherous journey, and many of the girls that came into the program wandered out—only to wander back later. Perhaps the story that stayed with her the most was the story of a young sixteen-year-old.

Chapter 37

She was a runaway like so many of the others. She ran away at fourteen with thirty dollars, a sack lunch, and a bus ticket. At fourteen, she seemed to think that would be all she needed. But the reality of the streets was harsh; night came, and she had nowhere to go. Thinking she was being smart while trying to swallow her terror, she went to the subway station and found a remote platform where she could sleep.

But instead, she was attacked. To her great joy, a man in his midthirties rescued her from the attackers. She did not realize he had orchestrated the entire thing for just that purpose. All she knew was that she was being beaten, and he had stepped in and saved her. He doctored her wounds took her in and gave her a safe place to live.

For the first time in her life, she felt loved. Love at least as she understood it. She had a warm place to sleep, food on the table and new clothes. It was several months before the violence began, then several more months before he began selling her.

Several times she had tried to find her way out, tried to find help. But he didn't allow her to be alone, she had no phone, no access to the internet although that was where she bought and sold.

Over time she had gotten pregnant by whom she had no idea. All she knew was that she was pregnant, and she desperately wanted her baby. She was terrified her "daddy" would force her to get rid of it, like he had with so many of the other girls, after all having a baby could cut into their profits. She had hoped for the first time in her short life that this child would complete her new family, change things.

But she had been mistaken on so many fronts. She had thought wrongly that he would no longer sell her. But that had not been true. He didn't care that she was pregnant. He had beaten her so severely that she feared she would lose the baby. She didn't, looking back, she wished she had, it would have been better than the fate that awaited her child. Much to her horror, there were plenty of men who were happy to pay for a pregnant woman.

She comforted herself with the idea that she would be a mother. That when the child was born things would be different. He would be different. Instead the unthinkable happened. She gave birth to a beautiful baby girl.

She had cuddled the beautiful baby in her arms drinking in her smell, bathing in joy. She had believed things were going to be different. But when he entered the room, she knew things would not be ok. She could see it in his eyes. He wrenched the baby from her arms as she struggled to keep her. She screamed and fought with a ferocity that she had never known in an attempt to save her child. But he head-butted her, knocking her out, taking her daughter and selling her on the black market. Not to a loving family, but to someone named Wanda. Someone who would raise her child in the life, selling her precious baby condemning her daughter to the same life of misery and suffering.

When he had finished the transaction of selling the child, he had come back for her. She had tried to fight, and she had paid the price. The Eleventh got the call in the middle of the night. When the Eleventh got to the hospital and saw the girl's small broken body, she had not expected the young woman to make it. Her pimp had carved his name on her chest. Her nose and jaw were broken. She had internal damage, and her kidneys had suffered severe harm from blunt force trauma. Her head had been partially shaven to accommodate the stitches in her head, others zigzagged across her face.

But the girl was strong, and she survived only to die. She had joined the Eleventh at Hope house and had been doing well. She attended classes toward her GED and was getting regular intense counseling. Something essential for all the girls. But the idea of her daughter being bought and sold living a life, the life, with no mother, no hope it proved to be too much for her.

It came as no shock when she set out one-day to find her pimp, find out who Wanda was and hopefully rescue her daughter. The Eleventh had not seen her again until she stood over the girl's ravaged body in the morgue. The mortician had commented that perhaps it was better this way. After all, who would ever want a girl like her? She was sixteen no one would ever adopt her. She was damaged and traumatized with little hope for a normal future. It wasn't like she would one-day discover the cure for cancer he commented. It was, in his mind, probably for the best.

The Eleventh had fought the urge to hit him. Why could no one understand? Why could people not see these girls for what they were? Victims. She was a sixteen-year-old girl in any other situation she would be treated with compassion. If she had been raped by an uncle or had sex with a teacher at her school, the men would be viewed as aggressors she would be recognized as the victim incapable of consent. Weren't there men rotting in prison for having sex with a minor? And yet these men walked free.

But because that same young girl had been labeled at fourteen years old as a prostitute, she was viewed as less valuable, unworthy. Society told itself that she had chosen this, that she wanted it and that she was capable of making such choices. She was a criminal to be locked in jail. A child that had been abused, raped, and mistreated-viewed as a criminal to be locked away with the murderers.

Society believed the lies she was forced to tell her johns. They ignored the fact that she was still a child that this was something she was forced to do that she was regularly beaten. They ignored that she lived in fear. All they saw was a harlot. Perhaps because that was the easiest thing to see. But the Eleventh knew that the easier thing was rarely the right thing because she had walked that path. She had been called a harlot, she too had once been judged and condemned.

Chapter 38

The Eleventh pulled into her garage and parked the car. She was tired. Remembering that situation had brought up emotions she thought she had buried. Something about today's interviewee reminded her of the other young girl. The memories had also reminded her of a promise she had made to the girl as she stood over her broken body. She had promised both the desperate young mother and herself that she would find Wanda and free the girl's daughter.

She wondered what had made her ever make such a promise. She supposed it was that she had no children of her own, well, none other than the one she had given up for adoption all those years ago. These girls had become her children, and she had committed to fighting for them as long as she had breath in her lungs. And so, she had made a promise that she was finding very hard to keep.

The Eleventh had dug deep to discover who Wanda was. But no one knew of any pimps named Wanda. She could find no wife-in-laws with that name. She had hunted down every girl on the streets with the name Wanda each lead was a dead end. Eventually one cold winter evening she was called to the hospital to the bedside of a young Ukrainian girl. The girl had been promised a job in America as a nanny. The pay was decent, more than she would expect in her home country and she was told she would receive free room and board.

She was quickly relocated to the States, but instead of the picturesque home in the suburbs that she had been promised, she was locked in a shipping container made into a heroin addict, beaten, and abused. She had been sold thousands of times since arriving in America. She was continuously moved from place to place under cover of night never quite sure where she was or even what day it was.

The young girl had fought hard against the drugs, against the abuse. But eventually, she allowed the drugs to swallow her. She welcomed the reprieve from the nightmare her life had become, and she welcomed the day someone would eventually kill her. In her mind, it was the only way she saw this ending.

But she had not died that day. She entered the program, and despite the challenges that she faced she stayed with it until the Eleventh could arrange to get her home. In the months they had spent together, the girl confided that she had originally responded to a want ad posted by a woman named Wanda.

When the Eleventh pressed for more information, the girl told her that Wanda was a recruiter. She worked at an American company in Tanzania recruiting nannies for wealthy Americans. They worked with only the best families. Of course, she had never actually met the woman, and they had only communicated via email. When she went in for the appointment, Wanda had been out of the office helping another applicant. Instead, she had met with a man in his mid-thirties. He was kind and attentive, dressed in an expensive suit.

The Eleventh experienced the renewed hope that perhaps she would find Wanda after all. But she had little else to go on for her search and time marched on. Women and girls kept pouring through her doors, and the day-to-day demands had snuffed out thoughts of Wanda. Sitting with her interviewee today had for some reason awakened those memories.

The drive home flooded her mind and strained her emotions. The encounter with the girl brought with it a myriad of memories.

The Eleventh knew that every ten minutes someone was forced into the commercial sex trade, many of them children who would never find their way out.

It was an uphill battle, and for some reason on the drive home, she realized just how hopeless it was. She could not save them all she could not stop human trafficking, and she would never cut the proverbial head off the snake. But she had hoped that she could at least find and stop Wanda.

There had been a time when she had been hopeful that she would be part of the solution. She wanted to make a dent to see these women and girls given true options in life. That had been enough in the beginning. But now, suddenly, she felt weary from the weight of it. With each mile toward the house, her heart felt heavier and heavier.

When she arrived home, she dropped her bag on the floor as she entered the house and placed her keys in the small dish by the door the clanking sound announcing her arrival. The smell of bacon and fresh coffee caught her attention, bringing a smile to her face despite her exhaustion. Her husband must be up. She caught a glimpse of herself in the mirror as she walked into the kitchen and she didn't recognize herself. She looked hard into the mirror and knew she was looking at a woman who had been beaten down.

There was a time when she had been full of life and fire. She had pushed, pulled, and clawed her way up with amazing results to show for it, always aware of those around her, always grateful for those whose shoulders she stood on as she clamored her way up. She had picked herself up from a mud puddle and found a way to bloom. But now that was all gone. She was tired of fighting. She was tired of pushing forward. That fire had fizzled to nothing more than a warm glow, a slight ember.

When she thought of all she had been and then looked in the mirror and saw what she now was, she felt disappointed in herself.

Sort of. Part of her was too tired to even be disappointed. Part of her yearned to climb into bed and stay there for a month. Those who were young still trying to make their way and prove themselves, let them be the ones to fight.

Once upon a time she had been optimistic, excited about the possibilities full of ideas. Now she just wanted to be left alone. Optimism and excitement had been beaten out of her. Thoughts of uncovering Wanda all but forgotten. She took a deep breath trying to push the ideas out of her head.

Titus stood at a great distance and watched with pleasure as the Eleventh looked at herself with a critical eye. Criticism, he himself, had arranged. It had not been easy given she could see the demons. He had to be very clever to cover her. He had selected two of his most subtle demons, Discouragement, and Belittlement. They had hidden under the Eleventh's car and scurried up her pant leg as she came out of her meeting with that horrible child, the one with hope. But the child had been well covered, and her spirit was nearly broken, so Titus felt confident that he need not bother with her, his focus instead was on the Eleventh.

Discouragement and Belittlement had managed to attack the Eleventh without giving themselves away. They could do considerable damage in a short amount of time; they should be enough to keep her from digging into Wanda. He smiled, he really was enjoying this mission. It required so much more creativity than normal missions; these eleven humans were challenging. He had to think "outside the box" as the rats liked to say. They tested his skill and cunning, but he enjoyed the challenge.

Chapter 39

The grass, if you could still call it that, was crispy under her feet as she walked a few paces behind her daughter. They were winding their way along a secluded path with no particular destination in mind. At least not one she was aware of. The path had started lush and beautiful many people had walked with them, but slowly without any fuss, the path had grown narrower, and there were fewer people until only her and her daughter remained.

Her daughter stopped suddenly and turned back toward her.

"Mom?" she began and then waited for the Twelfth to reply.

"Yes?" the Twelfth managed to get out as the path inclined steeply.

"Is the zombie apocalypse real," her daughter asked.

"No," the Twelfth responded, trying to navigate the rocky path.

"Will we see the end times?" her daughter persisted.

The Twelfth paused before answering, partially to catch her breath, and partially because it was a difficult question. Her daughter waited patiently, scratching at a random spot on her arm.

"Well, that depends," the Twelfth wanted to present what she knew without bias, being fair to represent what was known to be true compared to things that were a matter of interpretation.

"We won't ever see the destruction of the earth if that's what you mean," she offered.

"Why not?" her daughter asked, relieved to hear that fact.

"Well, that happens after Armageddon, which isn't until after the thousand-year reign of Christ, so that will be long after we are gone."

"So, what about the tribulation," her daughter asked. The path had gotten so steep and rocky that they were now climbing the rocks more than walking. It required significantly more effort and focus. The daughter waited patiently for her mother to maneuver the rock. When the Twelfth reached the top, her daughter offered her the canteen they were sharing. It was a good time for a short break.

With gratitude, the Twelfth took the canteen and suggested they sit down on the rock.

"The tribulation is seven very bad years on the earth," she offered after she had had a sip of water.

"Does that happen before or after Armageddon?" her daughter asked. The Twelfth wondered where this sudden interest in the end times was coming from, perhaps they had studied it in Sunday school?

"Before. The idea is that we will have seven years of tribulation on the earth. Then Jesus will return to rule the earth for a thousand years. During that time, the devil will be held in a cage. When the thousand years are over the devil will be released from the cage, and we will have the battle of Armageddon after which the entire earth will be destroyed by fire." She hoped she had gotten everything right it; wasn't something she had spent a lot of time studying.

"So where does the rapture come in," her daughter pressed on continuing to scratch at her arm. The Twelfth made a mental note to check her daughter's arm before they resumed their walk. If she had gotten into poison ivy, it could be troublesome.

"Well, that is where it gets sticky," she offered. "We don't know for sure. Some people believe we will be raptured before the seven years start. They think the rapture of the Christians will be the catalyst for the tribulation. Other people believe it won't happen until halfway through the tribulation when the Antichrist turns against Israel. And another group believes it won't be until the entire tribulation is over and Jesus returns to rule the earth," she again found herself hoping she had gotten it right. She wondered why she hadn't spent more time studying it.

"Why don't we know for sure," her daughter wanted to know.

"Well, the Bible isn't clear on that part. So different people read and interpret it differently. I guess when it happens, we will see who was right." She added with a smile.

"Which one do you believe?" her daughter asked, still scratching at the spot. But the question was lost on the Twelfth. Instead, she watched in horror as her child's hand scratched across her arm, taking the flesh off in the process.

Her daughter's eyes betrayed her fear and confusion, and so the Twelfth tried to conceal her own. She resolved to bring calm to her daughter by focusing on the medical issue and not on her motherly instincts.

"Let me see it," she said in a calm voice as she stepped toward her daughter and examined the arm. She found a strip of flesh missing where the girl had scratched. The muscle was laid bare completely exposed. "Does it hurt," she asked with her best detached, clinical voice. But the girl had already moved on to another itchy spot on her neck and as she scratched, the skin from her neck peeled away falling to the ground in a solid sheet. Four distinct lines of bare muscle showed where she had scratched.

"Stop itching!" the Twelfth ordered in more of a panic than she intended. But her daughter didn't seem concerned. In fact, she seemed mesmerized that she could peel off her skin. Reaching up to her face, she ran her fingernails across her cheek pulling the flesh away as she did.

"STOP!" the Twelfth screamed at her daughter. But the girl continued to scratch at herself each time pulling the flesh from her body. Sores began to form on her skin, they festered and blistered bubbling over the surface of what of the girl's skin until eventually, they turned black and crusty. Smiling the girl peeled off each crusty sore, her skin going with it. Soon the girl had skin remaining only on her fingers. She had peeled all the remaining skin from her body.

Horrified, the Twelfth tried to make sense of it, to formulate a plan, but before she could do anything her daughter suddenly doubled over in agonizing pain. Blood began to pour from her wounds, and she cried out to her mother for help her voice frightened and panicked. The girl grasped her throat, her eyes bulging with fear. The Twelfth rushed to her only to watch as the girl choked and gagged, eventually spitting out her tongue.

The Twelfth fought to control her fear. Stooping over her daughter, she searched her mind for what could be happening while trying to control the bleeding that now threatened her daughter's life. She screamed out for help doubtful there was anyone to hear, desperate for someone to be there.

As her daughter lost consciousness, the Twelfth screamed into the void. A man appeared in the distance, someone familiar although the Twelfth couldn't quite make him out. She called out to him in desperation begging him to move faster. Slowly he got close enough for her to see it was the Eighth.

"This is the plague with which the Lord will strike all the nations that fought against Jerusalem: Their flesh will rot while they are still standing on their feet, their eyes will rot in their sockets, and their tongues will rot in their mouths." He said as he approached. "This is the plague of Zechariah."

"Help me," she screamed.

Emeka, startled by the scream, drew his sword. But there were no demons around. Adiel too heard the cry and rushed to the bedside of the Twelfth.

"She must have had the dream again," Adiel offered Emeka. "I usually try to wake her up before she cries out," she offered as an unnecessary apology. The husband of the Twelfth also walked into the room coffee in hand. He quickly put the coffee on the night side table and sat down beside her taking her into his arms.

"You ok?" he asked.

"I had a horrible dream," she answered, trying to shake the fear away and resisting the desperate need to go check on her daughter.

"The regular?" He asked, feeling confident that it was. After all, she hadn't dreamt of anything else in two years.

"No."

Her husband stopped, surprise evident on his face. Adiel and Emeka shared a quick look before Adiel called for the other angels. With as much detail as she could recall, the Twelfth told her husband about the dream. The angels crowed about her listening intently to what they recognized as a powerful prophecy regarding the King's wrath.

The Twelfth's mind raced as she considered what, if anything, it could mean. Meir stepped forward and placed her hand on the Twelfth tickling something in the far recesses of her mind, a memory she didn't quite realize she even had. The Twelfth sent a quick text to the Eighth and then reached for her Bible to search for the plague of Zachariah.

Chapter 40 -The Eighth

A year ago, the smoke-filled tavern would have made him cough and seek solace elsewhere. Much had changed in a year. Now he was quite comfortable here. He liked to think the tavern was filled with others like himself, those who were lost, people seeking answers, looking to escape. But admittedly, he was lost by choice. He had grown tired of being himself; he needed a break.

He looked around the tavern and found it was not filled with the type of patrons he had always thought frequented such places. In fact, he could not categorize the patrons at all. A young couple sat in the corner snuggled together enjoying a bottle of champagne. He imagined they were newlyweds perhaps even on their honeymoon. He wondered how long it would last.

College students played darts and shared a pitcher. They laughed and joked in the loud carefree way that only college kids could. A table of suits sat as far from the college students as they could get. Most likely to avoid the noise. It wasn't the casual friendliness of co-workers out for a drink it was more stilted tenser. The Eighth assumed it was a business meeting of some sort. Possibly a new client they were hosting.

Most of the people in the tavern were there in groups at a minimum in pairs. He was one of the few alone, and so he had chosen a seat at the bar in hopes of making it less obvious, less pathetic. But there was no denying his life had become precisely that - pathetic.

He sat his whiskey glass down with a loud enough clank to alert the bartender that he needed a refill but not loud enough to annoy her. She was deep in conversation with another patron one who seemed to need to pour out their life story to any sympathetic ear. Another poor slob he thought here by themselves desperate to drown their sorrows just as the Eighth was trying to drown his. But he could not escape the pain of others, no amount of alcohol could drown that. He knew because he had tried.

A text came in on his phone at the same time the bell on the door rattled announcing the arrival or departure of a patron. Ignoring the message, the Eighth glanced up to look at the door because he wasn't doing anything else. A woman with wild red hair walked in disrupting his soul. It took him only a second to place her. She had held the door for him in Platitude. That seemed like a lifetime ago. How could she possibly be here halfway across the world from Platitude? A strange sense of familiarity with a hint of shame washed over him. She smiled as recognition and astonishment swept across his face. He could feel her joy, and for some reason, it incensed him.

"May I join you?" she asked while gesturing to the bar stool beside him. He was sure his mouth was agape.

"Please," he answered smiling, although he didn't feel happy.

"We met at Platitude College," he half stated half asked.

"We were both there weren't we," she responded. "How did that work out for you?"

"Fantastic," he replied sarcasm nearly suffocating the word.

"Tell me about it," she prompted gently. And so, he did. Because his story had been beating at the gates desperate to be shared and it was no longer able to be controlled. It took control erupting from his soul tumbling and spilling out before he even knew what was happening. He could only sit and listen as if a spectator to his own story as it rushed from his lips.

What are you doing? He caught himself thinking, but he was powerless to stop the flow now that it had begun. He felt a powerful connection to this woman, one he could not explain.

His words rushed forth tumbling over each other, each wound, each slight, more significant than the last. He had gone to Platitude with such high hopes. He was going to conduct research that would change the world. Instead, he had nearly lost his wife. He had lost his research. His career had been sidelined. But the loss of the Fifth... there were no words to describe the hole that had blown in his chest. The chaos and condemnation of the barley field, a time when they were supposed to be honoring her. Instead, they had attacked each other. The emotions had been overwhelming for him.

Standing in that field, he had been overwhelmed, first by their sorrow and then by their hate. Waves of emotion had washed through smashing into each other, wrestling to see which would win. He had nearly collapsed under the weight of it.

The chaos had ended as abruptly as it had started. But even then, the oppression and condemnation had continued in Platitude. There was no trust; people lurked in the shadows. Legalism had taken over smothering the institution in rules and judgment. People remained silent out of fear. The few who did speak up grew tired of the fight eventually or were "assisted" in "determining where the Holy Spirit may be leading them next."

The woman with the wild red hair and piercing green eyes had remained entirely silent as his words rushed forth. But at that statement, a laugh erupted from her startling him. He stopped speaking then, aware of how he must have sounded. But never once had she caused him to feel condemned. Never did he feel she had tuned him out. He felt only catharsis and peace as he poured his heart out to her. He felt—heard. And he hadn't felt heard since leaving Platitude.

With his story told, he paused and waited.

"Was there no one you could trust in that place? No one at all to support you?" She was sincere and yet knowing in her inquiry. He smiled, remembering his friends, remembering the Wednesday night group. He had drawn strength from them. He could have stayed there amid all the Pharisaical rules if the group had stayed together. But they hadn't.

"I had close friends there," he answered a little ashamed he had not included that as a more significant part of his story. He supposed it was normal to focus on the unpleasant parts.

"And now you don't?" she asked, again seeming to know the answer.

"Well, yes. I mean, they are still my friends. We keep in touch via Facebook and texts. Sometimes we chat. We pray for each other. But it's not the same."

"What a beautiful thing that has happened to you," was her response.

"Beautiful thing?" he stammered. "Which part? The part where my friend was driven to kill herself? Or the riot that followed? Perhaps the part where my entire support network moved away, and I was left alone in a place that didn't value me. Maybe you thought the part where my research got absconded by my "partner," and I do use that word loosely, was the beautiful part? Maybe me sinking into an abyss of depression and taking up drinking was the part you found beautiful?" Anger coursed through him. Who was this woman?

"None of those things on their own are beautiful. But the tapestry they are weaving is. I do not look at you and see a man who drinks too much. I see a man who feels too much and has chosen a poor way to handle it.

I do not see a man who was duped by his research partner; I see a man who was fortunate to get free of that commitment before the corruption was exposed." She paused. "I do not see a man who has lost his friends and support network. I see a man who had the great fortune to find himself in a place where he could develop powerful friendships. Friendships built on a strong foundation that cannot be broken by geography alone. Now those friends have branched out covering more ground, providing you support no matter where you go, at a time when technology makes that possible in ways that were unheard of before. Before me sits a man who is loved, a man who has fought faithfully for his family and for what is right. But perhaps he has also neglected some things that are important, and because of that he has lost his way."

Her words covered his wounds like a salve. He expected fain sympathy or perhaps outright condemnation, but not this. Not understanding. Not acceptance. Definitely not perspective.

"I drink too much," he blurted out like a child caught with their hand in the cookie jar.

"Can you stop?" she asked as one who wasn't worried.

"Yes. I'm not an alcoholic I just drink too much. I know it. My wife hates it." As if on cue the bartender arrived, having freed herself from the other patron who now looked even more morose. She lifted the bottle to pour him another whiskey. The Eighth placed his hand over the mouth of the glass and gave a grateful yet declining face to the bartender as if to prove to the woman with the wild red hair that he could. The bartender nodded knowingly and walked away.

The woman with the wild red hair smiled. "Then perhaps you should stop," she said as if it were the simplest thing.

"Perhaps," he answered because he lacked anything else to say. "What are you doing here?" He asked after a minute of comfortable silence.

"I am on my way to see to an important matter in Tanzania. I just stopped here to pick someone up." The answer seemed completely satisfying and reasonable to the Eighth. And yet her being here was still quite unnerving, serendipitous even.

Just then his phone rang. The woman smiled and looked away indicating it was ok that he cut their conversation short. He glanced down and was both shocked and pleased to see his cousin's name pop up on the caller ID.

"Hello?"

"I need you to go with me to Tanzania," the Tenth answered getting straight to the point. The Eighth's heart skipped a beat. Did he just say Tanzania? He turned his head toward the woman with the wild red hair, but she was gone.

Chapter 41

Kfir and Aegeus returned from the clinic with the Twelfth to find Mordecai sitting on the deck, the sun beating upon his face, a computer sitting on his lap and a small coffee on the round end table next to him.

Kfir sniffed the air, "Is that a Palomino?" he asked with a hint of desire.

"It is," Mordecai answered. "Would you like some?" He asked, offering the cup to Kfir with a smile. Kfir walked forward eagerly.

"Where did you find it?" Kfir asked, excitement in his voice as he readily accepted the cup.

"I made a quick trip this morning while you were out with the Twelfth."

"How?" Adiel asked as she joined them. "You haven't left?" Mordecai smiled more broadly.

"I don't have to fly there," Mordecai offered. "Sentinels can just "be" where they want to be. I popped into the shop, got a coffee and then popped back," he seemed amused by their looks of astonishment.

"Show us?" Kfir asked with excitement as he swallowed down the Palomino and let out a little groan of pleasure.

Mordecai put the laptop on the small coffee table in front of him "Ok." And with that, he was gone reappearing seconds later on the dock.

"What?!" Kfir exclaimed, clearly impressed. He pulled out his phone and began pushing buttons.

"What are you doing?" Aegeus asked Kfir.

"That was Tweet-worthy," Kfir said still typing on his phone.

"You have a cell phone?" Meir asked joining them.

"You don't?" Kfir asked surprised. Meir shook her head, gently laughing as Mordecai rejoined them on the deck.

"I read your blog today," Mordecai offered. "It's pretty good."

"You have a blog?" Adiel asked in shock.

Kfir rolled his eyes in an exaggerated manner. "We've been over this," he began.

"What happened at the clinic today?" Meir asked changing the subject.

The angels gathered around the small deck and Kfir, and Aegeus filled them in on the young woman with the strange carving in her stomach and the phone call to the Eleventh.

"Why would anyone carve words in their stomach?" Aegeus asked.

"What words?" Mordecai wanted to know.

"It said Slim Money," Aegeus answered.

"That's a pimp name," Mordecai said, sadness emitting from him. Meir walked to him and curled her wing around him, offering him comfort. He looked up at her a little embarrassed and smiled.

"Sorry," she said, blushing a little "it's a habit," she offered in explanation, but she did not remove her wing.

"I understand," he offered, "it's the tear with which I was forged."

Meir didn't respond; she saw no reason to mention that it wasn't the humanity she was reacting to but the sadness. She would have offered the same comfort to any angel.

"How did things go here?" Aegeus asked.

"We got the kids safely to and from Pine Tree Frosty," Adiel offered.

"Is that code for something?" Aegeus asked, wondering what was happening.

"Pine Tree Frosty is an ice cream shop," she answered winking.

"Meir, what progress are you making with the prophecies?" Aegeus groped for any development, anything that was relevant.

"I think we are getting close," Meir responded.

"Mordecai?" Aegeus asked, moving on.

"I did have a bit of luck," Mordecai offered while walking to the laptop and turning it toward the group, who moved closer.

"How," asked Kfir, baffled that Mordecai would be able to get through the concealment of the Keepers.

"Perhaps it is the tear that I am forged with?" he suggested.

"What is it?" Aegeus asked, stepping closer.

"I found the First and his wife."

Chapter 42 -The Wife of the First

The sound of the ocean lapping at the shore soothed her soul. The sun gently warmed her skin as if it knew that her veins ran with ice as if it understood that she needed gentleness. She dug her toes deeper into the sand and leaned back resting on her elbows and turning her face to the sun. With her eyes closed, she tried to bask in the peace of it. She let the sound of the seagulls creep in. It was so easy only to hear the waves and miss the soft cry of the seagull.

She concentrated on the feeling of the sand between her toes. How warm it was, how granular. She didn't want to miss the sand because the warmth of the sun distracted her. The smell of the ocean rose to meet her as she sat still and invited it in. The clean smell of saltwater mixed with a hint of fish. It was perfect, and if only for a moment, she forgot everything else.

But cancer is powerful, and it would not be forgotten, not for long. Five minutes was all she got. Five minutes to forget all the doctors' appointments, all the treatments, all the times when she had had to lay aside her dignity and just do what needed to be done.

The last two years had taught her humility. Two years of battling an enemy she could not see, an enemy that had taken refuge in her very body. And now? Now she knew she had lost. There was no more hope. Cancer had won.

Each day we all take a small step toward death. It is our unavoidable fate. She knew this. And yet seeing the finish line so close in front of her somehow changed things. It changed her. It changed the way she viewed not having children. For the first time in her life, she uttered a prayer to the King thanking him that he had not given her children, that she would leave no one without a mother.

She stretched out in the sand lying flat not caring that she had no towel or beach chair. She wiggled her body just a little to force herself a little deeper into the sand so that it nestled around her. She was ready. At this moment, hugged by the sand, kissed by the sun; she was ready. If she just slipped away now, it would be ok. But she knew that wasn't going to happen. From what the doctor had just told her it wouldn't be quite that nice.

How would she ever tell her husband? The sight of his face when she had told him she had cancer seared itself into her brain. She could not imagine telling him she was dying. She would not live to see another year. She would not live to see Christmas. Weeks maybe months was what the doctor had said. She had sat emotionless letting the words bounce off her; she could not allow them to soak in, she didn't want them to become part of her. She simply refused.

But now they nestled in and settled on her soul. She reflected on the last two years, the battle with her own body, the struggle against her fear and she realized she had lost. For two years she had neglected her friends, her relationships. Now? She feared it might be too late. Had it only been two years since she had been in Platitude surrounded by friends, a support group? It seemed like a lifetime ago.

Two years of battling cancer. She had found out right before the first of her friends left Platitude. But she hadn't told anyone. She couldn't quite bring herself to do it. Then, they were gone. One by one they had left, leaving her to fight alone. They had called and tried to keep in touch, but her battle with her disease had become her life. The timing had just never seemed right, and so she had never told them. Eventually, they must have tired of her never answering their calls or emails because with time the contact between them dwindled down to nothing.

Nothing. The word sat heavy on her heart. She had let her friendships dwindle to nothing. And soon, she would be gone, a mere vapor, a memory in only the minds of a few people. She left behind no legacy, no children, no story. She would amount to nothing. Her life had come to nothing. How would she tell her husband? She dreaded the look in his eyes, the knowledge that she was letting him down.

Emotions welled inside her each one fighting for control. But in the end, fear won. Fear of dying, fear for her husband, fear that she would not be able to accept the fate that God had handed her.

She let the tears she was holding back rush down her cheeks. Sobs racked her body, and she did nothing to stop them. She wanted to feel the hopelessness the sorrow. She savored the feeling of the wet tears pouring down her face. She was dying. Each and every experience was now invited, something to be treasured. They all seemed so beautiful now so perfect, even the sorrow.

She rolled onto her side and poured her anguish into the sand. There was no one to see her, no one to hear her cries, no one to pass judgment or offer comfort. It was just her, the beach, and her cancer. Or so she thought.

Chapter 43

Titus watched from the dilapidated dock as the wife of the First cried into the sand. How pathetic he thought. You could always count on the hairless rats to weep and wail when facing death. Titus found their utter lack of self-control to be disturbing. He prided himself on self-control.

The small dingy he was sitting in rocked gently with the ocean current, and he found the movement and sound of the waves slapping against the dock to be grating. The fact that he had drowned the boat's owner was of no consequence to him. The man had been an inconvenience.

Titus looked back down the beach at the wife of the First. Mere human eyes would not have been able to see her from this distance, but he was no human. She was lying in the sand blubbering while Ayo ministered to her. He watched as the angel knelt over the wife of the First cradling her.

Titus knew that Ayo was performing a covering. She had wrapped her wings around her charge and was drawing out words of truth and encouragement into the woman's broken soul. Words that Titus knew had been planted there just waiting to be found. It sickened him. He hated the very thought of it because it meant the King had planted them. He hated it because it meant that from the beginning, the King had known to create the ministering angels with this exact skill for this exact purpose.

He hated it because that meant the King had known this would happen. He had always known that some of his heavenly beings would fall to this forsaken earth and become darkness. The King had known every time he had looked into Titus's eyes that one-day Titus would be darkness fallen to earth stalking the wife of the First. The King had known that locked deep in Titus's heart was ambition and selfishness. The King had known that one-day Titus would choose wrong.

And yet he had allowed it. The King had known, and he had never even hinted at it. For all that time Titus had lived among the angels in the presence of the King clueless of his fate. But the King had known. He had known, and he had loved Titus, anyway. He had known that on this precise day Titus would stand in this place, this place that was so powerful and painful to him thinking these very thoughts. Reflecting on what had been; fearing what was to come. For that reason, Titus's hatred of the King and his children grew deeper every day.

The knowledge that he could kill the angel did not bring Titus any comfort. Everyone knew ministering angels, like their tormenting demon counterparts, were not trained in combat and carried no weapon. In Titus's opinion, watching a ministering angel transform into a tormenting demon was one of the most joyous transitions. To see a heavenly being so perfectly designed to offer comfort and encouragement slowly darken into a monster bent on tormenting those same souls... Well, it was something that Titus never tired of.

He was surprised that Lucifer had not armed them when they fell, but Titus never asked him about it. It was not wise to question Lucifer.

While there would be no glory in killing a ministering angel that was alone and virtually unprotected, it did not remove his desire to do so. After all, she was not truly unprotected. She did have the Light of God. The Light was particularly strong in ministering angels, and while it was their only weapon, it was more than enough.

With reluctance, Titus turned from the wife of the First and Ayo. While he hated New Orleans and was more than happy to leave this place and its bitter memories, he also regretted leaving the woman alive. It would have been quite satisfying to kill her. Perhaps it would have quenched his soul of the thoughts this place invoked. But instead, he walked away. Now was not the time to kill her. He had seen the fear deep in her soul, and he could use it to destroy her, perhaps to destroy them all. Using her own weakness against her would be more satisfying. For now, he would report to Lucifer what he had found.

Chapter 44

Lucifer rested his elbow on the table and twirled the girl's long brown hair around his left index finger. Her hair was silky and soft, softer than most and it smelled like peaches. The diner was small and quaint with the promise of fresh apple pie permeating the air. It created an environment that screamed of comfort and belonging. Ambiance was important to Lucifer. She felt safe here like she belonged here like nothing bad could happen here. That lowered her defenses.

With one simple touch, he had been able to read all her thoughts, he knew instantly what she was looking for what he needed to say and do to assure his success. So, he had become what she wanted. It hadn't taken much she was a tender soul, not like so many of them. She only wanted someone to truly look at her to look deep into her soul and give her their full attention. Deep down that was what so many of them wanted.

He listened carefully as she chatted about the life she was leaving behind where she was from her dreams for the future. He was careful to give her his full attention it was important to her, and that made it essential to his success. Lucifer smiled at her gently oozing charm as he did. He found immense pleasure in looking deep into her soul and discovering how to further lure her in. The urge to destroy her flooded through him it always did when he was this close.

His hatred for women was second only to his hatred of the King. But he had had centuries to learn to control that to conceal it. Instead, he looked up at her lovingly, his ocean blue eyes caressing her. His smile perfect and bright. His blond hair parted precisely as it should be according to her. He listened to each ridiculous word as it tumbled from her lips.

Runaways were easier targets than most. The girl had told him she was eighteen, but Lucifer knew that wasn't true. He knew that she was only fifteen. He knew she had been in and out of foster care since she was eight. He knew that she couldn't really remember her mother anymore, she remembered only the abuse she had suffered at the hands of her father. Her understanding of love had been tainted and distorted by years of mistreatment. Lucifer had seen to that detail years ago.

Destroying her childhood and corrupting her understanding of love had been both simple and necessary. He couldn't have her achieving what the King had sent her for. She was too important, it would derail his own plans. Sitting here with her now, he was pleased to know that soon he would take the last needed step to destroy her. He would lure her in with kindness he would take her off the street and pretend to love her. And then he would put a label on her marking her as his own.

The world would not be able to see past it. They would view her as a scourge to society. She would be rejected and loved by none but abused by all. Lucifer was once again reminded of the King's declaration to his children to love one another. It was so simple and yet so impossible for them. For this, Lucifer was grateful.

By destroying her and all those like her, he was, in fact, able to destroy the King's children. Each one of these girls they turned their faces against caused their hearts to harden just a little more. Each time they dismissed the plight of the downtrodden each time they averted their eyes from the anguished souls around them, they stepped a little further from the King and a little closer to Hell.

It pleased him to know he could manipulate the King's children. It was relatively easy to convince them to do his work. Often it was as simple as twisting their understanding of the King and his Word. Oh, the damage he had convinced them to do in the name of the King.

If he could attach a distasteful label to the person, the King's children would do the rest. It pleased him just thinking about it. The girl saw his smile and believed it was in response to the story she was telling him, the attention and approval caused her to blush. Lucifer smiled even more broadly knowing that soon he would damage her soul so severely that she may never blush again. He reached out and gently tucked her hair behind her ear, his hand caressing the birthmark that was nearly hidden on her neck just behind her ear. It reminded him of the fafanto, the symbol of tenderness, there was irony in the mark considering his plans for her.

He was concentrating so intently on the girl that he almost missed Titus coming into the diner and joining Morax a few tables over.

Chapter 45

Morax did not have any idea how long he and Lucifer had been working. Time was of no consequence except for one small detail he was using one of the hairless rat's bodies. Their bodies were so weak it utterly revolted him.

Lucifer did not have that issue, he shifted effortlessly between having a body the rats could see and one they could not. He took whatever form most served his purpose there were no limitations.

Morax however, was confined to the body Lucifer had given him for this mission. And it had physical limitations. For starters, it needed to eat. It needed sleep. And traveling as they did in defiance of time and space took a toll on it.

Lucifer had taken small measures to assure Morax's human form did not die, but his efforts were cruel in nature and Morax recognized them for what they were, punishment, not concern. He would stop to eat only when Morax's hunger became so severe he could no longer go on.

Morax hated the hairless rats and their food. Over the centuries he had learned to manage it by eating in the most exclusive places. But Lucifer did not stop in fine dining establishments with delicacies which were what Morax was accustomed to. No Lucifer would stop at dives. Places so filthy and greasy that Morax would have gastrointestinal problems for days afterward.

He had never even heard of chitlins before this trip now he doubted he would ever forget them. Their journey in had been nearly as painful as their journey out. Morax was objective enough to admit that the food itself may not have been an issue if the establishments had been better quality. But Lucifer had made it clear catering to Morax's taste preference was not a priority.

They had spent countless hours in America because the American's forged the way of freedom; they were a symbol of hope to the rest of the world. Stamping out their light was crucial to Lucifer. Had Morax not felt so sick, it would have been perfect.

The booths in the small diner were intimate with soft lighting. Morax had been hoping that once their work with the babies was complete, Lucifer would relent and heal him from the dreaded sickness that had overtaken him.

Instead, Lucifer had merely transported them to this small diner.

Morax had no idea where they were. The menu was in English, and it smelled American, so he assumed he was somewhere in the States. The diner had large windows on three sides, the fourth wall was exposed brick. Despite his best efforts and foul mood, he found himself liking the place.

With a pounding head and a churning stomach, Morax found a booth in the back corner. The vinyl creaked if you moved, so Morax attempted to sit unmoving as he waited patiently for Lucifer to finish whatever business he had with the girl. The waiter seemed to understand that Morax did not wish to chat. He brought a tall glass of water to the table with two small white pills.

"These will help," he offered. A tormenting demon clung to the boy continually whispering in his ear. The demon met Morax's gaze and nodded his head indicating his part in delivering the white pills.

"Thank you," Morax said flatly more to the demon than the boy. Despite his hatred of their food, he relented that he must eat; he settled on eggs with toast. His order placed, and the pills taken he leaned back in the booth and watched as Lucifer beguiled the female. He wondered what path he was sending her on.

Morax was so engrossed watching Lucifer and the girl he did not notice Titus sliding into the booth across from him. It was an unwelcome intrusion.

"What are you doing here?" Morax asked with annoyance. He had not forgotten that it was Titus who had betrayed him.

"I bring news of the eleven," Titus said as if everything was as it should be.

"What news?" Morax asked, making his displeasure obvious.

"I have found several of them."

"You reek of the sea," Morax spat out, knowing it would awaken old wounds in Titus.

"I have been in New Orleans," Titus replied without emotion. That was better news than Morax could have hoped for. A smile crept onto his face. Titus' face did not flinch, but Morax expected nothing less, Titus had mastered his emotions long ago. Despite the lack of reaction, Morax knew that a trip to New Orleans must have affected Titus. A demon could not visit the site of their falling without being affected.

"Ah, a visit to your old stomping grounds, how was it?" he asked, hoping to press what he knew would be a wound.

"I was not there to reminisce Morax I was there on the Princes' business." Titus's face did not falter or give anything away.

"Of course," Morax pressed on enjoying himself "but you could hardly deny the pleasure of being back in a place you know so well." For over a century Titus had served the King in New Orleans. "Tell me Titus, has it changed much?"

"I was not there as a tourist Morax. But soon enough you will be displaced from your position one you have taken lightly, and you will be free to visit New Orleans. Then you can see for yourself."

"I see your visit to New Orleans has ignited your insatiable desire for power," Morax said with as much condemnation as he could pour into his tone. "Tell me. Is Café Du Monde still there?" He paused briefly for effect before going on, "Perhaps when we are done here I will take a little vacation and visit New Orleans. I do love the beignets. You can show me around." Morax continued to press, he knew the mention of Café Du Monde would elicit a strong response.

"I thought you hated their food," Titus spat from his mouth, his emotion starting to get the best of him.

"I do," Morax answered honestly "but beignets are one of the rare exceptions. They are heavenly" he finished surprised by his own honesty. It was not often his corrupted mind, let him have memories of his life before, life in heaven. But there were rare instances when some small, unexpected thing would cause a little bleed through.

Those moments were precious and painful all at once. For a fleeting second, some minuscule sliver of his soul would experience a gentle reminder of what it was like to have peace, to know love. It was these small quiet memories that would disrupt his entire existence slamming into him like a horrible reminder of all that he had lost, all that he had given up. He loved and hated those moments all in the same breath. Eating beignets, even remembering them was unexpectedly one of those times.

Chapter 46

Titus sat across from Morax rage coursing through him. How dare he bring up New Orleans? There was an unwritten code among the demons never to mention their fall. For Morax to bring up New Orleans well, Titus didn't have words for it. Despite the rage that ravaged him, he sat still and calm staring at Morax as if he were an idiot. Titus refused to allow Morax, the upper hand. He would not betray the flood of emotions he was experiencing. He willed his voice to remain steady, his eyes to stare unflinchingly into Morax's. He painted a sneer on his face as he thought of the joy that killing Morax would bring him.

Despite his best efforts, his mind returned to New Orleans in 1868. Racial tensions were high, the city had had a significant riot only two years prior. The Mafia was in control, and Joseph "Peppino" Agnello was making a resurgence among the Palermitani family. But Titus had not been sent there to fight for race relations or against the Mafia, other angels had been assigned those responsibilities, Titus, a guardian angel at the time, had been assigned to fight the growing influence of voodoo and witchcraft.

Titus had been in New Orleans for just over a century. Initially, he had traveled home between missions, but as time passed, he often volunteered to take extra missions. As a result, he had spent very little time at home. Titus wanted results, and he had not at that time fully appreciated the wait. But as a celestial being time was a non-commodity. What were a hundred years in the big scheme of things? But so much time away from the King weakened him.

It was not until he became a demon, when for the first time his time was limited did he suddenly discover the beauty of patience. No longer did he care to rush anything. Rushing time served no purpose other than moving him closer to his inevitable fate, complete separation from the King. It was a horrible fate of unimaginable cruelty. Titus could think of nothing worse.

As a demon, he had come to hate the King, and yet even that hatred came from a place of love. It was a hatred that stemmed from being separated from the King. The King was love there could be no love without the King. Even separated as he was Titus remained in the world and the King's love was cast down upon the earth. Demons full of rage and hate and scorn still benefited from feeling the King's love as it rained down on creation. It was muted and less powerful than when they had been angels, but it was there in tiny droplets. In those small droplets, the demons found love and hope.

They corrupted it, of course, using it for their own purposes. They corrupted that love to fuel their own evil ambitions to motivate their desires for power and hatred. They aspired to nothing more than to destroy as many of the King's children as they could in their limited time. If they were to face complete separation from the King one-day, they would bring as many unfortunate souls with them as they could. It was the only way they knew to grieve the King. Mordecai had once likened the demons' plans to the tantrum of a human child. Titus had stabbed Mordecai for saying it. But in his heart, he knew it angered him because in many ways it was true.

But in 1868 Titus was still an angel, thoughts of separation from the King and hatred were far from his mind. His hatred was against evil the very demons he now embraced as brothers. At that time, he fought faithfully for the King in the battle against the influence of voodoo. Voodoo had been brought in by ship and had slowly be-

gun to mingle with true faith. The King's children had become confused and were being lured into dangerous practices of spiritualism.
Witchcraft was being intertwined with the Lamb's bride, and the
King would not tolerate any threat to his bride. Angels fought for her
integrity to keep her pure and holy.

Titus could still smell the horses on that fateful night when he
had traded in his Light for a life of separation. Of course, it is never presented to anyone like that. No Lucifer was much too clever
for that. Who would ever choose evil if it were presented that way?
For Titus, his mistress had been power. Seneca had enticed him with
promises of power and glory. And fear, it would never have worked
without fear.

It was a particularly warm night in the late summer. Titus accompanied his charge to Café Du Monde. The man had lied to his
wife about where he was going it had been Titus's first indication
that something was wrong. The man did not yet have the Light, but
his young son did, and the boy had called in the power of the King
as a protective covering for his father. Titus had been the guardian
called in to protect the man just days before the crocodile incident
that caused him to walk with a significant limp.

Only months before he had been on a house call to a home in the
bayou when he had had an unfortunate run-in with a crocodile. If it
had not been for Titus, the man would have been lost. However, instead of seeing his survival as the miracle it was he instead saw only
the pain and fear that he had experienced, and he focused on the per-
manent damage to his leg and how difficult walking had become. As
a physician using a cane was a nuisance and impeded his work and
his ability to get to all his patients.

Titus had had to save the man's life more than once. He had a
panache for getting himself into trouble. He kept dangerous company, company that was surrounded by destroying demons.

When they arrived in the French Quarter, the driver brought the carriage to a stop just across from Jackson Square. St. Louis Cathedral towered in the background. Titus accompanied the man to Café Du Monde; there were no demons in sight. Assuming the man was there to meet a secret lover, Titus left him sitting comfortably at a corner table while he did a patrol of the square.

While Titus was patrolling a beautiful woman entered Café Du Monde and joined the man at the table. When she arrived, he stood, as was the custom and removed his top hat. After a short greeting, they both sat down, and he slid a fresh cup of chicory coffee over to her. She smiled in return.

Titus was circling back to the Café when he saw the woman. He recognized her immediately, a voodoo queen named Marie Laveau. An epidemic was spreading through New Orleans, many had perished. The man seemed to be seeking Marie Laveau's assistance both in nursing the ill and in providing protection for those not yet infected.

Titus was familiar with her work. She was a woman of true compassion and power. But she mixed the truth with voodoo and witchcraft. It could not be permitted. Many fought to help her come into the light to help her see the truth and abandon evil.

Demons poised and ready for battle suddenly dropped from the sky surrounding the café. A horse from a nearby carriage neighed in the background pawing the ground nervously in response to the presence of so many demons. Powdered sugar floated in the air from the beignets filling the air with a slightly sweet scent as Titus drew nearer. Severely outnumbered Titus drew his sword.

The battle had been intense. Other angels joined Titus as he battled toward the table. Titus swung his sword with all his might removing demons from his path. Voodoo clung to the woman his talons deep within her. The woman sat sipping coffee and listening to the man with the top hat unaware of the battle that raged around them or the demon that clung to her. Voodoo did not flinch as Titus drew nearer. He seemed to have a confidence that Titus had never seen in any demon.

Mordecai called out to him, but Titus continued battling his way deeper into the horde until, without noticing, he was in the center, surrounded by demons on all sides. There were no angels around him. No one to offer him assistance. He had unknowingly gone deep into enemy territory, alone.

There were two demons between Titus and the table when suddenly a massive warrior with long hair and a distinct scar had dropped down in front of him. Titus did not know Seneca then, but he would never forget him. They had battled, but it did not take long for Titus to realize that Seneca was a far better warrior than him. Titus was not a warrior at all his combat training had served him well, but he was not equipped to fight a warrior such as Seneca. Within minutes Seneca had pinned Titus to the ground his sword poised at Titus's neck.

"It doesn't have to be this way," Seneca offered in a tone that conveyed his strength. "Do you see the woman?" He asked nodding his head ever so slightly toward her without taking his full attention off Titus. "She is powerful, compassionate and kind. She does great deeds, helping all those around her. She saves lives and destroys the wicked." He paused to allow the implications of his statement seep into Titus. "There is another way to fight evil. You see, the demon attached to her? It is extraordinarily influential. It can do good, save lives. You can have that kind of power." Seneca paused. Titus strained beneath him, in the distance, he could hear Mordecai calling his name.

"We can give you the power and influence you crave. You must make a choice now," Seneca said in a gentle voice. "You must choose to help her in her fight against evil, or you must choose death." Seneca pressed the tip of his blade into Titus's neck just enough to draw blood. There on the floor of Café Du Monde, surrounded by a horde of demons with no angels near him, the smell of chicory teasing his nose and powdered sugar floating in the air, Titus had made his choice.

Chapter 47

Lucifer slid into the booth next to Morax excitement lighting his eyes.

"I trust you bring good news," he asked Titus not wasting time with silly formalities.

"I do my Prince." Titus smiled bowing his head in reverence and shooting a gloating look at Morax as he did.

"I have just come from the Eleventh she is covered in demons. I have instructed them to remain with her tormenting her day and night." He did not want to overreach, it was not wise to make claims that were not yet assured, and so he withheld that he felt her destruction would come swiftly.

"Is that it?" Lucifer asked, annoyance evident in his tone. Morax smirked.

"The wife of the First has cancer." Titus knew this news would bring Lucifer joy, cancer was his creation. A sly smile slid up Lucifer's face as he turned toward Morax and raised his eyebrows in a gesture of pride.

"How is she handling that?" Lucifer asked with glee.

"She is dying, and the fear consumes her." Titus was pleased to be the bearer of good news.

"And the others" Lucifer pressed on excitement filling him as the idea of destroying the eleven began to seem more tangible.

"The Tenth is still in Platitude. I have assigned an entire unit of destroyers to him. Deception is in charge. The Ninth is working herself to death in the remote reaches of the world, some disease will take her soon enough, and the Fourth is isolated in a lab with very little interaction with anyone," Titus felt proud of how much he had discovered in such a short time.

"They are all still living?" Lucifer asked, disappointment clear in his tone. He looked to Morax with bewilderment. Morax shrugged his shoulder and offered a look clearly intended to insinuate that Titus was incompetent.

Titus had enough experience and wisdom not to answer. He could have explained that each of the eleven was well protected by some of the King's best, but he thought it wise to leave those details out.

"I believe my instructions were to destroy them, not to provide me with a book report," Lucifer said sweetly with eyes that betrayed the kind tone.

"Plans are underway my Liege. We find them isolated from each other with no real support network. Their isolation leaves them weak, vulnerable. But each is protected by prayer and the woman with the wild red hair is with them," It was a risk mentioning it, but weighing his options, he thought it best to do so.

"Prayer cover?" Lucifer pondered this. "You have not found the Second and Third?"

"No."

With lightning speed, Lucifer reached out and grabbed Titus by the throat dragging him slightly out of his seat so that he leaned over the table. Sulfur began to pour from Lucifer, patrons in the restaurant alerted by the display started to fidget uncomfortably in their seats. Lucifer noticed at once.

"A bee," he said to those in the bistro "he has a bee in his shirt," he smiled at them. Relief rippled through the crowd at the simple excuse. It was a perfectly reasonable explanation that meant they would not be required to respond to anything more difficult. Lucifer released Titus and sat back in the booth.

"When covered in prayer, they are not truly weak and vulnerable. Isolation is good, but you will not ever succeed if you do not find and destroy the Second and Third. Their prayers are helping protect the others." He spoke slowly and deliberately in a manner that was intended to be condescending but not raise the suspicion of those around him.

"What have you learned about their location?" Lucifer demanded.

"I know only that they retain a house in Platitude, but they are not there. They recently had a grandchild that is said to be heavily guarded by the warrior Omri, they may be with the child?" it was the best guess he had.

Bile washed up Morax's throat, and his eyes grew wide despite his best efforts. Hand trembling, he lifted his water glass to his mouth and took a nervous sip. There was little chance that the child they had visited, the one protected by Omri, had been a different child. His best hope was that Lucifer would not notice.

"They are not," Lucifer said with assurance. It was clear he had made the connection, but he had done so too late. Rage coursed through him making him even more determined to find them; their incessant praying was destroying his plans.

"Have you any other news or are you wasting more of my time?" Lucifer demanded.

"There is one thing. Perhaps it is nothing, but it seems a bit odd," Titus eased into it softly it may be nothing, but when the woman with the wild red hair was involved, it was never "nothing."

"Yes," Lucifer prompted impatiently.

"The woman with the wild red hair seems to be sending them to Tanzania."

"Tanzania?" Lucifer questioned. Titus only nodded slightly in response.

"What for?"

Titus thought this an unnecessary question. If he had any idea why he would have led with that bit of information. But he said nothing of the sort.

"I can't be certain, but I did hear the Eleventh mention the name, Wanda." It wasn't much, but it was all he had and apparently, it was enough. Recognition flashed in Lucifer's eyes, and the rage he held so close to the surface began to bubble over. He spoke through gritted teeth.

"Which of them are going?"

"All that I have found so far, although the Fourth is uncertain."

Lucifer's fury continued to boil within him. He struggled to control his anger, he did not care to transform into the beast in this place. It was becoming clear to him that the King was working to dismantle his plans. His operation in Tanzania was at stake, and it seemed the King planned to use these eleven humans to do it. Scales began to emerge across his skin in small patches, sulfur oozing from him as he began to lose control. He took several deep breaths as he tried to assure himself this was not the case. It was possible it was all a big coincidence. There was no way to know for sure which made his need to destroy them all the stronger.

Working hard to control his anger while making it exceedingly clear he was displeased Lucifer said, "I will take care of the Fourth."

"Titus," he added through clenched teeth, "Find the Second and the Third. They provide prayer cover for the others. Find them and destroy them or I will destroy you."

"Yes, my Liege." Titus left eager to leave Morax to deal with Lucifer's anger.

Chapter 48

Morax walked a few steps behind Lucifer down the sterile hall. The building was quiet, and their feet made a slight squeak as they walked down the well-polished floor. The smell of bleach and antiseptic filled his nostrils, and he couldn't help but wonder if they were in yet another hospital. If so this one was entirely different from the others. There were no patient rooms, and only a few tormenting demons flitted about.

They reached the end of the corridor, and Lucifer paused briefly. Glancing to the left, he smiled, dipped his head slightly as if in greeting and then turned to the right. Morax reaching the end of the corridor slightly after Lucifer, also looked to the left to see who was there. He was stunned to see a small unit of angels, all warriors, guarding the entrance to a secured door.

Morax quickened his step to catch up with Lucifer.

"What's in there?" he asked, gesturing his head toward the hall they had just passed.

"That is not our concern today," Lucifer said without looking back.

"What are we doing here?" Morax asked even more intrigued. Lucifer did not answer. About halfway down the hall Lucifer stopped abruptly in front of a closed door with the word Director etched into the glass. Smiling broadly Lucifer stepped into the large office.

A stocky man in an expensive suit was sitting behind a large desk, windows lined the wall behind him. The day was rainy and overcast encapsulating the office in a dreariness that could be felt. The man seemed oblivious as he poured over a thick file.

Lucifer entered the office as if it were his own. He settled into one of the chairs across from the man and put his feet up on the edge of the desk. Morax stood in the doorway hesitant and unsure of if the man could see him.

"He cannot see you," Lucifer offered. "Come in, sit down, this may take time."

Morax walked over and sat in the chair next to Lucifer. The hairless rat ran his hand through his hair in a way that let Morax know he was anguishing over something. Something that apparently had attracted Lucifer's attention.

"What are we doing here?" Morax asked again.

"I need him to make the right decision," Lucifer responded.

The hairless rat stood from his desk. He stuffed his hands in his pockets then stared out the window for several minutes. Lucifer rose from his chair and went to stand beside him.

"The source is in Asia," he said to the man without looking at him, "All the evidence points that way."

The man left the window and returned to the file sorting through it to find a report. He reread it, which one was it, he wondered? The unidentified virus had two possible sources, one in Tanzania and the other in Asia.

"The CDC thinks it's in Asia," Lucifer said again. Morax wasn't sure the man was convinced. Apparently, Lucifer wasn't either. "Send someone to both locations," he suggested.

The man pushed a button on his desk phone and leaned toward the speaker out of habit.

"Yes," a soft voice on the other end asked.

"Get T for me," he requested. His decision made, he settled back in his chair to wait.

Morax and Lucifer settled back into their chairs and waited patiently as well. T was a young man. Morax estimated him to be in his twenties. After an initial conversation with the Director, he left the office only to return after a few minutes.

"He's on his way," he said by way of a greeting. The director nodded slightly, acknowledging that he had heard the young man who now stood comfortably near the large desk. A third man shuffled in wearing scrubs with a lab coat and towel drying his hair.

Morax was disappointed to see the man had the Light and was flanked by a guardian angel. This task would have been much easier if they had all been without the Light. The guardian seemed surprised by Morax, but the presence of Lucifer was apparently even more unexpected. He drew his sword immediately taking his place between his charge and Lucifer. This amused Morax; a guardian was no match for Lucifer.

"Settle down," Lucifer said dismissively to the angel even as he began to scale over slowly showing signs of his true form. Morax knew this was a result of the man having the Light. It burned brightly within him making things more difficult for Lucifer.

As the towel dropped from in front of the man's face, Morax was startled to see it was the Fourth. Lucifer watched amused as recognition registered in Morax's eyes.

"He is from Platitude," Morax stated in astonishment.

"I know," Lucifer said. "That's why we're here. You squandered a great opportunity in Platitude. To make matters worse, we now have a prophet roaming about doing who knows what and two prayer warriors on a rampage disrupting my entire operation."

"You wanted to see me?" the Fourth asked, interrupting Lucifer without knowing it. The director did not sit nor, did he invite the others to sit. Instead, he got right to the point.

"Z1412 is a potential BSL4 virus. Some recent mutation of the flu, or so we suspect." He paused there for only a moment.

"We believe it has an R0 of twenty."

"Twenty?" the Fourth asked, sure he had not heard correctly.

"Yes," the director paused for a second, letting the gravity of that settle in.

"The World Health Organization is reporting two outbreaks of unknown diseases, both in separate locations. We suspect that one or both may be Z1412. The CDC is leaning toward the outbreak in Asia sending out epidemiologists to track the source and control the outbreak. Currently, no one is going to the other location. This disease, if it is what we think, has the potential to kill a lot of people. We need to develop a treatment, and I can't do that without samples."

Lucifer stood from his chair the conversation now reaching the part he was interested in. He walked to the Director and spoke to him as if the man could see him.

"He is your best researcher. You need him in Asia. You cannot trust this to just anyone. You can send someone else to Tanzania. It is highly unlikely that is the source.

"I don't understand why we care about this?" Morax stated, knowing he was unwise to do so.

"We care Morax," Lucifer said with obvious disdain in his voice "because the King is sending so many of the eleven to Tanzania. The more that are gathered together in his name, the more powerful they become. I have significant interests there, and I do not care to have them disrupted by such trivial matters as a simple disease outbreak!" spittle flew from his mouth as he shouted the final words.

"This, Morax, is me cleaning up your mess," Lucifer said with slightly more composure.

"You think the King does not already know of your interests? Will you never learn, Lucifer?" The guardian angel asked interrupting them.

Turning, Lucifer covered the short distance between him and the guardian before Morax even realized he was moving. Sulfur poured from him, and his scaly skin began changing into a greenish blue color.

"You dare speak to me," Lucifer said inches from the angel's face. The angel did not flinch his sword already drawn and at the ready.

The director, unaware of the surrounding battle, looked at the Fourth and said, "I need you to go to Tanzania; take T with you."

The angel slowly smiled at Lucifer. "Your pride has cost you again," he said.

Lucifer whipped his head around just in time to see the woman with the wild red hair walking away from the director. She smiled broadly and disappeared in a flash of light. Lucifer turned back around to the angel, now clearly understanding that the angel's initial comment was a distraction orchestrated by the woman. As he turned, he found the guardian now standing amid a small army of angels. Morax shifted uneasily where he stood.

"You are done here," The Guardian said, speaking with the full authority of the King.

Lucifer let out a cry of rage.

Chapter 49

Titus quickly took in his surroundings. An oriental rug lavished the sterile floor, and ornate bookcases lined the room. The books had matching spines and were neatly arranged to perfection. A Tiffany lamp sat on the edge of an expensive oak desk. It provided a quaint light that gave the exquisitely decorated office a warm, inviting feel. It was precisely the kind of office that Titus believed he deserved.

There was a small humidor behind the desk, largely concealed from view, but the sweet smell of the Cuban tobacco teased his nose causing his mouth to water. He reached for one just as the door to the office opened.

A woman dressed in scrubs and full of the Light ushered in the First and his wife. Her manner was professional yet kind which caused Titus to hate her. He watched from behind the desk as the woman invited them to make themselves comfortable, offered them a drink and then when they declined assured them the doctor would be in shortly.

It had been a week since Titus had seen the wife of the First bellowing on the beach making a spectacle of herself. He was pleased to see that her eyes were still red, her face gaunt and tired.

The First sat beside her holding her hand as Fear clutched his throat, her fangs were buried deep in the First's skull. This pleased Titus. Once in a different time, Titus had fought with all his might to protect his charge against Fear a powerful demon who could cause a significant amount of damage. Now he relished the fact that Fear was among them.

The doctor walked into the room, she welcomed the First and his wife and sat down behind her exquisite desk. Titus looked deep into her eyes and knew that this meeting was going to go his way, her eyes betrayed sadness. She would deliver bad news. The First could see it too, he gripped his wife's hand tighter.

The doctor discussed the results of the latest tests. Titus ignored her. He already knew what she would say. She would tell them that the cancer was not curable, there was nothing left that modern medicine could do. She would discuss end-of-life care and other such things. Titus had no concerns over these things. For he knew that these bodies were nothing more than packaging.

The transformation from this life to the next was quite beautiful, and it was all that really mattered. It was then that the soul entered eternity. The King's children didn't really think of themselves as immortal; that worked to the demon's advantage. But they were immortal creatures, the shedding of their earthly body like the transformation of the caterpillar into a butterfly. The caterpillar itself was not gone, was it not the same creature merely more magnificent than when it had begun? It became the best version of itself.

Fortunately for Titus and the demons, the humans rarely considered this. Titus walked over to the wife of the First and knelt beside her chair studying her carefully. Outwardly she sat still and emotionless, listening to the doctor discuss options for relieving pain and making her comfortable as her life ebbed away. She listened without comment, without question, and without emotional reaction. He considered how different this encounter was from that day on the beach.

Fear tore at her, clawing and biting and choking her. But outwardly she gave no indication. She smiled at her husband and offered comforting words of assurance to him and the doctor. She thanked the doctor for all she had done to help. Titus wondered what would cause a person to fight so hard against the Fear.

"Is there nothing more we can do?" the First was asking the doctor.

"I am sorry," she said, seeming genuine to Titus.

He walked over to her and whispered in her ear "you should have done more," then he stood and chuckled, thinking of all the grief it would bring her. Fear laughed in appreciation of Titus's work.

"What about experimental therapies?" the First asked, sounding desperate even to himself.

"We have tried everything we can," the doctor answered patiently. She would sit with them as long as was needed, and the knowledge of that infuriated Titus even more. His only comfort came from knowing that she didn't have the light. No matter how kind, no matter how loving, eventually she would spend her eternity with him.

He considered what a tremendous waste it was spending your life being kind. A "good" person, by the human standards and still ending up with the same eternity as the demons. He smiled at the thought perhaps that was the greatest of Lucifer's deceptions. He was so lost in the idea that he had tuned out the surrounding conversation. It was the word Tanzania that brought him back from his own thoughts. Panic flooded him. How had Tanzania come up? He looked frantically from the First and his wife who both sat silently looking at the doctor waiting for a response. She was pondering their question, carefully considering her answer.

"Yes," she began with caution. "I have heard of a healer," she was hesitant, weighing each word carefully.

"Then you know of Kikombe?" the First said hope in his voice.

"Yes. But there is no evidence that it works. Tests by the ministry of health were inconclusive, there is no scientific evidence that it would do anything," she was firm but kind knowing that he was grasping. Fear laughed, pleased with herself for driving them in this direction. Titus felt nervous, they were playing right into the King's hand.

"Thousands of people have gone to Samunge to see him," the First answered.

"And many have died," the doctor cautioned.

Yes! Titus thought Fear could grab hold of this.

"While waiting," the First countered in defiance, his voice both desperate and hopeful. The doctor did not immediately reply. Titus moved slowly, unsure of what to do. The First and his wife going to Tanzania would be problematic.

"Is there anything more you can offer my wife other than making her comfortable as she dies?" the First asked without animosity but with finality.

"No," the doctor admitted before Titus could stop her.

"Then we have no other hope," he said, rising from the chair. "We have nothing to lose," he took his wife's hand and led her from the room. He would take her to Tanzania.

"NOOOO!" Titus yelled in rage, sulfur pouring from him and filling the room with smoke.

Chapter 50

The Ninth had never been to a refugee camp before, and she was poorly prepared for what she found. She had been briefed that it was overpopulated and that supplies were low. Both had been substantial understatements. Because other countries were refusing them entry, they were forced to remain in a space that could not support them. The camp had nearly a hundred thousand more refugees than they were designed to house. There was a dire shortage of food, housing and fuel all essential items.

Those who had arrived early were issued standard tent-like structures for shelter. The Ninth had lived in similar tents in other countries. But the tents had run out long ago, and the families were left to build their own shelters most of them fashioning a simple one-room hut made of mud. The Ninth was assigned one that had been erected near the medical center.

The Ninth had been told that violence was an issue in all refugee camps. She supposed having that many people in such deplorable living conditions sort of lent itself to such problems. She wondered why the world used such a system. She thought of a time when the Christ child had had to flee his home in the middle of the night under the threat of death. She wondered what things Mary and Joseph had packed as they fled. And she said a silent prayer of thanks that Egypt had let them in and not placed them in a refugee camp within the reach of King Herod.

She had ridden into the camp in the back of a supply truck next to bandages, medicines, rice, and live goats. When they arrived, the goats had been the first thing removed. Without ceremony, each goat was slaughtered as it was pulled from the truck. They would be skinned and used to provide food for the families. The Ninth disembarked from the truck with no choice but to step in their blood.

There was no refrigeration system, so the goats by necessity had to be butchered and sold the same day. The experience had left an impression on her. As a result, she avoided the meat market if she could. The smell was overwhelming, and the sight of the goats in various stages of slaughter and butcher was more than she cared for. After being in the camp for a while, she realized that the arrival of goats was rare, meat was an expensive commodity.

But even without the goats, the overwhelming smell of death and rotting sewage covered the camp, perfuming your clothes and bedding. Despite the deplorable conditions, she had fallen in love with the people in a way she had never imagined possible. They had a love so pure and a sense of resiliency that she had never seen anywhere else.

Her heart broke each day as she worked endless hours in the makeshift medical center that was no more than an oversized tent, with grime clinging to the walls promising to spread disease to any who dared to enter. Unlike in American hospitals patients had little to no privacy.

The medical center had few supplies left, and what remained was either useless to their needs or severely rationed. Only the worst patients got bandaging or medications. But as she had learned from her prior posts, not having supplies did not stem the flow of those needing care, and so out of necessity, she quickly learned to be creative.

People would camp outside the medical center in hopes of seeing a doctor. The heat was suffocating, and those who were not suffering from heat exhaustion or heat stroke when they got in line usually were by the time they were seen. The Ninth felt discouraged that no matter how many patients were treated in the clinic the line never seemed to get any shorter. Most days she came in before the sun and stayed late into the wee hours, eventually collapsing into bed exhausted.

"Doctor," a soft voice broke her concentration as she worked to stitch up the foot of a young boy. She looked up to see a woman smiling at her shyly.

"I brought you some coffee and a potato," the woman said, offering what was to be the Ninth's only meal of the day. While it was a meager offering the Ninth treasured it no less, she knew the cost of luxuries such as food. She also knew that this simple gesture was one between friends, an offering from a woman who had little to smile about, and yet she found a way.

The Ninth smiled back and said a quick prayer for the woman she called M. M was the closest thing the Ninth had had to a friend in years. She had not intended to become friends with M, the woman was probably old enough to be her mother, although she didn't know for sure. But the friendship had snuck up on her, and she found that it was a welcomed intruder. In fact, it made her aware that her isolation over the years had cost her far more than she realized.

"Thank you," the Ninth offered, holding her gloved hands up to indicate she could not take the gift just yet. M set the coffee and potato on a nearby mayo stand, then left without another word.

Chapter 51

M was a businesswoman with a loving husband, a nice home, and three beautiful children or at least she had been. Now she was a widow living in a mud hut with only one young son remaining. Her face bore the scars of the physical trauma she had endured, but her eyes did not betray the horrors that she had experienced.

She had been in her modest kitchen cleaning up from dinner when she had heard the first shot. The sound attracted her attention, but it sounded distant like a neighboring village. The screams had been much closer. Fear and adrenaline flooded through her and she turned to run to find her children. Her husband had been right there, the look on his face telling her all she needed to know.

"Get the children; flee to your sisters. I will meet you there." His voice serious, his grip on her arms firm yet loving. She wanted to argue to refuse to leave him to insist that he come with her. But the screams were getting louder the gunfire more pronounced, and she knew there was no time to argue. She would flee with her children. She nodded her head slightly to signify she would comply, then she threw her arms around him, pulling him close, smelling him one last time.

"I love you," he whispered gently before releasing her. He lovingly wiped the tear that had slid down her cheek. "It will be ok." He tried to smile, but his eyes betrayed him, they both knew it would not be ok. The children rushed into the room their fear palpable.

"Papa!" his middle child clung to him sure that if she held on tightly, everything would be fine. He hugged her, not wanting to ever let go, knowing it was most likely the last time he would ever hold her. He said a silent prayer for them all.

"Listen to your mama," he said as his eyes met each of theirs. A loud explosion shook the house. "Go!" he ordered, rushing out the front as they ran from the back.

M carried the youngest child as they fled the house amid explosions and gunfire. She would lead her children to the edge of the woods, hoping they would be safer there. A stray bullet smashed into the back of her twelve-year-old daughter's knee, exiting through the front, and sending the girl tumbling to the ground in agony, unable to walk.

Unsure of what to do, M commanded her daughter to stay down while she ran the other two children the short distance to the woods. She looked at their precious faces so terrified, so young. She dug deep, searching for her own strength, "go to the cave. Stay there until I come for you. Do not leave for any reason!" She turned and ran back to her injured daughter who was so vulnerable and exposed.

But M was not the only one who had taken notice of her daughter. An insurgent had found her and was dragging her by her hair, while her daughter screamed and fought to free herself. M ran toward him catapulting herself onto his back, clawing at his eyes and face, rage taking over her body at the sight of her endangered child.

The man let go of her daughter long enough to swing at M's face in a desperate attempt to free himself from her grip. She continued to punch his face, biting, and screaming as she did. Suddenly, without warning the world went black.

M awoke disoriented and in excruciating pain. She could hear the screams of her daughter. But she couldn't make sense of what was happening. She felt a significant pressure on her body as if someone had laid a hefty sack of corn on her. She struggled to open her eyes to understand the screams that mingled with laughter. When her mind finally realized what was happening, she fought the man on top her, desperate to get to her daughter and free her from the beasts who raped her mercilessly.

But she was not strong enough. No matter how hard she struggled, she could not break free. She was beaten for her efforts, but there was no pain that her attackers could bestow upon her worse than what they had already done by forcing her to watch her daughter be brutalized.

For three days M and her daughter had been held captive repeatedly raped and beaten. Her daughter's cries had eventually stopped. Initially, M thought her daughter had been killed, but the girl had lost all hope, a fate much worse than death. M began to cry out begging the King for death, but death did not come.

On the third day of their captivity a firefight broke out, and the village was once again thrown into chaos. It had allowed M and her daughter an opportunity to escape. Fever ravaged her daughter's frail and broken body, a direct result of the untreated bullet wound. With her daughter unable to stand or walk, M put the girl on her back and carried her, desperate to escape the horrors of the village.

When she arrived at the cave exhausted and weak, she found her other two children frightened, starving, and alone, but alive. She lowered her oldest daughter from her back only to discover that her injuries had been too severe; she had not survived.

Chapter 52

When M and her two remaining children arrived at the refugee camp, the medical team had treated their physical wounds, but only God could heal her emotional ones. The Ninth had not known M then. She had not met M until the unthinkable happened.

Firewood in the camp ran out. If M had any hopes of feeding her family, she had to venture into the surrounding woods and collect more.

M and her ten-year-old daughter made the three-mile hike to gather wood. They had not seen the men hiding in the woods, but she had heard her daughter's screams as the men attempted to abduct her. Both M and her daughter were brutally beaten and raped. Believing the women to be dead their attackers left them.

When M regained consciousness, she placed her daughter across her back and crawled back to the camp. The Ninth was walking back to her hut at the end of a very long day when she saw them. She had worked tirelessly to save the girl, but she did not have the supplies she needed, the girl succumbed to her injuries.

The Ninth had no idea what M's real name was, the woman refused to tell her. Each time the Ninth would ask, M would shake her head and say, "Mimi ndio Mungu amesahau," Swahili for, "I am the one that God has forgotten." And so, the Ninth called her M because M sounded like it was short for something.

M was the first of many who eventually found their way to the clinic after being raped or brutalized. The Ninth treated two to three a week.

Young girls would go missing for days, only to later be discovered being held captive in the hut of a much older man. Finding them took time, time many of them did not have. Some of the girls never reappeared; the Ninth could only guess what happened to them.

The women of the camp were left in a precarious position. Most of them were widows and to cook and feed their children they needed firewood. To get firewood, they had to leave the camp and go to the woods where they were often threatened, kidnapped, or brutalized. They began traveling in groups, but often so did the attackers.

The women were faced each day with difficult decisions regarding leaving their children alone in the camp while they ventured into the woods or taking them with them. Neither option was void of risk. Many of the women began to bond together. They would leave their children under the supervision of a few women while the rest went to gather firewood. If any of them did not survive the other women would take over care of their children. No one went to look for those who did not return, it was not safe to do so.

A few months after the women began the new rotation cycle an American businessman showed up in a suit looking shockingly out-of-place.

"Who is that?" the Ninth asked M as they walked from the market back to the clinic.

"The devil," M said without hesitating.

The Ninth laughed at that and took another bite of the apple she was eating. It was particularly juicy, and she felt as if it were a treasured prize.

"He is here recruiting," M said more seriously.

"Recruiting?"

"Yes, he runs a big electric company a day's journey from here. He is offering high-paying jobs and housing." M said as if the man were selling mud pies something everyone had plenty of.

The Ninth stopped in her tracks looking at M in shock.

"M this could be your chance out of here away from this place!" But M only shook her head no and continued their walk toward the clinic.

"Why not?" the Ninth asked incredulously.

"I have watched him. He only takes the strongest men and young girls. He is the devil." She said it as if she were saying his hair was black as if she could not understand why the Ninth did not see what was so obvious.

The man continued to come to the camp every week, bringing with him chocolates and bottled water. Each week he would distribute his goods into the eager hands, grateful for the small treat. And in return, he would depart with his truck full of people quite willing to leave behind the dangers of the camp and venture on, to promises of a good job and a safe place to live.

As they approached the clinic M stopped. A serious look took over her face. The Ninth waited, unsure of what to expect.

"I need you to promise me something," she began, her eyes starting to well with tears; her voice shaking.

"What is it?" the Ninth asked. M had already endured so much, they had been through so much together, there was nothing the Ninth wouldn't do for her.

"My son," she began emotion cutting her words off before she could get it out. But she didn't need to say it the Ninth already knew. Every week when it was M's turn to go into the woods, she would leave her son at the clinic in the care of the Ninth. It was not a sanctioned thing to do, and the Ninth felt sure that if anyone noticed she would be told the boy could not be in the clinic. But fortunately, there was far too much chaos for anyone to notice.

The Ninth also fully understood from the very beginning what it meant. M was putting her son's life in the hands of the Ninth expecting that if she did not survive, the Ninth would take him in as her own.

The Ninth didn't think M fully understood how impossible of a request that was. The boy had no identification, no birth certificate, and no way for her to obtain a passport. In addition, the Ninth had no legal precedence for doing so. She doubted the Tanzanian government would even allow it, but admittedly she had no idea. If they were to allow it would the United States let her bring him into the country? She somehow doubted it.

The harsh reality was if M died the boy would become an orphan. She saw no reason to mention any of this to M. She knew her own heart, and that she was quite fond of the boy, in fact, she loved him and would be happy to care for him. She knew she would do everything within her power to honor the request. Her own eyes watering she put her arm lovingly around M and nodded to affirm. In comfortable silence, they continued their walk along the dirt path toward the clinic.

"Excuse me?" a familiar voice said. The Ninth looked up, startled.

Chapter 53

"Professor?" the Ninth said shock and disbelief clearly in her voice. The Fourth merely smiled in response, giving it time to register.

"Professor!" she threw her arms around his frame emotion swelling over her for a reason she could not explain. She clung to him longer than was necessary, longer than was comfortable but she didn't care. Seeing him reminded her that she was desperate for a connection. She had starved her soul for so long without even realizing it, but seeing him, in this place, reminded her.

The Fourth stood somewhat stiff, slightly taken aback by the unexpected emotional display.

"What are you doing here?" she asked, wiping the tears that threatened to spill from her eyes. Stepping back, she stared into the familiar face.

"I hear you have an outbreak?" he answered, his eyes raised in question.

"Um…" the Ninth hesitated only out of shock seeing him in this place was so unexpected. "Well, we have a flu-like illness going through the camp," she suddenly felt like she was back in school doing rounds. It had been a long time.

"You came all this way for a little bug?" her mind began to clear, and realization began clawing its way to the surface. The Fourth watched as she set her emotions aside and returned to her scientific mind a space he found much more comfortable.

Her eyes betrayed several things to him at once understanding that this illness was potentially more significant than she thought and that she did not care to discuss it while in the presence of the woman who stood beside her. He agreed with both.

"This is T." He offered, turning slightly to introduce the young man standing silently beside him. "We work together," he finished considering that a full introduction of all the essential points. T stepped forward with a broad smile on his face and extended his hand in greeting. The Ninth shook his hand and introduced M to them.

"M, perhaps you would give me a tour of the camp?" T suggested. M hesitated, looking nervously at the Ninth who nodded slightly, indicating it was ok she would be safe. M agreed although the Ninth could tell she was uncomfortable with the idea. Reluctantly M walked away with T secretly wishing they had just asked her to leave so they could speak privately.

When T and M were out of earshot, the Ninth turned back to the Fourth.

"What is it," she asked?

"We got a sample of a virus a BSL4," he paused for a second to let that sink in before continuing. "We think it may have originated here. I came for a sample."

The Ninth laughed in relief. What they had was no BSL4.

"I'm afraid you made a very long trip for nothing. And we have no equipment here for collecting samples."

The Fourth didn't flinch. "I brought equipment. I just need to see the sick. How many do you have?"

The Ninth again fought against the panic of being a student caught without having done her homework. She had no idea how many were sick. This wasn't that type of environment. They didn't really keep records there was no reporting mechanism, patients didn't really have charts. That wasn't how it worked here. Charts cost money something they didn't have.

"Professor," she began feeling slightly ashamed but unsure how to help him understand.

"I just need a rough estimate. Have you seen hundreds? Thousands?" while she clearly struggled to release their former relationship of professor and student; he did not. He viewed her as a colleague, he wanted her to move to that too. It would be much easier to get things done that way.

"Maybe a few hundred cases," she began walking with him toward the clinic suddenly nervous that she has missed something. He seemed so sure, and she knew he wouldn't have come this far if he didn't have some evidence that they were dealing with something serious. She had been practicing third world medicine so long that she felt self-conscious trying to explain things to a first world practitioner, someone who had been involved in her training someone who had taught her the way things were supposed to be done. He walked alongside her comfortably.

"Tell me about it," he asked as they walked.

She had to think hard. The clinic saw hundreds if not thousands of patients each day. Each day she had to tell a mother that her child would not survive. She held the hands of the dying and watched children starve to death. She scraped pus from wounds fighting nausea from the smell of rotten flesh. She had helped amputate limbs without anesthesia, she delivered babies only to bury them. Everyday women and girls were raped, brutalized, and left forever changed. What was a cough amid that?

"They present with a cough, dehydration and sometimes diarrhea. The cough is non-productive. Lungs usually sound clear. Low-grade fever, headache, body aches. A few have complained of dry eyes or blurry vision." She hadn't really been tracking. There may be more or less. Some of those symptoms could be completely unrelated. She couldn't be sure.

"We see lots of dehydration, so it is hard to know precisely which symptoms are related to the cough and which are the dehydration," she offered in defense.

"Understood," he said, continuing to follow her toward the clinic. "Any deaths?"

"Not within the clinic. If they die at home we wouldn't really know," had she just called their dwellings "home,"?

"Do you know the R0?" the Ninth panicked just a little searching her mind to remember what an R0 was. She dug deep remembering it was something epidemiological. That had been the course she had done poorly in. Finally, she stumbled across it the basic reproductive rate of a disease the higher the number, the more people a single person could infect. A disease with an R0 of four meant that for each person infected, they would infect four others. How could he possibly expect her to know that?

"No," she kept her answer simple. She knew from school that he preferred it that way.

"Any chance you have someone hospitalized with it?" he asked, hopeful but realizing that that was probably asking too much.

"No," she again kept it simple. She could have explained that they didn't really have a hospital at least not anything that traditional medicine would consider a hospital. They had another tent where they kept people too sick to allow to leave. But even that wasn't entirely true. Often, they sent people back to their own dwellings to die. It sounded so harsh when she had to say it aloud to someone who wasn't living it.

But the reality was they could only do so much. The hospital wing was reserved for those who had just undergone surgery or for those who they thought they could save. Even then it was not a guarantee that they would keep them. Sometimes they were sent back to their tent, and the family looked after them.

They arrived at the clinic and found M and T already there. M nodded at the Ninth and left. It was her day to gather wood. The Ninth said a quick prayer for M's safety and entered the clinic with the Fourth and T. She intended to show them around, but the Fourth didn't seem to need or want a tour.

"We brought supplies," he offered, and she found herself saying a quick prayer of thanks. A huge smile covered her face it had been a long time since they had had supplies.

"I also brought suits." He paused to give her a minute to process it. He wanted them to wear Biohazard suits?

"People will panic," she argued. They didn't even know if they had the virus he was looking for. She had been walking among them all day if they did have it he thought she probably already had it. Biohazard suits would serve no purpose other than to cause panic in the camp.

"I know. But if this is what we think it is, we need to take every precaution. We may have to quarantine the camp." He said it factually as if it were the most normal thing in the world. As if every reasonable person would see the logic in his words.

"Do you know how many people we have sent out of here in just the last week? The Wanda project has been taking them off in truckloads. If we have a BSL4 disease, we have already spread it. Putting on suits and issuing a quarantine won't do anything but incite panic," she offered her opinion and knowledge with gentleness and respect; he was, after all, her professor.

"I understand," he said, acknowledging her position, but not agreeing with it. "I have suits, and I am required to wear them; I am also responsible for T so we will be suiting up. You make your own decisions. But if we find it is a BSL4" he let that hang there for a minute. She nodded her head in understanding. If they had what he came here looking for, she was probably already contaminated, but she would put on the suit to prevent spreading it to others.

"Explain it however you would like," he said leaving that in her hands. "Whatever you think would cause the least amount of concern. T help me with the supplies?" he added. They walked from the small hut and headed back to a van they had parked at the entrance of the camp.

When T and the Fourth returned from the van, they were both in Biohazard suits. They made several trips back and forth carrying supplies. The Ninth rolled her eyes in an overly extreme way when the locals looked at her in question. She hoped the exaggerated gesture said, "crazy westerners" but she couldn't be sure. A few laughed, and to her knowledge, no one seemed to panic.

When the supplies were all unloaded, the Fourth went about putting them away in a manner that seemed organized and well thought out. He did it quickly, and without fuss, it was what needed to be done, and so he did. The Ninth watched in amazement. It was a scorching day. Inside his suit he had to be cooking, and yet he showed no indication of that. He just worked. When the supplies were where they belonged or at least where he assigned them, he started treating patients.

The Ninth was thankful for the help. Seeing him in action made her more comfortable. He was a great doctor, and the people loved him. She watched in awe as he seemed to intuitively understand what needed to be done and the limited supplies with which they had to work. He didn't ask questions he didn't need to, and he didn't expect her to chit-chat with him as they worked. He just worked, doing his best to provide compassionate care to each patient.

T was not a physician, he was a researcher, but even he made himself useful without needing to be asked or directed. He entertained the children while they waited, walked the line doing triage and brought patients in according to their complaint. It helped tremendously to keep things smooth and organized. Patients moved through in an efficient way that she had not experienced since arriving at the camp.

It did not take long before she realized that T was sending all the patients with the disease in question to the Fourth. It was, of course, intentional; he was drawing blood from each of them labeling the vacutainers and placing them in a cooler on the dry ice that he had brought with him specifically for this purpose.

Chapter 54

The hammock rocked gently in the breeze. The day was just a little cool in the sixties just the way she liked it. The sun was out in full force warming her face as the hammock swung gently coaxing her to sleep. She snuggled closer to her husband nestling into him, comforted by his scent. Mordecai stood guard beside her as she drifted off to sleep.

She was standing in a barren field with grass that was dry and sickly looking. The sun beat down on her mercilessly. The smell of dirt and rotting flesh rushed up to meet her. People swarmed about her their skin rotting from their bodies moaning out in misery. In the distance, she could see a fire, and she knew that it was being used to burn the dead.

It took a moment to acclimate and figure out where she was. Things were chaotic hectic, but there was an eerie silence broken only by the sounds of coughing and the murmuring of hushed voices. She looked around her trying to take it in trying to make sense of where she was.

"Doctor!" she heard a familiar voice call. "Doctor!" the voice called again. Suddenly, she realized they were calling her. For a second, she considered telling them she was a physician's assistant, not a doctor, but then the idea seemed strangely out-of-place given the circumstances.

She searched for the voice, but she didn't see anyone she knew she saw only the sick. The field with the sickly grass had been transformed into a makeshift hospital of some sort. No that wasn't true it was more of an emergency triaging station with thousands of the sick and dying.

"Can you help him?" the voice repeated. It seemed to be closer this time. The Seventh looked anxious, frightened even. The Twelfth realized she was kneeling over a young man who was dying. His eyes were shriveled and unseeing like dried raisins in the sockets. His skin was decayed and rotting away in large patches. His mouth hung open, and she could see that most of his tongue had rotted away, leaving him unable to speak, incapable of anything more than animalistic groans.

The Seventh's eyes were desperate, large tears threatened to pour over. She struggled to maintain control she looked at the Twelfth with a mix of desperation and hope. The Twelfth looked away from the Seventh; she could not bear to see the anguish. Instead, she focused on the dark-haired young man who seemed so important. The Twelfth said a silent prayer as she began to check his vitals and assess how bad he was.

She called out for medicines and supplies in a way that made her believe this place was familiar to her even though it wasn't. A news crew meandered through filming the dying. A beautiful woman walked backward in front of the camera offering commentary as she went. She spoke in a solemn tone the way you would in a funeral home. The camera crew approached filming the Twelfth as she worked to save the young man.

The Twelfth wasn't sure what to do. The Seventh wept gently beside her. A cracking sound caught her attention. She turned toward the young man who lay nearly lifeless on the cot, his chest pulsated as if the very life inside him battled to break free. The camera crew caught it all.

In horror, she saw his chest crack open, and the arm of a beast reach out. She fell backward grabbing the Seventh as she did. The young man seemed to turn inside out to transform before their eyes into a seven-headed dragon. He towered over them, the fire roaring from his nostrils caught the parched grass of the field on fire, and within seconds they were enveloped in thick smoke and a raging fire. The flames raced toward the makeshift clinic.

Panic engulfed the people, and they began to run tripping over cots the dying and each other. The Twelfth grabbed the Seventh and pulled herself to her feet trying to put space between them and the seven-headed beast. Holding tightly to the Seventh's arm, she ran toward a small building she could just make out in the distance.

The beast roared behind her thrashing about and snatching people from the ground so that he could toss their bodies into the fire. The Twelfth could hear their screams as their skin sizzled and popped from the flames, but they did not die. Instead, they suffered in agony with no relief.

She ran, dragging the Seventh with her until she felt like her lungs were going to explode. They reached the small shack-like building she had seen from a distance, and she raced inside slamming the door behind them.

Dozens of eyes looked up in shock at the sudden intrusion. The Twelfth was equally shocked, staring into the eyes of so many from Platitude. How was it possible that they were here? The Sixth rushed forward throwing her arms around the Seventh tears of relief tumbling down her cheeks.

Suddenly the roof of the small shack was ripped from the building and tossed to the side causing the ground to shake. The beast grabbed the Sixth flinging her like a rag doll high into the air, his powerful teeth snapping at her desperate to destroy her.

The Twelfth jerked awake disrupting the hammock and sending her and her husband careening toward the ground. Mordecai was so caught off guard by it that he could do nothing to soften their fall.

"What was that about?" her husband asked, laughing from the fall, and rubbing his tailbone as he stood up.

"I had the weirdest dream," she answered, accepting his hand, and pulling herself to her feet.

"Another one?" he asked, surprise filling his voice. After having the same dream for two years, it seemed strange that she suddenly was having new ones. It concerned him, but he thought better of mentioning that.

"Yes," she said.

Mordecai walked closer, he was eager to hear what new message she had received. He couldn't help but wonder how long it would take her to recognize her dreams for what they were.

"I think it may be about the same thing as the last one, the plague of Zechariah," she said with trepidation. She told her husband about the dream as the angels slowly arrived and listened intently.

"Do you think it means something?" she asked, afraid of hearing his answer. The woman with the wild red hair arrived and put her hand on the husband of the Twelfth.

"It may be time to consider that it's a prophecy of some sort," her husband said, struggling to believe it himself. The angels waited with bated breath. The woman with the wild red hair looked at their faces and smiled.

"Maybe," the Twelfth said not fully convinced. Foreboding rippled through her. The angels cheered. The woman with the wild red hair laughed softly then took her leave.

The Twelfth pulled out her phone, she needed to assure herself that her friends from Platitude were ok. Quickly she group texted them and waited anxiously for their replies. While she waited, she wrestled with what it could mean but even as she let herself accept that perhaps it was a prophecy, part of her felt foolish for entertaining the idea. Slowly, one by one, texts began to trickle in—offering updates, requesting prayer, sharing news, all but the Sixth.

Chapter 55—The Sixth

The Sixth sat at the small bistro table soaking in the sunshine. She loved the summer. Some people didn't like the heat, but she savored it. The temperature was causing a light sweat to moisten her skin and send her sunglasses slowly gliding down her nose. The waiter sat her drink down, and without a word, he laid a croissant with a pat of honey butter and a small knife slightly to her left. She nodded her gratitude and pushed her sunglasses back into place.

Her phone buzzed, and she glanced quickly at the screen. The Twelfth had been texting her for several days, and the Sixth had been ignoring it. Not because she didn't want to talk to her, but because she wasn't sure how she could ever explain how she was. And the Twelfth always seemed to know when she wasn't being honest.

With deliberate thought, she gently picked up the croissant and split it into two spreading butter on half. She had specifically ordered a strong red wine to complement the sweetness of the croissant and butter. She didn't typically have wine with lunch, but today wasn't typical.

The Sixth took a deep breath and tried to make sense of what she had found. It couldn't be right, she couldn't be right. And yet for months she had been digging, searching to find out what Project Gorilla was. Months ago, when she had first found the discrepancy during an internal audit, her supervisor explained it away. But the answer hadn't sat right with the Sixth. A small voice inside her just kept whispering that something was wrong. The warning slowly got louder and louder until the Sixth could not ignore it any longer.

It hadn't been easy to research it without raising suspicion. But the code name kept appearing in invoices and budget statements. Initially, it had been small amounts, well small for a corporate energy company. But slowly. without fanfare. larger and larger numbers began to appear. Sometimes the amounts were expenditures, sometimes revenue. The income far exceeded what was going out. Whatever it was, it was profitable, perhaps the most profitable thing the company was doing.

To complicate matters, project gorilla seemed to be a subsidiary of a larger project called Wanda. It was one small piece of what appeared to be a more massive operation. With enough digging, the Sixth found that without Wanda, and her feeder programs, the bottom line for the company was not healthy. She doubted the shareholders realized just how anemic the company really was. But Wanda kept the coffers well-padded providing millions of dollars of profit.

Then this morning it had happened. One of the senior associates was in a high-stakes meeting and needed some data they had not prepared. The Sixth was the only one available to retrieve it. The associate sent her a text message with the request and the password to access the data. After retrieving the information and sending it back, the Sixth sat staring at her computer for precisely eleven and half minutes struggling to decide what to do. She had the password she could sneak back in and find Wanda. But should she?

After precisely eleven and half minutes her phone rang, causing her to jump and draw the attention of the man in the neighboring office. Glass offices were not ideal for covert operations. The voice of the Seventh rang out from the other end of the phone. She was once again telling stories of the new man in her life, but mainly chatting about nothing.

"Something is going on with you. I can tell. What is it?" the Seventh pressed. The Sixth knew there was no point in trying to hide it, the Seventh knew her too well.

"I have the passcode, and all the executives are in a meeting" She didn't need to say more the Seventh knew about Wanda. But even that small amount of information had been a mistake. The Seventh was always one for adventure and had advocated for using the password to solve the mystery. Her hands shaking with trepidation, the Sixth had done just that.

Upon initial examination, Wanda seemed to the novice to be some type of safari experience. There were hotels, car services doctors, police pharmacies and clothing stores associated with it. All of them listed as expenditures. The Sixth let out an enormous sigh of relief. But why the secrecy over offering a safari experience in Tanzania it was common there? Then she found the link to all the other countries. The Sixth explained it away. People from those nations weren't precluded from a safari, were they? They would need services there as well to arrange their trips.

Further digging only led to more questions. The hotels on the list were shady. Surely a safari package that costs what these seemed to would not house guests in such low-level hotels. She dug and dug all morning until she landed on a list of names and prices. The list had had hundreds of names all female the first of which was Wanda. Beside each name was a column that read "acquired on." There was a date for each. Another column said, "sold on" some had dates others did not. There was also a running tally of cost for each. Purchase price revenue expenditures and sale price if they had been permanently sold. Some of them had an "out of circuit" column with a large black x in it. Wanda was out of the circuit.

The expenditure list was coded with a code key at the bottom of the spreadsheet. Codes covered things like clothing, medical treatment, medication, transportation, bail, etc. The Sixth plugged a USB drive into her computer and began copying files as quickly as she could.

"You've uncovered something big," the Seventh whispered into her ear.

"I haven't uncovered anything not really. All we've done is generate more questions. This could be completely innocent," the Sixth said trying not to jump to conclusions. Her hands trembled slightly as she willed the files to copy more quickly.

"Do you think they are dealing in illegal diamonds? You know that is a big industry in Tanzania," the Seventh offered. But the Sixth didn't think it was diamonds. She didn't want to admit what she thought it was, and she didn't have to because the senior associate walked into the Sixth's office. She jumped, startled by the intrusion, and quickly closed the files hoping she hadn't left too much of a fingerprint.

"Thank you, Miss. Evans, I will get those documents right over to you," she said into the phone. The Seventh began firing questions understanding that the Sixth had been interrupted. But the Sixth didn't answer the rapid-fire questions, she hung the phone up without another word trying not to appear suspicious, hoping the senior associate didn't notice she was sweating.

She didn't want them to know she had been looking. She wasn't even sure what she had been looking at. The senior associate thanked the Sixth for getting her the needed data and left without further comment.

The Sixth waited two minutes and then tried to log back in, but the password had been changed. She had only gotten a handful of files moved to the USB. She felt like it wasn't enough. She wasn't even sure what it wasn't enough for.

She wasn't sure what to do next or if she even needed to do anything. Couldn't she just ignore it? But something inside her knew she couldn't. She quickly called the Seventh back, which only seemed to complicate matters.

"All roads lead to Tanzania get on a plane meet me there! This can't be a coincidence." The Seventh was insistent, but the Sixth made no promises. Getting involved with this, whatever "this" was, didn't seem wise. And going to Tanzania? Honestly? It seemed foolish. Going there with the Seventh? Well, that was destined to be trouble. Fun, memorable, but trouble all the same.

Instead of deciding she opted to sit at this outdoor café eating baked goods and drinking wine in the middle of the day. She had chosen a Cabernet hoping it would help settle her. It was stronger than she typically liked her reds, but today she needed it. She took another sip, trying to calm her frayed nerves, and stop her shaking hands.

Chapter 56

The Sixth took several steadying breaths and tried to sort through what she knew to be factual. Fact: Project Wanda had nothing to do with electricity. Fact: Project Wanda was highly profitable with projections in the billions. Fact: Project Wanda had branches on every continent. Fact: it all started with their energy company in Tanzania.

Of course, that last one may not be factual. Perhaps it just seemed that way; the Sixth had more questions than answers, and she had no proof. She wasn't even sure what she was getting proof of. She had no idea who knew about Project Wanda or who she could tell. Who could be trusted? That part was easy. None but the Seventh. But even that wasn't foolproof. The Seventh was spontaneous, quick to rush to action slow to consider the consequences or seek counsel. But the Sixth knew despite the Seventh's spontaneity she just might be the only one the Sixth could trust.

It wasn't like she could march into anyone's office and admit she had used a password that wasn't hers to look at files she was not authorized to see. That would be a career-ending move with nothing to show for it. When she had approached her supervisor months ago, he dismissed it. He may even be part of it. Based on the expenditures listed on the balance sheet it was apparent whatever "it" was it was bigger than her.

"You know what is happening," the woman with the wild red hair whispered gently. But the Sixth resisted. She didn't want to think about it, she didn't want to admit what she thought she knew. Even considering it brought memories to mind that she had spent many years ignoring. Despite her best efforts her mind started to dust those memories off and pull at the scars of old wounds. A single tear ran down her cheek. The Sixth reached up quickly and wiped it away with the back of her hand, crying was not something she did, at least not publicly. She did not care to show weakness.

She pushed unpleasant memories back. She would not allow herself to think of such things. That was a long time ago. That girl had been young, too young to protect herself. She wasn't that girl anymore, she had learned how to defend herself, she had become an expert at keeping people far outside her circle of trust. Bitterness bubbled to the surface, even as she struggled to suppress the memories.

She had only been eight years old. She took another sip of the wine and then placed the croissant in her mouth the butter gave it just a hint of sweet as it melted slightly in her mouth. She focused on those sensations in a feeble attempt to keep the memories from overwhelming her.

The Sixth's story was so closely tied to the story of another girl. A young girl with beautiful brown eyes and jet-black hair that she always wore in pigtails. A young girl who found her courage and did what the Sixth could not. While the girl had never confided in the Sixth, she eventually found her voice and told her mom what the youth minister was doing to her. Even as a second grader, the Sixth had understood the courage telling had taken, because the Sixth had not had that courage. For over a year she had just endured, crumbled, tried to survive.

The girl's mother went to the church, and for months they did nothing. Where was her proof? He was a man of God, she was a young girl. Girls tended to be melodramatic everyone knew that.

These were grave allegations such things could not be left to the word of a young child it was, after all, this man's reputation on the line his career.

And so, while they tried to silence the girl and her mother, while they attempted to discredit them the Sixth continued to be abused by him. While they waited and debated, the youth minister began to offer the Sixth to other men, allowing them to abuse her in the same way he had. Still, she remained silent too afraid and ashamed to ever tell anyone, but secretly she prayed for the girl with the pigtails and her mother.

The Sixth listened as some members of the church debated the truth in the girl's claims. Few people at the church knew of course. No, this was the type of thing best handled by the deacons. But the Sixth heard the stories when her own mother would sit with the girl's mother late into the night comforting her.

Eventually, another girl came forward and then another. But still, the Sixth remained silent. Even when her mother asked her directly, she denied that anything had happened to her.

The Sixth's stomach lurched to recall it. She tried desperately to shove the memories back, to keep them at bay where they belonged. But the woman with the wild red hair pushed her forward straight through the middle of the worst of it.

Eventually, the girl's mother gave up on the church and went to the police. The church allowed the minister to resign, citing the sin of adultery as the reason. For a while, the Sixth believed he would walk away from it free while she would carry the scars with her forever.

But the girl's parents made sure that didn't happen. He was prosecuted and imprisoned. But the Sixth was imprisoned too. She had constructed her own prison and dwelled in it where it was safe; safe but in no way pleasant. She knew no joy.

The church criticized the girl's family heavily for violating the Bible when they took the issue outside the church. Her parents eventually changed churches and got her counseling. The Sixth had never told anyone what happened to her. When all the other girls spoke up, the Sixth had remained silent, and she had never quite forgiven herself for that. And then she had met the Seventh, and for some reason, she had trusted the Seventh with her deepest secret. The Seventh had proven trustworthy keeping the secret for many years.

The memories were unwelcomed, and the Sixth struggled to push them away, she did not care to dwell on them ever again. But the woman with the wild red hair pushed on because memories were to be treasured they were to be learned from they could be used to strengthen and inspire others.

For years the Sixth had rejected the church and all who went there. But eventually, she had found her way out of her prison. She had realized that she could forgive even when she could not resolve her anger and her pain.

Perhaps harder than forgiving him was forgiving herself. She had cloaked herself in shame and guilt. And in time she convinced herself that she was somehow to blame. What had she done to draw his attention? Why hadn't she told anyone? She couldn't answer those questions.

Eventually, she realized that she followed the savior, not his followers. Being in Platitude at the college with the other women she had met there helped her with her journey back. It was there amid all the madness that she determined this one man who had hurt her was but one man. She would not let him define her. She would not give him power over her any longer. She was finally able to acknowledge that one-day God would use this for his glory.

"This is the day," the woman with the wild red hair whispered to her. But the Sixth was not yet willing to hear it.

Chapter 57

Titus watched from a safe distance he was not foolish enough to risk getting too close when the woman with the wild red hair was present. And so, he watched from across the street. The battle around the Sixth was great. He counted six warriors and three guardians surrounding her. They fought with at least a dozen destroyers who seemed very determined. They did not seem familiar, and Titus wondered who they reported to.

In an attempt to assist, he called additional destroyers and tormenting demons. Without reinforcements, the demons currently fighting would not win.

Titus watched the woman with the wild red hair. She had the power to blast all the demons from the area. Self-Justification, one of the strongest destroying demons, clung desperately to the girl screaming in her ear. The woman with the wild red hair could easily flick the demon away, and yet she did not. Instead, she sat unseen with the girl holding her hand and whispering to her.

Titus would laugh at that if he had not seen it work so many times. Somehow, despite all the noise the King's children managed to hear the woman over all the other voices. But Titus also knew that just as often they did not, or at least they ignored her. He also knew that none of the other demons would ever get close enough to touch the girl. Self-Justification was the only one because, from the looks of it, she had already been there many years. The woman with the wild red hair would allow her to remain with the Sixth until the Sixth herself released her. Titus grinned thankful that the King was such a supporter of freedom.

The face of the Sixth contorted as she wrestled through the conflicting thoughts. One bearing truth the other lies. Which one would she believe? Which one would she allow to advise her? Titus wished he had popcorn. He found joy in watching the rats struggle against forces they could not see forces many of them did not believe existed. They tended to restrict demons and angels to mere bible stories something of the past something that did not apply to them. He chuckled; Lucifer really was the Great Deceiver. Titus admired his work.

"My Liege," the demon spoke quietly, his voice a low grumble. Titus turned grateful for the simple announcement of arrival. He gestured his head toward the Sixth.

"Provide aid," he said quietly.

"My Liege, the woman?" The demon stopped short, he knew the risk he took questioning his superior. But the woman with the wild red hair was a much bigger threat than Titus. Titus did not take offense all demons feared the woman and wisely so.

"It is training for the girl. The woman will not blast you. Free will and all that," Titus stated with a slight smirk on his face. "You need not get close to the girl. Scream out to her. Convince her that no one will listen; no one will believe her. Convince her that her very life is at stake; that the personal risk isn't worth it. That normally works."

The demon curled his lips into a sinister smile that did indeed usually work. So few of the King's children were willing to risk their own comfort and safety. Oh, if they were facing overt persecution, then they might, but the demons knew that. They took a subtle approach. How many would risk speaking up at a meeting if it would cost them their job? How many would speak up if they believed they stood alone?

The demons had become experts at keeping it subtle the King's children in response had gotten good at justifying their inaction. They had a family to feed after all. Didn't the King tell them to provide for their family? Was this little thing really that big of a deal? No one else was speaking up it probably wasn't necessary. They were probably making a big deal out of nothing. The excuses were plentiful, and the demons expertly handed them out.

When they did speak, the demons worked hard to make their responses condemning, hostile, and full of judgment. They filled the speaker with self-justification and pride whenever they could. Of course, the demons also knew that so few that carried the title were indeed children of the King. Few had the Light while many claimed to. He wondered if they realized it? After all the Word did say that many would stand before the King claiming to know him and he would cast them away declaring that he never knew them.

The demons drew their swords and walked purposefully toward the battle as Titus stood and watched.

Fear crept up the neck of the Sixth. Who would believe her? Heck, she wasn't even sure what she was suggesting. She had no proof of anything. But could she really turn a blind eye? If what she suspected was true, women hundreds of women were being bought and sold by her company. And she was profiting from it. It was too repulsive to even consider. This sort of thing didn't happen, not in real life. She laid her napkin on the table and tried to quiet the multitude of thoughts all vying for her attention. She closed her eyes and sat quietly soaking in the sun, its rays beating down on her, sweat glistening her skin. She willed herself to quiet her mind and expel the fear.

"What do you want me to do?" she asked.

Titus could not tell exactly what was happening. He had been distracted by a young couple that was walking by. Lust had latched onto the boy, and Selfishness covered the girl; it was almost cliché.

They were arguing over what movie they wanted to watch a seemingly silly argument, but one that Titus knew could be fed and stoked to become something more. Something that festered resentment. Titus had been drawn into their conversation this was turning out to be a good day.

But then the crack of the air snapped him back to the Sixth. She was praying. The demons began to be pushed back from her. Her Light flared stronger forcing them even further away until the angels stood unchallenged laughing at the demons who struggled to push against the prayer. But all of them knew there was no use. They had no power over prayer the King's children were in a place of protection when they prayed in the spirit. Titus shook his head at the futility of the demons. It was embarrassing they would be better served to wait it out.

When her prayer ended, she stood from the table with a sense of purpose. She dropped cash on the table, picked up her bag and walked away with a new assurance in her step. Titus could smell, even from this distance, that she was still nervous, but she had a plan, and she knew it was what the King would have her do.

Titus realized there was only one thing left that he could do, only one thing could redeem him in Lucifer's sight; he had to find the prayer warriors.

Chapter 58

With so many of the eleven on their way to Tanzania, it became evident to the angels and demons alike that the King was doing something. Lucifer felt convinced that the King was planning to dismantle his operations there, but Morax wasn't as confident. There seemed to be many options, and some demons whispered of the possibility that the designated time had arrived.

Titus dismissed that theory immediately because the fear of it was too much. No matter the reason, it was evident that Titus's only hope was to disrupt the plan, whatever it was. If they could find the prayer warriors that may be possible. He began a comprehensive search for the Second and the Third starting with obvious places and working from there. He called together every available demon pulling many of them from other jobs suddenly deemed less important. Finding the prayer warriors and destroying them became their top priority.

The demons searched every flight in or out of Tanzania; they weren't on any of them. They searched to see if they had gone there in the last six months or had a reservation to go anytime in the next six months, but they found nothing.

He ordered a search of every college in America, but they turned up nothing. He searched hospitals and ambulatory clinics around the country starting with those nearest where they had lived in Platitude–but still nothing. He searched his mind to recall what he knew about them, and he sent research demons to find anything they could they were somewhere, and he would find them.

They scoured social media watching their accounts. Eventually, they would give their location away, or post a picture the demons could analyze to determine where they were. Something, anything. He also put additional demons on the others from Platitude. Warriors who would find those they had not yet found, monitor them and report back any contact with the prayer warriors.

On the Sixth day, Kali joined Titus on top of the capital where he was perched. He has chosen this spot for many reasons, one of which was that it allowed him to monitor the Strongman while still overseeing the search for the prayer warriors.

"I trust that you bring news?" Titus said with as much contempt as he could muster. Kali smiled and handed him a folder.

TITUS JOINED MORAX and Lucifer in the back of the small church. A church business meeting was underway, and Lucifer looked up clearly annoyed to see Titus. It had become obvious to Titus that his plan to usurp Morax had been a mistake. It would not advance his position of that he was clear, and it was possibly making things worse for him.

Of course, there was nothing he could do about that now.

"You have something," Lucifer said with scorn.

Titus smiled. While he may have been mistaken to think he could remove Morax from Lucifer's right hand. He felt confident that he would be rewarded for bringing this news.

"I have found the prophet."

Chapter 59

Mordecai sat on the deck at a slight distance from the Twelfth and her family. The night was chilly, it usually was in Maine, and the husband of the Twelfth had built a bonfire. They were sitting around the fire laughing and telling stories. The angels positioned themselves around the family listening in.

The oldest boy sat on a camping chair sharpening the sticks he had collected to a fine point. As he finished each one, he passed it around to another member of the family. Mordecai watched as they put large marshmallows on the end of the stick and then roasted them. It was something he had seen lots of Americans do over the years, but apparently, it was new to Kfir.

"What are those white things?" Kfir asked, walking close to the family attempting to get a better look. He reached out and poked one just as the youngest child slid the marshmallow on his stick and placed it in the fire.

"It's spongy," he said, moving toward the Twelfth who was loading her stick with one.

"Kfir," Aegeus said in amused warning.

The youngest child pulled his flaming marshmallow from the fire.

"It's a fuel source?" Kfir asked, disappointed that it wasn't some new strange food to try.

"It's a marshmallow." Mordecai offered, standing up and walking toward the fire.

"A marsh what?" Kfir asked, just as the youngest child blew his out and slide it from the stick. The outside had transformed into something burned and crispy while the inside seemed gooey. Kfir stuck his tongue out toward the boy's marshmallow.

"Keef!" Adiel said in shocked amusement. "You can't-do that!" she laughed at the idea of Kfir licking the boy's marshmallow.

"What? Why not?" he asked, perplexed. But the distraction was long enough that the boy had popped the marshmallow into his mouth, leaving Kfir without a taste.

The Twelfth put a second marshmallow on her stick and placed it in the fire. Kfir watched carefully as it caught fire. The Twelfth was listening as her middle child was telling a story, and she didn't immediately notice that her marshmallow was on fire. Kfir saw this as his chance and reached into the fire, pulling the two marshmallows from the end of the stick, and popping them quickly into his mouth before anyone could say a word.

They had a sweet yet smoky taste. They caused his fingers to stick together. The angels watched with anticipation for his response. Kfir stuck out his tongue trying to scrape the white goo from his mouth.

"It tastes like cooked plastic," he tried to say while wiping his tongue and stringing marshmallow across his face. The other angels rolled with laughter.

"It's in your beard." Aegeus laughed as Kfir struggled to get the goo from his mouth.

"There is some hanging from your eyebrow" Meir laughed, pointing at him tears filling her eyes.

"It's disgusting!" Kfir bemoaned trying to get rid of it, but not making any progress.

"My marshmallow must have fallen into the fire," the Twelfth said, looking at the fire for evidence of where it went but not finding any. Her husband tossed her another one, and she started the roasting process all over.

"Don't eat it!" Kfir yelled at her in warning.

The angels were enjoying the family time, and the sight of Kfir with marshmallow strung about his face and hands. They were invested, in many ways, they had come to think of themselves as part of this family. Aegeus sat down by the fire and listened to the family tell stories and discuss the best marshmallow roasting technique which was better browning it evenly or catching it on fire? They seemed to have varying opinions on the matter, and the angels suggested that perhaps Kfir should try another one, one that was merely roasted and not toasted. They were so distracted by this that the demons arriving silently in the surrounding tree line almost went unnoticed. Almost.

Mordecai felt them first. He immediately stopped laughing and got serious something Aegeus and the others noticed. Instantly the angels were on their feet with their swords drawn. They formed a tight circle around the unsuspecting family. Aegeus scanned the tree line; he couldn't quite see the demons, but he could feel them, hundreds of them.

Aegeus looked at Meir, who stepped inside the circle with the family.

"You have to go," he said to her quietly concerned for her safety in the coming battle.

"I will remain with her," Meir answered confidently.

"Meir," he began.

"Aegeus, I serve at the will of the King. Do your job and protect her. You protect her you protect me. But I have a job too, and I will not leave her." She said it kindly with no malice, but she also spoke with certainty leaving no doubt that she would remain where she was.

With obvious reluctance, Aegeus nodded his head at her and then turned his face back to the demons. "See if you can convince her to move into the house we can protect her better there."

Meir nodded. She moved toward the Twelfth but before she reached her the woman with the wild red hair appeared beside the Twelfth and spoke to her.

The Twelfth stopped laughing and abruptly looked serious. Her eyes met her husband's, and he immediately detected the change in her mood the seriousness in her eyes.

"We need to go inside," she said suddenly getting up and starting to move the children in that direction. The warm wind began to pick up carrying a hint of sulfur on it.

"What is it mom?" her oldest son asked also standing.

"I don't know," she said, gathering the kids and moving toward the house "there is something out here in the woods. We need to get inside." Her voice was calm, careful not to incite panic.

Her husband looked towards the woods as the kids moved obediently with their mom toward the house. The angels tightened the circle, keeping their eyes on the woods. Aegeus could feel more demons arriving.

"Aegeus!" Adiel called in a loud whisper. He turned his head toward her. She had broken rank and was now separated from the other angels. The husband of the Twelfth had not moved from the fire. He stood straining to see what was in the woods. Adiel remained with him.

While Aegeus admired the man's courage and his desire to protect his family, it put Adiel at risk and having Adiel separated weakened the overall team.

"Meir," he called to her softly, knowing she would hear him.

"On it," Meir responded instantly flying to the husband of the Twelfth. She laid her hands on him and searched quickly until she found just what she needed to convince him that he would be best served remaining with the others. She reminded him that they would feel safest with him. He glanced back at his wife, and her eyes told him everything he needed to hear. He could see her fear whatever was in the woods had spooked her. He walked toward her, Adiel and Meir with him. Aegeus was grateful that the man had been willing to listen.

The Twelfth had just ushered the children into the house and turned back to watch her husband cross the yard when the demons flew from the wood line.

"Emeka, stay in the house with the family!" Aegeus yelled as the demons approached "Meir, get to the Twelfth!" Meir disappeared instantly.

Hundreds of demons flew from the wood, swords drawn, sulfur pouring from them, choking the air with thick black fog. Aegeus swung his sword, fighting to keep them from the house.

"Mordecai the roof!" he yelled as he sliced his sword through a gigantic warrior. Mordecai pushed off hard from the ground fighting his way toward the roof of the small cottage where a handful of demons had landed.

Aegeus lost sight of Mordecai as he disappeared into the house. A small dagger pierced his back on the left side. Pain ripped through him. He shoved his elbow back as hard as he could into the body of the demon behind him. It knocked the demon off balance enough for Aegeus to turn around and bring the full force of his sword with him dissipating the demon.

But hundreds more took his place there seemed to be an unending stream of them pouring from the woods. Adiel swung her sword slashing at demons as she escorted the husband of the Twelfth to the door of the cottage. She spun about kicking and elbowing demons that were too close to strike with her sword. She was near the door when a large warrior dropped from the roof of the house and sliced her cheek open with a small dagger he pulled from his boot.

She let out a yell of rage continuing to fight, pushing her way toward the house, protecting the husband of the Twelfth.

Aegeus was the last one in. He quickly took in the scene; the power was out the children were searching for flashlights and candles. Fear ran from one to the next twining his fingers through their hair whispering in their ears. Their Lights would flare sending him scurrying and howling toward the next child in hopes of latching on. While the Light protected them from severe harm, it did not prevent him from touching them feeding them irrational fears. If Fear were allowed to torment for too long Anxiety would be invited, and she was a strong destroying demon.

Meir held tight to the Twelfth drawing out ways to make the power outage seem like an adventure on this cold and blustery night. Meir suggested a board game by candlelight, and the Twelfth accepted it. She gave the children jobs to do, jobs that kept them all together while she went to find the game. Her husband stood at the window, watching, yet blind to the demons that flooded from the woods.

Demons began to drop into the cottage coming in through the roof and walls. Human structures could not stop them. The angels positioned themselves around the family who were gathered in the living room all but the Twelfth. Meir stood in the middle near the children bringing them comfort and peace fighting to keep them from understanding the battle that raged around them.

Aegeus, Kfir, Mordecai, and Emeka stood around the room, fighting the demons as they poured in.

"We need to get them out of here!" Aegeus yelled to the others. They would not be able to hold the demons back for long there were too many. Kfir shoved his sword through three demons at once, then used his foot to free his sword from their bodies. As each one fell to the floor, it dissolved into black smoke, leaving a hint of sulfur behind. The youngest child noticed instantly. He began to giggle.

"Who farted?" he laughed into the room, the other children laughed too. The husband of the Twelfth joining in and shaking his head that all the kids' conversations eventually came back to farts. Their joy weakened the demons making it easier for the angels to defeat them. Several demons dropped through the roof at once, they landed on Kfir knocking him to the ground.

He rolled to the side. Leaping back up, he pushed the demons back so that he could get a better shot at them with his sword. The Twelfth walked back into the room carrying several board games Self-Doubt clinging to her.

Meir let out a surprised scream as a destroyer broke through and grabbed her arm. The smell of burned demon quickly overpowered the room his hand blistered and smoked from holding onto her, yet he did not flinch he did not let go. Meir pulled back from him, her eyes, hair, and wings, turning a sickly shade of green. But his grip was tight. Aegeus ducked as a sword barely missed his head, he began fighting his way toward Meir.

Kali defiantly maintained his grip on her wrist as his hand continued to blister and swell. He could smell his flesh burning, but he did not let go. Stubbornness clung to him to ensure that he would stay the course. If they could destroy the ministering angel, the mission would be easier. If Meir could not provide them comfort, they would be more accepting of the demons. Kali jerked his arm and pulled Meir toward him so that her face was only inches from his. Meir stared into his dark eyes confidence and strength flowing through her. Instantly her eyes began to burn like flames, her hair turning bright red. She unfurled her magnificent wings, which were now also flaming red. She no longer pulled back, but she leaned into him reducing the small space that was between their noses.

"I am an angel of the King most high," she said, her voice unfaltering and strong. She filled the room with her power. Aegeus froze where he stood, the fighting stopped as angels and demons alike turned to watch. Meir was a mighty ministering angel. Aegeus had seen her comfort many of the King's children, he had seen her bring comfort to whole groups of people during a tragedy giving them clarity of thought so that they could make wise decisions. He had seen her remove all fear from those who were facing their death. He had seen her take their pain. He had been with her when this nation had met some of its fiercest battles and seen her stand amid the hurting and frightened and send out her comfort. But he had never seen her fight. He knew that she, like all the ministering angels, was powerful but until this moment, he had not understood just how powerful.

Many of the tormenting demons responded by sending out their darkness trying to fill the room with it. Meir did not remove her eyes from the demon who clutched her. But slowly the edge of her mouth curled up.

"Remove your hand from me," she ordered in the soft yet authoritative way that only Meir could. The demon snarled, his hand so blistered and red it no longer resembled a hand at all.

"Or what?" he snarled back at her. Instantly his hand exploded, light shooting out of it. He screamed in pain, clutching the stump to his body his hand no longer part of him. Instantly Meir stretched her wings out fully and leaning her head toward heaven she blasted all the demons from the cottage.

"Or else that," she said with quiet confidence after the carnage had settled.

The rest of the angels stood shocked and quiet. Meir's eyes still blazed from emitting the Light of God, she stood in the center of the room untouched power crackling from her. The humans went about setting up their board game unaware that anything had happened. All but the Twelfth who stood motionlessly, her eyes wide darting frantically about.

Kfir was the first to regain his composure. He pulled out his phone joy tumbling from him; his own light starting to overpower the room.

"I have got to Tweet this!" he exclaimed, opening the Twitter app.

The lunacy of it snapped Aegeus back to the present.

"Are you ok?" he asked walking toward her, but he knew from the way her eyes were still flashing that she was fine.

"Yes," she answered. Meir had never been one to waste words. "I will have to return to heaven."

Aegeus acknowledged this truth. Using the Light of God as she had required an angel to return to heaven. He was eager for her to go and return quickly.

Meir looked at the Twelfth still frozen in place glancing about her.

"Her human eyes cannot see, but she felt it. She doesn't know what she felt Aegeus, but she knows she has felt it only once before. In the woods, the night the Fifth died."

Aegeus nodded indicating he understood. But he also understood that Meir would not have the strength to minister to the Twelfth.

"I will help her," Mordecai offered stepping forward. "I am no ministering angel, but I do have some basic ministering capabilities." Meir smiled and nodded at him in appreciation.

"You require an escort for your return home," Aegeus said to Meir.

"No, you can't spare anyone," Meir answered matter-of-factly. "I will be fine," she reassured him.

"I will accompany her," Adiel said. It was not wise for angels to travel between earth and heaven alone, particularly ministering angels.

"Go, and return quickly," Aegeus directed.

"You don't have much time, Aegeus," said Adiel. "They'll be back. You need to get the family out of here." She was right of course. Meir and Adiel said goodbye to the team and departed for heaven. Now that the demons had found the prophet; she would have to be moved.

Chapter 60

Aegeus had chosen a secluded campsite a short distance from the cottage. It had taken a lot of planning and coordination, but one broken water heater, downed power line, and rodent infestation later, the Twelfth and her family had left their summer cottage and moved to the campground at Cupsuptic.

The campground was quiet and peaceful with just enough people there that the Twelfth felt like they weren't alone, but not enough to make her feel crowded or paranoid about how loud the kids were. They had rented a small camper for the few weeks they had remaining and, other than the Twelfth's shifts at the clinic they remained together in one place. Aegeus found that having them all in one spot made things considerably more manageable for the team.

The kids had popped in a Duck Dynasty DVD and were settled into their spots with popcorn and hot tamale candies. That should give the Twelfth and her husband just enough time to hit the public showers.

The husband of the Twelfth had his shower bag ready and was waiting patiently for his wife to gather her things and walk with him the short distance from the camper to the showers.

The showers were divided into individual concrete pods which were separated by a wooden walkway, each one about six feet from the next. The two stalls closest to the camper were open; he would take the one on the right knowing that she preferred the other one.

She gave the children last minute instructions about staying in the camper and keeping the door locked. He smiled to himself as she did. They were more than old enough to be in the camper by themselves for a few minutes. He gently grasped her elbow and steered her toward the door she had just reminded them to lock. Mordecai stood perched on top of the camper, his sword drawn.

Kfir and Aegeus walked with the Twelfth and her husband. The demon cover had been increasing steadily, and that could only mean trouble. Aegeus suspected the increased demon presence was the reason for the Twelfth's anxiousness although he doubted she recognized it as such.

She seemed to be getting more anxious, and her husband wasn't sure why. He hoped a hot shower and a few minutes away from the kids would help. Demons circled overhead. They darted in and out of tents, cabins, and campers taunting the occupants. Dogs around the campground barked aggressively as they tried in vain to warn the humans of the demonic presence. Aegeus walked close to the Twelfth his hand resting on the hilt of his sword in anticipation of the battle that was sure to ensue.

Her husband took her hand, and they walked together toward the showers. Her foot caught in a small hole, and she lost her footing, twisting her ankle slightly and losing her balance. He reached out to steady her, and she felt his gun brush against her hip.

"You brought your gun?" she asked only mildly surprised. Being a border patrol agent, he rarely went anywhere without his firearm.

"Of course," he answered amused. "You never know, we might encounter a bear," he said with a smirk.

"More likely we will run into a swarm of those black flies that are so common around here," she countered. Then, without warning, she jumped into a shooting stance and holding her hands like she had a gun, she attempted her best Charlie's Angels pose as if she were in an intense battle against the black fly swarm. He laughed aloud playfully shoving her. The pretend battle over, she slid her hand back into his for the few short steps they had left. For one fleeting second, she forgot the foreboding feeling that had been haunting her.

The shower facilities were clean and fresh, not what Aegeus had expected. The Twelfth took her time enjoying the hot water. Standing under the spray seemed to soothe her growing uneasiness.

She had just finished dressing and was gathering up her things when Aegeus first heard it. A low rumbling sound, something resembling a growl. It was still a fair distance away, so he couldn't quite hear it clearly, but even from a distance, he could feel the dark presence that accompanied it. He couldn't be sure what it was, but he knew it wasn't anything good.

He stepped outside the shower room to see. Kfir stood with the husband of the Twelfth as they waited patiently for Aegeus and the Twelfth to emerge. Her husband seemed to sense something was wrong and stood very still straining to hear. Kfir looked up, meeting Aegeus' eyes.

Aegeus shrugged. He took to the skies to get a better look. The woods around the campsite were thick, and he couldn't see what was coming, but it rattled the trees as it passed, and thousands of demons came with it. They were closing the space quickly and would emerge from the woods within seconds.

The growling sound rumbled again, close enough that Aegeus could hear it more clearly; his heart sank. There was but one thing that made that sound. This was no ordinary demon; it was the Beast.

Hundreds of demons began to pour into the campsite ahead of the beast. Some of them came in the form of humans, most did not. Aegeus rushed back to the Twelfth. She was just leaving the small bathroom when the ground shook slightly, and the sound of the beast rumbled around them.

The woman with the wild red hair showed up and laid her hands on the Twelfth.

"Get back!" she warned empathetically. The Twelfth's gaze met her husband's for only a second, fear and uncertainty in her eyes. Seeing her fear, he walked toward her, his own pulse suddenly increasing. His eyes questioning. She stepped back into the bathroom, unsure of why. The heavy door closed silently in front of her cutting her off from the outside world, from him. She felt threatened, frightened. Fear for her children nearly consumed her, and she reached for the door to leave the small bathroom once again. She could hear her husband knocking on the door of the pod, calling her name.

"Get back!" the woman warned again more forcefully. The Twelfth stood frozen, unsure of what to do.

She could hear what she believed to be a massive animal sniffing about the building and she knew she needed to hide. Her maternal instincts fought hard against the woman with the wild red hair. Her children were alone in the camper. Her husband stood exposed in the space between their two shower rooms. And she stood in a bathroom afraid of what? Protected how? But in the end, the Twelfth followed the woman's advice.

"You must hide," the woman urged, her hair flying out in red flames from around her face. The Twelfth looked around the small bathroom. There was nowhere to hide. The pod was small with concrete walls covered in wood paneling to make it seem rustic. There was a toilet and sink and a secondary space with a bench and a shower. The shower was separated from the bench with a shower curtain, but that would not be much of a hiding spot. A sense of urgency began to overwhelm her. Panic and foolishness also settled in.

Aegeus readied for battle.

The woman with the wild red hair took the hand of the Twelfth and directed her attention to a small space at the top of the wall. There was a small gap between the top of the wall and what could only be described as a form of skylight. The small space made a gutter of sorts. The area was much narrower than the Twelfth, but if she laid on her side, she thought she could fit. She went to the wall and reached up toward the gutter. She couldn't reach it.

"Jump!" the woman directed.

The Twelfth stood still, jumping was not one of her talents.

"Jump!" the woman repeated more forcefully. The Twelfth made a feeble attempt to jump up and grab the top of the wall. Aegeus shook his head in disbelief at the magnitude of her failure.

"Tell her again," he unnecessarily encouraged the red-haired woman. The woman nodded.

"You must jump," she repeated to the Twelfth. The sound of the beast was closer. A sense of dread and fear spread over the Twelfth like ice inching its way through her veins.

"I need help," she said into the air as she attempted again. She placed a foot on the toilet paper dispenser and another on the toilet. She reached for the ledge, but it was still too high. She attempted a jump. One foot landed squarely in the toilet while the other caused the toilet paper dispenser to crash to the floor with a loud bang. Fear and humiliation filled her. She once again heard her husband calling her name from the other side of the door. Most of her wanted to throw the door open and run to him. But the small quiet part wouldn't let her.

Hot tears escaped her eyes. The woman with the wild red hair prompted her to try again. Once more she jumped, reaching desperately for the small space above. Aegeus pushed as she jumped, nearly flinging her through the windows above.

"Thank you," she whispered as she clamored up the wall and crammed her body into the small space between the wall and the frosted windows above. Aegeus laid down behind her covering her body with his own just as the door flung open. The woman with the wild red hair instantly disappeared.

The Twelfth filled the air with silent prayers for protection for her children and her husband. Her body trembled slightly with fear and adrenaline. Aegeus pulled in close behind her once again wishing he could reassure her. He wondered for the first time if he had made a mistake by not becoming an archangel. If he were an archangel, he would be able to bring her comfort to communicate with her. Instead, he covered her body with his own concealing them both from the beast.

The smell of sulfur assailed their senses. The Twelfth prayed more fervently the air crackling with her prayer, her Light starting to fill the small space. Aegeus worked to conceal it from the beast.

"I know you are here," the beast said in a deep voice that was like marbled honey. "I smell you... Both of you." Aegeus laid still, not daring to even breathe. Those who were wise did not take on the beast alone. The Twelfth began to shake uncontrollably, and Aegeus wondered if she could hear the beast.

The beast searched the small room until finally, he was smelling the back of Aegeus' neck. Aegeus could feel the heat from the beast's nostrils burning his neck. The Sulfur in the room was so intense it temporarily blinded him. The Twelfth continued to shake. The smell of rotten eggs caused her stomach to churn. Dry heaves began to take over her. He put his hand over her mouth willing her to remain silent.

"I know you are here," the beast taunted. "Not only can I smell you, but I must also have brushed against you because I know. I know what you gave up to be here." He sneered, frustrated that he could not find them despite knowing they were close.

"Very well," the beast muttered. If you do not reveal yourself, I will draw you out. With that, he turned and left the room, his enormous tail smashing into the wall as he went.

Aegeus stayed in position for several seconds after the beast left. Then he jumped down from the wall and rushed out of the bathroom nearly colliding with the Twelfth's husband as he entered the room.

"You ok?" her husband asked as he helped her down from the wall. He cupped her face in his hands searching her body for injuries with his eyes.

"I'm ok," she said, visibly shaken but unhurt.

"What happened?" he asked, trying to make sense of her bizarre behavior. Suddenly, she felt humiliated. She couldn't explain what had happened, she buried her face in his chest, willing her body to quit shaking. She prayed desperately that she wasn't losing her mind.

He pulled her back gently and looked down into her fear-filled eyes.

"What happened," he asked again. Before she had to try to put it into words, the sound of screaming disrupted them.

"Stay here!" and with that, he turned and ran toward the camper. The Twelfth ran after him.

Chapter 61

The scream came from the camper. Aegeus flew toward it. Mordecai had already gone inside. In the few minutes Aegeus had been in the shower room with the Twelfth, thousands of demons had descended on the campsite. They were surrounded and quickly losing ground.

The husband of the Twelfth had covered half the space between the bathhouse and the camper when two demons, possessing human bodies, pulled their youngest son from the camper. One of them held a large hunting knife to the boy's throat. Hundreds of demons surrounded them.

"Where's the doc?" the man yelled, clutching the sobbing boy more tightly. The husband of the Twelfth stood still.

"Who?" he asked, stalling.

"The doc!" he repeated. "She took something of mine, now I will take something of hers!"

The Twelfth ran around the corner of the bathhouse, a strangled scream escaped her. Panic flooded through her bringing her to an abrupt stop. Bile danced in her throat. The scene began to spin around her, and her knees buckled. Memories she had fought to defeat flooded to the surface. For just a moment she was years away with another child. A child she had lost. A child ripped from her arms in the most unthinkable way. She tried to focus, to pull her mind back to this moment, but she struggled to separate them.

Her husband called her name. She could hear the concern in his voice, the pain, the evidence that he too struggled to suppress unwelcomed memories.

Finding her strength, she looked up into his eyes. Which quickly darted to her and back again. She saw the flicker of disappointment that she hadn't stayed put. He held her gaze just long enough to assure himself that she was ok. With a slight nod, he turned back toward their child. With great effort, the Twelfth pushed herself from the ground.

"Ahh, there she is," said the man from the clinic.

Horrified, she took in as much of the scene as her human eyes would allow.

A man held her son at knifepoint. Another stood beside him, blocking the camper door. He looked familiar. It took her a minute to place him, the man from the clinic!

Her husband stood poised slightly to her left but about 25 yards ahead of her. He was positioned almost perfectly between the men and her. His hand was slowly inching toward the gun in his waistband.

All around them thousands of demons had converged on the campsite. Aegeus and Kfir fought desperately to reach the camper. Aegeus could not see Mordecai inside the camper, but he could see flashes of light, and he could hear the clanking of swords.

"The Prophet!" yelled a powerful looking warrior demon who was standing on top of the camper. The eyes of all the demons looked at her. Aegeus sliced into the demon in front of him and turned back toward the Twelfth, suddenly realizing he had left her unprotected, vulnerable. Demons began to converge on her. Quickly Aegeus changed directions and started fighting his way back towards her.

"You took my property," the man from the clinic yelled in rage, referring to the woman the Twelfth had treated. The woman had agreed to go to the hospital where she had received medical care and assistance in getting free from trafficking.

"Now I will take yours!" the man yelled.

He signaled his hand, and four men, covered in destroying demons rushed toward her. More quickly than she could process what was happening, her husband pulled his weapon and pointed it at the men. Everyone stopped. The man with the knife pressed it into the boy's neck drawing a small line of blood and eliciting a cry of terror from both the child and the Twelfth.

The man from the clinic smiled broadly. He caressed the boy's face gently. "I could use a young boy such as this in my business," he said. "And your daughter? Well, she will bring a fair price as well."

"Take your hands off him!" The Twelfth cried out.

"It's your life for his, doc," he yelled.

The Twelfth's eyes met her husband 's for only an instant, but in it, she spoke volumes. She loved him. She had chosen to bond her life to his, to grow old with him. They had brought new life into the world. She knew that it was unlikely he would be able to save both her and her children. He must protect the children. She needed him to save them, she would not survive ever losing another one. She nodded slightly, and despite the pain that was evident in his eyes, he nodded back. He knew her heart.

She would gladly trade her life for her son. She started to move forward, and her husband's eyes flashed in warning stopping her. The woman with the wild red hair laid her hand firmly on the Twelfth and spoke firmly into her ear. The demons shuffled nervously.

There was a large drainage pipe nearly hidden just inside the wood line. The Twelfth's husband glanced at it quickly. But fear coursed through her. Her instincts fought against him. How could she run when her son's life was on the line? She twitched her head no.

Once again, he glanced at the drainage pipe and back at her, more insistent, he had a plan. She should make her way to the drain. If she could get there before they got to the woods, she could hide there, and they wouldn't find her.

The woman with the wild red hair leaned toward her and whispered firmly, "It is your best chance."

The Twelfth nodded almost imperceptibly, she would trust her husband's instincts and not her own. She owed him that much. It had only taken a second for them to formulate a plan. One second in which everything seemed to stand still. One second for Aegeus to be completely covered in demons, unable to reach the Twelfth.

With a final parting look at her husband, the Twelfth bolted away from her would be captors toward the wood line. The sound of her son screaming for her rung in her ears, ripping at her heart. Her mind yelled desperately at her to stop and go back to him, but she knew his best chance was her husband.

Her husband turned back to the two men threatening his child. He took aim carefully and exhaled as he expertly fired off two shots. The men dropped dead where they had stood. He turned quickly toward where he had last seen his wife and the men that pursued her, but they were already out of sight.

Chapter 62

When the Twelfth awoke, she wasn't sure she was awake. She blinked her eyes several times just to make sure they were open. Her body shook uncontrollably against the cold. All-consuming darkness filled the space. She was lying on a hard surface that felt like ice stabbing into her flesh. And then in one horrifying instant, she realized where she was.

The chamber was dark; so dark she couldn't see her own body. The floor was damp and cold against her bare feet. For a split second, she allowed herself to believe that it wasn't real. To believe that she was dreaming again. She had been here so many times in her dreams. But the reality of it was so much worse.

A scream of utter and complete terror filled the chamber bouncing off the walls. She didn't immediately realize it was her. She had been here in this room hundreds of times over the last few years and never once had she escaped. In no version of the dream was there hope, only pain, and suffering, only her own desperate pleas for death.

Her mind worked to make sense of how she got here, but the memories oozed in like thick sludge. Her head was pounding, and her brain felt foggy, her thoughts distant and far away. Little flashes of memories pushed their way through the fog. Memories of being at the campground, memories of running for the woods. She felt like she was running through mud, each step fighting against her heart.

Tears stung her eyes as she ran away from her husband, away from her children. The reality of that settled on her like a thick wet blanket nearly suffocating her. She closed her eyes against the darkness and tried to silence the condemnation.

As more memories crept in, she remembered being tackled and falling hard to the ground. She had not made it to the drainage pipe. Seeping through the fog, she had the vague memory of someone dragging her backward by her feet. She had kicked her feet, desperately clawing at the ground as she was dragged away from her family. And then, pain had shot through her head, and everything had gone black.

For several minutes the memories were jumbled and clogged in her aching head. Fear distorted them. She found it difficult to know which ones to trust, but somewhere in the far recesses of her mind, she thought she remembered hearing gunfire. And with that, it all came flooding back to her. Her son! What had happened to her son?

Panic filled her; she fought desperately against the chains that bound her ankles and wrists. Their cold metal bit into her skin. She had pulled at them a million times in her dreams, all in vain. But survival instincts were strong, and she pulled frantically, desperate to free herself from the chains and find her son.

The wooden chair she was in was splintered and worn. If she twisted about she could get better leverage. She pulled desperately on her chains ignoring the pain. She alternated between trying to pull the chain itself free from its source and trying to free herself from the shackles.

In time, a warmth spread slowly down her hands and feet. Gradually it became more intense covering more space. The smell of her own blood soon revealed the source of the warmth, but still, she pulled and fought, for she knew what was coming and her fear of him was stronger than the pain.

The beast chuckled at the sight of her struggling. The sound of it caused her to stop instantly, scouring the darkness to see the threat but knowing that there was no hope of doing so. He strolled toward her, circling around her. He slid his hand through her hair drawing in her scent, the sickeningly sweet smell of a prophet. She shrunk away from him, fear pouring from her, strengthening him.

"Do you know where we are?" he asked. She did not respond, he supposed he didn't really expect her to. "No, of course, you don't, you couldn't possibly." He added, remembering that her human eyes could not see in the dark. "Well, I have chosen this place just for Aegeus," he said resuming his slow walk around her, never removing his hand. When he was positioned directly in front of her, he slid his hand along her jawline then abruptly grabbed her by her throat.

"Let me explain exactly what is going to happen," he said, as she struggled to get air. "I am going to ask you a very simple question, and you are going to answer me. If you tell me the truth, I will kill you quickly. If you do not, I will take my time. Do you understand?" he asked.

The Twelfth nodded her head to indicate she understood. He released her throat and stood back as she gasped desperately for air. When she had recovered sufficiently, he posed his question.

"Where are the prayer warriors?"

The Twelfth was so dumbfounded by the question that she thought she had misheard him. Her silence angered him, and he struck her across the face. But she knew nothing. She had nothing to say. She didn't even know who it was he was looking for.

"Who?" she asked baffled. He leaned down into her face so close that their noses nearly touched. Still, she could not see him through the darkness, but she could feel him.

"The prayer warriors, where are they?" he asked in hatred. Her fog-ridden mind could not catch up, and she was at a loss.

"Answer me!" he yelled.

She uttered the only words she could, "Where are my children?"

He grabbed her face and squeezed her jaw until she thought it might break.

"I am the one asking the questions," he said with icy coldness. "Where are the prayer warriors?" spit flew from his mouth hitting her.

"I don't know," she cried in response. He struck her again out of rage sending her careening to the icy floor. She could feel his anger, the room pulsated with it as if it were an animated thing. She heard a metal door smash against the wall as it was flung open and then slammed shut. For several seconds she did not breath, unsure if someone else had entered or if the beast had left.

After several minutes she determined that he had left, and she allowed herself to cry. Her mind raced as she tried to figure out what was happening. The woman with the wild red hair knelt next to her.

"Why have you dreamt of this," she asked the Twelfth. The Twelfth wrestled to make sense of it. For two years she had dreamt of this chamber, of this beast. She had dreamt of the beatings and pain. But she had no idea why. She felt no closer to understanding now. The man at the campground had been a trafficker, so she reasoned the beast also had to be one of the human traffickers.

"He traffics human souls," the woman with the wild red hair said.

"What does he want from me?" the Twelfth asked.

"What did he ask of you?" the woman replied.

The Twelfth let her mind focus on his question. He asked her where the prayer warriors were. It was a strange question, not what she had been expecting. Who kidnapped someone to find a prayer warrior? Why would a human trafficker care about prayer warriors, what possible threat could a prayer warrior pose? None of it made sense to her.

Chapter 63

It took Aegeus less than two earthly minutes to fight his way free and fly after the Twelfth, but two minutes was apparently more than she had. He flew into the wood line just as the Twelfth was being loaded into a van and driven from the woods. In their glee, the demons paid little attention to him, he was but one. He followed the van from a safe distance, watching for an opportunity to free the Twelfth, but he was severely outnumbered, tens of thousands of warriors had been called in to guard the van and escort the Twelfth to wherever the beast was taking her. The coverage was so thick that soon, Aegeus could no longer see the van, all he could see was the horde, and so he followed it, waiting for an opportunity, waiting for backup.

The horde continued to thicken until the surrounding area and landscape were lost in a sea of darkness, Aegeus had no sense of where they were, or what direction they were going. The air smelled familiar, but it was saturated so heavily in demons that he couldn't quite make out where they were from the smell alone.

Eventually, the van stopped. Aegeus watched in horror as they dragged the Twelfth out, she had a hood over her head, and she squirmed and wiggled trying to free herself. One of the warriors struck her, and she stumbled to the ground crying out. Aegeus stood at a distance, his heart racing, his mind fighting against all the training Michael had instilled in him over the centuries. Thousands of years of training had taught him many things, one of which was that to rush into the fray, when he was outnumbered thousands to one, was not wise. He knew, logically, strategically, that waiting was the right thing. But waiting was not easy, and his heart yearned to draw his sword and run into the horde. How would she survive it? She was there, in the midst of the horde, and yet he stayed back where he was safe. It made him feel sick inside.

And so he paced, hoping reinforcements would arrive before he lost his resolve. The beast walked out of the building and approached with his hands raised. Aegeus drew his sword instantly, aware that alone he was no threat to the beast.

"There is no cause for violence, Aegeus," said Lucifer in his gentlest voice. "I am here to negotiate."

Aegeus bristled at the very idea.

"I do not negotiate with evil," he responded, "I serve the King."

"Ah, yes, I know. You are a mighty warrior Aegeus. Mighty indeed. In fact, I hear you passed up a promotion to archangel?" Lucifer paced slowly about, he felt it made him seem less threatening. Aegeus did not respond.

"I once was an archangel too," Lucifer continued. "We are not so different you and me." He added. Aegeus again did not respond. He kept his sword poised and ready.

"Oh. I see," Lucifer said. He tucked his hands into his pockets and paced around a bit as he pretended to ponder the situation.

"It's strange that the King sent you back so that you could protect the Twelfth, and yet you have spent very little time with her. Instead, he had you off on side missions, protecting the prayer warriors, searching out the others, protecting her family. Even now, you are not doing what he promised you you were sent here for; she suffers, and you do nothing." At that Lucifer shook his head and made a clucking sound with his tongue.

Aegeus flinched at the words. The twisted truth within them dug deep.

"You know I have the prophet," he went on. "But I find her to be a tremendous amount of trouble. She's been quite a bit of trouble for you too as I understand. She never quite seems to get it now does she?" Lucifer again paused, letting the comments rip at Aegeus's heart. But still, Aegeus did not speak.

"Perhaps you would like to see her?" Lucifer said, conjuring up an image of the Twelfth in the chamber.

Aegeus looked on in horror to see her lying injured and chained to the floor. Her body was broken, her light flickering and weak. His throat felt as if it were closing. He tightened his grip on his sword.

"Ahh, there is no need for that," Lucifer said, "I am happy to release her to you. No one needs to get hurt, especially not her." He paused there for effect.

"I serve only the King," Aegeus repeated. Lucifer laughed in response.

"That need not change Aegeus. It is very simple really. I will give you what the King will not. I can give you everything you want. I will release the Twelfth to you. Then you will not be needed on earth and can return and serve as an archangel. What harm could possibly come from that? It is, as the humans like to say, a win win."

Lucifer stood still, a look of patience on his face as if they were brokering a simple business deal or discussing what was for dinner.

"No," Aegeus said, although his heart ached with the words.

"Will you just stand there and watch her be destroyed?" Lucifer asked incredulously. Goading Aegeus, he asked, "Isn't protecting her precisely what the King sent you here for?"

"In his time," Aegeus answered with confidence, although his heart did not feel nearly as confident.

"It is the King that has allowed this to happen!" Lucifer said, his anger starting to bleed through. Gaining control, he took a slow breath and continued.

"How noble of you to allow her to stand alone Aegeus while you wait patiently for the signal from the King which may never come," Lucifer said, the smile fading from his face. "Are you prepared for that? Are you prepared that the King may let her die? He may have sent you on a mission you cannot win." Lucifer paused for a moment to let his words seep into Aegeus's heart.

Aegeus wasn't sure he was prepared for that. What if the King did indeed call her home? What if the King never gave the signal? He was not sure he could survive it. What if Lucifer was right? For one fleeting second, he regretted ever coming on the mission, ever having met her. For just a second, he wished he had never known the prophet because his pain for her was so great.

"I will kill her Aegeus, and there will be no one there to stop me. That will be on you when it happens. It will be your fault. You had a chance to save her, and you chose not to, putting yourself above her." His anger once again evident, Lucifer turned to walk away and then stopped and turned back to Aegeus.

"You know where to find me if you change your mind, but know that her time is limited, she isn't strong enough to make it much longer." Then he walked away.

Aegeus sheathed his sword then cried out to the King on her behalf and on his own. Quietly, without fanfare, the woman with the wild red hair appeared beside him. Aegeus dropped to his knee.

"Rise Aegeus," she commanded with concern in her voice.

"I am so glad to see you," Aegeus said, joy filling his heart. He drew his sword anticipating the battle. For alone, he stood no chance, but with the woman, the battle would be theirs. The woman walked toward him, understanding how difficult her next words would be. She gently placed her hand on his shoulder.

"Aegeus, this is not your battle, it is hers," she paused for a moment as emotions flooded through him. Aegeus looked as if he had been struck. He stepped back in shock and denial. The woman waited patiently for him to process the statement.

"But," he stammered, unable to voice what he was feeling. The woman drew closer to him, for she understood that what she asked was difficult.

"Sometimes, I ask very difficult things of people and angels alike," she said. She once again placed her hand on his shoulder, filling him with power and light. "But never, never do I do it without reason. Never is it in vain."

Aegeus staggered both from the power she imparted to him and the knowledge.

"I am with her Aegeus, and Meir will join us when it is time. But this test is hers alone. She must endure this, and she must come out stronger for much depends on it." Aegeus nodded his head in understanding. In truth, his mind understood, but his heart struggled.

"Did I make a mistake in returning to her? Should I have stayed in heaven and accepted the promotion?" he asked full of doubt.

"You know the answer to that Aegeus." She answered.

The woman watched with sadness as Aegeus wrestled internally to balance his love for her with his love for the Twelfth. The woman knew Aegeus's heart, but she needed him to know, she needed him to trust himself. She needed him to never again worry that his love for the human woman would cause him to stumble. When he walked away from this place, in his heart, he would know what she and the King already knew. His greatest fear would be set aside and forgotten. She waited patiently as he struggled.

"Is she ok," he asked.

"She struggles, but she makes strides," the woman answered.

"Am I to simply stand here and wait while she is attacked and destroyed?" he questioned, his voice straining at the very idea.

"Aegeus look where we are," the woman instructed, sweeping her hand around them and in so doing, clearing things so Aegeus could see. The reality of where they were caused him to recoil.

"Why?" he asked shocked.

"The beast has chosen this place specifically for your benefit," she said. Aegeus stood straighter, his fear was replaced with righteous indignation, and it exploded within him.

"She suffers because of me?"

"No Aegeus, she suffers *here* because of you."

"What is it about this place that matters so much?" he asked.

"In time Aegeus, in time," she said. "But I hope you see that by bringing her here, the beast was sending a message to you.

"I have failed her. I was to protect her, and I have failed her. I have failed you." He said with disappointment and anguish.

"She was always going to come to this place Aegeus. You have not failed, the battle has not yet truly begun," the woman assured him. "This is much bigger than her Aegeus, there are others. Inside this building, there are others, scattered throughout this nation there are others. Around the world there are others. And they too cry out for deliverance. The King treasures them every bit as much as the prophet. We must free them all."

"What would you have me do," he asked as his heart broke. He desperately wanted to run into the horde and free the prophet. Not just because she was a prophet, not just because she was his charge, but because he loved her. Standing by, allowing her to suffer was unthinkable.

"I want you to do what is hardest. I want you to leave her Aegeus."

Aegeus reeled from her words, he felt sure that he must have misheard the woman.

"Go and find her husband and help guide him here. Alert the Second and the Third, you will need their prayers. Cover her family, get your team, lead them here. For here, in this place that represents all that is wrong with the earth, we will begin the battle for them all."

But Aegeus did not want to leave her, his heart screamed out not to, he stood frozen in place, knowing what was right but struggling to do it. Finally, with great resolve, he turned to leave then quickly turned back asking, "Will she make it?"

"That is up to her Aegeus."

Chapter 64

He was coming back, she could feel it. Panic began to fill her. A sense of extreme dread preceded him. She had lived this so many times, knowing somehow made it worse. The chamber itself shook as he approached. A terrified scream escaped her bouncing off the walls and echoing throughout the room. He chuckled in response.

He seemed to pause, his hollow eyes studying her. Her Light was strong, but he had no fear of that. He had destroyed stronger.

Near the door where he had entered was a large crank. He turned the crank slowly filling the room with the sound of rattling chains. The chains tightened, pulling her toward the floor until she could no longer sit up. Her arms stretched above her head; her legs pulled tightly in the opposite direction until she thought her body may be ripped in two. He tightened and tightened the chains until a scream pierced the chamber giving him pleasure. He would enjoy this.

The cold floor penetrated the feeble pajamas the Twelfth was wearing. Slowly the beast walked closer to her, the chamber rumbling in response to each step. He positioned himself near her feet. She could see nothing but his horrible red eyes equally full of hatred and amusement. But she could feel him, he evoked such terror. She shook so violently that her chains clanged against the cold hard floor. Warmth spread down her legs.

The smell of her urine mixed with the scent of her blood. He laughed, a sound both insidious and melodious at the same time. It caused her hair to stand on end and yet it drew her in.

"I see you are making yourself at home," he spoke as if they were old friends. His voice hypnotizing in its cadence and tone. Her fear and humiliation too great to speak. A small sob escaped her throat.

He walked around her slowly taking in the so-called prophet. A woman, a mere woman! She was not young or strong nor even particularly pleasing to look at. What had the King been thinking? And yet, he reminded himself, Seneca had not been able to kill her.

"Tell me what makes you so important to the King?" he asked genuinely perplexed. The prophet did not answer.

"This doesn't have to be painful. I can kill you quickly, painlessly. Just tell me where they are."

The memories of the dream filled her mind. She knew that if she didn't tell him, he would beat her. He would kill her. But she knew nothing. She had nothing to say. She didn't even know who it was he was looking for. She uttered the only words she knew to be true.

"I don't know."

"Wrong answer."

Lucifer took one talon and pierced it into her thigh. A scream erupted from her, her back arching off the floor as she tried to escape. It filled him with desire and longing for more. He dragged his talon down her leg ripping the flesh and muscle as he went. Blood poured from the wound freezing when it hit the floor. He could taste her destruction. It had been many years since he had personally seen to such an event. Jubilation overcame him a carnal desire to destroy her surged through him.

He stopped himself abruptly. His pulse racing; his mind screaming to torment her, to finish her, and satisfy his intense desire to rip her apart. But he stopped. He would be patient. He would savor the job. He stood very still calming himself. His talon remained buried deep in her leg blood pouring over it. He focused on that as he collected himself.

The Twelfth trembled on the cold floor. Her skin had grown pallor. She pulled feebly on the chains that bound her, but each movement sent further pain coursing through her body.

Lucifer pulled his talon from her leg brushing roughly across the wounds as he moved away. It served both to bring her additional pain and to prevent her from bleeding to death. There was no sense in killing her too quickly.

Walking past the crank, he loosened the chains just a bit. Enough that she could pull her body into a ball. She laid on the floor weeping and counting the minutes until he returned. The woman with the wild red hair and bright green eyes knew that the Twelfth was reaching the end of her strength. Watching the beast taunt her and punish her for his own failings was difficult. But the woman also knew the importance of the lesson.

The King had allowed the Twelfth to dream of this event for over two years; a preparation of sorts. She must endure this trial, and she must learn from it. For much worse was coming. This pain and sorrow would work to give her strength, it was a blessing although the woman realized that it would not appear that way to the Twelfth.

The Twelfth slipped in and out of consciousness while she waited for the beast to return. She knew he would return; the dream had taught her that. And eventually, he would kill her. Many times, she had felt the life slipping from her body, her blood puddling on the floor. In her dream, her blood was an odd color, a swirling of red and gold. But the result was always the same; death was coming to the chamber.

The cold of the chamber was all-encompassing. But it had saturated her to the point that she no longer shook; she did not have the energy to do so. In fact, she laid very still, her skin a pale blue.

She mumbled almost silently, and the woman with the wild red hair leaned closer to hear the words that tumbled from her lips.

"For though I fall, I will rise again. Though I sit in darkness, the Lord will be my light," it was a quote from Micah.

The woman smiled, it pleased her to hear the Twelfth utter praise to the King. The woman with the wild red hair knelt closely beside the Twelfth and watched. She remained just far enough that the Twelfth would not feel her presence, it wasn't time for that yet. But she was there whether the Twelfth felt her or not.

The woman called her name gently, softly to awaken her soul. The Twelfth fought against the overwhelming desire to sleep, to escape this place and the evil that enveloped it. But some small part of her knew that she had to fight, she had to understand.

"You must not tell him where they are," the woman with the wild red hair whispered just loudly enough for the Twelfth to hear.

The Twelfth once again poured through her mind to determine who it was he was looking for. He had called them prayer warriors. She tried to think of people she would consider prayer warriors. There were undoubtedly those who prayed frequently, those who prayed powerfully, but warriors?

"Let those who have eyes see," the woman spoke.

And then, as if a veil had been pulled back, she could see clearly. The Second and Third were warriors. In her mind, she could see them cloaked in splendor, their prayers like a shield of protection covering others. Suddenly, she understood. And that realization cleared her mind as if she had been living blind.

The Twelfth knew she had lived as if she had no eyes to see, no ears to hear. It was as if she had somehow forgotten who she was. She choked on her own disappointment in herself.

"I am so sorry," she whispered into the air. She was a prophet. But she had lived as if that weren't true. Why? Because being a prophet terrified her. She was afraid of what people would say, what they would think, she was afraid she could never live up to the title of prophet. She was afraid that people would never hear the message, because of the messenger. She was afraid she would get it wrong.

Sobs ripped through her body, shaking her to her core. Shame flooded over her; she had failed. On so many levels, in so many ways she had failed, and she feared it was all she was capable of.

Her mind danced quickly through prophecies she had been given, messages she had delivered. They rushed through in rapid succession overwhelming her with the truth of it. Suddenly, she understood how wrong she had been, how much she had not understood.

She recognized that the dream was a prophecy, all of them were. She had been given an amazing gift, and she had squandered it, and now she felt the full force of that truth. Understanding flooded her. The woman with the wild red hair rubbed her hand over the Twelfth's back infusing her with a small surge of strength.

"You must never tell him," she whispered again.

Chapter 65

Meir arrived to find the chamber in utter darkness. The woman with the wild red hair knelt beside the Twelfth who laid on her left side chained to the floor, unrecognizable. Her arms were extended over her head her legs curled toward her in a ball. Her clothes were torn and saturated revealing bruises and abrasions. Her bottom lip swollen, one eye would no longer open. Despair covered her like a suffocating blanket.

She appeared to be singing softly, almost in a whisper. Meir's instinct was to rush to the Twelfth, to remove her fear, remove her pain but she fought that urge and instead looked at the woman with the wild red hair.

"She has done well Meir, Aegeus will return for you both," the woman said, standing up and gesturing toward the Twelfth in indication she was departing and that it was okay for Meir to approach.

Meir rushed to the Twelfth curling her own body and wings around her. The cold of the Twelfth's body was shocking to Meir, leaving her wondering how it was possible that the Twelfth was still alive.

The Twelfth continued to mutter softly, almost without conscious thought.

"The Lord is my light and my salvation, so why should I be afraid? The Lord is my fortress protecting me from danger so why should I tremble?" she repeated the Psalms over and over. Meir thought it an unusual choice. She took a deep breath and slowly allowed herself to merge with the Twelfth. Meir brought warmth to the Twelfth's frozen body, sliding a wing between the Twelfth and the floor. Her other wing covered over the top of the Twelfth like a blanket.

She knew her delicate wings would not protect the Twelfth. As a ministering angel, her wings were thin, they did not possess the protective features of a guardian or warrior. But they would help hold in the positive memories and encouragement that Meir would bring the Twelfth. And, it just seemed right.

Meir searched the Twelfth's mind while working to heal her body just enough to keep her alive, but not enough to alert the beast. He must not discover that she was here. She carefully searched through the Twelfth's mind to find memories Meir knew were stored away and could be used to impart comfort and strength. As she made her way to the memories she was looking for, she stumbled over a memory of Aegeus which the Twelfth was grasping tightly. It was the memory of the night in the woods, the night the Fifth had died. Meir tried to pull back from it, to move on to something else, something uplifting, but the Twelfth clung firmly and would not be moved.

Unable to move the Twelfth away from it, Meir was forced to watch through the eyes of the Twelfth as the Fifth shot herself. The pain and sorrow of losing the Fifth ripped deep into Meir. Agony flooded through her. She again tried desperately to move the Twelfth to another memory something that would bring her strength and hope. But the Twelfth fought her. Aegeus dropped to his knees in the woods crying out in anguish. It was that part of the memory that most haunted the Twelfth.

Meir realized that she and the Twelfth had been carrying around the same shared memory, the same anguish, the same guilt, the same thought that they should have seen it coming, that they should have done more. Of course, they carried different perspectives of the event, but their anguish was the same. Meir had been in the Fifth's mind. She had seen the utter despair that resided there. She had watched as Haywood tried desperately to protect the Fifth giving his own life for her and yet Meir had been helpless to stop it. The difference was that Meir knew how the story ended.

The Twelfth too lingered on her own helplessness, her guilt over not having done more. But ultimately, instead of her personal anguish, the Twelfth's memories focused on the anguish of the angels. The Twelfth had carried a burden for them, a burden for what they had experienced, for their sorrow. In that one moment, the Twelfth had seen and understood how desperately heaven fought for those on earth. It was the magnitude of that thought that overwhelmed the Twelfth, wrapping her in guilt. And it was the Twelfth's anguish and consideration of the angels that rocked Meir to her core.

"If you're here," the words came out faint, airy like the final words of a dying woman. "I want to thank you for trying to save me," The Twelfth paused gathering her strength. She tried to lick her dry, cracked lips, but the effort was futile. She kept her eyes closed as she continued, "I want you to know how much I appreciate you trying. And I don't want you to feel bad if I don't make it. I will be in a better place, of course, I guess you already know that." Tears dripped from her face onto Meir's wing. "But my husband," emotion strangled her voice, and it was several seconds before she could continue. "He... he will need help to get past it. And my children," she could not go on. Quiet sobs shook her body. "Please," she whispered, "please protect my children."

Meir suppressed her own emotions and snatched the thought away, it was too overwhelming for them both. Instead, she filled the Twelfth's mind with things that made her feel strong, invincible even. The Twelfth had fed her soul well, there was much to work with. Meir reminded her that the King was in control.

When the beast entered the chamber, Meir cloaked herself instantly. He must not see her; he must not even suspect she was there. Terror consumed the Twelfth, and she struggled, desperate to get her body off the floor. But as she tried to lift herself up, her frozen skin ripped from her body pulling part of Meir's wing with it. The Twelfth would have screamed, but she no longer had the energy. Meir wished she could speak to her and instruct her to lie still.

The Twelfth wondered how long she had been in the chamber; she had no idea. But she did know that the beast had been in the room many times. And while each time was different and each approach unique, ultimately, he was always after the same thing. This time he spoke directly into her ear. His voice was angry, hatred permeated every syllable. His hot breath burned her; a new sense of fear flooded through her. Her mind raced as she attempted to sort through what was happening.

"Where are they?" he demanded. His breath felt like fire against her face and neck. Was it possible that it was fire? Her skin screamed at the assault.

"I don't know," she was barely able to push the words out. She yearned for even a small drop of water.

"TELL ME!" he bellowed spewing utter and complete hatred.

Suddenly he stopped, and his rage seemed to subside momentarily. A cunning smile spread across his face. His voice softened.

"I know you're here!" He called out. "Why have you come for her? Look at her." He paced as he spoke straining to see any sign of the angel he could feel.

"Why does the King care for such a pathetic creature?" he continued to circle the room. "I can't quite tell what you are.... a mighty warrior I suppose. Aegeus, is that you? Do you lurk in corners instead of standing and fighting? Have you come to watch me kill her?" Lucifer taunted.

Meir did not flinch. She would not be drawn in by taunts. She had orders from the King; he had been very clear about her mission, and she would not deviate from it. But the mention of Aegeus sparked a small fire of hope in the Twelfth because she knew that Aegeus would only be there if the King had sent him.

Just then, the sound of a muffled sob made its way through the distance. The Twelfth inhaled sharply; she had not considered that there were others. She was not the only one being held in the chamber. Suddenly, the pieces began to fall into place. Suddenly, she was no longer fighting for her own life, but for everyone who was held captive by the beast. Suddenly, it was so much bigger than her, and it all came into focus. All the time in Platitude, the dreams, and Aegeus. Suddenly, it made sense.

In the clarity of that moment, she realized that indeed the King had sent someone to help her. She knew that she was not alone and that knowledge gave her hope. That hope caused her Light to blaze brighter than Meir had been expecting. Such a surge of hope and Light caused a quick surge in Meir briefly revealing her.

"My my, the King has not sent a warrior at all," The beast sneered.

He used what the Twelfth had once believed to be a whip covered in leather and some sort of scales to beat them. She now knew it was his tail, the tail of a hideous beast. The Twelfth had lost track of how many times and ways he had beaten her. When she was lucky, she would pass out and not awaken until he was gone. The whip tore flesh from her skin and pieces of Meir's wing with each strike. The smell of their blood mixing together filled the chamber.

The sound of his tail smashing into the Twelfth's frail human body and tearing the flesh from her bones with each strike emboldened him. But the sight of the angel's wings being shredded, her golden blood pouring from her, worked him into a psychotic frenzy, making him giddy.

He became increasingly excited, lashing her repeatedly. He was gleeful as the human's feeble screams bounced off the chamber walls. But Meir did not cry out, she wrapped herself tighter around the Twelfth. He swung the whip indiscriminately, bent on their destruction.

Meir's hair and eyes flashed from one color to the next as if she no longer had any control over it. She felt her life slowly seeping out of her as her blood dripped onto the Twelfth. Yet, she remained silent. She would not give Lucifer the satisfaction of hearing her cry out. The Twelfth cried out to the King for deliverance.

"He cannot help you!" Lucifer shouted in jubilation as he reared up on his hind legs to crush them both.

Chapter 66

Aegeus readied for battle, eager to rush into the abandoned building and rescue the Twelfth. It had been the hardest thing he had ever done walking away from the salvage yard and leaving her with the beast, but it had been the will of the King. Aegeus now more fully understood the struggle of the King's children. He now understood their temptation to take matters into their own hands, to follow their hearts in ways that seemed right to them. Because he had faced that same temptation.

He had struggled against his own heart, his desire to rush in and free the Twelfth from the clutches of the beast. But of course, he was not powerful enough to do that. Not without the King, and it was not the will of the King that he should do so. In fact, as he reflected on the entire mission, he realized that the King had purposefully given Aegeus tasks that often required him to be away from the Twelfth, pulling him away from what his heart wanted, submitting to what the King wanted.

He looked around now at the angels and humans that readied for the battle. The husband of the Twelfth was a warrior, Aegeus would be happy to go into battle with him. He had gathered a small group of humans including the oldest son of the Twelfth. The group knelt just outside the compound amid the abandoned and decaying cars.

They joined hands as their souls prayed to the King to bring them through the battle. It pleased Aegeus that the group seemed to understand from where their power came. Aegeus noticed the woman with the wild red hair standing among them, her eyes met his briefly, and power flowed through him, strengthening him for battle. She raised her arms in victory, and her strength flowed through the salvage yard, covering the angels and humans in her power and protection. The battle would be theirs.

Aegeus drew his sword, and the other angels followed.

"Kfir, stay with the boy, protect him at all costs," Aegeus ordered. He did not wish to rescue the Twelfth just to tell her that her son had been lost.

"As the King wills, so shall I do," Kfir responded, also eager to rush the compound.

Before Aegeus issued any further orders, angels from all around Platitude began to arrive. Some warriors, many guardians, each with their weapon drawn, ready for battle. Aegeus stood in silent awe, watching them arrive one by one. Soon, the old salvage yard was covered in battle ready angels.

The woman with the wild red hair smiled, "The Second and Third are hard at work," she said in response to Aegeus's unspoken question. "The power of their prayers will sustain the battle."

The husband of the Twelfth drew his weapon and signaling silently to the humans, they began their approach to the abandoned building that had once served as the meeting place of angels and now served as the dwelling of the beast.

Mordecai appeared at the front of the group and spread his wings wide yelling out in a loud voice, "Yahweh Nissi!"

The surrounding demons were temporarily stunned, unable to move amid such a powerful proclamation. The angels and humans rushed forward, led by the woman with the wild red hair.

Aegeus remained close to the husband of the Twelfth, slicing demons from his path. The husband moved expertly, dodging behind decaying cars, shooting with expert marksmanship, and blazing a trail closer and closer to the chamber.

As they got near, a warrior dropped from atop the building and blocked the path. Aegeus approached slowly toward Kali, his sword at the ready.

Kali laughed as Aegeus approached. "We have enjoyed our time with the prophet, Aegeus."

Rage flooded over Aegeus. Kali sneered, pleased to see he had struck a nerve. "You arrive too late Aegeus, the beast has crushed her. There is nothing left of her for you to save."

"Will you fight with your mouth or with your sword?" Aegeus responded, swinging his sword with precision. The sound of his sword smashing into Kali's rang out across the salvage yard. Aegeus glanced quickly toward the husband of the Twelfth, he had knelt just yards from the entrance to the decrepit building. He was meticulously picking off the humans that blocked his path. Mordecai fought beside him, so Aegeus turned his attention back to Kali.

"I too trained under Michael," Kali said as he swung his sword at Aegeus's head. Aegeus ducked and rolled to the left barely escaping the strike. Aegeus stayed low to the ground and did a front sweep of the demon's legs sending him careening to the ground with a loud thud.

Springing to his feet, he rushed to the demon and pressed his foot into Kali's chest. Raising his sword high with both hands, he was poised to thrust it into the demon's chest when he felt a blow on his back. The force of the blow sent him sprawling forward, his sword flying loose from his hand, his body rolling a few feet before skidding to a stop against the metal wall of the building.

Two demons approached him slowly, the smile on the face of the larger one told Aegeus that he had been the one to deliver the blow. Aegeus pushed himself from the ground searching for his sword. Suddenly, the demons stopped, their eyes wide in shock, causing

Aegeus's to be the same. Then slowly they fell to their knees before collapsing face down in the dirt, arrows sticking out of their backs.

Aegeus searched the battlefield for the source. Kfir was deep in battle with a group of demons with far less experience than him. Their power was in their numbers and not in their strength. A smile covered Kfir's face as he sliced through them, flinging them from his path. Mordecai walked nearly untouched across the field, it was as if the demons could not get near him, his sword was drawn, and he walked confidently forward, covering the son of the Twelfth who had moved away from the rest of the group.

Aegeus continued to search until his eyes found Adiel standing atop one of the old cars, arrows flying from her bow as quickly as she could fire them. Their eyes met, and he nodded his thanks. She smiled briefly and then turned to deal with the demon clamoring up the car. She kicked him in the chest sending him flying backward and smashing into a large truck at the end of the property. More demons rushed toward her. She pulled her sword and began slashing them, fighting her way toward Aegeus and the others.

The husband of the Twelfth was near the entrance of the building. His back was pressed against the building, providing cover to the others as they made their way to him. He would wait, they would go in together.

Chapter 67

The chamber door flew open, and Morax stood silhouetted in the light trying to catch his breath.

"We need to go my Liege," he said, slightly out of breath. The smell of gunpowder drifted into the room from behind him. Lucifer transformed back into a human form then paused to take note of the smell. A baffled look settled on his face as the smell of the gunpowder grew stronger. Angels and demons fought with swords or bows. They did not use guns. Guns were the tool of man. It took a moment for Lucifer to fully appreciate what was happening.

"A human has come for her?" he asked slightly impressed. A gunshot rang out from the hall as if in confirmation. Morax shifted uneasily moving further into the room. Lucifer glanced back at the Twelfth, she was nothing, a mere trifle. He could not understand why anyone would come for her.

"Her husband," Morax answered, moving quickly toward Lucifer. "There are warriors with him."

"Of course, I would expect nothing less," Lucifer said dismissively with a wave of his hand. There had been a time when Lucifer had been an angel of light, a time when he had loved. But he had long ago been consumed and now he was the incarnation of evil itself. As such he could no longer even conceive of love for anyone other than self. He understood the theory of course but knowing about something and knowing it were two very different things.

A look of utter fascination settled on his face. What madness must this man possess to have risked his life to come after his wife? Lucifer once again looked at her broken body lying in a puddle of blood. He was mesmerized by the strange color that her human blood and the angel blood made now that they were mixed. She was nothing. Utterly nothing. What type of love could motivate such a risk?

"How did he find her?" he asked befuddled, as sounds of battle grew closer.

"The woman with the wild red hair," Morax answered nervously glancing over his shoulder. He was troubled to note that Lucifer did not seem to be in any rush.

"Yes of course," Lucifer said nodding in understanding.

"We must hurry my Liege; they have breached the inner sanctum of the compound making it past all the hairless rats. We need to leave," Morax urged. The compound had been protected by nearly a dozen of the hairless rats all belonging to the Prince. Morax could only imagine how many the man had eliminated.

Morax stood beside Lucifer both eager to engage in battle and concerned about being trapped in this body. A hairless rat body was not ideal for a gunfight.

Lucifer stopped walking and turned to face Morax, "Surely you do not fear a mere human Morax?"

"I fear none but you, but this human body is not bulletproof. Did she tell you where the Second and Third are?"

"No." Lucifer said, "she claims not to know." His anger flared at the reminder.

"Perhaps she doesn't?" Morax suggested.

"She is lying Morax. Don't you think I recognize a lie when I hear it?"

Morax knew better than to respond directly. "Lock the chamber. She is nearly dead. By the time her husband gets to her, she will be.

There is no need for us to stay, no good could come of it," Morax said, glancing at the prophet and Meir who both lay motionless on the floor.

Just then, the husband of the Twelfth entered the room with his gun extended. Morax reached for his sword. The husband of the Twelfth fired.

Aegeus and Kfir ran into the chamber mere steps behind the husband of the Twelfth. Aegeus's heart was not prepared for the scene in the chamber. Lucifer's eyes met Aegeus's. He looked from Aegeus to the Twelfth and back. A coy smile slide across his face, "I told you I would kill her," he said. And then he was gone.

The body Morax had been using was in a crumpled heap on the floor, but Aegeus knew that a human could not kill a demon. The husband of the Twelfth had only destroyed the human body Morax had been using, but the demon within would not be destroyed so easily.

The Twelfth was chained to a wall, she had been beaten mercilessly, her body broken and torn. Her husband ran to her, cradling her frozen body, searching desperately for a pulse. Time on earth was different from time in heaven, but those few seconds seemed like a lifetime to Aegeus. He felt as if his feet would not move, his wings could not unfurl, his lungs would not breathe.

Meir, unseen by human eyes, laid motionless beside the Twelfth. Aegeus felt sick. He stood frozen, temporarily at a loss. The husband of the Twelfth was yelling out orders to the humans who had accompanied him in the battle. One of them spoke into his phone rattling off the address where they were, requesting assistance, reporting that there were others. The humans were searching the buildings desperate to find them all. Their hearts guided by the angels they could not see.

The Twelfth's husband was kneeling over her compressing her chest, willing her to live. Mordecai rushed into the room and ran straight to the Twelfth. He laid his hands on her head, working desperately to heal her.

Adiel was the last angel to enter the chamber. The agonized sound that escaped her was guttural. Meir's eyes flickered slightly in response, and her hair sparked a dull, lifeless gray. Her eyes met Adiel's, then Aegeus's briefly before they once again closed.

"Stand guard, do not allow any demons in!" Aegeus ordered Kfir and Adiel, as he rushed to Meir. Meir groaned as he gathered her to him.

"I will get you to the King," he said in reassurance as he scooped her into his arms preparing for what he knew would be an arduous journey, one she was unlikely to survive.

"Aegeus," she sputtered softly. Aegeus's eyes filled with anguish. He tried in vain to gently brush the blood from her face.

Meir smiled weakly and placed her hand softly on his cheek, trying to pour comfort into him. She coughed slightly. He worked in vain to heal her, but her wounds were too severe. Her only hope was the King.

"Aegeus," she began again, this time sounding slightly more urgent. "She has worn my blood Aegeus. We now share a bond that shall not be broken." Aegeus nodded his head in understanding.

"Mordecai!" he called. Mordecai's eyes met Aegeus's amid the chaos, but Aegeus did not speak. He could not. He didn't need to, Mordecai knew. A silent understanding passed between them. Mordecai pulled his eyes away and returned his attention to trying to save the Twelfth.

Gathering Meir into his arms she roused and attempted once again to speak, "Save your strength," Aegeus directed, emotion choking his voice, "I will get you to the King."

Chapter 68

The Twelfth had never seen such a magnificent tree. The branches reached out in every direction covered in leaves of every possible color. A warm glow of colored lights seemed to hide just below the surface of the rough, cracked bark. She felt as if the tree was whispering something to her heart that she yearned to hear but couldn't quite make out. She walked closer desperate to listen to the secrets that seemed just as desperate to reveal themselves.

A slight breeze caressed the leaves causing them to rustle and change colors. For a moment, they were all a glorious golden hue, then slowly they morphed into other colors. She stopped, standing still in awe of the beauty of this place. The breeze carried with it the sweet scent of lavender bathing the land in royal splendor.

But the tree beckoned to her and without realizing it, she again began walking toward it, feeling as if some part of her own story was contained just below the surface of its bark, swimming in the light that pulsed within it. The feeling that she had been here before washed over her. Slowly the memory emerged as if from deep within a cave. She had once dreamed of this place. In her dream, she had stood among the wheat and gazed upon this very tree. There had been three men beneath the tree, their joy and laughter infectious. As the memory bathed her mind, she recognized one of the men as Aegeus.

She had been so deep in the memory she was surprised when her feet touched the lush green grass surrounding the tree. She paused to register how soft and silky it felt to her toes.

She wore a white linen top and pants. She had her own body, only not the body she had had in the chamber, but a youthful body, one without blemish or fault. She couldn't quite remember ever having this exact body and yet she knew that it was her true form. She felt young, full of energy and completely at peace. Her skin shimmered slightly with a radiant glow.

She looked around in bewilderment. She did not wish to ever wake from the dream that could bring her to such a place. She wanted only to remain here with the tender grass caressing her feet and the sweet smell of lavender floating in the air as the ever-changing leaves rustled in the wind.

There was no sense of urgency here as if time were nonexistent. And yet, something deep within her stirred with a feeling of unease. A feeling that someone was calling her from far away, a feeling that she had forgotten something very important, but she couldn't quite remember what. If she strained her ears, she thought she could make out the faint sound of sirens. But the sound seemed so out-of-place here, impossible even, so she again dismissed it.

Slowly, she resumed moving toward the tree. As she got closer, she noticed it was covered in fruit. Each piece was unique. Each completely different from the next, and unlike anything she had ever seen. And yet, in her soul, she knew that this fruit was what she was always meant to eat. She lovingly caressed the piece closest to her. Its pink surface was smooth and warm. She was so distracted that she didn't immediately notice the man leaning casually against the tree's trunk. He had wavy brown hair and eyes that made her think of the ocean. He was whittling something and whistling softly. She couldn't quite make out the tune although it seemed familiar.

When their eyes met, power coursed through her sending her stumbling to her knees. Emotion choked her; her heart raced, tears of gratitude streamed down her cheeks. She had not seen the man move from the tree, but she felt the electricity of his touch as he laid his nailed scared hand gently on her shoulder. Joy rushed over her and with a suddenness that surprised even her, she flung herself into his arms clutching him tightly.

"It's you," she managed after a moment.

"Yes," he answered, releasing her from his embrace. She looked up into his eyes, but it once again overwhelmed her, and she sank to his feet. He smiled knowingly. The lamb reached down and took her hands in his own pulling her gently to her feet.

Her thoughts tumbled over each other as questions crowded her mind each fighting to be first to get out. But one simple thought nestled securely in the recesses of her mind found its way to the front.

"Am I dead?" she asked, regaining her strength.

Before he could answer, Aegeus arrived at the Tree of Life clutching Meir's broken body in his arms. Her hair, the color of rain, was disheveled and caked with her own golden blood. Her once beautiful wings were now tattered and gray. Large gashes covered much of her body. But it was her eyes that bothered him most. They stared up at him lifeless and void of color.

The Twelfth stumbled backward, her eyes wide with shock. Clinging to Meir, Aegeus sank to his knees on the lush green grass under the tree, its vibrant beauty standing in stark contrast to Meir's broken, colorless body. Aegeus clung to her, screaming out his anger and sorrow.

Angels from all over heaven heard his cry and began arriving at the Tree of Life unprepared for the sight that awaited them. The Twelfth sank to her knees, too shocked to notice the angels arriving around her, unable to remove her eyes from Meir's ashen body or Aegeus' anguish. The lamb walked to Aegeus and knelt beside him.

Slowly, one by one, angels of every type arrived. Each one placed their hand gently on the angel next to them until eventually they were all touching, all connected, all sharing in their collective grief. They bowed their heads and remained silent as Aegeus cried out, for the angels knew that there were no words that could shoulder such sorrow.

A delicate angel standing near the Twelfth knelt and laid her hand gently on the Twelfth's back imparting comfort. The Twelfth looked up, for the first time aware of the other angels. Her eyes met the beautiful crystal eyes of the angel who touched her. The angel nodded in acknowledgment and then closed its eyes. The Twelfth felt her sorrow now being shared among them. She felt their spirits lifting her own. She understood that by joining together under this tree and holding each other up, they were sharing the burden and sharing their memories of Meir.

Tears silently dripped from their angelic faces to the beautiful grass beneath their feet, and yet they remained silent, the moment sacred, only Aegeus broke the silence. He cried out for all of them, the sound of it unbearable for the Twelfth. The saints too began arriving silently, standing among the angels, standing together in honor of Meir, united in their sorrow. They carefully lined up among the angels, each laying a hand on the next until finally, all of heaven stood beneath the Tree of Life, connected in their mourning.

The King arrived without Aegeus knowing. Kneeling he reached out and gently took Meir from Aegeus's arms. Quiet tears dripped from the King's eyes as he closed hers. He pulled her close to him until she disappeared into his Light. Then gently, he laid his hand on the ancient bark of the Tree of Life. Light erupted from the King and swirled about his arm, enveloping Aegeus as it danced its way to the tree. The field was instantly covered with the Habenaria radiate, Meir's favorite flower. In the distance, they could hear the mournful wail of a loon.

Deep inside the trunk of the tree, lights flared and swirled beneath its surface. A new carving, the Fafanto, the ancient symbol of tenderness and gentleness, formed in the ancient trunk and etched itself onto Aegeus's chest. Aegeus rubbed his hand lovingly over the symbol that would forever remind him of Meir and her sacrifice.

But the Fafanto was more than that, it was a reminder of her character. A physical reminder to him to remain gentle, even in his strength. If he listened closely, he could just make out the sound of her voice calling to him from the tree, begging him to hear the wisdom of the past and promises of the future.

The Twelfth's skin began to glow and sparkle as if she were made from the most exquisite golden glitter. She turned her hands slowly over watching the way the golden sparkles of light emitted from them. A small Fafanto blazed forth on her right wrist.

Her eyes met Aegeus's and the swirling lights danced about her as they did. The Twelfth felt uncertain of what to say or do. She wanted to go to Aegeus, to tell him she was sorry, to beg his forgiveness. But when she looked at him, she felt shame.

The angel with the crystal eyes leaned close.

"Do not believe the lies of the evil one. You see only anguish in Aegeus' eyes, there is no malice, no accusation. Aegeus knows better than that," she whispered to the Twelfth. "He can see her in you, for you have worn her blood, the two of you have a bond that shall not be broken," said the angel with the watery crystal eyes. The Twelfth felt grateful for the reassurance, she knew that the angel spoke the truth, even if the Twelfth was not yet ready to hear it.

She looked again at the beautiful lights seeming to swirl and dance in her veins just beneath the surface of her skin and once again she got the sense that someone, somewhere in the distance was calling to her. Someone she couldn't quite hear. The lights began to change colors dancing in beautiful patterns that she could see but not quite anticipate.

The King laid his hand gently on Aegeus's shoulder, offering comfort, peace, and memories. Images of Meir danced in Aegeus's mind tripping over each other as thousands of years of memories rushed to the surface. Slowly, lights began to dance forth from the tree, swirling and changing until they took the form of a memory displayed magnificently for all to see. Heaven watched as highlights of Meir's life were splashed across the heavenly sky.

The Twelfth watched as the tree displayed in brilliant color the creation of Meir, the first of the ministering angels to be made. The tree revealed memories of Meir in heaven and scene after scene of her comforting the King's children on the earth. Thousands of angel's memories of Meir flooded forth filling the sky with their memories of Meir, all of them displayed in glorious light. The Twelfth watched them all, willing them to soak into her soul.

She stood in awe as she watched Meir comfort human after human and offer peace and joy to her fellow angels. She watched scenes of Meir walking with the Lamb in a field of flowers or laughing over a meal with friends. Eventually, scenes of Meir in Platitude flashed before their eyes and the Twelfth felt tempted to look away, but the angel beside her lightly rubbed her back, encouraging her to watch, to honor all that Meir had done. Scenes of Meir with the Fifth lit up the sky and a ripple ran through the crowd until it reached the Twelfth. Her eyes were drawn away from the lights for just a moment to the source of the ripple. Across the field, she saw the Fifth standing with her husband and daughter among the angels. The Fifth's tears joined the tears of the angels, and yet the Twelfth noticed that the Fifth seemed to have an inner peace that the Twelfth suddenly realized she didn't have.

Other memories followed, Meir in the Garden of Souls, Meir in Maine. Gradually, the lights faded down to a single memory, a conversation between the King and Meir. They were seated in a beautiful garden, the King had spoken to Meir, but the Twelfth had not been able to hear what he said. But an understanding flooded through the gathering and without words, without knowing how, they shared Meir's heart, her fears, her feelings.

Meir did not raise her eyes to look at the King. She took a minute to process what he had told her. She seemed to understand what the King was asking, but she remained silent. He was asking her to walk willingly to her own death. But it was more than that, it was an act of love.

"Would you have me choose another," the King asked, knowing it was not an option, but wanting Meir to see that as well. Meir did not meet the King's eyes, nor did she answer right away. There was no sense of urgency, the King was patient.

Instead, she allowed her mind to think through the options. Could you really deny your own mission? Plenty of the King's children tried to, but that never truly worked out.

Who would carry this burden? Handing this cup to another didn't feel right. Would someone else be condemned to die because of her fear? Who would be given a mission that was not theirs and take this cup from the hands it belonged in, to drink down so bitter a fate? No, Meir would not be responsible for that.

Lifting her eyes to meet the King's, Meir said the only honest thing she could, "I am afraid." The King's face filled with compassion and love. There was no judgment or condemnation; he understood Meir's struggle.

"The Lamb was afraid too when facing his own death," the King offered in a warm, tender voice. "He cried out for deliverance, pleading for another way." The King's voice broke just a little as he remembered the anguish of his son. Watching as he suffered had been unbearable. But having to turn his face from the sins of the world as they were poured upon his son had broken the King's heart.

The King had held his son's gaze as long as was possible, until finally, his son cried out in pain, "Abba!" It would be a gross understatement to say that had been difficult. But the King knew it was necessary, and it served a far higher purpose than a single act of suffering.

"Sometimes I ask difficult things of people. Things that are hard, things that scare you. But they are never without purpose. No angel understands this better than you. I am with you. I will always be with you," said the King.

Lifting her eyes to meet the King's, Meir said, "I am honored to have been chosen. I will gladly serve as the seventh angel."

The King and Meir stood from the bench where they had been sitting together, and Meir prepared to return to Platitude where the beast held the Twelfth. The Twelfth felt startled to see herself displayed in lights as Meir covered the Twelfth's body with her own while the beast beat them. She watched as Meir's beautiful colors slowly faded into an ashen gray, all but her sparkling, golden blood. It flowed over the Twelfth's wounds creating a unique effect. Neither lost its own identity. Instead, they seemed to mix into a beautiful red color with golden streaks of glitter. Watching, the Twelfth knew this was important, but she did not understand the significance. Slowly, the memories of Meir's life faded, and only silence remained.

Releasing Aegeus, the King stood. The last lights faded, and the Twelfth noticed that she, like the angels and saints, had a delicate dandelion puff in her hand. It was perfectly fashioned, and it seemed as if it were crafted of snow, yet it was not cold or wet. The Twelfth closed her eyes in honor of Meir and with a steady soft breath she blew the dandelion puff sending its seeds soaring into the air. She watched as the others gathered around the tree did the same before slowly leaving the same way they had arrived.

The Lamb walked forward carrying an ancient, tattered scroll with seven royal seals.

Turning toward the earth, with a loud voice the King declared, "Let those who are wise understand these things, let those with discernment listen carefully. There will be wailing in all the streets and cries of anguish in every public square. The farmers will be summoned to weep and the mourners to wail. There will be wailing in all the vineyards, for I will pass through your midst. My fierce anger will not diminish until I have finished all I have planned. For when I called, you did not listen, so when you call out to me, I will not listen. In the days to come, you will understand this."

Chapter 69

Morax could not fathom why Lucifer had insisted that they fly on a commercial aircraft. It was pure torture; they could easily transport themselves anywhere in the world. They had been, and now suddenly Lucifer wanted to fly commercial? What value was there in traveling like the hairless rats? It was miserable. And if it were completely necessary to do so, why wouldn't he have been issued seats in first-class with Lucifer? But his questions had been answered instantly when the first of the ten entered the plane. Morax's eyes had widened, and Lucifer had smiled.

"Your incompetence has cost me yet again Morax," Lucifer said with contempt in his voice. Morax bristled at the accusation. Nothing that had happened had been Morax's doing, none of it at his command. If anything, Titus was to blame. But he remained silent keeping these thoughts to himself.

"Now, you will sit here, among the steerage and you will cloud their minds keeping them from recognizing each other," Lucifer ordered before walking away. Morax stood momentarily in the aisle stunned and then found his seat.

Morax sat quietly on the plane, miserable but happy to be alive and finally sitting still. The long flight would give him some much-needed time to rest. An elderly woman with long tube socks and granny loafers ambled past Morax in the aisle. As she walked by, her carry-on bag hit Morax in the face. Something about it felt intentional. He couldn't be sure, but he thought he heard the old woman chuckle softly. She had a sense of familiarity to Morax, and suddenly he felt sure he knew her. But the woman's light was so bright that Morax could not look directly at her.

The plane was full, and there were many more children on board than Morax could bear. He had the aisle seat, and the man beside him overflowed into Morax's space. To make matters worse, he appeared to be from one of those nations that did not put much value on bathing regularly.

Someone near him had terrible gas and if that weren't enough the child behind him was kicking his seat. In any other instance, he would have turned around and shown the child the true face of a demon, that typically worked. Morax smiled to himself at the thought, it was a long flight with multiple stops, there was plenty of time to frighten the child. For now, he would try to focus on his good fortune at escaping the chamber.

In stark contrast to Morax, Lucifer seemed quite taken with the experience. He sat comfortably in his first-class seat and seemed to have plenty of leg room and shared the row with a beautiful woman.

The Seventh was pleased that she had spent the extra money to sit in first-class. It was a rare treat but so was this trip, so she had decided to enjoy it and pamper herself in small ways; a first-class ticket had been the first example of that.

The plane was full, and she could hear the muffled cry of babies from the back of the plane. She was grateful she was not back there. She had accumulated thousands of frequent flyer miles over the last two years. Why not use them for a free upgrade? She positioned her bag in the overhead compartment and smiled kindly at the gentleman sitting in the aisle seat of her row. She pointed meekly at her seat by the window and said, "excuse me."

He stood to let her pass, and she could not help but notice that he seemed very familiar to her. His salt and pepper hair was thick and stylish giving him a youthfulness that made it difficult to estimate his age. He had a mysterious appeal with intense, brooding eyes. His clothing was very expensive and surprisingly out of season for where they were going.

There was something about him that drew her in with an almost hypnotic effect. She had only met one other person that had that effect on her, and that was Damian. The man smiled at her kindly as she sat down and fastened her seat belt, something she found awkward when sitting next to a stranger.

"Business or pleasure?" he asked as they settled in for the long flight.

"Pleasure," she answered, smiling. Normally she would not have encouraged chit-chat, but something about this man with his piercing eyes and beautiful smile drew her in. "And you?" she asked out of courtesy as much as curiosity.

"Oh, unfortunately, business," he said, wrinkling his nose as if he had smelled something unpleasant. "Tanzania is an unusual choice for a vacation, do you have friends there?" he asked comfortably.

"My boyfriend is there on a humanitarian mission. I am surprising him," she added a little nervously. Lucifer smiled. Her soul was so tender, her gift from the King so evident, it was almost too easy.

"Well, it would be a foolish man indeed that was not pleased with such a surprise," he responded.

The Seventh smiled in appreciation, then opened her book and offered a last glance to the man with a "we are done chatting now" look. He smiled knowingly and dipped his head to signify he understood completely. He did not seem offended by the message which should have relieved the Seventh instead it distracted her.

Something about his expression hinted at a confidence that she found troubling as if although he accepted and understood her non-verbal cues, he also felt sure she would indeed talk to him. She thought she saw just a hint of amusement in his eyes as if he knew something she did not. Something about it gnawed at her reaching into the recesses of her mind and tap dancing on thoughts she couldn't quite bring to the surface.

It was quite unsettling, and as a result, she could not concentrate on her book, her mind completely distracted by thoughts of what it was she was missing. Snatches of random pieces of the puzzle flitted through her mind as she tried to sort out why the man was so comfortable with her ignoring him. She found herself fighting the urge to glance at him out of the corner of her eye for just a peek.

The flight attendant's offer of a drink, while they waited to depart, came as a welcomed interruption. The man beside her ordered a cranberry lime spritzer. The Seventh ordered water, then once again closed her eyes and leaned back in the plush chair dreading the long flight to Amsterdam where they would pick up additional passengers before heading off to Nairobi, and then finally to Tanzania. But despite her best efforts, her mind quickly wandered back to the man beside her.

Lucifer watched with delight as the Seventh struggled. He waited patiently, knowing he would take advantage of the flight attendant, returning with their drinks. The Seventh would be ready by then.

He fought to keep from laughing as she struggled to ignore him, sneaking sideways glances at him when she thought he wasn't looking. Lucifer did not concern himself with the Seventh's attempts to dismiss him, he knew that curiosity would eventually get the best of her. His lure was strong, she would not be able to resist, and so he waited patiently, knowing time and experience were on his side.

As he had expected, when the flight attendant returned with their preflight drinks, the Seventh attempted to restart the conversation. Lucifer answered her with polite but stilted answers and returned his attention to the magazine he was carrying. Patience was key, and it was something he had an abundance of. He would gently entice her, feeding off her emotions until she would become the pursuer. It was so satisfying, and he planned to savor every moment.

Slightly embarrassed, and perplexed that her attempts at conversation had failed, the Seventh quickly opened her favorite playlist on her phone and put her earbuds in. The airplane was just a little chilly, so she got out the thin red airplane blanket she traveled with and pulled it over her shoulders. Nestling into her seat, she hoped to forget about the man beside her and enjoy the flight.

Dinner came, and she asked for a glass of red wine with it hoping it would help clear her head and improve her sleep on the long flight. But the wine had been too strong for her and she hadn't been able to enjoy it. After several attempts to drink it, she had given up and handed it back to the flight attendant. The Seventh was glad Damian was not here to see it, he would have found it wasteful.

The thought of him warmed her spirit, and she once again closed her eyes, leaning her head against the window of the plane with just the small airline pillow between her and the darkness outside. Flying to Tanzania had been spontaneous, and for the millionth time, she wondered if he would find it pleasing or if he would fret over how wasteful she had been. But she had plenty of frequent flyer miles, and the flight and upgrade had been free. It was his birthday after all, wasn't that worth a little extravagance?

She pushed the worry from her mind; he would be pleased, she was sure of it. Lucifer watched her closely, enjoying the way her mind raced and struggled. She wore her tenderness like a cloak, something so tangible he felt certain he could touch it. Her lack of confidence was amusing sport.

He was glad he had chosen to sit next to her and not one of the others. Any of them could have been an amusing seatmate for the long flight, but there was something about the Seventh. Initially, he thought it was her artistic flair, the carefree way she carried herself or perhaps the innocence that flowed from her. He hadn't been sure exactly what it was, but it was enough to gain his attention.

He had waited patiently for her to join him, to slid past him into her seat. It was only then that he had smelled it, the scent of evil. It lingered about her like a sweet perfume. He had inhaled deeply, savoring the fading scent. It wasn't the normal scent of evil, the one that all those without the light carried, no it was something much more beautiful. The smell was faint, but it clung to her the way the smell of a campfire clings to those who have warmed by it, slowly fading over time.

Lucifer's pulse had quickened, and his mouth began to water at the smell. His first instinct had been to devour her instantly, but thousands of years had helped him learn to control those instincts. Lucifer was not the only one to notice the smell, the large angel disguised as an elderly woman wearing ridiculous tube socks also noticed.

The angel's eyes had met Lucifer's and recognition registered in them quickly. Unfortunately, Lucifer was at a disadvantage. While he clearly recognized the angel as such, he could not see through the disguise well enough to identify the angel behind it. He knew only that the angel behind the disguise was anything but frail.

Epilogue

The first signs of morning streamed through the shabby curtains in the dank hostel. Damian woke just enough to smell the stale air, cringe a bit and roll back over. He considered himself lucky that his roommate, a most persnickety man from Germany, had checked out the night before leaving him to have the room to himself. The man had snored terribly, and he smelled of cigar smoke and cheap whiskey. On top of it, he had complained about everything. Yes, the hostel looked nothing like it did on the website, and ok, the bugs were large enough to carry your suitcase for you, but what exactly did he expect? Damian doubted the man had traveled very much.

As he lay on the prison style mattress with the bed springs poking into his chest, he could hear that another guest was already up and moving about. He suspected it was the American down the hall. She would want a warm shower and early morning was her only hope of getting one. The sound of running water a few minutes later all but confirmed his guess.

He closed his eyes tightly and tried to will himself back to sleep. For a few minutes, as sleep and wake battled for control of his mind, he couldn't quite remember what country he was in. He dozed into a light sleep, half his mind listening to the sounds of the hostel waking and the other half tiptoeing on the edge of a dream he had had a million times. He tried to sink deeper into the dream, to ignore the light, the sour smell of the mattress, and the slight growl of his stomach, but apparently, the American had taken too long in the shower. The hostel keeper was banging on the door and yelling something in Swahili that Damian couldn't quite make out, but he understood the gist of it.

Begrudgingly, he opened his eyes and stretched his aching muscles. He had spent all day yesterday digging ditches in a small village. Eventually, the pipes would be placed into the ditches and water would be brought to the village but that was many years away. Today, if he remembered correctly someone else would dig. He was part of a small team that would be going to a nearby refugee camp to help build a temporary school.

He slowly sat up, accepting that morning had indeed come. Damian enjoyed the morning. He always had, it felt fresh and new, full of possibilities. Getting out of bed was the difficult part, but this bed was not as hard to leave as some. He threw on the jeans he had been wearing the night before and pulled a black shirt over his head as he slid his feet into his shoes.

There was a cloudy mirror on the far wall by the door which revealed that his black hair was sticking out in every direction. He picked up the cheap plastic comb he had and attempted, in vain, to help it lay down in a more civilized manner. But he knew the effort was really wasted. His hair had a mind of its own. It was thick with just enough wave to make it seem even thicker, but not enough to make it ever be described as curly. In truth, it was just enough to make it stick out in every direction. Throw in a cowlick on each side, and his head was—well he had worn a lot of hats in his time. He had finally come to terms with it years ago, truly embracing who he was, ridiculous hair and all. To his delight, disheveled hair was all the rage.

After patting his back pocket to assure he had his ID and his front pocket confirming he had some cash, he headed out. The hostel host offered him coffee, which he accepted with gratitude, although he knew he would not drink it. The thick mud like sludge in the cup did not exactly match the description of coffee, but it was what they had, and he did not wish to offend them. So, he took it with a gentle nod of his head and a soft but sincere thank you. Their eyes met briefly in the exchange and Damian could see the anxiety melt into pleasure in the man's eyes.

A young boy from the village had agreed to serve as a guide for Damian. The boy was sitting on the ground beside the hostel when Damian walked out.

"Habari Za asubuhi," the boy offered in his native tongue.

"Habari za asubuhi," Damian responded, grateful he spoke the language. Growing up the son of a U.S. diplomat, Damian had lived in many countries, thirty-seven to be exact. He had traveled to many more. It was one of his goals to visit them all. He quickly discovered much to his parent's delight that he had a gift for linguistics. Without any real effort, he quickly learned the language of each country they lived in and often, if he was going to visit a nation for any length of time, he learned its language in preparation for the visit. It just made things easier. People were more comfortable with you when you spoke their language.

Without thinking, he took a sip of the sludge coffee. It only took a second for the shock to register on his face and his lips to expel the coffee into the nearby dirt. It was not something he normally did, but he knew the boy would appreciate it. He was right. The boy's face lit up, and laughter poured from him over the silly American who couldn't handle his coffee. But Damian knew that this cup of coffee was no representation of what was to be expected here.

He laughed along with the boy as they made their way out of the village and toward the remote area where Damian would be working. A dirt path led the way. Tall grass grew wild around them, and he wondered if they would see any giraffes. He imagined they were a little too close to the coast for that.

Damian doubted they would see one, but he could dream. Hoping for one didn't seem like too much to ask. Giraffes were one of his favorite animals. His father had told him many stories growing up, stories of a Giraffe with great wisdom and many adventures. Giraffes, his father had told him, knew just when to stick their necks out and when to lower them. Damian's father had guided him toward this same knowledge, and it had served him well.

His father had not been thrilled with his decision to spend his thirtieth birthday doing missions in Tanzania. But to Damian, it seemed perfect. It was his first birthday since his mother had died and he was finding thirty to be much harder than he expected. He could think of no better way to get through it than by visiting somewhere he had never been and working to make it better because of him being there.

Damian asked the boy about his family and his interests. He praised Tanzania for its beauty and all it had to offer; the boy walked a bit taller a mite prouder because of it. Damian took in a deep breath as he and the boy walked along chatting easily. Africa had a smell that he liked, a smell that comforted him for reasons he could not explain. But Damian was not the only one smelling the air. Hidden in the tall grass along the dirt path, a destroying demon had been ambling about looking for a target when a wonderful smell sweetened the surrounding air, gaining his full attention.

The demon stopped in his tracks and closing his eyes he greedily drank in the scent. He searched the air slowly, meticulously until the wind shifted just enough that he was able to pinpoint the source. His eyes fluttered open in total bliss settling on the young man walking so amicably with the boy. A sinister smile covered his face as the scent of evil filled his nostrils. It wasn't the normal scent of evil, the one that all those without the light carried, no it was something much more beautiful.

A Note from the Author

My heart aches for those who are or have experienced human trafficking. I hope that in some small way I have been able to do honor to an issue that touches my soul. And I hope this book has changed you in some way. A portion of the proceeds from the sale of this book will go to support those working to end human trafficking.

Visit www. andeedwards.com[1] for additional content related to the book including a discussion guide for book clubs and an angel guide that accompanies the book.

If you enjoyed this book, I would be honored if you left a book review.

---

1.   http://www.andeedwards.com

Don't miss the next book in the series.
An Excerpt from Book 3

F ear remained at the elaborate dressing table brushing out her long hair. Morax shuffled his feet unsure of if she had heard him but unwilling to repeat himself. With great care, she pulled the ivory brush through her long tresses. She could smell his fear emanating from him, he tried to bury it under pride and arrogance, but he could not. It was, after all, a beacon calling to her, strengthening her. She pulled the ivory brush once more through her hair and then slowly turned toward Morax.

A cold shiver ran through him. He tried to conceal it, but there was little hope. A coy smiled slid across her lips in response. She knew very well her power, none were immune, sav the King. Slowly, with great deliberation, she laid the brush down on the table and stood filling the room with her essence. Shadows danced across the floor and reached threateningly from the far corners of the inky room. Morax tried to control his breathing and exude the power due him, but he felt sure he was failing.

Fear moved slowly, her elegant gown flowing behind her until she reached Morax.

"Show me the dossier," she commanded in a voice that would haunt his dreams. Morax showed her the file. Fear took her time reviewing it. She slid her hand caressingly over its worn pages slowly as if the very words on the page could be absorbed through her skin.

"She is powerful?" she asked Morax as she reviewed the file.

"Very," he answered. She smiled in response; they wouldn't have come to her if the target wasn't powerful. But the strength of the target meant nothing to her. Eventually, they would all succumb, none were immune. She turned purposefully back toward the dressing table, her back to Morax. Closing her eyes, she savored the scent of his fear, breathing it in deeply so that her own power might grow even as she drained his. She watched in the mirror as he shifted uneasily, eager to leave her presence. It pleased her to see him so uncomfortable.

"She has become a significant problem," Morax added unnecessarily. He would not have sought her help if the woman wasn't a problem. Fear once more turned slowly toward Morax allowing sulfur to pour from the hem of her dress. The sulfur cast dark shadows around the room. Slowly the shadows danced and swayed until they formed horrible forms with jagged teeth and beady eyes. Fear stopped, amused by the horror in Morax's eyes.

"All these years and this is still your greatest fear?" she asked gesturing gracefully about her. Morax's heart pounded in his chest, and he fought the urge to run from the room. He felt his resolve slowly fading and knew that he must escape her presence.

"Can you destroy her?" he asked trying to disguise his fear with anger. Fear smiled.

"Don't worry Morax, I will destroy your prayer warrior."

Don't miss out!

Visit the website below and you can sign up to receive emails whenever Ande Edwards publishes a new book. There's no charge and no obligation.

https://books2read.com/r/B-A-QKOG-EUCU

BOOKS 2 READ

Connecting independent readers to independent writers.

Also by Ande Edwards

The Prophet Series
The Prophet
The Seventh Angel

Watch for more at www.andeedwards.com.

About the Author

Ande Edwards is the author of The Prophet series. She seeks to explore the spiritual battle that rages around us through the eyes of an artist and a woman of faith and science.

Ande is a college professor living in the Midwest with her husband and four children. In her free time, Ande enjoys reading, photography, and gardening. She describes herself as "an artist living in a cupcake-loving scientist's body." Ande aspires to write stories of encouragement and hope by bringing the spiritual realm into focus

Read more at www.andeedwards.com.

www.ingramcontent.com/pod-product-compliance
Lightning Source LLC
Chambersburg PA
CBHW021443240626
47153CB00001B/270